the river beyond the world

also by janet peery

ALLIGATOR DANCE

janet peery

•

the river beyond the world

•

Picador USA

New York

THE RIVER BEYOND THE WORLD. Copyright © 1996 by Janet Peery. All rights reserved. Printed in the United States of America. No part of this book may be used or reproduced in any manner whatsoever without written permission except in the case of brief quotations embodied in critical articles or reviews. For information, address Picador USA, 175 Fifth Avenue, New York, N.Y. 10010.

Picador® is a U.S. registered trademark and is used by St. Martin's Press under license from Pan Books Limited.

Design by Songhee Kim

Library of Congress Cataloging-in-Publication Data

Peery, Janet.
    The river beyond the world   /   by Janet Peery.
        p.   cm.
    ISBN 0-312-14719-8
    I. Title.
    PS3566.E284R58   1996
    813'.54—dc20   96-19122
                                                                              CIP

First Picador USA Edition: October 1996

10   9   8   7   6   5   4   3   2   1

for

ORA SCOTT SAWHILL

1950 · 1974

a c k n o w l e d g m e n t s

I wish to express my profound gratitude to the Whiting Foundation, the Richard and Hinda Rosenthal Foundation, and the National Endowment for the Arts.

Of immense help as I worked on this story were these books: *Aztecs*, Inga Clendennin's study of the ancient Mexican belief system; *The Teachings of Don Juan: A Yaqui Way of Knowledge*, by Carlos Castañeda; *Memory of Fire*, by Eduardo Galeano; and *The Lower Rio Grande Valley of Texas*, by J. Lee Stambaugh and Lillian J. Stambaugh.

I would like to thank George Witte, Leigh Feldman, and Terry Perrel for their invaluable advice; Bill Peery, Essie Sappenfield, and Joe Boone for Texas talk; and my family, my children, and my husband, Cy Bolton, for the kind of help that matters most.

c o n t e n t s

It is told that when yet all was in darkness, when yet no sun had shone...it is said the gods gathered together and took counsel among themselves there in Teotihuacan. They spoke, they said, among themselves; "Come hither, O gods! Who will carry the burden? Who will take it upon himself to be the sun, to bring the dawn?"

—THE FLORENTINE CODEX

BOOK I

salsipuedes

1944

Below Los Olmos the Rio Grande breaks against its bed, braiding into bends so tight it seems the river would hold off the moment it will give into the Gulf. On the Texas side of the watershed, between the palm-lined delta roads, stretch great flat fields of cabbages and cane, tomatoes, cotton, groves of oranges and grapefruit. On the Mexican side, southwest of the dusted border towns, the land gives way to chinch-weed, cactus, and rock nettle, until at last the foothills of the East Sierra Madre rise.

Furred with sage and salt cedar, the limestone hills seem endless, rolling into one another until they fade—still only hills—into the distance of the high range. At first the land appears barren of people, but here and there a farmer tends his milpa, a woman carries water, a boy herds sheep out of a sand draw. On the eastern slope that leads into the first true canyon lies the town of Salsipuedes, whose name, depending on who says the word as well as on who hears, can sound a warning or a dare: Leave if you can.

In the winter months the west wind from the cordillera sets wooden doors banging, works nails from leather hinges, batters roofs until the squeals of rumpled tin become so piercing it would be a mercy if in the night they would blow loose to clatter down the canyon walls. But in the summer months great vines grow, as if to hold the town to earth. Buffalo gourd and loco melon, their stalks wrist-thick, the vines snake through cracks and into windows, beneath the vigas in the houses, through the rusting spokes of the bicycle a cattle rustler rode down from Monterrey in 1912, a vehicle that had leaned—after its rider vanished in the night—against the back wall of the pulquería for over thirty years. They grow under the '39 Ford truck parked like an offering in front of the rubble that had been the mission of El Corazón Sagrado, where the carburetor coughed the last fumes of rationed gasoline that had seen the truck from the border. Up the tires, along the running boards, into the wheel wells, they blossom overnight with orange stars that make the gray hulk look like a carnival parade float.

Those vines will grow around your feet, old women warn young girls, laughing as they wash clothes in the arroyo, if you stand too long with your mouths agape, dreaming about babies, houses, men. Higher still, the girls whisper as they nudge each other, until the vines twine around their ankles, growing green and strong, up their legs. Then, they whisper, we might never leave.

•   •   •

After many years of drought, in the rainy spring of 1944 at the time of Tocoztontli as the fields were being sown, the Río Sin Nombre burst its banks above the town. Like dirty curd on boiling beanpots, the water frothed and curled over the washing rocks, flooding the path into the arroyo. The youngest child of Fideo Rubio, who had disobeyed his mother to play Apache scout along a ledge, was swept away. The old women pursed their lips, nodding to the girls, saying that just as they had foreseen as they watched the reckless child run through the rain, La Llorona, the ghost who haunted streams and rivers searching for her own drowned son, had seized the boy. One for one, they said. It had always been so and would always be. At least the corn would grow.

For weeks the women of Salsipuedes had done little wash. This was because they had to depend on the men to carry pots of water. The men could hardly do this as well, not knowing exactly the place along the bank to draw from, exactly which rocks to fit their feet into along the path so the good washwater didn't slosh into the dirt. The men, the women muttered, had no idea what trouble this work was, how thankless, how important, especially when the men would wipe their oily hands on their pants legs and other practices too shameless to speak of, and which no woman should have to witness.

As for the men, they had grown weary of the task, as well as of the women's idea that the whole mess was the men's fault. ¡Zas! How could the women, who had no idea of the complexities, expect the busy men, who had countless things to tend, to perform such mindless work? The women had no notion of how lucky they were. They slept easily at night, safe only because the men beside them were wide awake, their heads heavier than lead with worry. In almost every house, the misunderstood men squared their jaws and stiffened their shoulders and tried to dodge the stinging, snake-tongued words of the misunderstood women.

In Barba's pulquería, those bachelors who had been wise enough to see from the start that the crooked path between the sexes led straight to one thing only, which was trouble, and who, if such trouble came to them, had foolproof methods that would quick as lightning put a stop to it, began to bet on which of the henpecked husbands would have it up to *here* and be the first to leave for Texas. Just when it looked as though there would be a tie between Chalo Ruiz and Filo Santos, the boy who had been sent to check the water returned, shouting that the washing rocks were at last clear.

1

the canyon

The night before, in the manless house of the two sisters Villamil y Cantú, Catalina's—the elder's—water had broken. Now it was noon. Time, Rosario the midwife said, to send the children from the house. While her mother was giving birth, the girl María Luisa, who was almost fourteen, would be sent to wash the clothes and to make certain her brothers bathed. Her mother allowed her only as far as the arroyo, but Luisa knew, as she stood waiting in the dim room for her mother to release her, that she would go instead to the river.

She was tired of talk. Of the gossip she knew she would hear at the washing rocks. The women could whisper all they wanted about her mother's sister, Chavela—most of what they said about her wild-haired aunt was true—but she didn't want to hear about her mother, hear the women when they whispered that if not knowing how to tell men no could kill a person, the gentle Catalina Villamil y Cantú would be four times dead. At least. It was not that her mother was bad, Luisa overheard the women saying, but that she loved too easily, and hadn't learned to tell a good man from a fool.

Now her mother lay on her side, waiting, her knees drawn toward her huge belly, resting her head on her arm, looking at Luisa. "Be sure to cover yourself when you bathe."

Old Rosario had hung blankets at the windows so los aires wouldn't blow through with any of their evil. Though the room was already so hot it was hard to breathe, Rosario had built a fire in the corner oven for tea because everyone knew it was bad luck to drink cold things. The midwife had tried to clear some of the clutter—neither Catalina nor Chavela would part with so much as a dented coffee tin—but she had given up trying to straighten the piles of paper scraps, bundles of string, the crates of bottles, broken pots. Now Rosario sat, sewing in the light from the oil lamp beside the bed. "This baby is feet first," she said to Luisa. "You'd better cover your ears as well."

Chavela, squatting just inside the doorway so she could blow away the smoke of the cigarette she'd rolled with wild tobacco, laughed, then coughed. "Maybe this means the new one will be satisfied on the ground." Smoke curled like a ribbon when she waved toward Luisa. "That one wouldn't hear the earthquake swallowing her feet."

Luisa scratched at the place a wasp had stung her arm the day before. The bump was tender, already sore and red, but she rubbed at it, trying to ignore her mother's sister. Luisa had wanted to be present for the baby's birth, but Chavela convinced the women that she would only get in the way. "Remember the time," Chavela had reasoned, "she ground the goatburrs with the corn? Her head takes her away, and she will be bad luck. Things have to be just so. One wrong move and . . ." Chavela hadn't finished her warning, but Rosario had begun to nod and Luisa's mother had given in.

Now Chavela reached out to tug at Luisa's skirt, taunting, "I heard Uncle Chu is out today. Better not let him see you."

Luisa wondered why Chavela never warned of the real dangers in the hills around Salsipuedes, of rattlesnakes and scorpions, of the cats that made their sound like crying babies, but only of ghosts and people. Sometimes Chavela warned of La Llorona, but most often she tried to scare Luisa with Uncle Chu, who lived in a hut near the high caves, where he kept his black bear. Many said he was a brujo, able to put spells on people. Her brother Memo said the Uncle peeled strips of his own skin and used them to dress wounds, that if he ran out of places to peel, he cut hide from the bear. Luisa didn't believe him. The bear was old and patchy from mange, its roar more like a mule's bray, and Uncle, no matter what people said about him, looked no more dangerous than an old, kind horse. Luisa didn't understand how one moment Chavela could say watch out for him and then, when he came to visit, smoke with him until the air was white and drink the pulque that smelled of celery, sour milk, and gasoline. For her part, she was not afraid, and she laughed at Chavela's threat.

Her mother raised herself on her elbow. "The water might still be bad in the arroyo. Don't let your brothers wander."

Luisa looked at her feet, thinking of what she could say that wouldn't be a lie. "I'll be careful," she said, and at last her mother blessed her and she was out in the bright day.

The speckled hen she called Dolores hurried across the dirt yard toward her, first pecking at Luisa's toes, then stopping, as if she suddenly remembered she was too proud to need attention, to ruffle her feathers and preen for mites. Under the fig tree Memo and Rafael played a game with bottle caps and stones. Luisa picked up the basket beside the doorstone. "It's time," she called to them. Today would be their first trip to the canyon. To make sure they wouldn't run back and tattle when they learned what she would do, Luisa planned to wait to tell them until they had gone too far to turn back.

She had found the place once when she had daydreamed past the big nopal cactus that marked the turnoff to the arroyo. At first she had been frightened, but the river there was beautiful and deep, so far from the shallow brown pool where the other girls and women slapped their wash against the rocks. No voices filled the air with who was sick and who was fighting, who had stolen what from whom and how who planned to get it back. Who did everything their husbands said and what two sisters could not trouble themselves with such a thing as husbands, two sisters named for haughty queens but in whose house—a house that when their mother left it to them had been grand, with thick adobe walls and sandglass in the windows, where now there was only crumbling mud and oiled paper—you could hardly find a clean place to sit down.

Twice again she had gone to the canyon and each time was better. She had found a secret hollow in the rock where she could stand and think, where she could make pictures in her head of the stories Señor Miller read at his school, and where the hidden girl who lived inside her chest—a higher, truer girl than the one who carried wood and milked the goat, who flinched when she reached beneath the hens to gather eggs—came out to fill her skin. God was in this place. The clean, pure God who didn't care about sins and who and whom. The beautiful, good God who saw straight into hearts.

"We're going now," she told her brothers. If they hurried, they could be back before dark and no one would know.

Memo caught a spotted lizard among the ololiuqui that grew by the woodpile, and as he ran to show her, the lizard's tail switched around his wrist like a small brown whip. He held the creature under the forelegs, laughing while Rafael tried to snatch it from him.

"Put it down," she said. "We have to go."

Memo held the lizard so its pale belly caught the sun. "He doesn't need a bath. See how he shines!"

Rafael reached out to pet the lizard's throat while the creature clawed the air, struggling. "This is don Ricardo." Her younger brother bent to look lovingly into the lizard's eyes. "Brave don Ricardo! So manly!" He inclined his ear toward the lizard as though don Ricardo were about to deliver a tiny, urgent message. "He says we don't have to wash. He says we should stay here to guard things."

"Maybe don Ricardo is a girl," she suggested.

Her brothers stared.

"Oh, bring him," she said.

She hurried past the ovens and pens and houses of the lower part of town. At the place where the path led into the chaparral she stopped to wait for her brothers, already lagging behind and fighting, as she had known they would, over don Ricardo.

She hoped the new baby would be a sister. She would carry her on her hip and tell her the names of things, show her Chula's fleece and let her touch how soft. They would play school, and she would say the beautiful long rolling words Señor Miller said at his school—*calvary, nativity*—to make the baby's eyes grow round and bright and solemn.

Though she knew it was wrong, sometimes she imagined what it would be like if something happened to her mother and she were in charge of her brothers and the new baby. Her first act would be to chase away Chavela, who was hard and strong and bossy, who often slapped Luisa for nothing more than being slow to answer. "Her high head gets her into trouble," Chavela would say if Luisa's mother cried about the trouble in the house. "I have to remind her of what's real."

Once, when her mother was grinding corn, Luisa had asked why Chavela was so mean. "Hearts are made two ways," her mother said. "Some are full with what they're given, no matter how small, and others can't forget what they can't have."

"She's mean," Luisa insisted. "And that's a sin."

Her mother stopped to cool the mano, then sprinkled new kernels onto the metate and blew on them to give them courage. She shook her head. "Forgive her."

"She never asks."

Her mother shook her arms, then resumed her rolling. The corn crunched between the stones. "All the more reason."

When Luisa said that Chavela could at least *try* to have the first kind of heart, her mother had pushed the mano even harder against the metate, but she had laughed. "Who told you we get to choose?"

Surely there were some things that could be chosen. You shouldn't just have to smile at whatever came your way, and act as though you liked it when you didn't. If she had a choice, she would also chase away Ralph Emerson Lopez, who was the new baby's father, who came from Texas any time he wanted and her mother let him and then Chavela acted even worse and this was why the women talked about what went on with the sisters Villamil y Cantú in the little house at the edge of town.

After they were gone she would throw out the boxes of cloth and paper, the jars and bottles, sweep and sweep and sweep. When everything was clean, she would arrange the furniture so the table stood beneath the window with a jar of poppies where the sun would shine on their scarlet heads. On the pretty table she would place the food on clean clay plates and everyone would smile and thank her and say how good she was. Maybe, when he came back from Mexico City, she would invite Señor Miller to see.

In the sand at the base of the nopal she saw a quick movement. Another lizard, this one shining and green as a chile, scuttled from the shadow of a rock and raced up the cactus between the spines to the lowest arm, where it stopped, its tail still as wire, just right for catching. She thought of telling Memo and Rafael, but they would prick themselves on the thorns. There would be crying and they would have to go back and who would get the blame?

She shifted the basket to her shoulder. "Hurry," she called. "You'll be left behind."

Just the month before, the nopal had been withered as old Rosario's fingers, its dusky flesh shrunken nearly to the bone, but the rain had filled it out so that now the tall body looked as though it might split open. The pretty fruits along its arms looked like the bursting red hearts in the scenes on the tiles of the church. The sight of this led her thoughts to her mother, and from there to what had been worrying her for the past months: what men and women did together, and how this made a baby.

In the big way of seeing things, it was like the nopal, how the rain brought something the cactus didn't have and made the flesh swell. Or it was like a town, like Salsipuedes above her. There were things the town didn't have. A truck had to bring them. Or Filo Santos in his loud gray bus with no roof. Letters came, and blocks of ice in nests of straw. Mangos and papayas from the jungle. Medicine. A crate of parrots, all dead but one, who flew away. The bus brought Señor Miller in his coarse black pants and jacket, his white shirt stiff and tight around his neck but not a button in sight, his strange beard that grew all around his mouth.

It was the same with people. The man drove the bus and he brought things to the woman. Not in a bus—she smiled at the thought of dirty Filo Santos in his sticking-up rooster-feather hat, honking his burro horn, bringing a big box of babies through the hills—but with the part the man had that the woman didn't, his falo. But the place had to be there for him: the cactus in the rain, the town in the hills, the woman lying down, her legs apart.

This was the big way of men and women, and she smiled to think how strange and sweet it was that she could know this from just the sight of cactus, rock, and rain. But she also knew that from the high way of things she would soon begin to think of the low. This part of it, as nearly as she could tell from listening to the women, was a sin. So before she could begin to think of how, exactly, when the parts met, they would feel, she shook her head until she was sure these thoughts had flown out of it. She called to Memo and Rafael to hurry them, making her voice loud so that if any low thoughts lingered, they would be scared away.

At home she kept hidden beneath the loose board under her petate a jar with which she kept track of her doings. For each good act she dropped in a bean. For each bad act, she took one out. As long as there were beans in the jar, all was well. One for one. She had already removed a bean for what she would do today, and she decided she didn't have to remove another one for her thoughts about the parts meeting. That would be covered by the bean for disobeying.

Just beyond the nopal the path split. One continued toward the arroyo and the other, steeper, banked by rocks so round they looked like great gray heads, led to the canyon. She waited to see if something in the air would stop her, but the day was still and bright, the sky so blue it took her sight beyond the color. She stepped onto the lower path. Her brothers, still arguing, followed.

It couldn't feel good. Chula bleated beneath El Coronel, who rolled his slotted yellow eyes and made a sound like coughing. Some nights she heard noises coming from the back room when Filo Santos visited Chavela, choking, low, harsh words, then crying. Her mother made no noises with Ralph Emerson Lopez, but she was quiet in all things. This didn't mean it didn't hurt.

Memo's voice startled her. "You took the wrong way." He had tied the string from his shorts behind don Ricardo's front legs, and the lizard, harnessed, scurried over his shoulders. With one hand Memo held the leash and with the other he tried to hold up his shorts. Rafael, sniffling, beat a palmetto stick against the dirt of the path.

"This way has better water. You can play in it and get clean and not even know you're washing."

Memo's look was stern. "They said we're not supposed to come here."

Rafael stood beside Memo, his sturdy legs set wide, and Luisa could tell he hoped that if he stood with Memo, he would win a chance to hold his brother's pet. She had to say the one right thing that would make Memo do what she wanted. Rafael would follow. They were almost there.

She set the basket on the path and faced him. "What a good boy you are," she said, making her voice smooth and sweet as milk, "to do what you are told."

When Memo stamped his foot and jerked his shoulders in the rough way of men, the sudden movement startled don Ricardo, and the lizard scrambled to the top of her brother's head. "I do what I want," Memo said, sticking out his chest.

Luisa turned away to hide her smile, hefted the basket, and when she turned back to the path, he followed her. Rafael tagged behind, trying with tender words to coax don Ricardo from his perch.

The women made the world sound worse than it was. Though the rains still swelled the river and along the wide sandbar there curved a flood ridge of sticks and leaves, the water ran within the banks. A tin can glinted on a gravel bar beside the sand. All was peaceful. She wanted to think of how the water and the river fit into the picture of the cactus and the town, but just then she heard a rustling sound from a willow stand. She thought of Tino Rubio. It was said that his skin had turned white as a rotten gourd. She thought of La Llorona, her ghostly fingers trailing like long willow leaves in the eddies, and then, with a shock of fear, of real things: wolves, bandits, javelinas. She held out her hand to stop her brothers.

"There's nothing," Memo said. "You're trying to scare us."

"Shh," she whispered. Her brother's voice had almost covered another sound, this one sharper—the chip of one stone against another. "Listen."

For a long time they listened, but from the willows came only the sound of a breeze in the leaves. She began to pick her way along the rocks and down onto the sand.

At first the boys stayed close as she took the clothes from the basket, but then Memo found a flattened tin cup, the bleached jawbone of a small animal, a shiny chip of gravel he said was Spanish gold, and at last the boys began to explore. She decided she had imagined the noise.

She started with Chavela's skirt, happy to be alone with her thoughts. The way her hands worked the agave soap against the cloth beneath the water made her think of her aunt's rough movements, and then, though she hadn't wanted to, of Uncle. She knew that every year he planted corn to make a baby so in the time of Atemoztli there would be a pregnant girl to ride the bear for Christmas. When she was younger and had heard this rumor, she had thought the women meant that Uncle planted real corn in the real earth, but now she knew better.

In the ten years since the town had had no priest, more and more people took part in the winter ceremony. It had gone on for hundreds of years, Chavela said, and no priest and not even Señor Miller and all his talk of peace and loving kindness was going to stop it. He wouldn't understand it, anyway, Chavela said, and he was just lucky the town would tolerate him. No one knew where he came from, what strange, spineless faith he followed, so how could he know anything? Besides, Rosario said, his name wasn't Miller at all and he was running from the war because he was afraid and who should listen to such a worm?

Luisa's mother spent long hours in the ruined church, her fingers moving rapidly over her beads. She didn't like the old ways and she pretended the winter ceremony didn't exist, so Luisa had never seen it, but she had heard about it from her friend Ana. People came from other towns because of Uncle and his father before him and his before him, but most came from around Salsipuedes, Ana said. Luisa would be surprised to see how many, and who. Even the old churchwomen who crossed themselves if they so much as saw coyote tracks where two paths crossed. The very ones who talked about how foolish Luisa's mother was.

The night itself was exciting, Ana said. The people danced around a fire and the pregnant girl danced until her dress was so wet it stuck to her belly. There were other things, Ana said, but when Luisa asked what kind, Ana would say only, "You know," and give a look that was at the same time hopeful and wicked.

Once her aunt had called Luisa into the yard, where she sat with Uncle on the bench beneath the catclaw tree. She gripped Luisa's shoulders and made her turn slowly. "What about this one?" her aunt asked Uncle. Chavela's face looked serious and shrewd, but under her voice there was a laugh. "In another year or two she'll be just right."

Uncle didn't look up from the greasewood stick he was whittling, but Luisa could tell he didn't like what Chavela was doing. She wrenched away from her aunt's grasp and ran behind the house, where she found Dolores stalking a beetle, and scooped her up and stroked her feathers until the hen was calm.

"Chavela can believe what she wants," her mother had said when she told her. "You don't have to listen. What will happen, happens, no matter what they call it."

A white moth flitted across the water to land on the edge of her basket, and for a time she watched the way the moth's legs moved one after another, soft and delicate and thoughtful, but then she caught herself and began to rub briskly at the skirt—Chavela's favorite, red and green checked—determined to keep her mind on the laundry.

"You forget," her mother had said when Luisa asked if having babies hurt, but that answer hadn't helped. What she had wanted to ask was why people did it in the first place if it hurt. Why Chavela, if she made such noises, had no children. And why and why and why. She had so many questions she didn't know how to ask them. What the men and women said to each other at the start. What they said after. How they learned these things. What made the women in the arroyo laugh and at the same time shake their heads and whisper.

A stone chipped at the water in front of her and she jumped. Then she heard a laugh. Memo appeared from behind a rock and Rafael scrambled up beside him, grinning, his hands full of stones. "We're bandits," he shouted. "Give us all your money."

"Take off your pants, bad bandits. I have to wash them." She made her voice sound stern and busy, but she was glad they liked the new place. When it was time to return, it would take only a little coaxing for them not to tell. She took the shorts they flung toward her, dipped them, then rubbed soap into the coarse cloth while her brothers splashed in the shallows. Their boy parts bobbed as they ran, the little sacks drawn up like small brown figs, a neat seam that looked as though someone had stitched them, the worm parts wagging.

Those were the parts they would someday put inside a woman. She tried to imagine this, but she couldn't think that this could feel anything other than silly. It was funny that the word for the sweet fruit their parts looked like could also mean that they were little pests.

Memo stopped in front of her, ankle deep in the river. Don Ricardo tried to jump, but the harness held and he dangled for awhile above the water at Memo's knees before her brother drew him up. Rafael thrashed through the water to stand beside Memo.

"Watch!" Memo called, and she saw a yellow arc. "All the way to the other side!"

Memo's effort had barely reached the channel, where the water was darker. Luisa laughed, but suddenly she wondered about something else. What if the man had to relieve himself?

Now Rafael aimed. When his squirt went no farther than he was tall, his shoulders sagged and he began to trudge through the water, away from the washing rocks. He would cry, she knew, and for this she loved him better. He was not like other boys, who bragged how strong they were. Even Memo, who was only nine, made himself bigger with tricks and boasting, like the silly puffing lizards with the leaf-thin collars they stuck out, hissing like great snakes when she tried to catch them, though they were smaller than her hand. Memo squared his shoulders just like that, his chin stuck out so far the sight of it made her want to hit him. Her mother and Chavela only laughed and said what a little warrior he was, which caused him to puff up even more. She loved Rafael for the way when something troubled him, it was as though a cloud passed over his face, and even when the women tried to say how big and strong he was, he seemed to grow smaller and everyone could see.

She scrubbed her mother's skirt, her brothers' shirts, some binding cloths, and wrung them until no water dripped from the twisted cloth, then spread the clothes on the rocks to dry. From upriver she heard her brothers' splashing.

She stood, brushed sand from her knees, and decided not to tell them she was going. If she said what she had to do was private, they would follow, trying to peek. Besides, she wouldn't be gone long, and she would set stones in the pattern her mother had shown her so the sun would tell her if she stayed too long. "Wash yourselves," she called. "Stay away from the deep water."

Down the river and around a jut of boulders lay the wider stretch of sand that she had found before. In the rock wall was a shallow cave, like a niche in the cool walls of Corazón Sagrado, and when she had first seen it she had known the place was meant for her. She stepped up onto the ledge and stood just inside the hollow, facing the river.

Her mother gave answers that were not answers at all. Chavela said her high head got her into trouble. Evil came from too much dreaming, Rosario warned. But she knew the women were wrong because when she stood in this place, in this way, their voices went away and she imagined she was like the statues in the crumbling church, their painted eyes so clear it seemed as though they saw so far into the distance, this had made their faces smooth. It was funny how in this place she was hidden, but at the same time found.

God made the world and all things on it, the water, rocks and sand, the plants and birds and animals, the men and women. The first man was made of dirt and God breathed on him. The first woman was made of the first man. He made it so they fit together and what it felt like when they did this didn't matter. There was no use wondering about it. What mattered was that this act made new people, so each could feel the way she felt now in the hollow, that the world was beautiful and full and good, in the beginning was the Word.

The marks Señor Miller made at his school made words. She hadn't been often enough to puzzle out all the letters on his slate—the lines and sticks and circles like fixing into place the sun and moon and stars—but she had loved the stillness of the room, the dry white smell of chalk. One by one his letters meant the talking sounds. The line that looked like a winding snake made the sound of hissing. The straight stick with the wing above it made the high sound of the wind. Like men and women, the marks married each other and made words that grew into all the words that had ever been said and this was the one big story everyone who ever lived had lived in.

She loved to stand behind the teacher as he sat on the low chair reading aloud, loved the way the wires of his glasses hooked around his ears, the place on his neck where the brown hair of his beard curled soft as Chula's wool. She wanted to place her fingers on his throat to feel the hum of his voice, a voice not like the quick, short Salsipuedes speech that hissed and rattled like the burro bus, but slower, lower, soft as water.

Even after he stopped reading, his stories went on inside her and it seemed she walked around in them, knowing all the people. Once, on her way back down the hill after school, the story of the three crosses on the hill came back to her, horrible and wrong, and no one had done a thing to stop it. Back along the crooked street she had run to tell him that if she had been there, she would have fought with the soldiers and the king, she would have taken off the crown of thorns and put cool water in the cup, not vinegar, she would not have let it happen.

It was meant to be that way, he said. From the beginning. Sometimes a bad thing had to happen to make way for the good, and nothing that came after could have happened if it hadn't. She felt foolish, but he looked at her and smiled and said that something large was in her. And then he said he knew that someday the name of María Luisa Villamil y Cantú would be called, and she would do some great, good thing.

Before she found this place along the river, she hadn't known what he meant, but now she did. Here the rock face caught the sun and held it, warm as skin, and it seemed the day was given to her as surely as her own brown arms were hers, as her chest that drew the breath to breathe the water-scented chuparosa, balsam and wild honey.

In the beginning was the Word. God said it only once but the breath of it had blown through everyone and everything and down to her. This was the message of the cactus and the town, the river and the rain. The Word was in them always and this was why, when she looked long enough at them, her heart swelled wide and she could almost know its meaning. At home, as she went about her days, working, breathing, sometimes she stopped before the question of why she had been set down on earth—*Why are you here?*—and she would feel her heart beat slow and even, her head lighter than air. But in this place, she knew that she was made to show how much she loved the world, and she wished the teacher would hurry back from Mexico City so she could ask him how. Would she give money to the poor, bread to the hungry? What-ever this act would be, she knew that he was right, for even to imagine such a thing made her feel as though her legs stretched down to become part of the trunk of the great tree at the center of the world, her arms grew into branches reaching to the stars. As she rested her back against the rock, she began to hum low in her throat, a song with no words but with a sound that was a place—high, quiet, cool—herself inside it, large with waiting.

She had forgotten to wash her dress. She jumped down from the hollow and took it off, soaped the cloth, rinsed it, wrung it dry before spreading it on the gravel. She would wash herself just before she went back. She had forgotten, too, to set out the time stones, but she knew she hadn't been too long away from her brothers. If she had, they would have come looking for her. She found a flat rock and sat, her arms around her knees, listening to the buzz a locust made in a saltbush on the op-posite bank.

There were thin, dark hairs between her legs. When she first noticed them, she tried to pull them out, but this stung and soon there were too many. There was a line of hairs down her belly, and on her chest were breasts that had started out as hard lumps that hurt when the cloth of her dress rubbed against them but now were growing. Chavela teased about them. "Little walnuts," she'd called them. Between the little wal-nuts was a hollow, like a secret place itself, a shadow in the rock. She put her fingers against her skin where the bone curved and felt her heart beating beneath it. She scooped a handful of wet sand and, leaning back to hold it, molded it into the hollow, thinking of her heart, of how it beat beyond her choosing. More than anything else, she wanted hers to be the grateful kind, but it came to her that if she wanted even that, it was the same as having the second kind, the one that wanted what it couldn't have.

The sky was big and she was small, but there was so much in her. Who could she ask if it was wrong to feel both small and holy at the same time, so full of want as well as full of love? She sent a message to the sky to say how glad she was for everything, to say she didn't mean many of her thoughts, but that they came to her without her wanting them and she was sorry.

When the mold was dry she rolled over to ease it into her hand, warm as one of Dolores's eggs in her palm. Carefully she lowered her hand into the water, where the sand grains swirled before the water took them. With her finger in the sand she made the letters of her name, careful to remember that the little bowl came before the dotted stick. Whoever saw the writing in the sand would think *Luisa at the river in the bottom of the canyon.* She lay back and tried to match her breathing with the locust's whir.

She thought she heard a shuffling noise from the ledge above her, the chink of stone on stone, and she lay still, listening. When the locust ceased its rattle, she listened harder, but there was nothing.

Her stomach gurgled, and so she scooped sand onto her belly to quiet it, then began to pile it higher, smoothing the sides to make her body look like her mother's. She smiled at what she was doing. Her mother had told her to cover herself, and, in a way, she was. The mound was warm and heavy and she had just begun to think of Señor Miller, wondering what his face looked like beneath his beard, when suddenly, starting in her belly and moving to her legs, her arms, the low part of her hips where they pressed against the rock, a strange strong feeling seized her. On her chest the little walnuts felt suddenly tender. A sound rose in her throat as the pile of sand began to crack and slide, and it seemed a canyon opened deep inside her and in it were all things—trees and God and babies, rocks, the sun, the moon, the great wide roundness of the world—but these were not enough. She felt her heart slide up into her throat, shuddering and warm beneath her neck, piercing like two horns of a bone she had once swallowed.

Tears welled, hot and stinging. The women went about their work and if this feeling came to them, they gave no sign. The other girls talked of boys and babies, but not of this. The wasp sting on her arm began to throb, to tell her that she had the second kind of heart, and she felt as though Chavela with her hard flat hand had struck her.

She heard a shout and looked up to see Memo running toward her. She hurried to put on her dress, trying to brush away the sand as she pulled the damp cloth over her head. Memo had put on his clean shorts. "You were naked," he said, narrowing his eyes. "Why?"

For a moment she couldn't think, couldn't remember the reason she'd removed her dress, didn't understand why now sand clung to her skin beneath the cloth, scratching her. "Where is Rafael?"

Memo shrugged. "What are you doing?" He picked up a flat stone and threw it in the river. "Someone was watching you," he said. "Uncle Chu. He went away when I came."

She wanted to shake him. "Where is Rafael?"

But Memo only shook his head.

As though the voices of her mother and Chavela and Rosario accused her, her own voice came back to her from the canyon walls as she ran, calling for her brother. She had lied, she had come to the river, she had left him alone, she had forgotten. For these wrongs there would be a price.

On the rocks she stumbled, but she kept climbing until she could see the washing place, the bright clothes on the river's edge, but beyond them only the willows and the rocks, the water. She hurried across the cobbles and onto the bank. Rafael's shorts were gone. She snatched the rest of the clothes from the gravel and put them in the basket. The sun had moved past the rim of the canyon, shading the lower reaches and making the flood ridges in the sand look like thick, dark snakes. Each time she thought she had found a footprint or the trail left by his stick, it turned out to be a rock, a root, a shadow. She made herself look at the river, at the current in the center where the water seemed to boil.

Among the willows near the bank, she saw a flash of white, and she ran toward the trees. Behind a rock she found him, his head down, picking at a scab on his ankle. His face was streaked with dirt and tears. He had been hiding all along, she could tell by his stubborn look, and she wanted to shake him. "I lost my stick," he said, wiping his nose with the back of his hand. He wouldn't look at Memo. For the first time she noticed that the lizard was gone and she turned to Memo. "Where is don Ricardo?"

The failing light cast a bluish shadow over her brother's eyes. He dug his foot into the sand. "He ran away."

There was more to this than she could know, and it came to her that it was what people hid inside themselves that caused all the trouble. This was why Chavela warned of people. You knew what scorpions and snakes would do, but people could look one way and think another and there was no way to tell. These feelings had no names, and like the beans in her jar they became so mixed up you couldn't tell one from the other.

She spit on her fingers and began to dab at the dirt on Rafael's cheeks. "We'll find a new stick," she promised. She gave Memo a hard look. "And a lizard, too. In Rosario's yard there are more than you can count."

On the way home Memo and Rafael were quiet and the only sounds she heard were the coyotes yipping from the arroyo and from higher in the hills the dogs of Salsipuedes barking in return. The way was growing darker, but with each step upward she felt better, farther from what might have happened. All was well, and there would be no price. Patient Chula would be bleating in her pen, ready to be milked. Dolores would be inside her box, settling herself in her warm feather skirt. There would be a baby.

When they reached the end of the path she stopped and lifted her foot to pull out a thorn. Memo tried again to tell her about Uncle, but she flicked her fingers at him and didn't think about it again until later, for when they drew in sight of the house, she saw that the blankets had been taken from the windows, folded, and stacked neatly on the bench. A group of women gathered outside the door. They ceased their talking to watch as she and her brothers approached the house. Luisa worried that Uncle had come to tell what she had done. Chavela stood with the women, her smoke rising white in the dark air.

Before she could ask about the baby, there was Memo saying, "She took us to the river," and Rafael began to cry into Chavela's skirt.

"She took off her dress," Memo told Chavela, "and Uncle saw."

Luisa set down her basket and looked away from her aunt toward the canyon, where the night seemed to rise, spreading dark and purple. She thought of the way she had felt in the hollow, and the girl who had wanted to do great acts, to be so high and pure and good, seemed far away and foolish. Luisa, the girl who walked around in the world of real things, couldn't do even the small ones right.

"It doesn't matter," she told Chavela. "The clothes are clean and nothing happened." She looked at her feet, waiting for Chavela to berate her.

"Everything matters," Chavela said, her voice wavering before it went brittle, then broke into a cry. "Don't ever forget that." Chavela wiped her nose with the heel of her hand, then put her fingers in her mouth and bit them, hard. "Your mother called for you. Over and over. Just before you got here."

Until Rosario, her old face creased and sorrowful, a fan of wrinkles, came to stand in the doorway, Luisa didn't understand.

"Chavelita, stop," Rosario said. "That isn't true. She died early in the afternoon, daughter," she said to Luisa. "See the hole in the back of the house where they took away her body? The baby died only just now."

On Rosario's huipil were stains, some bright and red, blooming like blood poppies on the coarse white cloth, others faint and delicate as the veins of leaves, or dark streaks that looked as though they had been brushed by the wings of birds. Luisa wanted to turn from the sight, to run far away from Salsipuedes, from the way the scatter of the stains looked like a picture of the wrong that she had done, but when Rosario held out her arms, she went into them and made herself stand still.

2

chavela

For whole days in the weeks after Luisa's mother's death, Chavela lay in her dark back room, asking to be brought her combs, a cool drink, tobacco, weeping and saying how lonely she was for her sister, but if Luisa tried to comfort her, she pulled away. "What do you care about me?" Chavela cried. "What did you care about her, to do what you did?" Other times, she raged through the house, sweeping furiously, knocking dust and cobwebs from the vigas, swatting flies, angry that Luisa had forgotten to fill the lamp, had left milk in the sun to sour. Then, as if nothing had happened, she would tell a joke or make a face, so happy and funny that Luisa would think she had imagined the Chavela who stormed, who had thrown a bowl of rice against the wall, who had begun telling it all over town that Memo and Rafael were the sons she had had with Ralph Emerson López.

"Our sons," she would say, "are growing into fine men like their father. But that one," pointing to Luisa, "gives me trouble. She is quiet like my sister, but a little ghost like . . . that other one."

Luisa could not remember when her brothers were born, or who their father had been, but Ralph Emerson López had not yet come around, so that part was a lie. Her own father had died when she was small. Once, after she had asked about him, her mother had led her outside, pointing toward the broken walls of Corazón Sagrado. "He was the Old Father."

Luisa could picture a black stiff robe with a rim of dust at the hem, but no matter how hard she tried, she couldn't make a face come into view above the black. She had not forgotten going with her mother to sweep the stone floors of the mission church, to dust the holy figures and polish the shining cups, and she remembered the day she had been playing under a bench with gourds and seeds while her mother cleaned. Just as she noticed how her mother's hands looked like dark stars against the white of the statues, the ground began to shake and her mother seized her from the floor and ran outside. The church behind them crumbled into dust and tiles and splintered beams. Old Father had been inside. In the days after the earthquake, her mother moved slowly at her work. Now Luisa understood this slowness. Her own arms and legs felt heavy and nothing mattered and sometimes when she looked at familiar things—a bowl, the sky, her hand—she had to wait a long time before their names would come to her.

Twice Ralph Emerson López had been to see them. The first visit was in the time of Tlaxochimaco when she and Chavela and Rosario were chopping peppers and tomatoes in the shade of the fig tree. It was one of Chavela's good days, and her aunt had stuffed tomatoes under her dress to mimic the size of greedy Silva Barba, who ran the store beside her husband's pulquería in the zócalo. Daintily she held out a small, worm-eaten chile. "One for you," she said, dangling the shriveled pepper in front of Luisa's nose, "costs twenty." She scooped a pile of the good chiles toward herself and with a sly look said, "And twenty-five for me. Free."

They were laughing when they heard the chug of an engine and the squabble of village dogs chasing the gray truck through the narrow street. Chavela, hiking up her skirt, ran with Memo and Rafael. Luisa ran too, in spite of herself, and when Ralph Emerson López jumped down from his truck, she was surprised at how glad she was to see him. His little brown dog, Santa Rita, was with him, and she barked at all the attention, jumping up to nip at Memo when he reached to pet her. Everyone was laughing, and for a moment Luisa forgot that her mother wasn't with them. Then Chavela told him what had happened, and he cried, wiping his face with a red handkerchief. Luisa liked him even better for this, and she wished someone would suddenly say, "Oh, we forgot to tell you. Ralph Emerson López is your father, too."

When he gave Chavela the money he had brought from Texas, her aunt cried and said she would buy food for her sister's poor hungry children. She told him the baby had been a girl, that he should be glad he didn't have another mouth to feed, that she was tired from tending three children, never mind a baby, and so even though she was sad, it was best this way. She led him into the house, touching his chest and arms and saying how cutting cane had made him even stronger than before, how tired he must be from the long drive from the Valley. She hurried to prepare a plate of rice and beans, sending Memo to Rosario's for a bit of pork, then ran to the yard and picked some yellow flax. When she put them in a jar before his place, saying that she always made sure to have fresh flowers at all meals, Luisa, remembering how she'd dreamed of the pretty table for Señor Miller, felt as though she'd seen into Chavela's wanting heart, or worse, that her aunt had seen into her own.

He brought gifts from Texas. For Memo and Rafael, toy guns that clicked when they pulled the triggers but which soon lost their silver paint. For Luisa, a round glass dome that when he shook it sifted snow onto houses with bright yellow windows and roofs like sharp peaks. For her mother he had brought a pair of shoes the color of ripe limes. When he left, Chavela took the shoes for her own and wore them when she went to the zócalo, flashing her eyes in a proud look, her hips high and rolling beneath her skirt. She told everyone how rich Ralph López was, that he had brought the shoes for her, that he had asked her to marry him and move to Texas. No one believed her. In Silva Barba's store one day Luisa had heard the women laughing.

Once when Chavela was napping, Luisa tried on the shoes, buckling the straps, extending her legs so they looked long and brown and beautiful. She tried to walk like Chavela, rolling her head, swaying her hips as though she were dancing, swishing her skirt so that it made a pretty movement, but when she pressed her knees together and lifted her skirt, the feeling of the sand crumbling at the river's edge returned. But this time there was before her the vision of Ralph López's face. She hurried to take off the shoes and wipe them with a warm white tortilla to make them shine.

The next time he came it was in the barren days of Nemontemi, when Rosario and some of the old ones fasted in their houses for fear of evil. But these dark, short days he brightened with a box of oranges, each fruit wrapped in blue paper and sealed with red and green and yellow stamps that Memo and Rafael stuck on their foreheads. Luisa could hardly look at him for remembering the feeling of the shoes. Again he brought money and gifts for Luisa and her brothers, but he brought nothing for Chavela and she pouted until he said, "Well, let's see what I can find for you," and went outside to his truck.

He was gone a long time, then finally returned with a crumpled package of El Toro cigarettes and a magazine. On the cover was a picture of an enormous fish twisting from foaming water, its mouth open to show terrible teeth, a hook, streams of blood. Chavela snatched the cigarettes, but looked at the magazine as if it were a scorpion. "What am I supposed to do with this?"

Ralph López looked at his feet. "Maybe you would like the pictures."

Chavela flipped through the pages, stopping at a picture of a woman in a tight black dress that showed most of her chest. The woman's pale hair fell over one eye, her mouth was open, and she looked as though something had surprised her. With a cry Chavela hurled the magazine to the ground, where the pages flapped in the dust. "This is what you want!"

He looked confused.

"Go to your other women! Never come back!"

He began backing toward his truck while Chavela, screaming, shook her fists. Santa Rita, who had raced ahead and jumped onto the running board, yapped. Chavela grabbed an orange from the box and, making a sound like a dog's growl, hurled it at Ralph Emerson López, who at that moment had turned to walk away. The thin blue paper blew off, fluttering like a bright butterfly. With a thump, the orange struck his back.

Watching, Luisa wanted three things at the same time. One was to tell him that Chavela didn't mean most of what she said, that if he stayed around and learned her ways they all could be fine and happy in the house. The second was that he would go away and never come back. She watched the truck all the way down the road from Salsipuedes until it disappeared into the hills. The third thing she wanted was to run behind it.

• • •

Now it was planting time again, but the wind held on and the rains had been so rare that even the gourd vines were slow to send off shoots. The town seemed sad and quiet. Most of the men and boys had gone to Texas to pick early vegetables. Even Rosario had left with her nephew to work in one of the rich houses in the Valley.

One evening as Luisa crossed the yard from milking Chula, trying not to spill any of the milk from the wide bowl she carried, she heard voices from the house. From behind the woodpile she heard the sounds her brothers made as they fought a duel with maguey swords. Chavela had a visitor. Memo's dog, Lobo, hackles raised, sniffed at a leather bag that hung from a nail beside the door. When he saw her, he left the bag and came to sniff at the milk, pushing his wet, black muzzle against her leg. When Memo first brought Lobo home, Luisa had spent a long time brushing his fur and scratching his ears, but then the dog had killed Dolores, and now she couldn't look at his black wolf face without seeing the torn body of her pet and the sad pile of speckled feathers. With her knee she pushed his head away. Lobo wagged his tail as if to say it didn't matter. He went back to sniffing at the bag. Uncle carried such a bag, and Memo said that in it he stored the breath of the dead.

Careful to make no sound, she went to a side window and looked through a crack in the paper. On the cluttered table, a new clutch of bottles glinted green in the lamplight. Chavela's visitor was Uncle, and in the part of her that knew things without knowing how she knew them, she knew that he had come for her.

She turned and started back across the yard. Between two branches of the catclaw, high enough so Lobo couldn't reach, she wedged the milk bowl. Then she hid behind the tree, watching the house.

All winter Chavela had talked of the ceremony, and at Christmas she had taken Luisa into the hills to watch. She asked about Luisa's monthly time. Did she know which days to eat cold foods, which days she should eat only hot?

She heard a scraping sound, as of chair legs on the wooden floor. Lobo, now lying by the door, head on his paws, pricked up his ears. Light fell across the yard and then Chavela, in the doorway, called in a voice that sounded sweet, "Lucha!"

She stood—nothing made Chavela angrier than when she didn't answer—but she couldn't open her mouth. She held still, her heart so loud she was sure her aunt would hear its thump. Memo and Rafael appeared from behind the house and went inside, Rafael pulling at Memo's shirt, each trying to enter first. From the goat pen Chula bleated. A cricket trilled in the woodpile. Again Chavela called. Just when Luisa began to fear that something in her would answer, would make her walk across the yard toward the light, Chavela turned and closed the door.

Stupid Lobo followed her when she left the yard. When she reached the high path he edged past her, then loped ahead, settling into a trot, and she could tell that in his foolish, proud dog head he thought he was guiding her. She was nearly halfway up the hill when she stopped. If she continued on the path, she would reach the caves by Uncle's hut, so she turned back and cut behind a stick pen to thread her way back down.

Light streamed from the door of the jacal where Ana lived with her grandmother. Luisa thought of stopping, but then gave up the idea. At Christmas, her friend had come to stand beside her at the ceremony as Luisa watched the girl Socorro—who didn't seem the same chattering girl she knew from the washing rocks, but a new, quiet Socorro, womanly and mysterious—pass by on the bear, her belly swollen and rolling with each step as Uncle led the procession up a path lit with candles set in clay pots. The way Socorro's dress shone in the flicker of the torches made it seem as though she were passing through the town from another world. Now and then a dancer broke away from the rest and ran to kiss Socorro, who smiled but kept her gaze ahead, as though watching something far away. The drums and rattles were loud in Luisa's ears, the chanting of the dancers like a slow heartbeat. In the firelight, Ana's dark face seemed to glow, her forehead glistened. "Look at her dress," Ana whispered.

Socorro wore a white dress, full and gathered, embroidered in blue and red with birds and roses, beautiful. Luisa nodded. "Why do they touch her?"

"For luck," Ana said. "For the baby Jesus."

They watched until the dancers led the girl, now with a rebozo over her head, into the shed where Otón Ruiz stabled his mule. The bonfire, Ana said, would come later. "Next year you'll be the one," she whispered. "Everyone knows that." Luisa had looked at her, wanting to ask how Ana could know this, but she held her silence. In her friend's voice she had heard envy.

Now, she turned away from Ana's and climbed the slope to a stand of piñons and sat on a flat rock where she could see the town below. Lobo nuzzled her, his hot, wet breath against her neck, but this time she didn't push him away. Below her the lights looked small as candles in the gathering dark. She heard faint, tinny ranchera music from the radio at Barba's pulquería. Somewhere in the world there was a war, but here all was still and peaceful. To the west the great head of a storm cloud rose above the hills. In the night it would rain. Though it had been a long time since she had, she decided she would pray, and she gathered a handful of piñon needles, meaning to count them like beads, but she couldn't remember the words her mother had whispered, and so she sat, bending the needles to release their sharp, clean smell, hoping that in the smell there would be an answer.

And then it was as though she woke up from the long sleep of the past year. As she looked east into the face of the moon, which shone upon the distant road across the plain and lit it like a silver path, she saw the answer, heard it in the stillness of the night as clearly as if the moon had spoken words. The one moon shone on the one road, but the road went two ways. It brought and took away, went in as well as out. Always—*always*—it offered both. Whoever walked on it could choose.

Lobo bounded beside her as she ran down the slope. Sometimes he raced ahead, then returned to run excited circles, scooting his hindquarters through the dust, as though he was the one who knew exactly what to do. By the time she returned to the yard, the wind had picked up and in it was the smell of rain. The moon had risen toward the cloudhead and now slipped behind it, pulling with it all the shadows and casting the house into new darkness that made it seem the light had not been there at all. The bowl of milk was gone. A sly, hard part of her hoped Chavela would be angry, would shout. For the first time, she would shout back.

The house was quiet. Memo and Rafael sprawled on their straw tick in the corner, sleeping. At first she thought her aunt was not at home, but then Chavela, sitting at the table, struck a match to light the lamp. "I waited for you."

Luisa didn't move toward her, but stood by the door. "I'm sorry about the milk."

Chavela pushed the lamp to the center of the table. "Sit," she said. When Luisa didn't move toward her, she said, "Pah, the milk. It doesn't matter. They ate eggs."

Luisa sat. For a long time Chavela looked at her. Then her aunt began to speak calmly, as though she had prepared her words. "There are things we have to do because they are expected of us. Sometimes we don't like the things, or we're afraid of them because we don't understand why they are important." She gestured toward Memo and Rafael. "Look at me. I take care of you and them. These are the things we do." She shrugged. "For duty. Love. Because no one else can. These are our sacrifices." Chavela smoothed her dress. "What Uncle does is not for himself, but for all of us. For God."

She talked on, but Luisa stopped listening to the words and heard only her aunt's low, patient voice. It had been a long time since she'd heard her mother speak of holy things, since Señor Miller had read the stories, and now something in Chavela's voice sounded familiar and soothing and at the same time made her feel as though she should do what the voice said. For a time she sat looking at her aunt's folded hands, thinking of the story of the angel and the shepherds, the baby in the manger, thinking of how Socorro was like the Virgin, but then she remembered a question that had troubled her the winter before and she asked about the bear.

Chavela leaned forward, her face lit by the lamp, and for a moment Luisa saw a glimpse, in the cast of kindness around Chavela's eyes, of her mother. When Chavela spoke, her voice was gentle. "All things stand for something else. How is the priest's bread like a body? Or wine like blood? Think of the bear as the great back of the world."

They were silent for a while, then Chavela stood and walked to the window. "We do this to show that we remember old things as well as new. That we honor them, and with our bodies make up for our wrongs." With her finger she traced a crack in the yellowed paper covering the table. "The priests want us to think God started far away from here and only comes to us in the ways they say. I watch you and I know what you are thinking." She peeled a strip of paper and let it curl around her finger. "I know you know that God is not only in a church."

Luisa looked away. For the many times her aunt misunderstood her, there were those few when Chavela seemed to see into her heart, and one of these disturbed her more than a hundred of the other. "What if I say no?"

At first Chavela's voice was sharp. "You think you are too good for this?" But then her gaze softened and she lowered her voice. "No one has. It's an honor." She reached for Luisa's hand, pressing it gently. "Can you tell me one good reason you can't?"

In the warm light, in the quiet room, with her aunt's fingers clasped around her own, with the even rhythm of Rafael's breathing and the rustle of Memo turning in his sleep to lull her, she couldn't think of a reason, and she knew that even if she were able to put words to what had troubled her before, they wouldn't matter, for she had seen—in a vision sudden as the little wind that now blew through the room and caused the lamp to flicker, to wash the air with the promise of rain—a vision quiet and certain as the moon when it had slipped behind the cloud: herself in white, her gaze clear and serene, looking far beyond the hills toward the great, good thing.

uncle

Sheaves of dried weeds hung from the vigas in the low-ceilinged room where Uncle sat at his table. The oily smell of tarbush made her think of the medicine her mother had given for stomachache and the saltbush made her sneeze, but the yellow sweet-by-night and the orange zempasuchitl the women had woven into her hair as they prepared her made her feel beautiful and good, just as Chavela had promised. When he called her from the doorway, Luisa went to sit across from him.

In a pool of wax in the center of the table stood a single candle, and inside a gourd bowl were what looked like small knots of lechuguilla rope rubbed smooth. A brasero smoked with the sweet copal that she had smelled before, though not this strong, on Chavela's clothes when she returned from the caves. When he stirred the smoke, moving his hands across the brasero in a gesture that looked like washing, she felt her throat thicken with it.

He explained what they would do and what it meant, that like the gourd the two of them were only vessels. She watched his eyes. They were deep and brown and solemn, and something in them made her understand that she had known them for a long time. As he talked, what they would do made even more sense to her than when Chavela had explained it. She knew how important their act would be, and though she felt as though birds were fluttering beneath her heart, lifting it so high that when they swooped she felt that she was falling, she was glad she had come. When she smiled to show him she was eager to begin, he took a knot from the gourd and placed it in his mouth, then held another, smaller toward her.

Bitter, it tasted, and old, like dirt. She felt odd stings along the sides of her tongue, as though she were chewing something sharp, then she felt the knot grow softer, shredding like cut cane. Water filled her mouth and yet she was thirsty. When she asked for a drink he seemed not to hear her, but when she tried to spit out the chewed knot, he stopped her and told her she should swallow it. Suddenly her throat was filled with burning water, pouring from her mouth. He waited, and when she raised her head, he put a cup to her lips so she could sip a liquid that tasted of piñon and agave.

As though from a distance, he began to speak, but this time the words were strange and in another language and soon they faded into lines that pulled each other back and forth until instead of two lines there were two of her, then two of him, a high part and a low part, and the words they said together were a language that she understood before she heard it, and when she wondered how the earth and sky had turned around and where, in all the turning, had her body gone, the words told her the reason.

She shivered at the vision of a figure at the far end of a tunnel. She was not afraid of dying, but of meeting the dead, for among them there was a soul she had abandoned. And then the figure disappeared.

Now the lines, smooth and slow and green as glass, moved in waves that passed beneath her until his voice above her took on weight and color. A frail, clear blue, a drawing back, then bright orange in a push, like the flesh of brilliant flowers dense and crushed together. Blue again, then orange, blue and orange, and it was only when she woke and found her eyelids raw with salt that she understood that she had had a dream and in it she had cried before the vision of her body as a blossom and a bell.

Seven times she went to him. Sometimes it was evening when Chavela came for her, the sun a fine red line across the cordillera; at other times, full day. Once her aunt woke her in the middle of the night, when the only sounds came from the scuffing of their feet in the dust and the soft chitter of doves in the algarrobo. Other women joined them on the walk up the hill to Uncle's, where they left her at the door.

He fed her no more of the buttons that made the colors come, but each time when she smelled the sweet copal a hard knot loosened in her to think how easy it was, how good, the opening of legs and the secret act of men and women solved. Though at first her body had been sore, she now knew that the cries she had once wondered about were not for pain alone, and she knew what it had been that she had longed for at the river. During the day she stumbled over rocks to think of what they did together, and once when she was milking Chula she was held so long inside a memory—like a shimmering blue moon—of the way his hand had pressed on her belly that she was surprised to see the goat had strayed into the pimientos.

And then the visits stopped. At first it was good to rest, but by the third day when the shadows drew out long and blue across the hills and Chavela went about her business with no mention of Uncle, she grew sick with longing. Three times that evening she had brushed her hair, had rinsed her face and neck and under her arms. Each time when she drew the cloth between her legs, her hand grew weak as she remembered. Now she stood by the door, her back against the adobe so she could feel the stored warmth of the day, hoping to see the white sight of the women coming toward her down the path.

At last Chavela came into the yard. She didn't come for Luisa, but went to sit on the bench beneath the catclaw. Luisa walked out to sit beside her. She was just about to ask when it would be time when Chavela said, "So, you're ready?"

Luisa stood.

Her aunt rocked back on the bench, smiling. "Aren't you in a hurry!"

Chavela looked at her for what seemed a long time, then rose from the bench. "This part is over. He's gone into the mountains. He'll come back when it's time." Her aunt started for the house but paused at the doorway, looking sharply at Luisa. "Only a fool," Chavela called, "would expect a sacrifice to be easy." From across the yard Luisa heard her low, rough laugh before she drew the door closed, saying, "I should have known you'd like it."

4

the gods arrive

At the time of Teotleco, when the vines began to rattle in the dry wind, people began returning to Salsipuedes. First came Rosario bringing silver thread, a washtub full of lily bulbs, stories of palm trees and fine houses, of dirt so rich the cannas grew taller than her chin. The braceros came back from the great fields, packed into truckbeds, shouting, drinking. Among them Lobo sniffed out his former owner, who had brought back a greyhound bitch in season, and the dog returned to live with him. Memo, for the first time Luisa could remember, cried. The men held cockfights, fought among themselves, set off Roman candles in the hills. One night someone stole Silva Barba's cash box, and when she discovered the loss, she ran through the streets dressed in nothing but the flowered doorway curtain she had yanked from its nails, accusing first one, then another of her neighbors, accusing the widow Hinojoso because once she'd argued over the price of a one-legged chicken, badgering Loco Lo, who had begged to trade his gold tooth for mescal and then told the town she'd cheated him. For days Salsi-puedes had talked of nothing else. In all the excitement the robbery was forgotten, and the news that enormous Silva Barba slept with no clothes on swept through the town more rapidly than the news that the world war had ended.

Just when the scandal began to die down, someone else returned. On this morning Luisa had gone up into the hills with her brothers to gather piñon. The smell of sun and dust on the needles had just reminded her that winter would not be far away. When they heard the rumble of Filo Santos's bus as it chugged up the hill, Memo and Rafael dropped their bundles and ran, but Luisa hung back. She was still not used to the thickness in her middle, the stretched feeling in the joints where her legs met her body, and she had learned that it was difficult to move quickly. Watching as her brothers joined the children in the zócalo below, she lowered herself onto a rock to see who had arrived.

These days it seemed she cried often, but when she tried to put a name to her trouble she could not. Now, at seeing the way the children crowded around the visitor, the way he patted them and smiled, it seemed that all her yearnings fixed onto their true source, and she un-derstood, with a catch of breath in her throat, how much she had missed good Señor Miller. She threw down the kindling and began to walk, first in slow, determined steps, then, before she knew it, she was running, laughing at the clumsy, heedless way she crashed through the branches like a big round loco melon bumping down the hill.

Jarred and out of breath, just past the first of the houses of the town, she stopped when she remembered she was forbidden to see the teacher. "You don't know what he'll do," Chavela had said. "A long time ago there was a priest who tried to stop things. He took the girl away and she never saw her family again. The next summer wasps ate the corn down to the stalks."

Rosario nodded. "The people starved."

"Besides," Chavela added, "if I were you, I wouldn't go near a priest. Look at all the trouble it got your mother in."

Memo, who in these days reminded her so much of her aunt that she almost believed Chavela's lie, had told her three times to stay away if the teacher returned. She had heard from Ana that Memo was to be the escogido, chosen by Uncle, even though Memo was not his son, to know his secrets, chosen for some feat he had performed. She imagined this feat had to do with her brother's pets. A few weeks before, she had seen her brother sewing shut the mouth of one of his lizards with agave fiber drawn through a cholla thorn needle. "Why?" she asked, horrified. "So she won't talk, of course," he'd answered in his hard-faced, knowing way.

She waited to catch her breath, then turned back for her load. She would take the back way home. To keep it from poking her belly, she shifted her bundle. But then something made her look one last time below, and she was glad. If she had failed to turn, she would not have seen the sight she knew she'd been meant to see: From around the corner of the crumbled church came the girl Socorro with her son on her hip, the baby's brown legs dark against the white of his mother's skirt. Luisa waited, watching to see what Señor Miller would do. When he saw them, he walked toward Socorro, took the baby from her arms, and kissed him.

All afternoon an idea grew and by evening she had settled on a plan. She had been a fool not to see the great design all along. She saw how she had been put in one place just so she could move into another, how the days were doors, like many doors to walk through but only one would open at a time, and it was only when you stood before the final one that you looked back to see the way they'd opened for you from the start. How stepping through the right one could make up for all the ones that had been wrong.

Though lately she had been hungry enough to eat clay, this night she could scarcely swallow for thinking of the questions she would ask on her way toward the plan, and she gave her bowl of onion rice to Memo. Chavela had left early for Rosario's, where they would have their coffee, but it was a long time before her brothers quieted down. Lying on their tick, they played their rule game. Memo made the rules and Rafael had to break them. "I build a jail with stone walls," Memo began.

"I would hammer a hole," Rafael said.

"Hammers aren't allowed."

"I would get a log."

"There are no trees around. And you can't get out."

"I would dig a tunnel in the floor."

"No shovels, and the floor is thicker than a house is high."

They played the game often, and Luisa wondered why Rafael seemed never to understand that no matter what plan he made, Memo would make a rule to stop him. Just as their voices trailed away, Rafael would think of a new plan, and their murmuring would begin again.

When she was sure they were asleep, she put on the green shoes. Chavela hadn't worn them for weeks. She took the blanket from her bed and wrapped it around her body; it would be best for Señor Miller to learn things slowly. As she pushed open the door to leave the house, taking care that it didn't squeak on its hinges, she felt large and looming as Silva Barba in her curtain, but at the same time silly and excited, as though she were lighter than the chill air.

When she reached the catclaw she heard a noise behind her. Rafael had followed. "Go back," she whispered. "Sleep."

"I'm coming with you," he said. His hair stuck up in two points from his forehead, making him look like a grasshopper. "I know where you're going."

"Maybe I'm just going for a walk."

"You're going to see the teacher."

"What if Memo wakes up and finds you gone? He'll tell. Then we'll both be in trouble."

He looked at the house, dark on the moonless night, then back at her. "Memo is mean."

"Go back to sleep. Don't tell and I'll bring you a surprise."

He brightened. "A book," he said, "a red one." Then a look of doubt crossed his face. "You're not coming back."

If she knelt to comfort him, he would cling, and so she moved away. She thought of taking him along, but to take him might spoil the way the doors had opened, might shut one. And how proud he would be tomorrow when he came to school and found his sister at the door beside Señor Miller to welcome the pupils, handing out pencils and paper, tracing the letters on the black slate, making the children wash their hands before they touched the books. She straightened her shoulders, shifting to keep her balance in the shoes. "Yes," she said, "a beautiful red book.

"You're going to have a good surprise tomorrow," she told him. "I promise. Go back to sleep and when you wake up it will be time."

Rafael rubbed his eyes and she could tell it would not be long before he was asleep. "Red. Don't forget."

She bit into her forefinger to show tooth marks as proof. "I won't."

* * *

A lantern glowed in Señor Miller's window, and she was watching it so intently as she approached that at first she didn't see that the teacher sat outside on a wooden chair. His voice startled her. "Well," he said, "my best pupil. And in such beautiful shoes." When he smiled she saw the whiteness of his teeth. "You weren't with the others today."

She looked at the ground to show that she had heard his compliment.

When he placed his hand on her shoulder, she felt as though a pot bubbled deep and slow within her. "Come inside and we'll put your name in your book," he said.

She looked at his shoes, dusted nearly white from his trip. She would like to shine those shoes until they shone black as beetles, so the shine of them would make it so that he had never been away.

He guided her into the room behind the schoolroom. In it were wooden boxes, a folding cot with a Saltillo blanket, a metal chair, two tables piled with books. "Bibles," he said. "From Mexico City." He took a book from the stack and held it out to her. "Do you know who Cárdenas is?"

She shook her head, but he seemed not to notice and went on talking about things she didn't understand. "We can thank him for these," he said. "They're old and used, but good."

She took the book from him and smelled the sharp scent of dust and cloth and paper. Gently, she opened the covers. Words marched along the lines and there were pictures, one of a coin, another of a tower built to the clouds, lightning striking, people falling. She imagined the tower was in Mexico City and she wondered if he had seen such a sight. Though it was not among the questions she had planned, she asked, "Do you come from Mexico City?"

He laughed. "No," he said, "from Nebraska."

She had never heard the word, but its sound rustled like book pages, beautiful because he had come from such a place, and she thought what a miracle it was that he had come from so far away but now stood before her. And what was going to happen in her plan, too, was a miracle. Like the angel and the Virgin. It was true that sometimes bad things had to happen to make way for the good.

All afternoon she had practiced her questions, and she began, looking at the collar of his shirt and wondering briefly how he kept it so clean. "So," she said, "you don't have a wife?"

When he laughed she looked at the floor.

"It isn't wrong to ask," he said. "You're curious about me. The whole town is, but people are too stubborn to ask." He began to straighten the books, evening the stacks. "Or maybe they're just being polite."

He pulled out the metal chair, indicating that she should sit. She sat, but then, thinking it might not be right that she sit while he did not, she jumped up, knocking over the chair.

"I don't have a wife," he said, righting the chair, his voice gentle and slow. "I'm from a town even smaller than this one. My church believes that war is wrong, but I wanted to do something to help. Before I came here I was a teacher and I had studied Spanish and so—"

Forgetting all the questions she had practiced, their order, how important it was that she ask each one in turn, with a sudden burst of pride in her own accomplishment she said, "Well, I'm going to have a baby."

He blinked.

Even later she could not remember how the threads of what she had hoped became so tangled in the threads of what she had forgotten. The moment she told him about the baby, the question she had asked him about a wife seemed to coil itself around and back onto her in a way she hadn't considered—did she have a husband?—and she thought of the women at the washing rocks, their whispers, and in her alarm that he would think of her what the women thought about her mother and Chavela, she began to explain about Uncle, talking faster than she had believed herself able. She told him that a husband didn't matter, all that mattered was what you had when you were done, a new person. A boy or a girl. She hoped, she told him, that hers would be a girl because of her lost sister even though it was better to have a boy because that was more like the baby Jesus. She explained that this was done so that the spirit of God that turned the world would keep on turning it, knowing the people remembered how it had started in the first place. She told him what she had just that moment realized: that nothing was a sin if you did it for the right reason, and that the God who made the river and the rocks and trees would not make it so that only what the people did could be a sin. She talked on, noticing that he had begun to pace, stopping each time he passed the table to run his hand across the books. Finally, when she realized that he was no longer listening, she fell silent.

He sat so heavily on the cot at the back of the room that its legs wobbled, and he was quiet for so long she wondered if he was praying. Then he spoke, so sorrowfully she felt as though she had taken something from him. "You're just a child. How old are you?"

She started to tell him, but then she understood that the answer didn't matter.

She wanted to remind him of Socorro and her baby, of the scene in the zócalo. She wanted to explain about the great, good thing and how it was because of him that she had come to understand that being the chosen girl could be part of this, and how because of this she had seen the plan to help him in the school, and how, if he liked her help, they could be married and how perfect this would be. She wanted to make him see the great round chain of all of it, but her plan seemed suddenly a web spun in the wind between impossible things, and she was left with only herself at the center, tottering in the shoes, the fool who thought things would be easy.

Once with Uncle she had wanted to tell him that even though she knew that what they did was toward a higher purpose, she loved him also in the low way of their bodies, but when she tried to say the words, her tongue grew heavy, so she had gone to stand behind him as he sat in his low chair, had wrapped her arms around his neck, pressing her cheek for a long time against his. He stroked her arms, and when she broke away she felt as though he had understood what was in her heart.

Now she crossed to the cot and stood before the teacher, meaning to kneel and rest her head in his lap. In this act would be the message that she understood why he was troubled, that she was sorry, that it didn't matter; she would come tomorrow like the rest and he could forget what she had told him. But as she leaned toward him he jumped up, nearly knocking her aside, and his one word, "No!" seemed torn from his throat.

If he called out after her, she didn't hear. Outside, the sky seemed low, the air thick. There was no moon to light the way. A flock of doves wheeled from an acacia as she reached the lower road and turned toward the chaparral. She thought once of turning around, but there was nothing in the air to draw her home. She had been carrying the green shoes but now she dropped them. Far to the east, where the foothills flattened toward the wide valley, sheet lightning shimmered in a haze over the plain.

• • •

In the old days young men went into the mountains to lie in a pit and wait for visions, but for her there was nothing but a great sand-colored dizziness and walking. When she looked up from the ground she couldn't tell if the spots she saw before her were stars or creosote bushes. Her hands were stained pink as melon from the juice of the bitter tuna she'd plucked from a stunted cactus, and the nettles from the fruit still stung her lips and tongue.

She had meant to stay far from roads, but when, on her third day past the hills, she found herself beside a road, she stepped onto the hardpan to ease her feet, and then, because it seemed easier, she stayed on. She had meant, if anyone passed, to cut through the chaparral, flatten herself against the earth, but when she heard a rumbling noise behind her, she kept walking along the road. When she felt the shudder of the ground, the stir of grit as it peppered her legs when the truck drew to a stop beside her, she turned to look. A man got out and walked toward her. As he drew near she saw that his face was nearly as pink as her fingers where the juice had stained them. She did not remember the questions he must have asked or the answers she must have given, and later, she did not remember the long ride in the back of the truck. She remembered only the sight of his hand, the way the sun's glare caught the pale hairs at his knuckles and made them gold and green and violet, as he held it for her to take. He led her to the truckbed, lowered the tailgate, and boosted her toward a woman in a black rebozo drawn against the settling dust who reached out to pull her in.

BOOK II

•

the summer of the ants

rio paradiso, texas

1947

•

Not every soil can bear all things.

—Virgil

a dinner party

The town of Rio Paradiso, at a bend in the river at the southern border of Hidalgo County, was just a farmer's cafe, a pump station,
a few bracero shacks, some farmhouses from the turn of the century,
and acres of groves and fields. The place had been named by a Mr.
Sabhaill of County Cork, who intended to settle in New Zealand but
embarked on the wrong ship and wound up in Galveston Harbor, from
which he made his way along the keel of coastal Texas to the Rio
Grande to stake his claim on the bank of a sandbed tributary, giving it
the hybrid name that had now lasted a century. No one at the land office
had pointed out, or perhaps even knew, that while *Rio* was Spanish
enough to fit into the history of the place, *Paradiso* was most certainly
Italian. From time to time, a purist insisted that the latter word should
be the Spanish *paraíso,* and everyone agreed, some saying that this was
what came of allowing the Irish to name things, but no one did anything,
and so the name stuck. Sticklers for accuracy, such as Edwina Harmon
Hatch of Lynchburg, Virginia, who when she arrived in 1944 and spied
the birdshot-speckled town limit sign said to her new husband, "That's
not right," were bound for frustration. "You'll get used to it," Thomas
told her, and he was right, for after three years, in the face of mistakes
far greater, the error no longer seemed to matter. The nearest actual
town was Martha, five miles away and not that much bigger, but with
a store-lined Main Street and the Ardmore Girls Academy, where during
the school year Eddie taught to orphans what shreds of schoolbook Latin
she remembered from her two terms at Sweet Briar College.

From the back porch, where she had gone to escape the heat of the
kitchen, Eddie could see the row of royal palms that lined the road to

town. It was July, high summer, and heat shimmered over the pale caliche of the Mile Six Road. Her husband had gone to Weslaco to look at—she couldn't remember exactly—root stock, cultivars, bud sports, something for his new project. She watched for the column of dust that meant his gray Paradiso Fruit truck was returning. She hoped he wouldn't be too much longer. There was no ice; in the heat even the icebox had given up.

All afternoon she had cooked at her new electric stove. Buttermilk fried chicken and plump ears of sweet corn, string beans with salt pork, biscuits, fried tomatoes from the bushel of green vinefalls, a pineapple cake. It was Thomas's birthday and she planned to use the occasion, her hard work, and her many sacrifices to ask again for a house in Rio Paradiso. Other growers were building fine estates on the outskirts of the town, and there were large lots for sale. Upstairs in the bottom drawer of her bureau beneath a stack of tatted dresser scarves lay her plans, a sheaf of drawings she had worked on for the past years, penciling in a dining table for eight, only to erase it, elongating it to seat twelve. She kept lists of colors, scraps of fabrics, party menus, and as she worked over the stove, she considered: When the day came, should she hire a Southern cook or try to train one of the Mexican women?

She'd taken off her dress to work in her cotton slip, which now had flour on the hips where she'd wiped her hands. Because she'd had to show the maid Guadalupe for what seemed the hundredth time how to use the new iron to press the crease in Thomas's khaki trousers, she had left the pineapple cake too long in the oven, and it had dried at the edges. When she turned the cake onto the plate the syrup stuck hard and brown to the pan. She'd pieced the pineapple back into its sunburst pattern, but the glaze was ruined. To make it look better, she'd sprinkled coconut and powdered sugar over the top, but the cake looked as bad as the heat rash on her chest. Finally she'd given up, throwing a dishtowel over the cake, tucking in the edges so the ants wouldn't get at it. The insects had been bad this summer. Thin lines swarming at the windowsills, braiding up the chrome table legs, caravans along the shelves of the pantry. Sometimes in the mornings around the hood light of her new stove they clustered thick as spilled black pepper.

She lifted her heavy hair from the back of her neck and bent to look at her reflection on the side of the pressure cooker she stored on the back porch. Though she tried to stay out of the sun, her freckles looked worse than ever. Her face seemed to melt sideways with the curve of metal, with the heat, her mouth smeared in and out of shape, as though she were a spot-faced clown looking into a fun house mirror. "Heat rash," she said, savoring the words for their hot, sweet sound, savoring how damp and overblown she looked. She plumped her cheeks, working air in and out, fishbreathing. "A big heat rash."

Rising from her collarbones, along the side of her neck, redder than her freckles, spread a blotch of blisters, the Mexsana she had sprinkled earlier now caked along the cracked-looking seams. Guadalupe had told her that if she broke off a leaf of aloe vera and smeared the white ooze over the rash, it would heal immediately. It might even rid her, Guadalupe suggested slyly, of her many spots.

"Like magic, Madama," the maid had promised, smiling, squeezing the stalk, and Eddie had tried, but the viscous white felt even worse, as though the unguent sealed in the heat. From bitter experience she knew that nothing—bleach, bicarbonate, witch hazel—would make the freckles go away. She would be piebald all her days.

Now in the chickenyard Guadalupe scattered meal, and Eddie could tell by the languid way the girl let the grain sift through her fingers that she, too, watched the road. All the Mexican girls idolized Thomas, though she couldn't understand why; usually girls like Guadalupe spent their time on more dangerous-looking men, braceros who circled each other in low-slung jeans, their elbows held in tightly, guarding like boxers, or else held out as though to draw knives, their necks rigid. Fierce, wolfish men who looked as though they could kill for what they wanted, a bottle of Pearl beer, a woman, vengeance, an apology. Compared with these men, her husband, Thomas, looked mild, pink with perpetual sunburn, frightened. Shorter than she by two inches, with his thin-boned, long face, his small nose too wide at the bridge, his weak eyes startlingly magnified by Teddy Roosevelt glasses, he made Eddie think of the jackrabbits that loped along through the Valley scrub. Sometimes, when she and Thomas drove their dove-gray Packard along the road at night, a jackrabbit would freeze, lightstruck, its eyes pale and glowing, and Eddie would almost laugh, imagining herself as the car—large, pale, predatory, her teeth a wicked, leering grill—as Thomas braked, flicked the lights, honked the horn until the creature bounded away, as though in some way he were sparing his own life.

For a time she watched Guadalupe, the hem of her blue uniform swaying around her knees, as she fed the chickens. Again the girl had shortened the dress, had tied a yellow chiffon scarf around her neck, though Eddie had forbidden decoration. Through Guadalupe's earlobes ran the gold hoops Eddie had just that morning told her not to wear. "You'll catch those things on some máquina and tear your ears off," she'd said. "Only gypsies wear earrings."

"No, Madama," Guadalupe assured her, waving dismissively, looking at the ground in that maddening way they all had of not meeting her eyes. "They are nothing. I forget they are there."

Also maddening on this day had been the hour she'd wasted trying to prod a blacksnake from the high shelf in the washhouse. Around mid-morning Guadalupe had run across the yard toward her, screaming, "Una víbora!" and pulling at Eddie's arm, pulling until they stood in the doorway of the shed, where they kept the wringer washer. Guadalupe pointed to the ledge just beneath the corrugated tin roof. "There!" she said, and finally Eddie saw the snake, thick as her forearm, stretched nearly the length of the ledge, its black skin dusty looking in the shadows of the rafters. She could see the creature breathing, a lump just behind its head which she guessed was a mouse or an egg.

"It's just an old blacksnake," she said. "He won't hurt you. See that bump? He's having his dinner. His comida. He's half asleep. Duermes, see?" She made the palms-together gesture for sleep, then a snorting, snoring noise that hurt her throat. She felt foolish, but sometimes when Guadalupe became upset she forgot her English. Eddie suspected a selective memory.

"Sí," the maid had said, lowering her eyes to hide a smirk which also maddened Eddie, but Guadalupe refused to enter the shed until the snake was gone. Eddie had sent her for one of Pompilo's rakes, and for a long time she'd prodded the creature. The snake would inch forward slightly but was so sluggish that it would barely raise its head. Finally she had given up and for the rest of the morning the pile of wet towels had lain mildewing on the concrete floor. When Eddie'd checked that afternoon, the snake was gone but the towels remained.

Now Eddie called across the yard, "No más today. Go on to your casa." Eddie took pride in her facility with languages, making sure to sprinkle Spanish into her orders.

Guadalupe lived behind the oleander hedge in a low-ceilinged shed that had once been a brooder house. Thomas had installed glass in its single window, had run water pipes for a sink and shower. Behind the shed he'd built a johnny house. To Eddie the place looked like the rattiest of shacks, but Guadalupe, for all her airs, seemed happy to have the house and the monthly ten dollars and all the giveaways. Eddie knew she was lucky to have a maid who lived on the property; most of her friends made do with day help. Still, it was often more trouble than it was worth. Guadalupe was eighteen, and when she wasn't willfully misunderstanding Eddie's orders, she was carrying on with some man or another from the bracero camp. Through the vines and trash palm and scrub pecan behind the brooder house there was a path beaten toward the levee blockhouses that served as quarters for the Paradiso field help, the crews Thomas oversaw. Eddie knew who used the path: Fat Polo the racketeer with his Pancho Villa mustache and his promises of wooden cases of Coca-Cola delivered pronto to Eddie's door anytime-day-or-night for only dimes and quarters, pocket change; thin, loose-jointed Perfilio, slit-eyed, white-smiled, his fingers black from tuning engines at the Chevrolet garage; Tito, Chalo, Tino, Chuy; she couldn't keep them straight. Guadalupe held first one suitor in favor, then another. Often they fought over her and it was at these times, it seemed to Eddie, that Guadalupe was most happy, complaining in rapid, passionate Spanish to her sisters—by Eddie's reckoning there were at least eight, and how they fit into the brooder house, God knew—when they visited, their voices a swirl of vowels, trilled r's, clipped consonants, anguish, and umbrage. Eddie tried to picture Thomas fighting for her, but the image was comic. Here she was, plunked down in the land of passion, defended by the Bunny Bread Man. Laughing louder than she'd intended, she startled Guadalupe.

The girl waved, but went on sifting the meal through her fingers, scattering grain in dusty arcs.

"Pronto, Guadalupe," she called again, louder. Though she tried to match the Spanish pronunciation of her maid's name, the syllables always burst haywire from her mouth—*Whatta-loopy*—and her efforts sounded flat and foolish. "Right this minuto." Again Guadalupe nodded but made no move to stop; it was as though Eddie were invisible.

The air seemed thick as bathwater. The late afternoon sun beat orange on the dun-colored silt beneath the live oaks, where the carpet grass wouldn't grow. In the stillness Eddie felt her own flesh giving off heat. She marveled at the odd feeling of sudden bulk, surprised, despite the pounds she'd put on in three years of marriage, to remember that she took up space and air. And she was no cooler than when she'd left the kitchen. Hotter, maybe. Her anger settled on Thomas. She straightened, turned to go back into the kitchen to finish preparing the meal, peeled her sticky slip away from her chest, decided: She'd come to the supper table in her dad-gum slip. He'd never notice.

Six times, she would tell las girls—her friends, the wives of other growers—if she had less pride. Six times for . . . *it*. She would slap her cards onto the poker table, hold up her hands, fingers splayed. What did they think of that? *It* six times in three years of marriage. The rest was pecks and pats, a peck when he left for work, a pat on the head good-night.

The buzz of conversation would cease, her friends fall silent. She could taste the women's shock as it traveled around the table, bitter as the gin and grapefruit juice she would sip, but sweet, too, sugary and rich, with the lingering, dark snap of molasses.

For whole days sometimes she forgot. Then, suddenly, the sight of a boy kissing a girl outside the Rialto theater in Martha would stun her. Her knees would weaken when she looked at the photographs in *Life* of soldiers embracing their girls. Even words could do it: *derrick, gusher, flood;* a conjugation—*amo, amas, amat*—could send her into a forlorn swoon. She was thirty-seven, but she felt eighteen, seeing *it* in every-thing, *it* in everyone, a bunch of hogs, every one of them snorting at the trough but her. And Thomas, who didn't seem to care. The times when the girls played poker were the hardest, when at the card table they talked of how their husbands couldn't keep their hands away.

At a party the month before, Nila Nimrod, whose husband, Buzz, had made more money than he had any right to disking under acres of cabbage, had giggled, smoothing the tucks in her blouse. "Mister Pes-ter," she'd said, her smile prim and at the same time salacious and some-how catlike. "That's what I call him. You know, his thing." She flicked a card into the discard pile. "Don't tell anyone. It tickles him."

Ann Dell Jenkins cut a look at Nila's maternity smock. "Looks like old Mister Pester tickled you right back."

Eddie sipped her drink and pretended to consider her hand, the jack and ace of diamonds, three nines—clubs, hearts, spades—trying to think of what to discard.

Joan Baines said, "Buddy calls his the Major. It's the Major's birthday next week and I have to make a party for him. I'm supposed to give him a present."

"A paper hat," Ann Dell said.

Nila said, "Sew it up a uniform."

"He wants . . ." Joan leaned over the table, whispering the name of the act he'd requested. "I could never figure where they got that name for it. There's no blowing whatsoever."

Ann Dell laughed raucously, laying down her cards. "Yes, but it sure as hell is a job. I fold."

"Stop it," Nila pleaded, giggling. "You'll make me wet myself."

Eddie, making sure she laughed the loudest, thought of the time she had gingerly lifted the sheet, gingerly brushed her lips across the wiry hairs on Thomas's belly, holding her breath, hoping.

Joan said, "I blame it on the war. They'll never be the same. They heard . . . things."

"I'm tired of *things,*" Ann Dell said.

"One time Buzz wanted me to hum," Nila said. "I couldn't stop laughing."

"What song?" Ann Dell wanted to know, and the others laughed. "Try 'The Eyes of Texas.' "

Eddie realized that Joan had been nudging her. "I asked if you want hit, Ed."

"What?"

"More cards?"

"Three," she said, laying down the nines, ridiculously hoping for the ten, queen, king of diamonds.

Ann Dell gave her a heavy-lidded look as she dealt. "Don't you all have a name for Tom's?"

Eddie picked up the cards and pretended to consider them, aware that the girls were looking at her, waiting. She thought of telling them, blurting out the sorry facts, but before she could think further, her mouth was moving, her voice too loud, too shrill. "I hardly ever think about it," she said, sliding the cards—the two of clubs, the four of hearts, the king of diamonds—into a fan. "He's after me all the time. I just tell him," she went on, hearing her voice grow ragged, strident, veering toward the edge of anger when what she'd hoped for was a blasé, joking tone, "to pull my nightgown down when he's done."

The women—all younger than Eddie, all with children to their names—looked at the table, at their hands, anywhere but at her, and it seemed to Eddie that her friends had grown suddenly interested in counting and separating the buttons they used for poker chips. She wondered if the bitterness she tried to conceal was as obvious as it felt—a stain, a scar, festering like the heat rash she suffered every summer. At that moment, no matter how hard she was tempted, she vowed never to tell. They would blame her; she could hear Ann Dell's suggestion that perhaps it was her added weight. "They like a little meat on the bones," Ann Dell would say, "but not the whole pot roast." Eddie had told Thomas she'd gained five pounds. To the girls she confessed ten. It was twenty-five.

Three years before, when she had first come to the Valley, workers in the bracero trucks had whistled at her, had clicked their teeth, made kissing noises, called out a name that sounded like *Wetta*. She couldn't find the word in her Spanish dictionary and she'd had to ask Thomas what it meant. Blondie, he told her. "They like your hair." Even that fool, the yardboy Pompilo with his liquid, half-wit leer, mowing the carpet grass around the farmhouse, trimming the crotons by the clothes-line, carting palm trash, looked long at her brassieres when Guadalupe pinned them on the line.

But then, without her knowing when things changed, that kind of attention had stopped, and something had gone out of her. Something she could feel, like starch bleeding into washwater, swirling into milky bluish threads, and she could feel the loss of whatever it had been that held her up while she had been Edwina Jane Harmon of Diamond Hill, Lynchburg, Virginia, sassing back the cook when she swatted her fingers from the sweetdough; sassing skinny Mr. Farnsworth Lucifer, the piano teacher who'd made her play "L'isle joyeuse" until her fingers hurt, who'd licked his lizard lips until they were chapped crimson; sassing boys, turning away suitors because their eyes were too close set, their prospects not shining enough; while she had been Miss Harmon, giving music lessons at the Steinway in the upstairs hall at Aunt Bean's in Rich-mond; while she had been pert Eddie Jane, a hatcheck girl in black taffeta ruffles at the Jefferson Hotel, declining offers more shadowy, suggestions more urgently proffered, husbandless for no reason she could determine, until at the age of thirty-four when she met Thomas when he'd come to Richmond on a tobacco-buying trip, gave up and married him, turned into plain Eddie Hatch, a farmwife in a cotton housedress her mother with her summer linens and winter velvets would have died to see, and the sassy, hopeful thing that held her up through all those years had left for good and she plumped out, the pounds arriving like a mess of piglets following their dam to swarm about her in a free-for-all.

While the other growers and their wives built big houses on Grand Texas Boulevard just outside Rio Paradiso, planted acacias and royal palms, poinsettias that grew tall as the eaves, she grew thicker, pound after pound, living on the flat dusted land beside the levee with Thomas Hatch—he of the surname it pained her to say for there having been sharecropper Hatches near Lynchburg—who oversaw the work crews in the Paradiso Fruit Company fields, who in his spare time tended his own farm he called the Hundred Acres, though it was only eighty, grew his vegetables and cotton and conducted his experiments with tobacco, grapes, and now with his pet, a strain of pink lemon more sweet than sour which he hoped to develop.

He was a man made stingy by his grandfather's loss of their dust bowl Oklahoma farm. She'd had to fuss at him for the electric icebox; long after other farms had hooked into CP&L, Thomas held back. It had been just this summer that she'd gotten the electric stove, the fans, the iron, the pressure cooker, and only after she'd stamped her foot. He had plenty of money, she knew, but about her urging that they buy a lot and build a house in town he was immovable: Until he saved the money to put down cash for every speck of dirt and every stick and brick, she was stuck in the slat-sided farmhouse with paint the color of old cob-webs, stuck five miles from town where not twenty years before there had been bandits and border wars, stuck in the moonlight parade of Mexicans across the river a half mile to the south, the smell of burning mesquite, and the scrabble and cluck of chickens. And now these ants. She pinched one from the windowsill and with her thumbnail severed its head from its thorax, then crushed it between her fingers, where the mangled body released its musky smell of bitter oil and coconut. When she looked for Guadalupe in the chickenyard, the girl was gone.

Often Thomas gave rides to workers, who slouched off toward the river, and so she thought nothing of it when his truck pulled into the lane and she could see a passenger. But when from the cab a tall man dressed in pressed khaki jumped down, holding in one hand her own burlap ice bag, in the other a green bottle, she grabbed her housedress from the doorhook and hurried upstairs. He was no Mexican, and it looked as though Thomas had invited him for dinner.

As she dusted her chest and underarms with gardenia talc, she remembered the ruined cake and decided not to serve it. She put on her best—the navy linen skirt she'd had to let out twice, and whose jacket she could no longer wear because it looked tight and short as a trick monkey's bolero, and her new lilac voile blouse. Though the blouse was of sheer fabric, it was loosely cut, mandarin-collared, would almost conceal the rash. She dabbed on lipstick and secured her hair at her temples with her mother's tortoiseshell combs.

On the landing she hesitated, listening. Thomas was saying, "Canned orange juice will never go over. Folks just like grapefruit too much. Maybe in England, or someplace where they're desperate. But not here."

It felt strange to have a visitor in the house, and she realized that in three years, except for the girls and Thomas's first hand, Joe Bonillas, no one had paid a visit to the Hundred Acres.

She intended to make a grand entrance, but the creaking steps spoiled her effect. When she reached the bottom of the stairs, she saw that the men stood in the kitchen doorway, coffee mugs raised toward her. Thomas smiled. "Grapefruit wine from California. This is my wife, Edwina. Eddie, Bobby Israel."

Before she knew what she would say, she'd said, "Can't you use the glasses, Thomas?"

Her husband looked at his boots. Bobby Israel stepped forward. "A pleasure, ma'am," he said.

Thomas had met him at the Reno, the cafe in Rio Paradiso where the growers met for coffee. Bobby Israel ran a family vineyard in the Salinas Valley, but he was more interested in invention, had come to south Texas to look into using the culls, imperfect citrus fruit either too large, too small, too bruised, in order to make wine. As he talked about his work, Eddie tried to place his accent. His speech was slow and liquid. When he said he'd gone to Duke, she decided North Carolina but a good family, and she warmed to him.

Thomas produced a glass and Bobby poured. He watched as Eddie tasted the wine. He seemed boyish. He was, she decided, still in his twenties.

The wine tasted of lemon oil and Lydia Pinkham's tonic, but she said, "It's delightful."

When Bobby Israel smiled, she saw that his front teeth were widely spaced, and as though from a great distance, she remembered what her mother used to say about such teeth. "A gap in the teeth, a gap in your heart." The memory gave her a thrill; before the ruin of her family, her Sweet Briar friends loved to visit Lynchburg to listen to Miss Alice hold forth on the Seven Signs of the Bounder. Just now, though, Eddie couldn't remember the other six. The wine seemed to spread through her body, to settle in her knees.

"Tom tells me you're a Virginia girl," he said.

"Yes. From Lynchburg. Diamond Hill."

"I suppose you miss your family?"

"My parents are no longer living."

Here in Texas she could preserve the illusion that her former life continued at its gracious pace, and she hoped that Thomas had not been forthcoming about her background, that he hadn't told Bobby Israel her family had lost everything in the Crash, her father his foundries and quarries, his holdings, her mother her pride—they'd had to sell Laurel House, their silver and jewelry, just to eat and pay taxes—and that before they died they'd lived like rickety old ghosts in a cottage behind the great house with only the cook, Noon Nulan, to tend them.

Bobby Israel nodded but seemed not to know how to respond. She had become accustomed to Thomas's blunt manner of speaking, had been so long away from the gentle manners of the South that she hadn't realized his inquiry was a polite invitation for her to go on. About anything.

She felt a flutter return to her voice. "You know, I was just thinking about home today. About what I miss? People were . . . loyal. The funny thing is, and don't laugh, the person I miss most is our old Noon." She told him about the cook, who had taught her to bake, told about how contentious Noon had become in her old age, especially when Eddie's father—who had served two terms as mayor—would hold forth on the subject of a classical education. Noon would eye the Laurel House library, where crimson rows of the *Book of Knowledge* lined the shelves. "Except for the Good Book," ran Noon's wisdom, "and a pile of them red ones to make a girl walk like she somebody, ain't no use for a book but to collect dust and confound a otherwise straight-minded person." Noon had called the stacks she arranged on Eddie's head "your lady books," balancing them on Eddie's unruly hair and saying, "Proud, now, Miss Edwina. Walk long, long-necked." Noon always pronounced the word "nekkid" and how Eddie had laughed. Eddie's mother had joked that if Laurel House caught fire, she herself would be in the street in her nightgown clutching only her little dog, Pom, while Noon Nulan would be inside, taking the portraits from the walls and wrapping them in damp sheets. It was Noon who seemed to care most about the family's standing and to take its loss the hardest, but this last Eddie did not tell Bobby Israel.

As she moved about the kitchen taking platters from the oven, she felt her posture straighten. She heard her voice grow husky, dipping into the low-slung vowels and gentle diphthongs of her mother's Tidewater accent. She realized she had talked more in the past minutes than she had for months on end. And to a man. Not her husband, not Joe Bonillas, not Pompilo the yardboy. A man man. She wished she had worn a dress that showed her bust, which had in the past years, in the way of the women in her family, grown large, but then she remembered the heat rash. When she put her hand to her chest to make sure the rash was still hidden, she saw that Bobby Israel had noticed her gesture. Suddenly, she suspected she had appeared too eager, and so she moved to stand by Thomas, resting her hand on her husband's arm. "Does California agree with your family, Mr. Israel?"

"Call me Bobby," he said, smiling, "or you'll make me think I'm my own daddy." He set down his cup. "My wife grew up there. The business is her family's and so she's happy. I miss certain things, though, too." He smiled, lifted the napkin from the platter of chicken. "Like this kind of cooking."

She swatted his hand away, pleased, then shooed the men from the kitchen in order to set the table. "Well, don't expect too much," she called after them. "The chica was no help at all and it was so hot today I could scarcely draw breath."

At the table, Bobby talked of problems with migrant workers at the vineyards, and he asked if they had any border trouble.

"It's getting better," Thomas said. "The bracero program's a mess, but it's better than nothing." He began to explain the plan that allowed workers over the border, begun during war years and now extended so the growers could maintain what had become their dependence on stoop labor. Bobby appeared to listen, but Eddie was embarrassed by her husband's plodding explanation, and she interrupted. "I heard they found a woman in Mercedes with fourteen children. Can you imagine? No papers for any of them. Lord knows what she fed them all. Stolen vegetables, no doubt." She peeled a string off one of her beans. "And they put a bunch of wetbacks on a bus up at Laredo. Just stopped the whole passel at the river and marched them into the bus and carted them right back across."

Although to Eddie her attitude seemed the more realistic, Thomas was touchy about her views concerning Mexicans. He changed the topic to agriculture, and for a time she was silent, nibbling at her chicken wing, picking the breading off her tomatoes. She realized, oddly, that she was not hungry, and she remembered the days when she would pick at a watercress sandwich, and Noon had to fume and hector every morning just to get her to the table.

"The Valley's behind the South," Bobby was saying, "especially with cotton. One mechanical picker can do the work of fifty field hands."

Eddie, feeling dangerous, said, "Or a hundred Mexicans."

When Bobby laughed at her remark, she noticed his lower lip was full, like Gary Cooper's. That had been warning sign number two. The Lip of the Libertine.

"The cotton's dirtier," Thomas said.

Bobby Israel winked at her across the table. Winking: number three—or was it four?—Butterfly Eye. "And they don't breed."

Eddie laughed, but Thomas looked away. When she'd first come to the Valley she'd been surprised to learn he allowed Joe Bonillas in the house. Joe smelled of unwashed work and the wild tobacco he rolled. He smoked in the house, sprinkling flecks and dried leaves on the table and around his chair. The two would sit at the kitchen table over a pot of coffee, drawing out planting plans, irrigation blueprints, while the kitchen filled up with the smells of machine oil and stale smoke. Finally she told Thomas not to ask him in. "He's filthy and they've all got tuberculosis."

He had looked at her for what seemed like a long time. "You need to remember that they were here first. This was their land, Eddie," he'd finally said. "For centuries."

She'd shrugged. "Well, finders keepers."

Thomas hadn't spoken again of the exchange, but he now conducted his business with Joe in the barn.

Her dinner was a success. Bobby exclaimed over the food and, with more wine, even Thomas seemed expansive. Behind his glasses, his eyes took on a blurred quality. He smiled at her more often than he had for a long time. She could tell he was proud of her, and she was touched. It seemed impossible that just that afternoon she had allowed herself to be angry with him. To anyone looking in on this scene, to Bobby Israel, the two of them would appear to be any other married couple, comfortable and happy. She had been a good hostess. She wished the girls could have seen her: Texas-grown, they had what her mother had called outpost manners, wouldn't know a salt spoon from a toothpick. She thought of her house plans, pictured a table of well-dressed guests, herself the sparkling hostess engaging everyone in conversation.

She told the story of Guadalupe and the víbora, exaggerating Guadalupe's hysteria, the snake's size, the length of time she'd spent prodding it. "You be careful, now," Thomas told her. "Up near the King ranch there's a real bad rattler problem."

She smiled at his proprietary remark, at the way he sounded like Will Rogers, trying to be courtly, his gallantry undercut by his flat, nasal Oklahoma tones.

Bobby folded his napkin. "That was the finest meal I've eaten for a long, long while."

"Your wife doesn't cook?" Thomas asked. In his voice Eddie heard a tinge of smugness.

"She's done with cooking, she tells me." He smiled, and again she saw the space between his teeth. "She's had her family. They're grown and gone. She's busy with causes . . ." He broke off, folding his napkin carefully, and Eddie, curious, adding and subtracting, determining that his wife would have to be at least fifteen years older than he, waited for him to continue. She pictured a thin, mannish woman, pictured a vineyard surrounded by an ancient stone wall . . .

But Thomas was not ready to drop the subject of snakes. "By the way, we've got coral snakes here, too," he said, leaning forward, his eyes magnified by the thick lenses of his spectacles. "Pretty darn deadly. Stub-headed and little. They don't have fangs like a rattler, just little old teeth they grind into you. Coralinas, the men call them. But they mostly stay out of sight." He crumpled his napkin into a ball, though Eddie had asked him over and over not to. "I'm always afraid I won't remember that little rhyme quick enough. That one about how to tell the stripes? I'll be standing there scratching my head, trying to figure if it's black and yellow, red and—"

"Red and yellow, kill a fellow," Eddie broke in. "My mother used to say it about trashy clothing. Red and yellow, catch a fellow. Red and white, to be polite."

When she rose, saying she would make coffee, Bobby produced a cigar. "I'll just step out onto the porch," he said.

"Oh, my, no," she said, "it's fine. You sit right there. I'll be put out if you don't. I love the smell of a good cigar."

Thomas looked at her in an odd way, but Eddie merely smiled.

In the middle of telling the story of how because she'd run out of sugar, Noon had once made a birthday cake out of a whole ham, frosting it with mashed potatoes and studding it with peas and carrot candles, she remembered one thing and realized another: Thomas's birthday, and that most of her conversation had revolved around food. Mortified, she changed the subject to the heat. Thomas, too, seemed to have forgotten his birthday, and she decided not to bring up the occasion. But it did seem the evening would be better with something sweet.

"It's just a poor old pineapple upside-down cake," she said as she brought it to the table. "I had an awful time keeping the ants away. It's all a mess because I had to cover it."

"Some weather coming, I reckon," Thomas said. "They're really something this year. Swarming." As she placed his dessert plate before him, he said, "Now doesn't that look dandy."

While Thomas smiled at his cake, Bobby looked at Eddie, holding her gaze a moment too long for comfort. "Your power lines draw them," he said, lifting his fork, smiling. "They're attracted to the buzz in the wires."

"I don't know," Thomas said, licking a coconut shred from his thumb, "years ago there was a big sugar plantation over by Pharr. They might still be around from that."

When it was time to take Bobby back to the Reno, where he had left his car, Eddie walked with them to the front porch and stood for a long time after they had gone, pleased with the evening. The haze of the afternoon had lifted and the air was soft and moist. In the live oaks the chachalacas fluttered, bickering before they settled for the night. Cicadas chirred from the hackberry. From the blockhouses by the levee came the wheeze and swing of accordions, the thrum of guitars, shouting and singing, the noise of the camp that would go on far into the night. It had been so hot for the past days that even the heavens had seemed clouded, but now she could see stars, a universe beyond the heat. She stood on the porch until she could no longer see the red smear of the taillights, then she went inside.

When she looked at her reflection in the bathroom mirror, she saw that the wine had made her eyes greener, narrowed, glittering. The end of her nose was the squashy, boneless tulip bulb of her father's family, and she had always hated it. Now she pinched it, pulling it out, and was delighted to see that she looked . . . foxy. She arranged her brow in a lascivious arch. She looked prettier, not the same person who had squinched her garish clownface in the pressure cooker. Even her freckles seemed to blend into a pretty blush. Slimmer, wolfish, she looked to herself, sly, and she laughed, thinking of Guadalupe's men. "Hubba

hubba," she said, then giggled. Beneath the lilac voile she felt her chest rise, and she felt as though her next breath might lead into something unforeseen and marvelous, but when she exhaled, her chest seemed to crack into shards that pierced her as she realized, at that moment, what was missing.

The word *exigencies* came to her as though from a long way off, and suddenly before her she saw her florid father, home for the midday meal, patting his large belly—"Noon, that was one of your finer offerings"— drawing his fob from his pocket, consulting his gold watch—"Miss Alice, I believe it's time. The . . . er, ah, exigencies." Her diminutive mother rising, smoothing her skirt: "Oh, Parker, you and your exigencies." In addition to the boneless nose, she had inherited from the mountain-bred Harmons the curse of lust. Haunted by the memory of her mother's thin-lipped capitulation, she had vowed never again to approach her husband, even if it meant waiting years. The trouble was this: All her life she had wanted a child. A daughter. Time was running out.

She ran a tub for her bath. With a chug and blurt came the cantankerous flow from the rust-eaten tap. She dropped in Epsom salts. A dollop of orange water. She waited until the tub was nearly full, then eased into the water.

In the second month of her marriage, when she hadn't yet accepted the idea that Thomas was different, there had been another night when she had felt this kind of desire. Though she'd had boyfriends, even suitors, boys who had begged and to whom she had occasionally allowed a liberty, she had kept herself for a husband, had waited thirty-four years, and on that night she wanted what was coming to her.

All day she had seen flesh. Flesh in the blush of Star Ruby grapefruit, the veined translucence of tangerine sections, the muscular heft of squash, even the deep, leaf-shaded lettuce hearts. At the sink the way a peach stone clung to the red center of the fruit had made her belly pull taut and the word *passion* had come to her, rising, thrashing, liquid. And on that night—it had been summer then, too—she had taken off her clothes and walked to the front porch where Thomas leaned against a pillar, smoking meditatively. She had cleared her throat, willing him to turn, to see the moonlight on her body, round and dappled as an apricot, a muscadine, a Seckel pear.

"You're beautiful," he said. "I don't deserve you." Then he began to cry.

Something in the sound made her think of Dr. Remillard and his
houseboy, Pet, who had lived two houses down in Lynchburg, the
heartbroken strains of Caruso's *Pagliacci* wafting from the open windows,
the pretty way Pet moved his hands over the rhododendrons that lined
their walk, how the two men had sobbed bitterly when their beautiful
Pandora, the gray Persian cat who often lazed in the great bow window
overlooking the street, had been struck by the ice truck. With a terrible
clarity she understood, and though the understanding provided a reason,
the wretchedness of her mistake seemed to pierce her heart.

But when she tried to tell him she understood, he said, "It isn't that.
Believe me, Eddie. I've thought of that, and it isn't so." He told her
how sorry he was, that he blamed himself. He had hoped that with her
he would be able to overcome his feelings.

"What feelings?"

His long sigh seemed drawn from the depths. The trouble, he told
her, had started when he was a boy in Oklahoma. He'd grown up tended
by his grandfather, Jack, and the hired girl, Mella. His mother had died
of typhus and no one spoke of the boy who had been his father. But
despite this, he told her, he had been happy. Mella was gruff but loving,
her hands raw and red from work, and he liked the way when he called
her name it sounded like *Mama*. Down the road lived Faye and Lorna,
his playmates, and though the children had to work hard, they spent
long hours playing in the shade of the Chinese elms that ringed the
turnaround lane. The girls' play names were Numnie and Peachy; his
was Boswell. Numnie and Peachy strung rope to make the walls of a
playhouse, served Boswell currants and wheat paste from bits of broken
crockery, then sent him off to work. Laddie Stew, they called their
mixture, though he couldn't get them to explain why. They spooned it
into his mouth, giggling, coaxing him to eat just one more bite. Sometimes even now the taste of raisin bread reminded him. The days had
seemed long and dear and sweet.

He was sixteen when the bank took the farm. For reasons he never
understood, Mella left for California. His grandfather took a job as a
man-of-all-work at a dairy farm outside the town of Cimarron, and
he and Thomas moved into the low rooms under the roof of the
milkhouse, which they shared with mice and rusted milk cans, pigeons
and barn swallows, spiders. Thomas quit school and went to work
cleaning the barns, mucking out the stalls and milkrooms. He was
only three miles from Faye and Lorna, but the distance now seemed

vast. Every day he wanted to run the ribbon-straight red miles across the hills to their house and his old life. It was then that he began saving money.

There was a separating-room hand, a trapper named Bodie Gilstrap who was fired because he made the milk smell of skunk, and from him Thomas learned about the Rajah Rabbitry, which supplied animals for furriers. They could always use rabbits, Bodie told him, and they paid a quarter a pelt, and so in the evenings when the cottontails came out to feed, Thomas hunted along the hedgerows and each week traded five or six pelts for dollars and change he stored in an El Ropo cigar box under his mattress.

He hadn't yet learned how weak his eyes were, and so he wondered how it was that other boys seemed to bag so many more rabbits. Though he hated hearing the squeals, hated carrying by the legs the limp, still-warm bodies with the sweet tufted fur on the underbellies, with each rabbit he shot, gutted, skinned, he kept his mind on Faye and Lorna, knowing that when he'd saved enough money he would ask one of them to marry him.

The trouble came when he tried to picture which one he would ask. Some days he was certain it was Lorna, for the way the tip of her nose pulled down when she talked, for her teasing, for the way she had of seizing him in hugs. Other days it was Faye, for her milky, grassy smell, for her voice, soft as the pigeon sounds that rustled above him nights as he went to sleep, for the way she lost herself in looking at the veins in an oak leaf.

All that summer he hunted, and by fall he had saved enough to buy an old Model T, its seats stripped and replaced with wooden chairs secured to the chassis with baling wire. Jack called the contraption Fool's Chariot, but the car ran, and now he was able to see the girls more often. With each trip to the farm on the bend in the Cimarron River, deciding became more difficult. One miserable evening as he drove across the bridge on his way home from a visit, he saw a fox streak across a sand wash culvert and into the timber. He knew the pelt might bring as much as three dollars, and he began to stalk the animal, following the bent grass of its trails, and at last he found its den in an elderberry thicket on a bluff at a bend in the river.

Somehow, he told Eddie, all his indecision and desire became bound up in that fox, and he vowed to bag it. Several times he'd caught the fox in his range, but by the time he'd clicked the shotgun's safety off and taken aim, the animal was gone. Though the practice went against all the rules Jack had taught him, he took to hunting with gun shouldered, safety off. And finally, one day in late October when it seemed that all the reds and browns and yellows of the timber merged into one enormous tree, he caught the creature in his sights.

If he had waited one more second before squeezing the trigger, he would have seen her among the trees, her brown skirt swirling as she rose. He would have seen that the white he'd thought was the fox's tail was the dish towel bundle she had been using to gather black walnuts, and that at the very moment he had squeezed the trigger, she had raised her hand to greet him.

It had been an accident, everyone said, one of those awful accidents, and no one's fault. No one blamed him, not Lorna, not her parents, not even Faye, whose face would heal, they said, but whose eye could not be saved. That no one blamed him was worst of all. He ached for punishment. But in the way of small Oklahoma towns where they forgave, he told her, far too much, people only shook their heads over him. First Methodist put on a bazaar for Faye's doctor bills, the Missionary Baptist held a pie supper. Thomas's first eyeglasses had been donated by the Odd Fellows. Kindness, he told her, could be a scouring thing, and finally he couldn't stand it. He caught an empty cattle car on the Katy Railroad and headed for the Valley, where he'd done day labor, saved, lived a bachelor for the twenty years before he'd come to Richmond on his tobacco trip.

It was a terrible accident, she thought, but surely twenty years was enough time to forget. He could pretend it hadn't happened, and soon the pretending would be the truth and he could be just fine. To blame the past, she believed, was the weakest of failings, and she held this against him, over the years traveling back to this fault as though to a scar, prodding it to see if it was still sore. It always was. And this, too, she held against him.

She asked him why, in Richmond, he had sent flowers every day, sweet notes asking her to see him.

"You were sassy. Funny and smart."

She nodded, believing him; she had been that girl.

"Your crinkly eyes."

"Crinkly?"

"They squint up when you smile. It makes you look happy all the time. It's me," he had assured her. "It isn't you."

But this—as though the opposite suggestion had been waiting all her life to attach to her, like the pounds that had plumped out her behind— she had not believed.

"I'll try harder," he said.

Stung, she wanted to say, "Don't bother," but he knelt before her. Often he'd talked of how he loved to come in from work and find her in the kitchen, of how fortunate he counted himself that she had married him. He was not good with what he called "love talk," but he loved her truly, he said, devotedly, and he promised to do right by her all his days. "Will you still have me?" he'd asked that night. She'd put her arms around him. "Of course I will."

Over the years the weight of what she had done by marrying him, and by staying, pressed on her head like a stack of Noon's lady books, and she couldn't seem to shake her head to shift them. Something in their balance had become important; they would stay straight only if she carried herself a certain way. She came to understand three things: that she had married him in the belief that he'd wanted her enough to make up for her own lack of wanting him; that he had saved her from something shameful; and that there was a deep and terrible sweetness in being wronged, a sweetness that with each new wrong grew deeper, more terrible, and more sweet. Worse than these three was a fourth: that the line separating what she thought she ought to want from what she truly wanted became so blurred she could no longer tell the difference.

The water had gone cool. Eddie rose from the tub, dried herself, and put on her best gown, apricot silk, recently pressed by Guadalupe. She took her silver brush and mirror from the dresser and carried them with her to bed, planning to present a picture of white, uplifted arms, a nimbus of hair, but when she heard Thomas on the stairs, she instead tucked the brush and mirror under the mattress, smoothed the sheet over her breasts, and composed herself to make it appear that she had just dozed off. When Thomas asked, "You asleep, or just playing possum?" she let out a sigh designed to sound serene.

Thomas settled himself in bed. She waited until his breathing slowed, then rolled onto her side, facing his back. For a while she lay there, breathing, then slowly slid her hand beneath the sheet. She would . . . see. It was not making the first move. It was just . . . seeing.

He lay still as she stroked the backs of his thighs. Encouraged, she moved closer, the stir of her body beneath the sheet releasing the faint scent of orange and warm gardenia, until she pressed into his back. She continued stroking, letting her hand graze upward, lightly, gently, until at last she felt him stir.

"Hot today," he said. "Must have been ninety-eight."

"In the shade. I had the girl move the fan up here." She continued stroking. "Isn't it nice and cool?"

"Good dinner," he said.

She listened to the sound of the fan blades, lulling and at the same time slicing the air with *You owe, you owe.*

"Those stories about Noon," he said, "I wish you hadn't . . . I don't know . . ."

She wanted to say that if he'd had any upbringing beyond an Okie reprobate and a rat-run milkhouse, he'd know how to take them, that the stories were told with love and affection, and the coloreds themselves told them on each other, especially to whites, and that if you couldn't tell a story on your own help, who could you tell one on? But she held back. Of the skein of desire she had begun with, a strand remained.

Again she began to stroke, this time his back, but it seemed that his flesh had gone cool, like the skin on a pudding.

"I need . . ." she said, but the words hung above the bed like a thick web she couldn't brush aside. She began again. "I want . . ."

She waited for him to ask her, listening for his question, not knowing what answer she would give—there could be so many, all of them true—until from his throat she heard the first soft rasps of deeper breathing.

Furious, but at the same time seized by an odd joy, she flounced over, thrilled by the rush of air from the mattress. Her heart pounded. She tried to settle herself for sleep, but she couldn't, and she sat straight up in bed. *You owe me a house in Rio for this;* she wanted to spit the words into the moonlit room where her discarded clothes hung on the chairback like rebuke, but she stopped herself. There would come a time when he had wronged her so deeply, a time when she had done nothing—not tell a story, not have an unkind thought—when her behavior had been so . . . unimpeachable that when she asked, he could not refuse. This wasn't yet that time.

She could feel the tension in the bed.

"What's the matter?" he asked.

Willing herself not to speak, she concentrated on the slice of the fan blades.

"Is something wrong?"

"Guadalupe," she blurted, surprising herself. Again the syllables went haywire.

He rolled over, squinting owlishly at her.

"That girl is a hussy and a mess!" she cried. "I need you to get me some decent help."

She crossed her arms over her chest and flumped down among the pillows. "So there!" she said. The spectacle of her own petulance almost made her laugh. She rolled to her side and let her gaze travel toward her bureau in the shadows, thinking about the sheaves of drawings. In her imagination, she yanked up a floorboard and installed a foot bell under the dining room table. *Bring in the spinach, Noon!* Setting her mind to the satisfying dilemma of choosing between a chair in butternut leather for the hunt room or a recamier in lemon shantung, she drifted off to sleep.

2

a wild pig

Two days later, when she was in the yard making sure Guadalupe didn't crimp the clothes as she pinned them to the line, a Paradiso Fruit flatbed rumbled down the lane and into the yard. It stopped in front of the porch and Bobby Israel swung down from the driver's seat, calling for her to get a shotgun.

"What's the matter?" she shouted back. He yelled something about a wild pig but kept running toward the house and so she dropped the clothespin bag and ran inside to take one of Thomas's guns—a Winchester—from the gun cabinet.

He had taken the gun and was nearly out the door before she remembered. "It isn't loaded," she called after him, rummaging in the drawer for a box of shells. She found a battered El Ropo cigar box at the back of the drawer, bound with thick rubber bands. She lifted it, but found it too light to contain shells. She was just about to give up when through the glass of the cabinet a green Remington box caught her eye. She grabbed the box and ran back out. Guadalupe hovered on the porch, fiddling with her hair and earrings, patting into place her chiffon scarf.

"Get in," Bobby told her when she reached the truck. "You might have to drive, depending."

As he drove he cracked the gun and loaded, telling her that as he was passing along Old Military Highway, he'd seen Thomas in the tomato fields and stopped to speak to him. As they were talking, a javelina boar had come upon some pickers at the far end of the field. The braceros had thrown tomatoes to drive it away, but the javelina wouldn't retreat. Thomas and Joe Bonillas drove the truck down the field road, where Joe jumped down, pulling out an old pistola, but when he shot, the gun blew up in his hand. The javelina lunged and fell, then scrabbled up to chase Joe as he ran for the cab, goring his leg with a tusk. Thomas had taken Bobby's Dodge to drive him to the hospital at McAllen.

At the field, the braceros squatted on the corrugated tin roof of the box shed. One of the men had produced a deck of cards. The workers smoked, taunted the pig, from time to time throwing cigarette butts. Thin-haunched, its black hide ridden with mange, saliva hanging in strings from its tusks, the beast sat with its head lolling, hindquarters canted, on the packed dirt at the edge of the field.

"Scooch over, kitty," he told her as he braked the truck, patting the seat, motioning for her to put her feet on the pedals. "Keep it in gear. Cut out if I give you the sign. I'll jump on behind."

She had driven only twice on the farm-to-market routes of the Valley, each time with mishaps—a flattened mailbox when a hornet buzzed into the car, a dead tomcat.

"I can't," she said, but she slid over, placing her feet where he showed her. The truck was huge, the gearshift that rose from the floor so large, so loose that the shift knob rattled like maracas. "I can't," she said again, but he was already on his way along the furrows.

Straining to keep her feet on the pedals, the pedals down, she watched as he raised the stock to his shoulder. His first shot spanged into the dirt. The braceros hooted. The javelina began to lurch toward him, stumbling sideways. Eddie could hear its low snorting. She wanted to roll up the window but she was afraid she wouldn't hear if Bobby called. Though the muscles in her neck and belly felt as though they would tear from the strain, she gripped the steering wheel, one foot on the brake, the other on the clutch, trying to remember: gas, clutch, brake, gears, but the names blurred into one another, rattling and rigid as the gearshift. He reloaded.

Again he sighted, and this time the shot was true and the javelina collapsed into the dust. The braceros cheered, throwing their hats into the air, then climbed down from the boxshed to kick the animal to make sure it was dead.

When he returned to the truck, Eddie's legs were quivering and she was near crying. "That was horrid!"

He leaned into the cab and cut the engine. She felt his breath on her arm, breathed the hot starch smell of his shirt. "It was just a pig, Eddie. I had to."

She let herself give in to tears. "It isn't that."

He waited until she had finished and was wiping her eyes on her apron hem. "You can't drive, can you, kitty?"

"Of course I can. What a ridiculous thing to say." She glared out the window at the rows of tomato plants. "I'm not a kitty."

He put the shotgun in the truckbed and opened the cab door. "Well, you are, too," he said, grinning. "But not much of a sidekick."

For a moment she was angry, but then she saw that he meant to be playful, and she slapped at his arm.

"I ought to make you drive home," he said. "To pay for your crimes."

Something made her daring. "I'll show you how an accomplice behaves," she countered. "Hop in, Clyde Barrow. Miss Bonnie Parker's going to take you for a ride."

They laughed at the way she lugged the truck, causing them to jerk in their seats like toys, at the way she ground the gears. They laughed when he bit his tongue as the truck jolted over the railroad tracks, and when she bit her own while laughing at him. When they came in sight of the Hundred Acres, though she could feel the sweat runnels down her back and between her breasts, her hair out of its pins, springing in unruly wires and plastered to her neck, she was sorry the ride was over. She pulled the truck into the drive at the front of the house, braking smartly. "What do you think about that?"

"I think you're a hotshot," he said, "and a kitty."

In the kitchen she pulled the bourbon bottle from beneath the sink and made drinks, and after Bobby had called the sheriff to pick up the javelina, they carried their glasses to the lawn chairs in the shade of the oleander hedge. She felt energized, as though a thrumming wire were stretched between them. Bobby drew out a package of Lucky Strikes and offered one to her. For a time they smoked, talking about the heat, the javelina, the braceros, again the heat.

A lull in their talk seemed to blanch the afternoon of light and color, and into the emptiness slipped the memory of herself in bed with Thomas, his refusal, and she cleared her throat. It was suddenly cool in the oleander shade. She sipped her drink.

Smiling, he said, "You don't seem like the same woman who served me a chicken dinner the other night. So stiff and formal. Miss First Families of Virginia. Look at you now. You're a mess, but you're beautiful."

She was taken aback. She had thought herself gracious and serene on the night of the dinner party.

He leaned toward her and the lawn chair creaked. "How long has it been?"

"I beg your pardon?"

"You know." Then he lowered his voice, the tone smooth and even. "You have a beautiful mouth." He set his empty glass in the grass beside his chair. "How long since anybody kissed it?"

She stood too quickly and was light-headed, her vision clouded. "I need to start supper."

"Stay," he said, standing, reaching for her hand. "Please. We can tell each other all about it."

"There's absolutely nothing," she said, "to tell." She turned and walked across the yard to the house, holding her spine straight, not looking back. When she heard the truck start up, she sank into a kitchen chair.

the baking fool

Troubled by dreams she could not recall, she had not slept well, and the next morning, though at nine the kitchen was already warm, Eddie was seized with a desperate desire to bake. She started with Noon's angel cake, then made a banana pudding, then a chess pie with walnuts and dates. When one dessert was done, she began another. She had always been a meticulous cook, exacting in her measurements, but on this morning she baked by jots and pinches, handfuls, helter-skelter. Lemon ammonia cookies that took her breath away as she beat the batter. Blond fudge in taffy-colored squares, studded with filberts and pecans. If he happened by, she would be busy. *I'd invite you in, but as you can see* . . .

In the middle of the afternoon, she started a Lady Baltimore cake, only to discover she had used all the eggs. She sent Guadalupe to reach beneath the laying hens, but the girl came back empty-handed. With her apron still around her middle, Eddie hurried down the lane and crossed the road to the neighboring farm, a place she'd vowed to avoid. Chez Wingo, she called it, or Dogpatch, entertaining her friends with imitations, playing Opaline Wing sometimes as Mammy Yokum and other times as Moonbeam McSwine.

Her neighbor was gap-toothed and garrulous, taller even than Eddie, but lank-boned and spare, her lap a floursack-aproned scaffold. When Eddie had first moved in, Opaline had brought over a bundle wrapped in a dish towel. "It's a present. You have to guess what it is."

Hefting the dense package, her mind on the lazy door she'd been trying to prop open, Eddie had exclaimed without thinking, "A doorstopper!"

Opaline wrung her chapped, large-knuckled hands. "It's a loaf of bread."

To return the favor and, she hoped, make up for her gaffe, Eddie had baked and boxed a lemon meringue pie, the delicate foamy peaks browned perfectly. She'd wrapped it in yellow tissue paper and decorated the package with lemon drops and mint, paper flowers and grosgrain ribbon. Though the Wing farm was just across the road, she decided at the last minute to take the car; this would be grander. Driving in first gear down the Wing's lane, the pie beside her on the seat, she'd seen the tabby barn cat as it bolted from the mesquite, routed by a pack of whooping children, but to brake suddenly would have sent her gift flying, and so she'd punched the gas pedal, hoping to outdistance the fleeing cat.

Opaline had assured Eddie she'd done them a favor in the long run—Barnabas was old and he sometimes killed the new baby kitties—and that she was just glad it hadn't been one of the children, but the next morning Eddie had found, scratched with sticks into the dust of her lane, a drawing of a dead cat, tongue lolling, x's for eyes, under which was printed in wriggling letters HOME OF THE CAT KILLER.

Now Opaline stood on the porch, yelling at her ragtag brood—after Eldon, Jr., Eddie couldn't keep their towheads straight—while they clambered like goats over a rusted butane tank on which they'd built with slats and chicken wire and sheets what served them either as a castle turret or an Indian howdah. "Run for your lives," yelled the biggest one, Eldon, Jr., his strap overalls unhitched and dangling over his behind like a barn swallow's tail. Another, wielding a hoe handle, beat a warning on the butane tank.

"All of you hush," Opaline hollered, banging a ladle against a pot lid. "A body can't hear herself think!" She gave the lid a final bang, then smiled and asked Eddie in. "I been hoping for company."

"I can't stay," Eddie told her. She asked for six eggs, hating the sound of her own voice as she heard it trilling, "I don't know what's got into me," and "I've just been a baking fool!"

Opaline placed eight brown eggs in her basket, then cocked her head and gave her a curious, inspecting look that made Eddie think of a suspicious hen spying a caterpillar. Opaline drew back, considering. "Yepper," she said, "freckled women always show it around the eyes, first thing. You got that haunted look. I'd bet a dollar you're in the family way."

Opaline cast a look toward the window, outside which Eddie could see that now the children were holding what appeared to be a puppet show, their heads and torsos poking through the trapdoor of a ram-shackle rabbit hutch, manhandling two white rabbits and setting them upon each other in a burlesque of threat and retreat.

Opaline asked hopefully, "You all got something in the oven? You and the mister expecting?"

"Expecting company," Eddie said, too fast. She'd meant it as a back answer, but when she realized what she'd said, she nearly dropped the egg basket. She thanked her neighbor, and then, casting about for an excuse to get away quickly, opened the screen door and exclaimed, "Oh, dear! You'll have to excuse me. I forgot my gas!"

She was out the door before she remembered that she'd told Opaline not two weeks before about the new stove.

"That gas . . ." she shouted over her shoulder, then, realizing how ridiculous this sounded, turned to walk backwards, meaning to explain herself to Opaline, who stood on the porch, hands on her hips, head cocked. "Wait. I didn't mean . . ."

The little Wings, ragged bird dogs on point, stood still, alert and smirking, puppets poised. Even the rabbits, lop-eared, limp-legged, watched her.

Opaline called, "That's natural, honey. Don't worry. Gas is just natural. I had just a terrible case with my last one. You never saw such. What you do is lay down on the floor with your bottom up . . ."

"It's gone," Eddie called. Then, to make it better: "We had it taken out."

The puppeteers regarded her with eyes older than dirt.

She tried one last time, facing Opaline, squaring her shoulders and hoping for dignity. "We are now one hundred percent electric!"

The junior Wings began to produce, with bare underarms and cupped palms, the juicy sounds of prolonged and frantic farting. Opaline's guinea hens honked at her as she passed beneath the tree, where they had flown to roost, showering her with a gray and white rain of their speckled feathers.

• • •

That night she was sick from sugar, butter, batter. Her legs jerked so violently that Thomas took his pillow to the spare bedroom, and she herself could hardly sleep. She tossed, and planned what she would say when Bobby Israel returned: that he had his nerve, that she was happy, that she knew the kind of man he was and enough to stay a mile away, that in Richmond his kind was a dime a dozen. That he was at least ten years younger than she, that she was married and happy. If he wasn't, that was not her problem. If he thought she was lonely, he was sorely mistaken. She was fine. Just perfect. Thank you. *He could play in his own backyard.*

Several times she rose to look out at the moonlight on the road, at the dark tossed tops of palms in the wind. Toward morning, as she watched the gray glimmer of first light along the horizon across a haze-bound beanfield, she decided there was no fool like an old one.

The next day she sent Guadalupe, with a laden wheelbarrow, to disperse the baked goods at the bracero camp. She allowed Thomas, who was so touched by her gesture that it embarrassed her, to think charity had been her intention all along.

A week later, in the lazy afternoon hours when the work crews took siesta and Guadalupe disappeared, as Eddie napped on the sofa, she imagined that there came a knock at the back porch door. In her mind's eye, when she answered, he would take off his hat and dust it against his thigh. "Tom went to McAllen for a part," he would say. He would bow, shamble comically like a tramp, smile, say: "Missus, can you spare a man a spot of branch?" And when she saw his face—for she could remember every feature, pore, and hollow—blurred by the lint-flocked gridwires of the screen and hazy in her naptime vision, all she would be able to say would be, "Oh," and she would unlatch the screen door to let him in.

"We can go as slow as you want," he would say.

In the Valley telephone book she looked up the number for the Casa Cortez Hotel and copied it onto the white part of a Calumet can. For two days she looked at the number. On the third day, she wrote it in the flour she'd spilled while making noodles. On the fourth day, she dialed, but then hung up. On the fifth day, when he answered, she said—in for a penny, in for a pound—"Meow."

fruit of the poisonous tree

In just six weeks she had exceeded the record of the past three years. Of her life. They met once in the laundry shed, another time in the cab of his truck, once at the tomato field, her back against the boxshed. Most often, he would pick her up by the mailbox at the end of the lane, and they would drive to Martha and sneak up the back stairs to his room at the Casa Cortez. They were careful to space the days, but each Friday, when Thomas oversaw the long afternoon pay line, was set. For his part, Bobby avoided the Reno Cafe and Thomas. When Thomas suggested they invite him to dinner again, she pleaded headache, and if he talked admiringly of Bobby, she shrugged. "He strikes me as an opportunist," she said. "Sounds as though his wife has all the money." But she adored him, and over every daily task she carried out ran the blessed words: *It isn't* me.

Her appetite departed. Day by day, she grew slimmer. Bobby loved her freckles, reciting parts of "Pied Beauty," improvising when he couldn't remember a word. He teased, trying to convince her he'd written the poem himself, but she told him she wasn't that big a fool. " 'Margaret, are you grieving,' " she quoted, " 'over Goldengrove un-leaving?' I wrote a paper on Hopkins. At Sweet Briar."

"What if you had to write a paper about me?" he'd asked as they lay in the slanted light that streamed through the venetian blinds at the Casa Cortez, twirling a strand of her hair around his finger. "What would you write?"

She laughed.

"Wouldn't it be about love?" he'd prompted. "How much you . . ."

She'd reached for him. "It'd be about this. He'd be the main char-acter—"

"The hero."

"Yes. And how he went around getting into trouble and then his mouth would have to get him out of it—"

"But it would only get him in deeper . . ."

She'd put her arms around his neck and pressed herself into his chest. "Yes. That's right."

More, she prayed. Of this feeling, of the way skin felt on skin, his mouth on the hollow of her neck, her arms wrapped around his back, could there ever be enough?

In September, when lint from the cotton gin furred the CP&L power lines, weighting them so they hung like thick ropes, he began to speak of how hard it would be when it was time for him to return to California. She brushed off his worry. Older than he, she now knew, by fourteen years, she felt wise, as though she looked down from a high place on what they did below, saying to him, "Well, we knew the rules," but at the same time she knew she was ignoring them. He was a charmer and a smooth talker. He filled the bill on all the Seven Signs and most likely more. But it was talk she wanted, and she knew that if he suggested that they buy a painted circus elephant and set out for Timbuktu, she wouldn't take the time to pack a bag.

•   •   •

On a Sunday afternoon toward the end of September as Thomas sat at his desk in his little office going over his accounts, she lay on the sofa, passing in and out of a doze. Her bones felt long, her flesh soft, she felt twenty, not nearly forty, and it seemed that time itself stretched out before her like a long, sweet nap. In her dreamy gaze, she considered the gun cabinet across the room, thinking of how, if she hadn't realized the shotgun wasn't loaded, how, if she hadn't run after him with the shells, none of this would have happened.

Thinking of that day reminded her of the rubber-banded cigar box she had meant to investigate, but before she could think to get up and move toward it, her thoughts traveled to a memory of an afternoon in the washhouse, where the smell of soap had made them sneeze, which made her consider why, behind her eyes, there had been—for days now—a thick, full feeling almost on the edge of headache.

Her husband stood at the foot of the sofa, holding the funny pages of the Sunday paper. "It's Fearless Fosdick in 'Dick Tracy' today. It's pretty good. See, old Fearless is after—"

"I read it," she said.

He moved closer and patted her foot. "How are you today?"

"Fine."

He walked around and knelt beside her. "You seem different."

She stretched. "Same old me."

He put his hand on her shoulder. "So," he said, "you're well?"

She nodded. "Never better."

For a time he looked at her. "Well," he said finally, petting her hair awkwardly. "I thought maybe we could . . . try."

Any other time, she would have jumped at the chance. Jumped. Now, though, even as she gave her excuse, gave it because it was the best she could come up with, because it was the reason to which her imagination took her first, she realized she had forgotten what she'd known from girlhood, had forgotten to count the days, and that the very opposite was true. She said, "I'm having my time."

He removed his hand, shrugged as though it hadn't mattered, but from his expression she could tell he was hurt. *This is what you get,* she wanted to say.

"Well, that's fine," he said, "in a few days, maybe?"

She rolled over and stared at the pattern of the sofa, at the waves and arabesques in the mock damask and the way they swirled before her vision, how one line swooped into another, then another then the next and there was no way to follow the pattern to its end and how maddening this was, and before she knew what she meant to do, she had pushed herself up from the sofa and was standing, staring angrily at the way a stray hair in his eyebrow curled over the rim of his glasses like a wayward insect feeler, screaming at him, "Is that all you can say?"

Thomas retreated to his books, his shoulders hunched meekly, which made her even angrier, and she threw herself back onto the sofa and let her tears soak into the fabric.

Later in the day, after she had slept, when her senses returned, she told him she was sorry, she was worn out with the heat. She confessed a headache. "Maybe you're going through the change," Thomas suggested. "Maybe that's it," she agreed, grateful that he had provided a reason for her to ask if he would drive her to the doctor in McAllen the next day.

•   •   •

On Friday when Bobby came she was waiting at the end of the lane where the trumpet vine grew over the mailbox, watching the wasps dip in and out of the throaty orange blooms and flicking at the red tin mail flag until it vibrated. She had spent hours planning how to tell him, imagining his reaction. Courtly, gently reared, he would take the blame. They would discuss doing the honorable thing. And then they would part. The beauty of it was that she had nothing to lose, for in the past days since the doctor had confirmed the news, it was as though the part of her mind that she'd lost on the day of her reckless baking had returned. Now she measured and calculated. All would be well. She was to have a child, and she knew exactly what she had to do. In the meantime, there was this scene to play out. And then she would never see him again. It seemed a small price to pay.

They drove to the levee, to a shaded rise between the river and Old Military Highway, where in the curve of the embankment there was a carrot field bounded by mesquite. She helped him spread the army blanket, feeling young and tragic as the breeze stirred the folds of her full skirt. She had worn white eyelet and pique, many years old and far too young for her, but who cared: It fit. Into her waistband she had tucked a spray of orange blossoms. Before he could pull her down beside him, she said, "We have a problem."

He laughed. "Us? Bonnie and Clyde?"

She'd imagined high seriousness, somberness to match her own. She put her hands on her hips, but then, feeling ridiculous and matronly in the pose, let her arms fall to her sides. "It's not funny."

He reached for her hand, tugged to pull her down beside him. "First let's kiss a little," he said. "After that, you can tell me what's so," he made a wide-eyed face to mock her graveness, "not funny."

She yanked away her hand. "Stop it," she whispered. "I'm pregnant."

Again he laughed. "You're kidding."

She wanted to shake him. "Why is that so ridiculous?"

"I thought you were . . . You've got to be at least . . . I assumed . . ." His gaze was imploring, as though he were willing her to save him, to fill in the idea, and in an awful instant she understood that he'd thought she was too old.

And there was something else she hadn't thought of. The lie she'd told las girls at the poker party came back to her. She had told Bobby Israel the same story, changing it a bit to cast Thomas in the role of lusty yokel, ham-handed bungler, herself as merely . . . unfulfilled.

She took the blossoms from her waistband and threw them into the carrot field. "Oh, hell," she said. "Just take me home."

•   •   •

That night she went to the grove to search out Thomas among his bud sticks. She found him standing at the edge of the grove, in the rows where he'd planted his progeny, fingering the grafts of his pink lemon tree. When he saw her he smiled. "Looks like this little sport might take. Another month and we'll know. What I need is a mutation that . . ."

She reached for his hand, surprised herself with the comfort the act gave her. She felt beaten, tired. "Say them," she said. "The names of all the oranges."

He closed his eyes to recite. "Joppa, Jaffa, clementine. Satsuma, Parson Brown. Temple, navel, Hamlin. Valencia, murcott—"

"They sound like a poem," she said, knowing it would please him to hear this, sorry for the times she had kept silent, her own want causing her to withhold a kindness.

"How's your head?" he asked.

"Oh, fine," she said, "it was just the heat."

They were quiet for a time. From across the grove, across the road, she heard a gaseous honking and knew that Opaline's guinea flock was surging toward the grove on its nightly insect rounds.

"I found a helper for you."

"But we already have . . ." she began, but then remembered the night she'd shouted about Guadalupe. It seemed so long ago. "You found someone else?"

"She has a little boy. He's about two or three, I think. She's been working at the camp since she got here. A few years ago I found her south of Reynosa, all alone and pregnant. She's intelligent, a hard worker. I thought you might want her to help in the house."

She had been asleep, she now realized, for nearly two months, and the word *house* shook her awake. Again the measuring part of her took over. "How's old Joe Vanilla, by the way?"

He gave her a curious look, as though surprised that she should ask, but then smiled. "He lost his thumb and forefinger. But it's almost healed over. And there wasn't any rabies, just a sick pig. I'll tell him you asked after him." His expression contained such gratitude that she had to look away. "So, do you want her?"

"Does she have one of those cockeyed names I can never say?"

"Couldn't be much easier. Luisa Cantú."

"Good," Eddie said. "I can never . . ." For a fleeting moment she wondered if something deeper lay beneath his desire to bring this particular girl to the Hundred Acres. Just as quickly, though, she dismissed the thought, knowing that her own guilt caused her to think in such a way. "What about Guadalupe?"

"There's an opening at the canning plant. I already talked to them."

"Better tell him to make room for all her boyfriends," she said, then, without warning or intention, she began to sob. For the first time she realized how lucky she'd been not to be caught. Hot tears coursed down her cheeks. "I'm sorry. I didn't mean that. You're a good man, Thomas. I need you."

His gaze softened and he leaned toward her, and at the sight of how touched he seemed by her compliment she was humbled and at the same time emboldened.

She moved toward him. "There's something else I need."

Hoping even as she said the word, the sign for the khaki-shirted, bespectacled person before her who was Thomas, innocent and solid, bruised, too, by want, that she could learn to mean it, she said, "You."

At that moment the guineas entered the grove, rushing toward a pile of rotting fruit from which the sharp smell of ferment rose into the cooling air. Like squat gray turkeys, they wheezed alarm and discovery, then squawked and scrabbled over the pile where the fruit sugar had drawn a swarm of ants. By morning, Eddie knew—as she kissed her husband with a battered, complex passion from which she understood that until this moment she had mistaken ardor for love—in their squabbling but somehow methodical way, they would have picked clean the pile, and unless he looked closely, a person wouldn't be able to tell it had been there at all.

BOOK III

•

rio paradiso

1948

•

I have forgotten, if perchance I ever knew,

the language of the sun.

—Octavio Paz, *Laughter and Penitence*

two tomatoes

In the plaza at Nuevo Progreso there had been strings of
colored lights in the jacaranda trees, conjunto music, sparkling showers
from a ring of Roman candles over the church of San Juan Bautista for
the evening of the Feast of the Assumption. The girls wore full skirts,
gathered blouses arranged so the cotton lace dipped gently off their
smooth, round shoulders. Many of the men wore uniforms: soldiers on
their way from Brownsville to Fort Hood.

How good it had been to be out in the air, the night, away at last
from her son, Gustavo, and his needs. Luisa's friend Amparo had tried
many times to get her to cross the river to the border town of Nuevo
Progreso, where the other pickers went each time there was a feast day,
but she had been afraid. Each time, when the trucks returned, Amparo
would be flushed and happy, imitating first this one, then that of the
dancers in the plaza, and Luisa, though she laughed, would feel a great
bright longing, round as the moon. But this one time she had gone—
on a night in August when the stars fell across the sky like flung sand—
leaving Gustavo in the care of her neighbor.

The swaying movements made her feel the wicked way she'd felt in
Salsipuedes when she'd first tried on the green shoes and swished her
skirt around her knees, but she had danced. The wine had tasted at first
like thickened water from a rusted cup, but then like blood and bread
and flowers, and the soldier's kisses had tasted the same. His words were
quick and soft, hovering like hummingbirds. Yes, she had said again as
they walked along the riverbank, Yes, when he spread his smooth green
coat in a packed-earth hollow beneath a water willow and pulled her
gently down beside him, Yes; but when they rose she felt even farther

from what she'd hoped to know, farther from the answer to the mysteries of men and women.

Now, on a morning when two things came to her at once—the feeling just beneath her chest that told her once again there would be a child, and don Tomás's offer that she come to work for his wife—she was leaving.

Amparo was helping her pack. From a peg on the wall her friend took several cotton dresses and shook them out one by one, preparing to fold them. "I am telling you, Lucha, don't do it. All you will get is work and feet like frying pans. And his wife . . ." Amparo broke off, making a warning face, her eyebrows pointed and dire. "Guadalupe says she is the devil herself."

Luisa went on folding her son's shirts and shorts, packing them in an orange crate. "At least you know what the devil will do."

Amparo snorted. "That's just the trouble." Amparo hunched her shoulders and became a sneaking crone with a long nose, sniffing at Luisa's dress, at the boxes, the blanket on Gustavo's cot. "This devil will sniff your sheets."

Amparo reminded Luisa of the funny Chavela. In the years she had lived in the blockhouse, she had waited, watching for the bad Amparo to reveal herself, but the girl remained the same, and at last Luisa saw that there was nothing hidden in her friend. One of Amparo's boyfriends worked at the Paris Gum Factory, and Amparo chewed one lump after another, cracking the gum so the noise sounded like the clicking calls of chachalacas. She went to sleep clicking her gum, and beside Amparo's cot each morning there was a new pink wad. Sometimes she would offer some of the sweet, dusty squares to Luisa, and they would chew together, arms linked as they walked through the camp to board the trucks for the field, Amparo shouting, "We are not tomato pickers but two to-matoes *bound for Hollywood*. The world will soon *adore* us."

Amparo shouted certain words. At first Luisa had thought something was wrong with her friend's speech, but Amparo explained that this was the way it was done in the movies; this was how you got what you wanted. This kind of speaking was, she said, *dramatic*. Amparo's voice sounded more like the old radio from Barba's pulquería—low, fuzzy music, then a sudden burst—but this Luisa didn't tell her friend. Amparo went often to the Mexican theater in Martha, and when she returned she acted all the parts for Luisa, who had stayed home. First she would be Amparo the dark-eyed lover pursuing his love with slit-eyed, smoky looks: *Come to me, my little soft one.* Then Amparo the proud beauty who at last overcome with passion and surrender would fall into a swoon across her cot: *Eduardo, oh!*

Amparo adored all the actresses, but Esther Fernández was her favorite. "Don't you think her name is so beautiful? You must call me that. I am no longer Amparo Gil, but *the beauteous Esther.* Say it."

All one Sunday Amparo would answer to nothing else, and by evening Luisa had fallen into the part of handmaiden. "Fetch me my *wildly expensive lipstick,*" ordered the beauteous Esther, lying on her blue blanket, waving toward the tube Luisa knew she had bought at the Woolworth's in Martha. "Now my *jeweled mirror.*"

Luisa hurried about, curtseying, giggling. That evening when she stood outside to look at the stars, she felt her heart catch in her throat to think of the backward way her life had gone, to think that at the age of seventeen and as the mother of a little boy who ran his toy truck across a scrap of tin to hear it rumble like a real one, she had played.

Amparo stood for no insult, no complaint. She was always right. "I gave La Chencha a *piece of my mind,*" she told Luisa. "She accused me of using more than my share of soap, and I looked her *straight in the eye* and I told her, 'You,' I said to her, and she was stung, you should have seen her old potato face, 'are the *long black hair in the mole on my backside.*' Oh, Lucha, I got her good." Amparo told Luisa that when Joe Bonillas suggested that she not pick so many green tomatoes and dirt clods to fill out her baskets, she had said, "You'd better look out for the rest of your fingers if you *shoot your mouth* like you shoot your gun."

Luisa wished she could be as funny as Amparo, but she knew it was not in her. She took all things to heart and only later did she think of clever things to say. Once, irritated with Amparo for the way she flounced off to *important things,* leaving the big atole pots for Luisa to clean, she had spent days thinking of the perfect thing to say. She practiced, making sure she got the words right and that she would not trip over her own tongue, and the next time Amparo began one of her tales of telling off someone, Luisa said, "You'd better watch out. If you keep giving people a piece of your mind, you'll wake up one morning and it will be all gone!"

In the awful buzzing moment after she had said this, Luisa realized that she would rather scrub a houseful of atole pots than ever again have to give someone a piece of her mind, especially someone she loved. But Amparo, unstung, had laughed. "The more you give it away, the more returns to you." Luisa imagined Amparo's mind like a thorn vine, beautiful and lush and green, winding around all complaints, all insults, always growing, with little thorns that pierced, and no matter where you snipped it, always more. She decided that for such a woman, life was much easier.

Amparo talked often of the fools some of the camp girls were for becoming trapped with children—"Not you, of course," she had assured Luisa, "but those who think a baby will bind them to a man"—and so it was her fear of this sharp tongue that kept her from confiding in Amparo about what had come of the dancing in Nuevo Progreso.

The two went on packing, Amparo shaking her head at each shirt, each dress. "Well, the only thing *good* I can say is that at least you might get *a fan to cool you off.*"

Amparo talked on, her voice like the whirr of a wasp, now faraway, now closer, sometimes an alarming thrum at the back of her ear, but Luisa worked quietly, determined not to let Amparo's warnings cloud her excitement. About the new baby, she would worry later.

On this day in late September it had been so hot in the tomato field that when she'd returned at midmorning with the other women to prepare the noon meal, the burnt, peppery scent of tomato leaves stayed with her. She could not get away from smells. The powdery white poison Paradiso Fruit put on the plants to keep the bugs away clung to her arms even after she washed them. Sweating as she stood at her place behind the serving line, heaping the workers' plates with beans and rice, she nearly choked from the thick hot smell of garlic, from the clouds of steam that rose from the enormous pots. And later, even after siesta, when the men went back into the fields and the women, who under don Tomás's plan did not return but remained in the camp, tended the children and prepared the evening meal, she still felt sick, as though a thick ball of wet bread were lodged in her throat.

Gustavo, who usually ran among the rows of houses, pestering the other children to play, trying to coax one of the yellow dogs to run with him, sat listlessly on his cot, dangling his feet and whining for a cut of the sugarcane he knew she kept on the ledge where the concrete walls met the roof.

For what seemed the thousandth time since he had come out of her, blue and writhing, straining against the cord around his neck, she had wondered what would become of him. At almost three, Tavo was stocky and strong, his hair so thick and curly it looked like black fur, his skin dark. At the cotton gin in McAllen she had seen a black man for the first time and she now understood Uncle's agate eyes, the dusky cast of his skin. Tavo wore the white loose shorts of the other children of the camp, but his he made her tie at the waist every morning with a length of electrical cord, the knot at his back so that it looked like the curled tail of a piglet that jiggled when he trotted along the dusty paths of the camp.

She could not believe how much time it took to worry about him. It was as though the midwife had forgotten to sever the cord that wrapped his neck and it was still attached, stronger, even, so that when the other children teased him, called him Pavo, Pavito—"Little Turkey"—it pulled at her own belly. Yanked it, when the camp girls who watched the children in the morning tricked him into eating chicken dung, telling him the lump was Paris gum. She understood now why her mother and Chavela had urged her brothers to be strong. Tavo, like Rafael, was too full of feeling. And there was no end to his wanting. She knew the world was set up to betray his hopes and that when this happened—again, again—each time he would be surprised, the hurt as fresh the hundredth time as it had been the first.

The night before, she had had the dream, the same one always, of a crowd of people in a tree above him, thick as fruit and humming like flies, all of them waiting to swing down from long grass ropes and kick him. And so that afternoon, when don Tomás had knocked on the door and after she finally understood his reason for coming, she could not say yes fast enough.

Now from the open doorway she heard the calls of the other children in the camp. Beneath their voices, thunderlike, was the rumple of the corrugated-tin well cover they were forbidden to jump on but jumped on anyway. "Stay here," she told Tavo, who had heard the noise and was heading for the door. "Don Tomás is coming for us."

Head like a bull and proud for all his tender longings, he charged outside but stayed close, running his red truck on the slab just outside the door. Soon she heard a contented song, Tavo singing of Papá and his truck. Like the other camp children, Tavo loved the patrón and called him Papá.

"You have to *ask yourself*," Amparo was saying, "*what would Esther do?* I'm telling you for the *last time* that Guadalupe says she is the *devil*. Oh, sure, you'll get your own house, but—"

"It was her idea. Don Tomás told me so. She wants someone to help."

She wrapped twine around a crate, tying it fast against the splintered pine, then added proudly, "Someone smart."

When Amparo made a spitting noise a bit of pink juice dribbled from her mouth and she slurped it back, wiping her chin with the back of her hand. "How smart do you have to be to say, Yes, Madama, No, Madama? How smart do you have to be to keep your mouth shut? You wouldn't believe how many times my cousin had to tell her off. She is bossy and picky and . . . and . . ." Luisa could tell her friend was angry; not only was she at a loss for words, she had forgotten to be dramatic. "I'll tell you all the English you need to know," Amparo continued. "*Work, work, work. Clean, clean, clean.* They think everything is dirty and that everyone wants their husbands. That everyone is a whore but them. They act like . . ."

Luisa picked up the floursack that held her household articles and slung it across the doorsill. "I like to clean." She looked over her shoulder at Amparo's strewn clothes, the jumble of her friend's possessions. "I think."

"Stay here," Amparo pleaded. "Did I tell you about my other cousin, Rutila? She worked twenty years in the house of a rancher in Presidio *who promised to leave her all his money* and all she got was . . ." Amparo broke off, looking at the ceiling, sighing.

Luisa gave a last look around. She knelt to check under Tavo's cot and felt the blood rush to her ears as she crawled under it to reach for a shirt. As she backed out, she felt Amparo standing over her. "And do you know, *as I was saying,* what she got?"

Luisa stood, dizzy, but smiled at her friend. "No, but I *know* you won't stop until you tell me."

Amparo huffed, then shook her head exaggeratedly. "It's too terrible to tell. You don't want to know." Then she seized Luisa in a hug. "You are so little. You are such an Indian. You tell me if she mistreats you." Amparo spanked her hands together. "I will be there as fast as that to give her a piece of my mind. And don't say I didn't warn you."

Luisa smiled, knowing that for all Amparo's bluster, there was a sadness in her friend that made it hard for her to believe that there was goodness in the world.

Amparo made her a good luck gift of the lipstick, and Luisa was ashamed that she had not thought to make a gift for Amparo. As don Tomás waited in the truck, Tavo on his lap and playing with the steering wheel, they said good-bye. "I'm going to send you something nice,"

Luisa said. "A gift." For the first time since she left Salsipuedes, Luisa remembered the red book she had promised Rafael, and she was seized with sorrow—for herself because she suddenly understood that in her life what she wanted to do would be always higher and better than what she did, and for the loss of Amparo, for she realized how much she would miss her. In her heart, she vowed never again to make a promise she did not intend to keep.

She hugged Amparo. "I'll send you something really good."

"You'll be too busy," Amparo said, dismissing Luisa's intention with a wave, but Luisa could tell that she wanted to believe. Luisa stepped into the truck's cab, and as they pulled away from the camp, she waved until she could no longer see the dusty row of houses in the ring of mesquite trees behind her.

2

the hundred acres

The low clouds of the hot afternoon, streaked violet from the setting sun, had moved out over the Gulf, and the little farm at the end of the lane of pecan trees looked beautiful in the slanting light. Don Tomás parked the truck in front of a house white as clean cotton where on the porch sat a pale-haired woman in a yellow dress. Even from a distance, Luisa could see she suffered from her thin skin. She was white as an egg, but with reddish speckles that reminded her of her old pet Dolores. There was a cracked, tired look around her eyes, and Luisa knew that despite Amparo's warnings, somewhere in this devil woman there was something kind. With all her heart, she vowed to love her.

Don Tomás stepped from the truck and went around to lower the tailgate. Tavo ran around the truck and don Tomás picked him up and ruffled his hair before he set him on the concrete walk. Don Tomás's wife looked suddenly stern, disgusted, and for the first time, Luisa felt afraid.

His wife called some words to don Tomás that made him look at the ground, then he turned and walked toward one of the sheds behind the house.

"My name," the woman called to Luisa, thumping her chest with her fist, nodding rapidly but speaking slowly, "me llamo Miss Eddie."

Luisa nodded, approaching the porch. "Sí, Madama." She thumped her own chest. "Luisa."

The woman made a noise that sounded like "Hump!" Then she stood and brought her hands to her eyes, making small circles of her fingers so that she looked like a raccoon. Then she waved toward the back of the house where don Tomás had gone. Luisa understood: She meant don Tomás. "He is el Mister Hatch. Don't let me catch you calling him anything else, hear?" Madama cupped one hand behind her ear, shook her head, stamped her foot against the floorboards of the porch, then, suddenly, hopped on one foot, holding the other. "Ow!"

Luisa nodded, though this time she hadn't understood what her mistress was trying to say. "Sí, Madama." She wondered if she should call Tavo to present him, but he had followed don Tomás.

Now la Madama twisted and wiggled like a hen having a dirt bath, patting her sides, her lap, her chest, saying something Luisa could not interpret, so she nodded and smiled until the woman said a word she understood: *lavada*.

Stunned, she looked at the ground. It was just as Amparo had said. Don Tomás's wife had called her brazen. "No, Madama, nunca."

To her surprise, Madama laughed. "Well, at least you can string more than two words together," she said, "hablar es posible, and that's bueno." She went with her wild movements. She ran her hands along her sides, then she bent and made scrubbing motions, nodding, then shaking her head. Then she crouched and ran in a tight circle like a dog chasing its tail. Suddenly, she stopped. "Hold on a minute," she said, and she picked up a little book from her chair and leafed through it. Then she yelled out some more words. Luisa caught only a few: *girl, dirty, baby, wash,* enough, though, to learn that rather than calling her brazen, Madama was interested in cleanliness.

Abruptly, Madama turned and went into the house and returned with a blue and white bundle which she set on the rail of the porch. "This is some ropa. And come back when you're all limpia." She went into the house and the screen door banged behind her.

The cloth was of a fine blue weave, crisp as a leaf. A dress. It smelled of clean salt, and she wondered why the woman wanted it washed. She stood for awhile, waiting for Madama to return and tell her where to wash it, wondering what she should do next, but then don Tomás came back around the corner and motioned for her to come with him.

When they were out of sight of the house, he picked up Tavo, who had been pulling at his pants legs, and he led her around the farm, pointing out the barns and sheds, explaining things she knew she would never remember. She worried that la Madama would be angry if she didn't return soon with the dress, but she told herself that don Tomás was the patrón, and that whatever he did must be right. At the hedge that skirted the big house, he stopped to tell her that these bushes were oleanders, and poison. She should not let Tavo touch them. Then he pointed to a building she had not seen before, tucked behind the oleanders, a low-roofed shed with a wide glass window that had been propped open like the window of a fruit stand. Beside this little house was a small yard fenced with wire. Don Tomás held open the door for her, explaining that the shed had been a chicken house, but that he had made improvements. The moment he said the words, "This is where you will live," something caught in her throat, and her easy tears reminded her of the old time in Salsipuedes—all she had hoped, all she had thought possible—and her sight was so clouded as she looked upon the place that she could know only that the little house was beautiful.

Though the room was dim, she could see that the wooden floor had been swept clean and in the center lay a rug with flowers the color of a rooster's comb. Along the white-painted walls were wooden crates nailed up to serve as shelves, their fruit company labels colorful and bright. Inside the boxes were stacked pots and pans, dishes, cups. In one corner of the room were two beds, a large and a small, with two thick mattresses, nothing like the thin pads on the cots in the blockhouse. A table and chairs stood in another corner, and over them hung a string which don Tomás pulled. With a tiny click, a warm yellow light fell over the room. In the center of the table, someone had put a jar of pink and red flowers, and she thought of Madama in her itchy skin, making ready for the day of her arrival, picking them to welcome her, gathering the flowers as she gathered the hope that all would work out well, and she was touched. Something had already told her that the woman was so made that nothing said between them would be straight, but always sideways, and she promised to remember this in the times to come.

When she looked up, don Tomás was gone. She scooped Tavo from the corner where he had pried open the little latched chicken door, and she hugged him harder than she had for a long time. "This," she told him, "is where you will live."

In another corner was a cinderblock shower like the ones in the camp, and she turned on the water with a laugh, for again the right solution at the right moment had come her way, and into the scrubbing of the blue dress she put all her gratitude. Then, with the wet dress in hand, she gathered up Tavo and went back to the porch to show Madama.

She tapped lightly at first, then knocked harder, but no one came to the door. If she stood just so, she could see down the long tunnel of the house to the kitchen, where Madama moved in and out of the light. Outside, the shadows grew longer and longer while she waited. Don Tomás's truck was gone, so she couldn't ask the patrón what to do.

Tavo whined. They had had nothing to eat since the noon meal and now it was dark. Beside the porch there was an orange tree. Most of the fruits were green, but on one branch she saw a ripe one. She started down the steps to pick it for Tavo, but then stopped. Madama mustn't think she was the kind of girl who took things, and so she stood, growing more and more miserable with the pressure in her bladder. Worn out, Tavo at last fell asleep, curled like a small dog on a braided rug by the door.

The many birds, nesting in the trees around the house as the light waned, had grown silent by the time the headlights of don Tomás's truck lit up the lane. The patrón looked surprised to see her still there, surprised at the damp, wrinkled dress she showed him, but then a look of understanding crossed his face, and he explained that Madama had wanted her to bathe herself, and that she should, from this time on, use the back door. He led her to the back porch, where there were two napkin-covered plates beside the door. She could tell they had been there a long time because a line of ants moved across the stiff white cloth. It would be several days before she understood that she was to wear the fine blue dress.

•　•　•

In just a week she had learned more than she thought possible, and she woke each morning in her own, the softest of beds, eager to begin the new day. In the big house she swept webs from high places and dust balls from the low. With toothpicks she cleaned the tiniest of crevices around the sink, and with clean sand she scrubbed the rust stains from the toilet bowls. She learned Madama's difficult ways, and, miraculously, she understood everything the woman said, though she used much English, bad Spanish, and broad actions which often had little to do with what she was saying. The slightest nod, the slightest sound, Luisa saw, could mean something important, and she learned to interpret these movements and sounds. Madama's "Hump!"—depending on how she said it—could mean "Oh, I see," or "Is that so?" or "I don't believe it," or all of these together. She saw that it was Madama's way to be harsh sometimes, but that this was toward a higher purpose, which was to teach her how to do things right. The lesson of the door was for her own good, she knew, and she was grateful.

Even the machines, which she had at first thought would be confusing, made sense, and it was as though she knew without being told how everything worked. Her favorite was the squat washer on its sturdy legs, like a helping friend that when you fed in sopping clothes and cranked the handle out came shirts and pants and socks, flat as tongues, to drop into the waiting basket. It was as though she had been born for this work, and all things came to her as easily as the pressed clothes dropping from the wringers.

Almost every night, don Tomás stopped by to bring her things she needed. A coffeepot, some pale green towels, a butter dish, some rolls of toilet paper that at the camp the people fought for, once a paper sack of lemon drops. Luisa divided the candies between herself and Tavo, and hers she savored, allowing herself one each day. His, Tavo ate all at once, except for two, which he sucked on to make sticky, then placed against his closed eyelids, squinting, and they laughed at how he looked like a little bug-boy. Don Tomás told her the gifts were from his wife, and she understood that Madama's pride would not allow her to make the trip down the flat stones to the little house. Don Tomás told her, too, how happy the Madama was with her work. Though she knew he did it out of respect, she wished he would not call her Señora Cantú, but Luisa; after all, he was the one due respect.

Though she loved working in the big house, she lived for the nights in the little house, when for hours she shifted her belongings here and there, never tiring. Sometimes she stayed up half the night arranging things in her house because each new pattern looked more beautiful than the one before. The same outside. When don Tomás brought seeds and cuttings, she planted them in the soft, silty ground, where she found the many bits of shells which the patrón told her were the bones of ancient sea creatures. By moonlight she watered, loving the scent of the moist earth, its chalk-and-bone-and-vegetable smell, and by day, when she inspected what she'd planted, she marveled at the growth.

She thought often of the story of the first man and the first woman, how they had been sent from the garden. Before, when Señor Miller had told the story, showing a picture of the weeping two, she had not understood why they were so distressed. The world was wide and bright and beautiful, and to go out into it did not seem such a bad thing. Now she understood that some things, some places were more beautiful than others. The secret, she saw as she gazed from the back porch at her little house already blooming with poppies and portulaca, was to know what you had to begin with. If the first ones had known this, they would never have eaten the fruit.

3

chickens

The first thing Tavo broke in the big house as he followed her through her day was a china figure, a lady with a shepherd's crook and a full skirt that looked like frosting on a fancy cake. Luisa was careful to sweep up all the shards. She set the figurine, the skirt broken and jagged, back on the table. Waiting for Madama to find out, Luisa was sick with worry. Finally, unable to bear it, she told Madama about the broken lady. "Hump," said Madama. She looked suspiciously at Tavo, but said only, "El Mister Hatch will take it out of your dinero." After Madama had gone upstairs, Luisa realized that she had forgotten to say it was Tavo's fault, but something told her it would be best if she did not mention this.

Next, when she hadn't been paying attention to him, he left dirty footprints on the walls of the kitchen. He liked to lie on the floor as she cooked, running his trucks on the squares of linoleum, his feet propped on the walls. This she could not explain as her own mistake, and Madama was angry. "The niño did it," she said, pressing her mouth into a thin, ugly line. She told Luisa she would have to discipline her child, and that she would watch to make sure she did. Dutifully, Luisa spanked

Tavo, though she didn't see that some dirty footmarks which she could easily wash away should cause so much trouble.

The end came when one day as she was dusting the plates and glasses in Madama's cabinet while Tavo was napping on a mat in the kitchen, Luisa looked up to see that he was not asleep at all but climbing up the curtains. "No!" she shouted, running toward him as he swung from the beautiful thin cloth, but before she could reach him, the curtain rod broke. The clatter and then Tavo's howling brought Madama running, red-faced and angry. The niño, she made clear to Luisa, was a pest. A danger. He was to stay in the little house while she worked. She could return to him at mid-morning, at lonche, and for siesta. In the meantime, he should stay in the little yard. And if that didn't hold him back, well . . . they would see.

Outside all day, Tavo tried to follow don Tomás around the farm. He grieved when the gray truck left and was happy only when it returned. Luisa, watching, remembering how she had felt when Ralph Emerson López departed in his own truck, knew he felt forsaken.

One day Madama overheard Tavo call the patrón Papá. This, Madama told her, was very bad. People would talk. She wouldn't want that. It would displease Mister Hatch and Luisa would have to be sent back to Mexico.

For her part, Luisa tried to be tender with Tavo, to understand that for him the days were long and confusing. But for her they were filled with delight at each new job she saw that she could do well. Though she only half-believed it, she told herself that having to stay in the little fenced yard would toughen him against what would be a difficult life.

•   •   •

One Sunday Amparo came down the path through the oleanders to visit. Luisa served her coffee from her own pot, sugar from her own bowl. "Look at this!" Amparo squealed over the cozy house and all the fine things inside it, but Luisa waved away her compliments; she did not want Amparo to feel envy.

On packing day when Amparo had talked of what would happen on the Hundred Acres, the buzzing wasp part of what she had said had to do with don Tomás. Amparo had predicted that he would soon begin to seek out her company, that there would be trouble. "Some men are like deep dry wells; no matter how much it rains, they can't be filled." Now her friend asked, "And how is don Tomás?"

Luisa told her about his generosity, and about how happy la Madama was with her work. Amparo nodded, but Luisa could see she was skeptical, and when she rose to start more coffee she felt Amparo looking at her body. As she took her place again, Amparo said, "And how does she feel about"—she pointed toward Luisa's belly—"that?"

Luisa told her about the soldier in Nuevo Progreso.

"What color hair did he have?" Amparo wanted to know. "What color eyes?"

"Brown," Luisa told her, "and green."

"You'd better hope for a dark baby," Amparo said. "What does *she* say about it?"

"She doesn't know."

Amparo rolled her eyes. "Does he?"

"The soldier? Ben?"

"Fool. Don Tomás."

Luisa shook her head.

Amparo stood up. "I'll help you pack."

•   •   •

Although Amparo had guessed, no one else would be able to tell yet, she was certain. Still, she knew she had to tell them about her baby. It troubled her that while Madama had grown great with child and she herself had begun to feel the thickness along her sides, the front part of this baby did not swell, but felt like a little gourd, hard and hollow. She worried that the baby was dead inside her. If it was, she knew the reason: She cared too much about what went on between Madama and don Tomás, and this took away the baby's strength for growing.

At night she watched the big house for the patterns of light and shadow which meant they were moving about. She knew when they passed each other on the stairs. When they sat. When they went to bed. Rarely did they stay in the same room. Madama sat often at the little desk in the bedroom, working at her plans. Cleaning, Luisa had found the papers with their blue ink lines, pictures of houses, rooms, tables and chairs and curtains. Don Tomás worked in the little room next to the sala, at a bigger desk, and through the windows she could see his pale hair in the circle of light from a gooseneck lamp. Some nights, he would tiptoe to the stairs and cock his head, listening. If Madama's light was out, he took his hat from the peg beside the kitchen door and clapped it on his head. His shoulders became straighter then, and once she had seen him prance back to his desk, high-stepping like a silly soldier. She watched as he saluted the stairs. Once he stuck out his behind and wiggled it. Another time, she had seen him hold his arms as though holding a woman to dance; he swirled and dipped around the room, a moving shadow in the yellow light. Something, she knew, had happened between them to cause them to have secret lives at night in which they were more themselves than when they walked around, living, by day.

There grew in her, though she tried to stop it, a belief that she could make him happier. She, Luisa, when he sat alone at the big desk, would make a cup of coffee with two spoons of sugar just the way he liked, she would rub his shoulders with sweet oil, on hot nights she would smooth cool cloths across his forehead. She would, when he held his arms out in his lonely dance, slip inside them.

Sometimes don Tomás lingered at her door in the evening and they talked about her garden, which overnight seemed to grow jungly and thick around the little house. He noticed each new leaf, each runner, each bud. At these times, when she saw his soft gaze, his eyes so close behind the glass of his spectacles, she saw that he was the kind of man whose nights were filled with longing, who, when he woke up in the morning, was surprised to find his same heart beating, surprised to remember that the same man felt it. She knew what filled his heart, for the same want, though it had no name, filled her own. It was this nameless want that caused their hearts to wish to burst from their chests, but the poor hearts could find no path toward this desire but through the body. This, she understood, was the stubborn, sideways way of men and women, and it fooled them into thinking this desire was somehow linked with the great, good thing. And perhaps it was, but how, she wondered, could they know? Now it was as though Amparo's words had twisted onto her: She was the deep, dry well.

One night, after he had left but the smell of his tobacco lingered in the cocopomosa, as the moon rose over the far palms, it came to her that there was a certain kind of person who, looking into that well of another's want, would ache to fill it, would pour himself into the well until he himself was left parched and dry. She understood that don Tomás was such a person. He would never be the first to act, but one word—the sighing, whisper-breath of it—would bring him into her bed. Of all the doors she had walked through without knowing what lay on the other side, before this one she stopped, considering.

• • •

The waste in the big house amazed her. Heedless Madama threw away good lard pails, bottles with lids that fit, plates with just one chip, towels with just one hole. She laughed, thinking of her mother and Chavela and how they would fall upon these things like zopilotes on bones, picking through the treasures, bearing them home to the clutter of the house in Salsipuedes. Pack rats, they had been, and she, for all her scorn when she was a girl, now saw that she was just as bad. She began to store jars and bottles under her bed, to line up pans and pails behind the little house. Into some she put the rich soil and planted seeds, in others she stored sugar, coffee, beans, and salt. Some she simply kept. It was better to have something you might want than to want it and not have it. And if you kept it in plain sight, among the many other articles you might want, you wouldn't be likely to forget it was there and yearn for it.

On the nights he visited her, it was don Tomás's practice to sit on the little bench outside her door, to smoke one cigarette, cupping the burning end in his palm so that the smoke curled slowly, but one night in mid-winter, when it was chilly enough for a sweater, he finished the first and then lit another. From his body came the scent of tobacco and laundry soap, salt, and beneath those odors the scent that was truly his, milky, vegetable, as hard to catch as the smell of ripened corn.

She was accustomed to the silences between them but on this night those silences seemed loud. Don Tomás was behaving strangely. He stood, began to pace. She heard him swallow, as though his mouth were dry, but she did not offer water. When she looked into the sky, the stars seemed far away and separate. She feared that one would fall, as such a star had fallen on the night she'd gone to Nuevo Progreso, and she would take it as a message from the heavens that she should move toward don Tomás, just a little, so the heat from her would touch the heat from him.

When he drew a third cigarette from his pocket, she jumped up and told him she felt ill. She turned to go, and she did not let herself look back to see his face as she closed the door.

Awake long into the night, she remembered her Salsipuedes bean jar, smiling to think of the way she'd tried to keep track of her acts, seeing that it hadn't worked. She would try harder, now that she was older. The next morning she took a beautiful blue bottle from beneath her bed and into it she dropped a bean. For the baby growing inside Madama, that the child would make things well between the couple. The one bean looked lonely, rattling as she shook the bottle, so she dropped in another for Madama, so what was broken in her would be healed. A third one would be for don Tomás, though she didn't trust herself to wish the right thing for him. This wish would have to come from a higher place that knew better what he needed. A fourth she dropped in for herself, so she would remember the great, good thing and be wise enough to know it when it stood before her, waiting to be done.

The next night, after Tavo fell asleep, she did three things: She took Amparo's lipstick from its silver box and put it on, using the bowl of a spoon to help her see; next she set the blue bottle in the center of the table; and then she pulled the cord on the light to cast the little house in darkness. When don Tomás knocked, she licked her lips, which tasted of beeswax, soap, and sweet clover, and she imagined how it would feel to kiss him. Through a crack in the curtains, she could see him, hat in hand, waiting for her to answer. Three times he knocked, each time louder, and three times she started for the door. But she looked each time at the blue bottle, and each time it would not let her answer.

She heard a rustle at the door, a thump on the doorstone. She watched through the window as he went slowly back up the path and let himself into the kitchen. Her gaze traveled up to the bedroom window, and there she saw the form, the shadow of Madama, watching, her hand parting the curtains. Better than the saints she'd wished to feel like as a girl, statues that looked beyond the earth to higher things, she felt honorable and good, a holy soldier on the earth, looking straight into the face of what stood right before her, guarding the house from wrong.

Suddenly tired, her legs aching, she went to sit at the table, in the dark. She poured the last of the cool coffee into a cup and sat for a long time, lulled by the sound of Tavo's soft breathing, watching the way the wind blew the fronds of cocopomosa against the screen. She imagined the rasping green fringe as a great broom that whisked the sky clean, clean.

The next morning she took in the bag of onions don Tomás had left on her doorstone, kissed Tavo, and walked up the stone path to the big house. With a clear heart, trying to use as much English as she could, she told Madama that she, too, was expecting. She told about the soldier. Madama looked at her. Then she "Hump"-ed. And that was all.

Madama's baby was born small and stringy on the last day of April.

Luisa, serving Madama's breakfast on her first day home from the hospital, thought he looked like a tiny red armadillo. But don Tomás seemed not to notice, and she saw that her bean prayer had worked. The patrón was smitten. His eyes grew moist as he looked at his little son, who was called Raleigh, a name Luisa could pronounce only with a rolling *r*, which made them laugh. He fussed over the cradle, covered up the baby, then worried that his son was too hot, drew back the blankets, only to worry that he was too cold. Often, he would sneak away with the child. Once they caught him with the bundled baby in the grove, where don Tomás was explaining what made oranges grow. So many times did he want to disturb his son that she and Madama had to chase him from the house and back to work. Luisa began to tease the new father, telling him that she believed he would crawl into the cradle if they didn't watch him. Though Madama was short-tempered during these days, Luisa was as happy as she had ever been. Don Tomás continued to bring her things, but he no longer lingered.

Every other week, don Tomás brought her an envelope of money, which she tucked into one of the coffee cans. Each time he had asked if she would like a ride to the store, she had declined, but not wanting to appear ungrateful she assured him that she had everything she needed. Now she couldn't wait to buy gifts for everyone, and the next time don Tomás asked if she needed to go into Martha, she said, "Woolworth's," and was amazed at how quickly she and Tavo were left standing on the sidewalk before the big red glass windows and amazed at what a rich lady she had become, for the salesgirl treated her like a queen. She bought cloth and thread and needles to make things for the coming one, a beautiful slip, red satin with black lace, for Amparo, and for don Tomás's baby she bought a playsuit onto which had been printed a red tie like the ones the Anglo bosses wore on Sundays, already there so you didn't have to tie it, perfect buttons, and red suspenders. For Tavo, who clamored for everything he saw, she bought a package of toy horses to be pulled in the red truck, a toy shovel, a brown cowboy hat with a wooden bead to tighten the chin strap. When he wasn't looking, she tucked into her basket a box of crayons to give him later, when he tired of his new possessions. She found a bottle of shampoo that smelled of the oranges and charcoal of the sweet-by-night the women had woven into her hair before she went to Uncle, and she stood in the aisle for a long time with the open bottle, sniffing, thinking of that time, wishing

Chavela could see her now. "Jasmine," the salesgirl called the shampoo, and Luisa bought two bottles, one for herself and one for Madama. She found a wedding ring just like Madama's, which she paid for at the special counter just for jewelry, and she fit it snugly on her finger.

For a long time she shopped for a gift for don Tomás, but it seemed that nothing was right. "What does he like?" the salesgirl asked after showing her the trays of pocketknives, the leather belts coiled in their boxes, ties with stripes and running horses, rows of leather wallets. "Fruit," she finally said, "and flowers." The salesgirl rolled her eyes. "I give up. Get him a box of cigars."

Luisa was at the pay line when she saw the perfect gift: a box of chocolates, each one in its own brown paper nest. The perfect part was the box. Across the golden cover were cross-stitch designs of birds and flowers and houses. They reminded her of the embroidery her mother had taught her, and of everything don Tomás loved.

A week later, she felt a pain, this time a catch in her back that moved up under her arms as though someone had tied a rope around her chest to bind her, so that at first she thought the trouble was some peppers she had eaten, but the pains grew worse and at last she went to the big house so Madama could call the midwife.

If Tavo had been the child of her confusion, this one was of contentment, for Antonia came easily, as though the world were water and she were a sleek fish slipping in. Her mouth was tiny, her fingers delicate and pale, flaking with skin angels. The soft spot on her head smelled to Luisa of a smoky, dusky meat, deep and human, from where the head had pressed into the bone and muscle of her own insides. The pull of the baby's mouth at her nipple shot straight to the place between her legs, and at first she felt ashamed when this happened, but then she thought she understood the reason for it. Years later, when she would have this feeling with a man, her body would remember. Madama gave her some days off, and she loved the drowsy afternoons when she sat in her soft chair with the baby and it seemed the whole world napped.

Antonia was a month old when Tavo, unwatched, pulled up a tomato stake from don Tomás's big garden and marched into the little house where she sat nursing the baby. "I'm fighting with my sword," he announced, brandishing the stick close to her chair and sprinkling clumps of dirt on her clean floor. His face was fierce, but she saw that behind it there was something else. With her finger she gently broke the seal of Tonia's tiny mouth. The baby whimpered but then slept, and Luisa put her into the blanket-lined crate and took Tavo onto her lap.

"The new baby is bad," he said. His look was hard and at the same time hopeful. "You should spank her."

His body smelled of dirt and salt and metal and the oily scent of his black cord belt. His arms and legs seemed crude and enormous compared with the delicate bones of the baby, but she rocked him for a long time, singing the baby songs she sang to Tonia, but putting in Tavo's name at the right parts. When he was calm, she gave him the crayons and they sat at the table to draw pictures on the butcher paper Luisa had saved from the big house. Luisa drew the hen Dolores and made Tavo laugh at her funny crooked comb, her quick black eyes. Then she drew a nest and in it she drew two eggs. "The eggs will be two chickens," she explained. She drew a jagged line on one of the eggs. "See how the shell is cracking? There's a new chicken ready to be born. Here he comes! Chicken One, and that is you." She drew a chick with small reaching wings and then a silly hen smile on Dolores's face. "How happy the mother is!"

Tavo petted the chick. "Chicken One."

She made the second egg crack. "Oh, here comes Chicken Two." She drew a smaller chick. "Not as big. Not as smart. Not as strong."

Tavo frowned at the smaller chick.

"The mother loves them both the same."

She spun a story of the mother hen and her two chicks, and when she lay down for a nap, Tavo went on happily drawing chickens and eggs. As she dozed, listening to his peaceful murmuring, Luisa felt proud of herself that she was the mother of two children, and that this, too, she knew how to do.

She was awakened by Tavo's wailing and Madama's shouting. She scooped Antonia, wet, now squalling, from her crate and ran outside to where Madama was pulling Tavo by the piglet tail of his belt toward the little house. Tavo, head down and fists flailing, tried to wriggle out of her grip. When her head cleared, she saw the cause of Madama's anger. Along the clean white boards of the big house, Tavo had scribbled a row of sticks and circles, and many blue chickens with yellow feet, red beaks, black eyes.

Madama pointed, yelling words Luisa couldn't make out until she heard her mistress say that Mister Hatch would punish Tavo. Luisa could only nod that Madama was right. What Tavo had done was bad. But she herself was at fault, she tried to tell Madama, for not watching him.

Madama didn't care.

It was nearly dark when don Tomás came home. She heard voices inside the big house, after that a long silence, but then Madama, holding a hairbrush, came to the back porch and shouted for Luisa to bring her son.

When he saw don Tomás, Tavo ran to meet him, and Luisa thought how strange it was that the same boy who had that afternoon in her lap felt so large could now look so small, his shoulder blades like the small wings of Chicken One.

Tavo cried as if his heart would break, though don Tomás struck only once, and not hard. It hurt don Tomás, she knew. When he had finished, he turned and went into the house where she knew the first thing he would do would be to pick up his own son and vow never to strike him. She saw that just as his new love had entered don Tomás, another had gone out of him, and in the great light of his own child, it was as though the lesser light of Gustavo Cantú had flickered, dimmed, and then blown out.

That night she put a bean into the bottle for Tavo, for forgetting him the first time she had offered up her hopes, and then another for the wish that what she'd told him about the hen who loved her two chicks the same were true. Into the bottle she dropped a third bean, for fearing it was not. Years later, when she would learn he had been lost to her forever, she would know the truth, and that no beans or hopes or wishes could bring back what was gone.

•　•　•

She had been at the Hundred Acres for almost two years when Madama said, "I've tried and I've tried but I can't say your nombre right and so I'm going to llama you Lu."

Though she understood exactly what Madama was saying—and that the new name was probably better than the sound Madama made when she tried to pronounce *Luisa*, a sound that was a swing and a screech—Luisa pretended she didn't understand. She shook her head. "*¿Cómo?*"

Madama tried again. "Tengo no poder for llamar your nombre."

Again Luisa shook her head.

Each time Madama repeated her statement in Spanish that grew worse and worse, Luisa made her expression more confused, until Madama grew frustrated and said, "Oh, hell."

She could not have said why it was exactly at this moment that something would close inside her, only that a small, hard place in her chest told her she could not love Madama in the way she'd wanted to when she'd first seen her, and that for this loss, Madama would pay a price. And so she became Lu, the name that fit her when she put on the blue dress, and part of being Lu was that she couldn't understand Madama without a struggle, without many explanations and repetitions. Until the day Ralph Emerson López found her on a street corner in Rio Paradiso, she would hear no one call her by the name Luisa.

BOOK IV

•

the queen of magic changes

1954

•

That which is crooked cannot be made straight: and that
which is wanting cannot be numbered.

—Ecclesiastes 1:15

the hacienda plan

Mad at the heat, Eddie gunned the engine of her new Chevrolet. Mad at the children, she slammed into reverse. Mad at her maid, she backed out of the driveway, and mad at the world, she shifted to first and peeled down the lane, leaving a satisfying cloud of dust to settle on those who had conspired to make her two hours late for the only thing she wanted on this June day, which was to be in this car rolling up this road, on her way to McAllen to make the final decision about the house she and Thomas would at last build on Grand Texas Boulevard just outside Rio Paradiso.

The car was an oven. Her canary linen suit with its starched organdy ruff, so crisp in the morning, now looked like the crumpled cellophane of a Kitty Clover bag, and her white lace hankie drooped from her breast pocket like a tattered Kleenex. Four knife-sharp creases across her lap, smeared with silvery tracks from where Raleigh had wiped his nose, made her skirt resemble an angry, furrowed brow.

It had happened like this: Tavo, nine, and Raleigh and Tonia, six, frenzied at the prospect of an afternoon together at Lu's little house, where there were beds for jumping and tin tubs for the building of pirate ships, had gotten into the back porch Deepfreeze, when Tavo, inspired by watching *Beat the Clock* on Raleigh's television, had promised the little ones a prize if they would stick two black-eyed peas into their nostrils. The ruckus—wailing, jabbering, and finger-pointing—erupted just as she was ready to leave. The children had to be taken to Rio to the doctor, but Lu, distracted, had locked all the keys—big house, little house, car—in the kitchen. They'd had to break the glass of the pantry window and boost Tavo in to unlock the door.

Lately there had been a string of burglaries in the towns along the river. Rumor at the Reno Cafe placed the blame on the criminal Kid Mapuche, so called for his nocturnal marauding, the black mask he was said to wear, and his habit of taking only the smallest of valuables. He would pass right by a heavy silver coffee service and find the ruby ring the lady of the house had left on the toilet tank. He would ignore the Philco television set and take the velvet bag of silver dollars. In the colonia, Eddie had heard, people accused the vandal sons of Anglo land-owners, who, spoiled by plenty, had nothing better to do with their time. The Anglos blamed the hoodlum sons of their yardmen. But the imaginations of the young boys—Anglo as well as Mexican—were fired by the tales of his daring, and they played the Adventures of Kid Mapuche from dawn to dusk, skulking from tree to tree, crafty and sly, trinket by trinket growing richer.

In the past years the Valley had been overrun with Mexicans. The *Evening Monitor* reported that in just three months, the border patrol caught 156,000 and returned them to Mexico. Half of that number simply walked back the same day. The patrol had resorted to airplanes, flying the illegals farther into the interior to make it harder to return. Every day, eight to ten full flights left the Brownsville airport. Lu was terrified. Though she didn't mean a word of the threat, if the maid became fractious, all Eddie would have to say was "I've half a mind to drive you down to Brownsville," and Lu would straighten up.

For the first time since they'd lived in the Valley, Thomas locked the house at night, and he instructed Eddie to lock the doors even in the daytime. Thomas had made Lu two keys, which he had strung onto a chain for her to wear around her neck. Lu complained that they got in her way, and she removed the chain—just until the scrubbing was done, she always promised—only to misplace them. Then a hysterical hunt would ensue. Lu's keys turned up in the oddest places—the oven, the silverware drawer, once in the bathtub, stretched from the hot water knob to the cold. For all her stolid loyalty, the woman was a scatterbrain.

After they'd retrieved the keys, Tavo fussed to come to the doctor's, too, and she'd had to be firm with Lu. Then, on the way down Mile Six Road to the doctor's office, just as she reached the peroration of her lecture on responsibility and her voice had begun to quaver convincingly and Lu looked contrite and only a little sullen, they came upon an accident in the road, Sheriff Hartley Rowell presiding. Eddie stopped the car.

It was a town joke that the angle of the sheriff's Stetson telegraphed his attitude: On this afternoon he wore the hat pushed back from his sweating forehead, indicating peeve and resignation. He told Eddie that as a blankety-blank graduation prank, the blankety-blank senior class of Harlan Bloch High had chopped down a blankety-blank royal palm. He pointed to the ditch, where a ramshackle bus lay on its side. "Bunch of blankety-blank Penitentes from Jim Hogg County. Up at the Sam Fordyce Field they got a Jesus face on a storage tank. Just water rust, but try to tell them that. Bus swerved to miss the tree. They think it's a sign."

Some of the Penitentes, in white robes and thorn necklaces, crept like stunned moths in and out of the open windows of their gray metal chrysalis while others milled about on the sun-scorched road, burning their bare feet in the tar. Two deputies strained to roll the palm tree off the macadam. "Miz Hatch," Hartley said, "there's no use waiting. It'll take a couple hours to fix this mess." Eddie'd had to back up and take the long way into Rio.

In town at last, just outside Dr. Bonney's office, a gangster had accosted Lu. He would have looked like a zoot-suiter if his jacket hadn't been so fitted, his trousers tight enough to show the cluster at his crotch. Bullfighter pants, Eddie thought, and she didn't like the look in his eye. He stood too close, smiled too brightly, his manner too familiar, oily. She could tell Lu didn't like his looks any better than she did. Though often her maid was nearly inscrutable, this time it was clear: The girl was miserable. As she pulled Lu away, she could smell liquor on the hoodlum's breath.

They'd had to wait in the doctor's office. The nurse sassed Eddie, told her to stay put in her chair and wait her turn. Raleigh screeched at the approach of forceps and swabs. Tonia had a nosebleed. By the time they were back in the hot car and headed home, Raleigh and Tonia were fussing over who deserved the grape Saf-T-Pop the nurse had given them and who had to settle for the lime. Lu was no help; she sat between the two, acting stunned as a branded cow.

Eddie told them to hush or she'd stop the car and make them walk. They didn't hush and she didn't stop the car. She told them one more peep and they'd be sorry. Raleigh peeped. There was nothing to do but make good on her threat, and so she braked the car on the shoulder, turned around in the seat to yell into their three astonished faces, demanded both Saf-T-Pops, threw the green one out the window, jammed the purple in her mouth, and drove on. Everyone needed a nap.

Now, driving up the highway toward McAllen, on her way at last, she added to the company of offenders: her husband. For years she had spoken of a house in the Greek Revival style, columned, colonnaded, great doors giving onto balconies. It was her dream. The plans were drawn. The lot—three acres on the outskirts of town—paid for. At the last minute, and when they finally had enough money to build the house without having to sell the Hundred Acres, Thomas had delivered the galling pronouncement that his heart was set on a long, low ranch. "Eddie, I know you think Thomas Jefferson hung the moon from a solid gold peg, but I'd feel like a fool tricked out in such a fancy house." The Rambler was what he wanted, and each time the word came out of his mouth, she winced. It was such a giddy, inconsequential name, boxy and Nash-like, low-class, Anglo-Saxon. The Monticello model, however, spoke of gentry, family land, the grand Latinate. Today she was to look at the Rambler with the architect in McAllen. She knew better than to dismiss her husband's plan outright—he would defend his opinion—but she knew, as the breeze from the open windows at last began to cool her, that she would prevail. She had ways: She had not lived with the man nearly ten years for nothing.

She tried to make herself feel better by looking at the scenery, which she had come, finally, to appreciate. The Citrus Exchange promoted the region as the Magic Valley, and it was true. In the subtropical climate, in the rich delta soil with its irrigation canals, everything grew. The chamber of commerce had begun a campaign to bill the Valley as the "World's Largest Vegetable Patch." Billboards dotted the roads. The Burma Shave people had come through and the roads were to get three cute messages. So many boxes and baskets and cans of food were being shipped that new roads and railroad lines had to be laid. Even poky old Rio Paradiso was up and coming: There was a new public school so the children didn't have to go all the way to Martha, a new private school so there would be a choice, a Rexall, a Piggly-Wiggly, the La Mode Shoppe, where she'd bought the canary suit and the spectator pumps to match, a Texaco, a Little League ball diamond.

For years the land companies had brought down trainloads of Midwestern farmers to interest them in buying land; now most of the land not under Spanish grant had been sold. Still the people came, this time as tourists whom the locals were encouraged to call winter Texans, though they called themselves snowbirds. After over a half-century of living through prairie winters that had turned their bones brittle, their joints contentious, and their skin to latigo, they behaved as though they'd been set down in the land of milk and honey. The farmer snow-birds weren't so bad; at least they understood that you didn't stop the car along the road and pick a bushel of tangerines from someone's grove, but the city snowbirds thought nothing of raiding the fields of broccoli and cauliflower, onions and tomatoes, cabbage, beets, and lettuce. Not to mention what they did to limes and lemons, oranges, grapefruit, avocadoes, tangerines. All clotted the post office, the few doctors' offices, and their trailer houses sprung up overnight where once there had been only cholla, tuna, and mesquite.

Down on the Gulf Coast, South Padre Island was building up: a causeway over Laguna Madre Bay, hotels along the sand. She'd pleaded with Thomas to invest, but for her efforts received only his speech about borrowed money and borrowed time, dry wells, foreclosures, and the everlasting dust bowl. Besides, he told her, to get in he'd have to sell part of the farm, and this he would never do. "It's a gold mine, Eddie, and when the time is right . . ." Because of a rounded rise at the river side of the property, Thomas suspected a salt dome concealing oil. "Hump," she always said, but he held firm.

Thomas had gained weight on Lu's cooking and now looked like a robust banty rooster. Though he was mild by nature, at fifty he had cultivated a habit of occasional bombast. A regular helium balloon. So wound up did he get with some of his opinions that Eddie thought he'd surely levitate. In times of dudgeon, she called him Mr. Phineas T. Bluster. But he only laughed and seemed to like it. Having grown up in the house of Parker Harmon, whom her mother had sometimes called "that Old Volcano," Eddie knew how to handle his outbursts. She ignored him. Well, not completely; she would listen attentively and agree to everything he said, but then she would do as she pleased.

Thomas was invited every year to give a guest lecture in the introductory botany class at Texas Southmost. She'd accompanied him once, expecting little more than boredom and embarrassment at hearing his talk on the history of citrus fruit. Grapefruit, he told the class, probably came from Malaysia. First mentioned in Palestine in 1187, it was known as Adam's apple and considered poisonous. It reached the New World in 1670, when a Captain Shaddock brought seeds to Barbados. At this point, it was called a pummelo, and was thick-skinned, rough, and unpleasant-tasting. A mutation of the pummelo came to be called a shaddock, although even into the 1700s it was still referred to as the forbidden fruit. Eddie covered her mouth to hide a yawn.

But when Thomas reached the 1850s, Eddie had sat bolt upright to learn that while in Brownsville on court-martial duty, Robert E. Lee had written to his wife about the beautiful citrus trees. Lee in Brownsville! Not five miles from where she sat! Eddie made a note to look up the family of Mrs. Richard King, who had hosted the general. They would have a common bond. One of her mother's favorite stories had been of a girlhood outing to Lexington, where she had stayed in the president's house at Washington and Lee University with one of Lee's daughters. The girls had strung a rope from the back bedroom window and had prowled the grounds by moonlight. Eddie *thought* it had been his daughter. It might have been a niece. But that didn't matter. It was still a small, small world.

The oldest citrus growing on the Texas side, Thomas told the class, was the sweet orange at Laguna Seca Ranch. Around the 1870s a priest on a visit to the ranch of Macedonio and Mercedes Vela had given orange seeds to their little girl, Carlota. Seven had grown, had borne, and one still held. Thomas suggested a field trip to Laguna Seca to visit Miss Carlota Vela, who at eighty-seven was a beautiful moth of a woman. If he ever bred a new strain of orange, he told the class, he would call it a Carlota Vela. Eddie was sorry when the class was over, even sorrier to learn in June a year later that the aristocratic Miss Carlota had died before she, Eddie, had had a chance to visit.

Thomas had flourished. He was respected by growers and beloved of the workers. Jefecito, they called him. Babies had been named after him. His crops had done well. His method for processing citrus molasses into cattle feed had been patented. Even the weather was on his side. The Hundred Acres had been untouched by the freeze of 1951, when many lost their groves. During the drought of 1952, his water conservation methods had saved the cotton. At the dedication of the Falcon Dam the October before, he had stood on the dais just behind President Eisenhower. His proudest possession was a photograph of the event. Framed in gold leaf, it hung in his office, the L-shaped room off the sala that had been used, in the border-war days when the house had been built, for wakes. In the photograph, Thomas stood nearly as tall as Ike, and only Eddie knew he had ordered for the occasion a pair of elevator boots.

Prosperity had made him even more generous than before, but had also revealed a hidden seam of vanity. She had learned to appeal to this seam, and was nearly delirious with joy on the day he had emerged from his office and announced, "Well, Miss Eddie, you've told me I'm a pillar of the community so often, I reckon I ought to at least have a post to hitch my mule to. Why don't we see about that house?"

Their sex life had improved some—it was still infrequent, but orderly and calm, oddly comforting. Such concerns, however, once so vital to her, had ceased, really, to matter. It was funny, Eddie sometimes thought, how things could turn out. Physically, Raleigh took after the Harmons, was tall, broad, and fair. "He's like me on the inside," Thomas had said after they'd gone to the Rialto to see *Dumbo* and both males had emerged red-eyed and tender-mouthed, "he's got my heart." Eddie, only mildly touched by the movie, dry-eyed, had nevertheless squeezed Thomas's arm. "Yes," she said, "he does."

They heard from Bobby Israel once a year at Christmas, when he sent a case of wine from the family vineyard, now famous, and a card that said he would never forget their hospitality. When Thomas remarked the generous gesture, she "Hump"-ed, and she would not touch the wine, and so the cases piled up in a storage room on the north side of the machine barn.

The weight she had lost in those weeks had returned with the pregnancy and had stayed, but she no longer cared. Her mother's prissy thinness had done her a grave disservice, she now realized. In the way of the Harmons, she was born to be big, and that was fine. Her skin, at nearly forty-five, looked firm and pretty, the freckles having mysteriously vanished, and she loved to look at her naked flesh in the mirror. Ripe, she looked, and womanly. Stately and substantial. She looked good in her clothes. Or at least she had earlier this day, when she'd first put them on. Now, she wiggled around in the car seat, yanking at her skirt, trying to fluff up the organdy ruff. She was almost there.

In McAllen, she parked the car in the broil of the architect's parking lot. To ward off Thomas's irritation, she entered the office of Sawyer and Soames in a pet, railing at roads and heat and Mexican help. Then she allowed Son Sawyer and Thomas to calm her.

The ranch house they were to look at was three miles out of town on Lower River Road, but before they arrived at the site, Son casually pointed out, set at the end of a palm-lined drive, the Spanish-style house he had just built for himself. "Stop!" she and Thomas shouted in unison, and when they saw the terra-cotta urns ablaze with bougainvillea and hibiscus, the earth-pink stucco walls set with painted tiles depicting market scenes, the red-tiled roof, the balconies, the filigreed iron gates of the hacienda plan, they stared at each other as though seeing themselves together for the first time, on the ribbon-cutting platform at the grand opening of the world.

"It'd go even better on your lot in Rio," Son told them, but they were already sold.

When he told them the construction would run half again what the Monticello would cost and twice the price of the Rambler, Thomas waved away the concern. Eddie was speechless.

Outside the office she hugged Thomas so hard he coughed, and she was so excited that all the way home she gripped the Chevrolet's steering wheel, alternately shouting, "Oh, lucky me!" gulping air, and bursting into hot, fat tears. By the time she arrived at the Hundred Acres, she had scrapped all her old, fusty Colonial decorating plans, had installed beamed ceilings, cool tile floors, low couches and copper sconces, a carved refectory table for twelve—no, sixteen!—and she raced into the farmhouse to begin planning the luncheon at which she would announce to las girls the wonderful news.

2

kid mapuche

When Luisa saw Ralph Emerson López on the street in Rio Paradiso, she knew he would come for her. Nervously, she awaited his arrival at the little house. One night a few days after the trip to the doctor's office, as she sat at the table showing Tonia how to cut paper flowers, she happened to look out the window. Approaching slowly down the rutted back lane that only Joe Bonillas and don Tomás used was a dark car with no top, gleaming silver teeth. A wide fish of a car, alligator green, it was the same car that had been parked at the curb in Rio Paradiso on the day of the black-eyed peas.

In Rio, she'd recognized him only by the bluish mole on the side of his cheek, for he had shaved his mustache, exposing a scar from lip to nostril, poorly sewn. She hadn't remembered his lisp, and it had shocked her to hear him try to pronounce the name of the town they had come from. In Salsipuedes, he had worn the coarse white shirt and loose pants of the pickers, a straw hat, sometimes blue jeans. In Rio, he had worn a tight black suit. Today he wore a loose white suit with a pink shirt, a tie with a picture of a monkey climbing a coconut tree, rattlesnake boots.

"I'm not going to take you back," he said, smiling through the screen wires. "I just want to see how you're doing. A courtesy call."

She was not sure she believed him, but she invited him in and offered him the brown chair don Tomás had given her the week before. Tavo and Tonia remained at the table, quiet but alert. He made small talk for a while, commenting on her pretty house. He wanted to be called Sonny.

"Well," she finally said, "how is Rafaelito?"

"Big. You wouldn't know him. He works for the Mennonite. He's going to send him to Mexico City to study at a big school."

"He works for who?"

"That Jacob Miller guy. The Mennonite."

"Rafael," she said, though only to herself. She thought of the clinging little boy, her debt of the beautiful red book, of how strange it was that in the circle of things, that book, as well as many more, had come to him. She looked around the house, at her children bending their heads over their work, precious, soft in the lamplight. And this had come to her. Rafael, grasshopper boy. Suddenly, she ached to see him, wondered if he remembered her. So many years had passed. Now weeks went by, months went by, without her thinking of him; for him it could be no different. He had been so young when she left, too young to remember.

Sonny López was talking and she'd hardly heard. ". . . but he's kind of strange, that Rafael. He cries a lot. Not big tears and noises, just that his eyes get watery all the time. People see him roaming around, reading and crying. He writes things, too. The Mennonite says he's an artist."

"What kind of things?"

Sonny López shrugged. "Who knows? One time the Mennonite invited everybody to a big party to listen. Poems or prayers or something. I didn't go, but I heard nobody could understand a thing he said. Big words. Aztec stuff. Eagles and corn and snakes with feathers. Bloody hearts. Rafael cried when it was over, and the Mennonite acted like he was Mister John the Baptist. People were pretty disgusted."

"What about Memo?"

"He went to Monterrey to work in the tin yard, but there was some trouble. Some guys got him drunk and then dared him to walk this board over some bad chemicals. His feet got eaten. Nobody knows where he is now. He came back to Salsipuedes once when . . ." He broke off. "Chavela is dead."

She nodded.

"Some say it was bad food, but it was probably poison. They say she coughed up her own liver. Whole."

"Who would poison her?"

He rolled his eyes.

Luisa laughed. "The whole town."

"Probably Silva Barba. See, Chavela decided to be in love with Silva's husband and she started hanging around him. She followed Dagoberto everywhere, hanging around the pulquería. She started saying things around town. Silva told her to stop, but you know Chavela. They found her . . . she looked pretty bad. Her hair was gone. Somebody cut it off."

Tonia was wide-eyed, and Tavo had slid off his chair to move closer.

"You know all that trash in the house? After you left, I heard it got worse and worse. When the women cleaned it out, well, guess what they found? Old Spanish coins, gold and silver, lots of them. Who knows where they got it." He shook his head thoughtfully. "All that time."

Tavo sidled up to the visitor's chair and made a muscle.

"You're a strong little guy," he said. "You can call me Uncle Sonny, okay, kid?" He began to throw mock punches. "Hey, Jack Dempsey, put up your dukes."

Tavo asked what happened to the gold and silver.

Sonny took out a bone-handled knife and began to pare his fingernails, arranging the sharp little horns in a pile on his knee. "Who knows? I'm in the battery business, myself." He explained how people threw away good Delco batteries, but that they could be melted down for lead. "I'm pretty rich, now. You wouldn't believe all the stuff people throw away."

When he replaced the knife, his jacket lapel fell away to reveal the black strap of a shoulder holster and the butt of a gun. Tavo was enchanted.

Sonny patted the bulge under his arm. "It's for protection, kid. Don't get any big ideas. Business can get pretty rough."

On his way out the door, beyond the children's hearing, he leaned close and said, "They say Chavela said some pretty bad things about you. She said you stole. Money and things. She was pretty mad."

"Look around," she told him. "If you find any gold and silver, let me know."

•   •   •

She wished she hadn't been nice to him. He began to visit often, and she grew to dread the sight of his alligator car nosing up the little road. As he had in Salsipuedes, he brought Santa Rita, now old, but whose brown belly was stretched taut with pups. He wouldn't tell her where he lived. "I move around a lot," he'd said. Tavo and Tonia ran to him each time, and it disturbed her that she'd caught Tavo with a kitchen knife tucked into his shorts. He brought gifts: bottles of Grapette soda, Eskimo Pies packed in dry ice, gum from Paris Bubble, which she liked in spite of herself for the way it reminded her of Amparo. For Tavo, he brought a stuffed bobcat, sewn at the belly like Raleigh's football and poised on a log with green moss. He gave the boy the nickname El Lince. "Because you're a tough, square-headed little guy," he said. To Luisa, he said, "He's the Uncle's kid, all right."

She began to wonder why her mother had liked him, or if she had liked him at all. But in her mother's honor, she tried to be kind. He had done nothing yet. "A friend of the family," he called himself. Still, she wished he would go away.

He gave the children one of Santa Rita's puppies, a female long-haired Chihuahua brown as dark coffee and no bigger than his hand. Tonia, excited about the teacher she would have for first grade in the fall and in love with all school things, named the dog Miss Evelyn Posey.

"You can't call him that," Tavo had protested. "Call him something tough. Zorro, for his sharp little nose. Or Chacal. See how his fur looks two colors? What he really looks like is a bat."

Tonia held her ground. "She's a girl and she's smart and her name is Miss Evelyn Posey."

"Oh, man," Tavo whined. "That's stupid. Make her name him something better."

Although she often tried to make things up to Tavo by shorting her sweet-natured daughter, something caused her this time to side with Tonia, and though she came to think of the dog as Zurullocita, for the foul little rolls Miss Evelyn Posey left about for all to step in, she insisted that Tavo use the name Tonia gave her.

One evening, as he sat in the brown chair with the children at his knees, Sonny López looked at her and said, "You and me could have a pretty good life."

She could hardly believe that she was the same girl who once would have settled for Ralph Emerson López and Chavela as parents. She pretended she didn't hear, made herself busy washing dishes, and soon he left.

The next day when Madama called her into the sala and told her, "Lu, I don't mind if your mujer amigas come to visit, but no me gusta that hombre on our property," she was relieved.

When she told Sonny López, he spat. "I can go wherever I want. Who does she think she's dealing with?"

He strutted around the little house for a while, muttering, but then he said, "Well, then, we'll have to go out on dates."

He began to take them for rides in the car. Up and down the Valley roads they drove, and with each new outing she felt trouble in the wind that swirled through the car and made her hair fly. He gave her a silk scarf to tie around her hair, and as they drove he talked about how someday the Valley would belong again to the people. She noticed that he drove up and down the same farm roads, and before some of the grander houses he stopped, looking for a long time. "You wouldn't believe how rich some of these guys are. And all of it off our backs. Stoop labor, man. Our sweat. And they keep their money under their beds."

Suddenly she remembered the broken pantry window. She hoped Madama had told don Tomás. Riding along, she reminded herself to remind Madama.

Sonny said, "Pretty soon I'll be going away for a little." His tone was mysterious. "Tomorrow I want you to come with me for a ride. Alone. The kids can stay home. I have some important business to talk about."

She knew he was going to ask her to marry him. She started to tell him she would be busy, but then she understood that she would have to tell him to stay away, and that she would have to do this without the children. She nodded.

The next evening she went to the end of the lane to meet him, and they drove toward the river and stopped by a cabbage field, where the dust and moonlight made the pale heads look like a field of sugar skulls. Sonny cut the car's engine. She waited, trying to decide whether she should speak first, or hear what he had to say. Either way would be bad.

Alone with him, she was afraid. The night was oddly quiet. When a coyote howled from the levee, she jumped. At last he broke their silence.

"You ever been to the circus?"

She shook her head.

"Well, I grew up in one. We went all over Mexico. The coast, even Mexico City. My father ran the ponies and the monkeys and my mother was the Queen of Magic Changes. She had this high-wire act. . . ."

She must have looked puzzled, for he began to explain. "See, they got these ladies in little shiny suits and they go way up a ladder with only a pole in their hands and they walk this thin little rope all the way across the ring. Sometimes with no net to catch them.

"My mother did this thing. She gets to the end of the rope, see, and she loses her balance. People go crazy. She just hangs there, balancing, almost falling. At first everyone screams, then the whole tent gets real quiet. Everybody watches my little mother, up there in her red and gold spangle suit, wobbling. And nobody breathes. Finally, when she can't hold on anymore, she drops. While she falls, she quick tears off her long black wig and underneath there's a golden one and she strips off her red suit like the husk on corn so that when she hits the net she's all in blue and silver. She rolls off the net and lands on her feet and it's like a different lady comes down from the one who went up.

"You don't know it, but you're like that, this little pretty queen. But no magic. No net and no other suit. You fall, you hit the dirt, hard."

She looked into his eyes, trying to determine what was coming next. Again she thought of her mother.

"I did some checking. Your kids are okay because you had them on this side. Automatic. But you're not, and they got you where they want you. Your boss lady can get mad at you and there you are. Back in Mexico." He gazed straight ahead to where the moon rose over the levee. "You don't know how bad it can get over there for a good-looking woman like you."

He was quiet for a while, and she felt worry fill her. Amparo had warned her of the problem of papers, but she'd brushed away her friend's concern. Over the years she'd wondered exactly how such things were done, but so much time had now gone by, she was afraid to ask. Suddenly she was glad she hadn't spoken first.

"So, I been thinking about how to fix that for you." He rested his arm across the back of her seat and began to toy with the chain around her neck, drawing it up, then releasing it to slide, weighted by the keys, back down. "I think I got a plan to help you out. You been at that place for a while now, right?"

She nodded. "Six years at the house. Two before that, almost three."

He appeared to calculate. "Too long. You better be thinking about what to do. Everybody knows about that girl of yours. She's too light. About ten shades lighter than your boy. It's all over the camp, and it won't take much for her to find out. Somebody could tell her Tonia's the patrón's kid and you'd never know what hit you."

She couldn't make herself speak.

He moved closer. "A woman like you needs a man. For lots of things." When he smiled the scar on his lip blanched white. "Chavela told me—"

"Stop," she said, "no." She tried to explain her life, her choices, her wishes and pledges, but each thing she said made her life with Madama and don Tomás sound worse, and with each explanation his face looked more evil and knowing.

He gripped the back of her neck, pressing his fingers along the side of her throat where she could feel the blood pulse. "Around here you got to take what you can get. They'll use you up and all the time you don't know what hit you because, see, you think you're better than they are for putting up with it. That's how they get you." He stopped, as though considering what he might say, then softened his voice. "I have a lot of pull around here. People do what I say. If you were smart you'd hook up with me. Your kids need a man around. That Tavo's going to give you trouble when he gets older. I can protect you. . . . You heard of that Kid Mapuche?"

She didn't want to hear any more, and she fumbled with the door handle, trying to open the car door.

With his palm, he slammed down the lock button. His voice was a growl. "You're not acting too smart right now."

She said, understanding as she said them that the words were true, "My mother didn't like you. She was just afraid."

His mouth went hard and mean. "Who do you think you're talking to?"

This close, beneath the smell of his sharp cologne, she caught the odor of motor oil and sweat, and although she was afraid of him, something made her laugh—the memory of the orange Chavela had thrown at him, lofting through the air as though the fruit contained everything about him that she hated.

He glared, but again she laughed, this time because a piece of her mind had rolled onto her tongue as though by magic, and because she did not feel for Ralph Emerson López in the way she had felt for Amparo Gil, she did not feel the sick shock of alarm but the hot joy of a hard sneeze as her answer flew from her mouth, "I can tell the difference between a good man and a fool. And you're a fool!"

While he was still stunned, before he could raise his dropped jaw, she drew up her legs and kicked him away, then bolted from the car. She ran. She had reached the far side of the cabbage field before she realized what she had done.

3

independence day

Luisa heard the children laughing behind the oleander hedge. In a few days it would be the Fourth of July, and everyone was excited. But this day was to be even better, Madama had promised. In the afternoon don Tomás would take his nest egg and return with the paid-in-full bill for the house in Rio. Building could at last begin. Madama was having a party to surprise las girls with the news. For Luisa, though, beyond the promise of a new little house in the back of the big one, a bathroom, this meant only more work and more worry about Sonny López.

She had done all the cooking the day before—baked chicken to be served cold, tea rolls, a shortcake with berries—and the kitchen was cool and spotless. Madama had shown her a magazine picture, and in the refrigerator were four peacock salads made of pear halves dyed blue. Madama had supervised as Luisa arranged lettuce and melon balls, sliced olives, cut citron for eyes, maraschino cherries for beaks, cinnamon stick pieces for legs and feet. Because Madama didn't want the kitchen heated up from ironing, Luisa had set up the board on the back porch to press the red and blue runner that would decorate the table. All the work was done now, except to arrange the table and to catch Miss Evelyn Posey and put her in her box so she didn't bark when las girls arrived.

Wasps buzzed above her as she ran the iron along the hem. She couldn't see where the children had gone, but she hoped their play did not disturb Madama, who was upstairs trying to nap.

Each time before las girls came over, Madama was in a foul mood, and often it took days for her to recover from one of her parties. This time could only be worse because today especially Madama wanted everything to be just right. She'd made Luisa practice serving, practice clearing, practice offering mixed nuts, practice making cocktails.

From the hedge she heard the pop of the firecrackers Madama had forbidden the children to play with until after the news was announced. A smell of phosphorous and punk drifted toward her. Raleigh, Antonia, and Tavo appeared, yelling, then ran into the Valencia grove. Laughing not three blinks of an eye before, they were again fighting. She hoped they would settle it themselves. Just now, she didn't have time to chase them.

Above her the water pipes clanked, which meant that Madama had risen and was preparing her bath. When she heard the water cease, she braced herself. Madama would soon lower herself into the tub and remember that she had forgotten a towel, the soap, a cloth, and she would call down the stairs.

"Lu!"

She started upstairs, counting steps, knowing that between the seventh and ninth, the call would come again, as though it was Madama who was so busy and overwhelmed by duty.

She knocked at the bathroom door.

There was the sound of water sloshing. "Se me olvidó that amarillo bathrobe, Lu."

Luisa went to the closet and took the robe from its hook. She went back to knock at the door.

"Well, it's not doing me any good out there, is it?"

Clouds of steam gusted into the hall when she opened the door. Madama sat in the bath, her black shower cap a fat, wrinkled prune. "Deja that on the hook allí. Did I hear one of those tricky-trackies go off outside? There was a pop."

She draped the robe on the hook. "No, Madama. No más que un coche."

"Momento, Lu," Madama said, extending a bathbrush. "Scrub my back un poco."

"Los niños," she said, but Madama tapped the brush on the tub rim, arranging herself to be scrubbed.

In town, when other maids spoke of the ladies they worked for, they too told stories of children missing lunch, of pronto-this and pronto-that, of silly rules and ridiculous ways of doing things, but none had ever said anything about this part of it. Because the others envied her working for don Tomás, Luisa had been too ashamed to mention some of the things Madama made her do. Most often it was the back scrubbing, but once when don Tomás was away and Madama had been with las girls and had too much to drink, she yelled out the window for Luisa to come to the big house. When she arrived in the bedroom she saw that Madama was naked before the mirror, holding her large pale breasts. "You don't think I'm too big, do you, Lu? Grande?" Luisa had run from the room. This had never happened again, but she'd been on her guard ever since.

Now Madama batted at her hand. "Cuidado, girl. You'll peel me raw."

"Sí, Madama."

"Do you remember . . . let's go over it one more time. How do we serve?"

Luisa sighed but quickly covered it by pretending to sneeze from Madama's bubble bath. She held out her left arm.

"Take away?"

She held out her right, then set the brush in a tray and reached for the cloth just as Madama let it go.

"Oops, it dropped in the agua," Madama said.

Outside, a child shrieked.

Madama fished in the water for the cloth. "Don't just sit there like a bump on a log."

Luisa hurried downstairs and through the kitchen. On the back porch she stopped to unplug the iron, which she'd left resting on the table runner. There was a scorch. Just then the children raced by, shouting, Miss Evelyn Posey yipping and romping behind them.

During their last fight a few days before, Tavo had blackened Raleigh's eye. Because Raleigh had refused to stay dead after Tavo had shot him the magic three times, but instead got up and ran away. Because Tavo had dragged out the dead count on purpose. Because Raleigh had called him a name. Because Tavo had . . . something. For no reason at all. Her children spoke more English than Spanish, and all of it seemed shouted into her ears so that she could hardly tell who was saying what.

She caught up with them at the live oak at the foot of the lane. Tonia had climbed into the lower branches, but Raleigh, probably afraid to risk the time it would take to boost himself up, dodged around the trunk, out of breath, crying, while Tavo menaced him.

It turned out that they were playing pirate and Raleigh was trying to boss the treasure. Tavo had seized a handful of nickel slugs from their treasure box. Raleigh had called him a name. Tavo had hit.

She grabbed Tavo by his shirt and tried to pull him toward her, but he wrenched away. Shoulders squared, fists up, he faced her. She raised her hand to strike him, but then, as sudden as the slap she'd meant to deliver, she realized he was too big, too old. Worse, she saw the moment this same knowledge passed across his face. He watched her. She stared at him, making herself hold his gaze.

He was first to look away. "Kid stuff," he said, and he flung the nickels into the field behind the tree, then stalked off.

Tonia jumped from the tree to comfort Raleigh, her sundress ruffling like butterfly wings. Raleigh sat crying in the dirt between the exposed roots. He had wet himself.

She told him to change and hang the wet shorts on the clothesline, though she knew that, like every other time, she would find them in a ball in the back of his closet.

The boy, looking over his shoulder at Tavo, who had reached the end of the first field, began to cry. "He started it, Lu. I found the treasure and I was in charge of it. I didn't call him a name."

She nodded as he went on, his child's voice like an insect in her ear. She knew what the name had been. The same one always. *Bastard.* Once don Tomás had spanked Raleigh for saying it. She'd heard don Tomás say, "Never call a name you wouldn't want to wear." Now at the back of her mind ran the words of Sonny López's warning, and she knew she had to do something. But she could never ask Madama, and to ask don Tomás about the papers might seem ungrateful.

She interrupted the child, patting his head. "Sí, Raleigh." She reminded him about the wet shorts and turned to go back to the house to set the table, remembering as she hurried that Madama had told her to wash the blue glass ball in the front yard. The yard ornament attracted chachalacas, who pecked at their reflections and left their chalky smears down the iron pedestal. She stopped walking and stood, trying to decide which to do first. She chose the table, thinking that if she hurried at the task, she would have time to run back outside to clean the bird ball.

• • •

Pleased with what she had seen outside—Lu had finally given her hoodlum son what-for—Eddie let the bathroom curtain fall back across the window. Long ago, she had tried to like him, once asking him, "How was your little day at school?" and for her trouble had received only a sneer. Another time she'd saved a cardboard cutout of an Indian headdress from a cereal box just for him, only to find it later, torn to shreds. She worried that his ways would rub off on Raleigh. But just as sure as she started to lecture her son about the differences in people, Raleigh would defend Tavo. She now realized that mixing had been a bad idea. She should have gotten it off on the right foot in the first place. The Valley was not the South; no one knew his place.

The week before she had caught Tavo at this very window, perched on a tree limb like a beady-eyed crow, staring in at her as she dressed, his dark eyes older than his years. In a curious way, the incident had thrilled her, and she had made her breasts jiggle lewdly before she yanked down the shade.

"Just keep your window closed," Thomas had told her, refusing to share her outrage. As usual, the upshot was that she'd had to listen to another of his lectures on her treatment of the help—Pompilo complained that she threw rocks in the grass before he mowed, that her blue yard ornament made a big mess, that she shook his bottle of Coca-Cola before she gave it to him, making it spurt.

"He's a little hooligan," she'd complained of Tavo, "a thug."

"He's just a boy," Thomas said. "Give him a chance." But she knew the time was coming that she would have to order him to stay away from Raleigh. Then there would be real trouble. Raleigh adored Tavo and Tonia, and although it seemed they fought from sunup to sundown, their bond seemed only to strengthen. After each fuss, when she tried to talk to Raleigh about Tavo's influence, he took the blame on himself. It was sickening. She regretted that she agreed to his latest plan, which was that today while her party was going on, the three would be allowed to watch television in Raleigh's room. She had instructed Raleigh to wash his hands before and after, to make sure he didn't sit too close. Polio germs were everywhere.

She comforted herself with the knowledge that all this was going to change. At the new house, things would be different. There was no doubt that she would take Lu with her—which meant her children would have to come—but the rules would change. Thomas could rail all he wanted, but she would put Raleigh in the new private school. Tonia and Tavo would walk the half-mile to the public. The little house would be farther from the big house. She'd had it designed so that no window in the little house would face the big house.

Now she opened the bathroom door to let out some of the steam and began applying her makeup. She wanted everything to go well. Lu had been jumpy for weeks—even more distracted than usual. As she dotted foundation over her chin, she tried to anticipate any mishap she might prevent. She could think of none.

She went downstairs. The table looked perfect. Lu had outdone herself. How wonderful that this would be the last time she had to serve a luncheon on two card tables jammed together. When she moved the blue bowl of calla lilies to set the blooms to best advantage, she saw in the center of the table runner a dark iron scorch that Lu had no doubt tried to hide. She drew in a breath to yell for her, but then, oddly, she laughed. The woman had probably dithered for an hour, trying to wish away the scorch, another hour trying to conceal it. For a moment so brief and sharp it was nearly painful, she felt her heart expand to contain the hapless creature who was her maid. For the first time, she realized, she could repeat the phrase her mother had used for Noon—"She's just a treasure"—and mean it. "Good old Lu," she said. She shook her head; to ask for perfection would be asking too much.

seed money

Nothing went as she planned. Thomas was nowhere to be found, and Ann Dell Jenkins arrived a half-hour early, eager to spill the news that a bounty hunter had come all the way from Carville, Louisiana, for the oldest daughter of the Dub Sissoms's yardman. Nobody knew who turned her in, but it was sure-enough leprosy, Ann Dell said, sores all over her elbows. They'd sent the rest of his family packing back to Reynosa. Then Joan and Nila arrived and there was nothing to do but begin the luncheon.

Lu served the peacock salads upside down. The maraschino beaks had bled red into the honeydew heads, which had rolled to the side to rest in the lettuce beds. The salads looked like trussed turkeys hung by their feet, the instant after the ax. The pear-half bodies stained las girls' teeth a dull, sick-looking blue. Just after one o'clock, Thomas, covered in field dirt, swaggered through the kitchen, picked a row of strawberries off the cake, lit a cheroot, then went into the bathroom off the kitchen intending, she imagined, to fog it up with his shower. She followed him, her voice a hiss. "Where have you been?"

Shaving, his mouth a skewed *O,* he lifted the razor and said, "Why is your mouth all blue?"

She fixed him with a look. "Don't ask. We're almost done, Thomas. I don't know how much longer I can—"

"Miss Eddie, the world does not revolve around your theatrical productions."

Chastened, she'd returned to las girls. When she entered the dining room, she saw the signs of suppressed mirth, and she could tell they'd quickly changed the subject of their talk.

At last Thomas came through the dining room, hair slicked back with Brylcreem, dressed in a Western-cut suit, a bolo tie, and his crocodile Tony Lama boots. He greeted them, then with a wink at Eddie said, "Well, ladies, I'd love to stay and visit, but I've got a little business to attend to. Miss Eddie can tell you all about it."

"Come on, Tommy," Ann Dell teased, "you can tell us. Where you going all got up like Hopalong Cassidy?"

"Oh," he said mysteriously, "to see a man about a dog." He went into his office.

Eddie picked up her tea glass and said airily, "Well, it wouldn't be a surprise if I were to tell you before it happened."

"Speaking of surprises . . ." Nila began an involved tale of her day girl, Elodia, a pressure cooker, and chicken parts on a kitchen light fixture, but Eddie could hardly keep her mind on the story. If he hurried, Thomas could be home with the papers by the time she was ready to serve dessert.

Thomas appeared in the doorway. "Eddie Jane, have you been in the gun cabinet?"

She set down her fork and wiped her mouth. "What on earth would I want in the gun cabinet? You know I hate guns."

"Has Señora Cantú?"

"Lu? I'd think she'd have better things to do than snoop around in . . . Thomas, we're trying to have a nice luncheon."

"Edwina." His voice was stern. "Call her in here."

"She's fixing more tea, Thomas. I can't very well—"

"Now."

When the maid entered, Thomas asked her in Spanish if she'd ever forgotten to lock the door.

"Never," Eddie said. "I've been here every little minute."

"Let her answer, Eddie."

"No, señor."

"In the last few days have you ever left the house open?"

Lu shook her head nunca.

"Of course not, Thomas," she said firmly. "Can we not worry about this now? If you can't find one of your guns, well, just buy yourself a new one. This is hardly the time or place to . . . don't you have an errand?" To prompt him, she nodded vigorously. "The bank?"

His words were faint, but they reached her. "I've already been."

The ruin of her family rose before her. "The money . . . was it closed?"

"I went a week ago. I was keeping it in that candy box. Eddie, it's gone."

•   •   •

Luisa, remembering at that moment that she'd forgotten to tell him about the pantry window, ran. Out the back porch door and down the path to the little house, where she stood before her door, trying to catch her breath, looking at the rusted wires of the screen as though she had never seen them before. For a long time she stood, unable to think. Then she turned and started back up the path.

The big house was quiet. Las girls had driven off, she imagined, to spread the news. Madama's car and don Tomás's truck were no longer parked beside the house. She listened for the children, then, when she heard only the drip of the kitchen faucet, went to search for them. She found them upstairs in Raleigh's bedroom, watching a cartoon cat, unaware of the trouble in the house. When she asked where Madama and don Tomás had gone, Tavo shrugged and Raleigh said brightly, "See a man about a dog?" Tonia didn't know.

If they'd gone for the sheriff in Rio Paradiso, she could have saved them the trouble. From the kitchen drawer she took the boning knife, sharpened it along the whetstone, and wrapped it in a dishtowel, then she set off down the path to the camp, determined to find Sonny López. First she would get the money back. Then she would kill him.

No one in the camp had seen him. Angrier with every step, and more determined, she walked the five miles to Rio Paradiso. When a boy in front of the barbershop made kissing noises at her, she drew out the knife and said in the perfect English phrase she'd practiced all the way, matching her steps to its rhythm, "I'm looking for the bastard Sonny López."

The boy backed off, hands up. "You and the rest of the Valley, lady."

No one in the colonia had seen him for days, and as she made her inquiries, she learned that no one liked him, that at first everyone had thought he was the bandit Kid Mapuche but soon had seen that he was too much a coward and a snake, and that he owed a lot of people money.

On her way home, on the outskirts of town, just past the new vegetable billboard, she saw don Tomás.

He idled the truck beside her. His smile was kind. "The brave Señora Cantú," he said. "You were going to avenge me, weren't you?"

At first she didn't understand, but then she remembered the knife. She tried to hide it behind her back.

"Come here," he said.

She approached the truck but kept her gaze down.

"Go on home," he told her. "Don't worry. Everything will be just fine."

When she looked up at him, he smiled. "It will be all right."

She asked if he had found the money.

He nodded, then began to speak in English, something about some papers, then low, soothing words that she didn't understand, but she knew that in them there was something important, something about love, some promise he was making.

She smiled back, feeling foolish that she thought she could have found Sonny López. "I'm going home," she said. Using her best English to repeat his comforting phrase, she said, "Don't worry." She waved as don Tomás pulled away, going slowly, she knew, so as not to raise the dust.

The long walk calmed her, and by the time she reached the Hundred Acres, she felt better. When don Tomás returned, when all the excitement died down, when things were calmer, she would ask what he had meant about the papers.

The children were lighting sparklers on the grass of the backyard beneath her avocado tree. The year before when don Tomás had brought sparklers, she had twirled and twirled along with the children, holding the metal rod of spitting fire, laughing. Now they called for her to play with them. She shook her head and told them she had work to do. As she made her way to the back door, she looked in the west windows to the wreck of the party.

She found Madama, brisk and angry, upstairs in the bedroom, yanking clothes from the closet, a tangle of hangers at her feet. "I'm packing. He can sell this stupid finca. Thirty thousand dollars in a box!"

Luisa told her about seeing don Tomás on the road and that he'd said everything would be all right.

"Oh, yes," spat Madama. "Everything will be just fine. Fine as a froghair. My foot!" She sank onto the bed and began to cry. "If he comes home without that money, I'll kill him."

•   •   •

Around midnight, Eddie was relieved to see lights at the head of the lane and she hurried downstairs, but the car wasn't Thomas's. Hartley Rowell, large in his khakis, chest crossed by his Sam Browne belt, his Stetson set square, brim hooding his eyes, stood on the porch. "Tom here?"

"He's still out looking. It's that Kid Raccoon, isn't it?"

The sheriff batted away a june bug. "The Rangers think he crossed into Mexico up at El Paso a couple of weeks ago, so unless he can be two places at the same time, he's probably not the one. Eddie, I been checking. There's been some guy hanging around your maid. Some kind of uncle or cousin or something?"

"Just some lowlife. I told her to keep him off the property and I haven't seen him since. Lu's good as gold, Hart. She never stole so much as a penny pocket handkerchief."

"I know that, Eddie." He shook his head and prepared to leave. "We'll let you know what we find."

•   •   •

Toward morning, Hartley Rowell knocked on the door a second time, hat in his hands for the first time in her memory. His forehead was pale above the hat line; below that his face was brown as hide, his eyebrows bleached white. Even from a distance she could smell sweat and bourbon. There were pinholes in his khaki shirt where earlier his silver badge had hung.

"It was that El Raccoon, wasn't it? I know how he got in . . ." She had remembered the pantry window and she started to tell him.

"Edwina, I'm going to ask you to sit down."

When she protested, he said, "You got to. Now."

She sat.

"I'm going to tell you one time what happened, and then I'll never mention it again and ever after it's got to be another way. You hear? Whatever way you decide." He pulled a crumpled handkerchief from his pants pocket and wiped his brow. "I'm going to tell you some things nobody ever ought to have to say and nobody ever ought to have to hear, and when I'm done I'll deny every word I said and you'll deny you ever heard 'em. If that's what you want. We clear?"

Speechless, she nodded.

"Tom's dead."

She jumped up from her chair but he took her hand and held it. "You need to know how." His voice caught, and he cleared his throat. "About ten o'clock or so, I got a call. Mary McManus heard some shots down by the levee. Eddie, Thomas shot himself in the head."

She wrested away. "He did no such thing!" She began to pace.

"That's just ridiculous! It must have been an accident . . . maybe he . . . he was after that robber . . . maybe it wasn't him."

"A man don't buy a brand-new .45 by Samuel Colt when he's got a gun case full of shotguns. He don't walk out in the middle of a cotton-field and set his glasses on his hat and lay himself down like he was fixing to rest. He don't take a towel to make it so nobody has to . . . He don't put the barrel to his head and pull the trigger by accident."

She couldn't seem to take in what he was saying. "Mary said two shots . . ."

"Said *some*." Hartley pinched the bridge of his nose. "He nicked his scalp. Had to do it again."

She felt her face collapse.

He put his hand on her shoulder. "Now, I did some things out there that . . . I need to ask you a question. Did he leave you protected?"

At first she didn't understand—guns, towels, glasses, cottonfields . . . "You mean insurance?" She pointed toward his office. "It'd be in there."

It seemed she moved through water. In a file drawer they found a folder labeled INSURANCE. When Hartley pulled it out, a choking sound came from his throat, and he sank into Thomas's chair.

She stood over his shoulder. "What is it?"

He swung his head back and forth, and the mournful, bull-like move-ment angered her. "What?"

He handed her the file. "I can't feature how a man who'd write so neat could put thirty thousand dollars in a Whitman's Sampler box."

Eddie looked at the folder, opened it, but could make nothing of the words and figures.

"You understand the company won't pay if it's . . . when there's . . . if he did away with himself?"

She nodded, handing back the folder. She felt oddly calm. "Suicide."

He ran his finger along the policy, pointing to a figure that stunned her.

"Five hundred thousand?" In the quiet room, her voice sounded loud even to her. Hartley drew back at the sound.

Again he pinched the bridge of his nose, rubbing his thumb and fore-finger into his eye sockets. She heard moist clicking sounds. When he looked at her, his gaze was bloodshot.

Suddenly she understood, and though she was ashamed of the mea-suring thoughts that came to her, she accepted them, for the events of the night had gone far past the place she could have stopped them, if ever she could have, and it seemed her whole life had been hurtling headlong toward this moment. She felt sick. Her mind raced to the oddest things—her mother's dressing table with its fine dusting of talc in the flutes of a crystal bottle, the granite foundation of the back porch in Lynchburg, where as a girl she'd chipped at the mortar with a butter knife, wondering how deeply she could dig before the stones gave way—anywhere, anything to keep her thoughts from coming to rest on what was happening to her heart, which seemed to crack, powdery and dry as ash. "Say what you have to say, Hartley."

"I need to tell you a story first." From his hip pocket he withdrew a silver flask, uncapped it, offered her a drink. She declined. He shrugged, took a pull from the flask. "It's a long one." He rose, offering the chair to her. She sat.

He sat on the edge of Thomas's desk and wiped his mouth. "My daddy brought me up to believe that if there was no law against stupidity, there might as well be, because every stupid thing you ever did would come home to roost on your shoulder and squawk at you until you . . . If I could tell you some of the dumb things I did, you'd wonder what kind of lawman you've got protecting you."

"Hart, I've just heard the worst news in the world. I need you to help me out, not—"

"I'm trying to." He shifted. "I wish you could've seen Tom when he first got down here. Nineteen thirty-one. Just a scrawny Sooner pup. Runt of the litter. Little-bitty old glasses. Got so sunburned you thought he'd just curl up like cooked bacon in a pan. But work? Started out picking cotton, worked up to suction at the ginyard, then foreman. Working and saving. Pretty soon he got on at the canning plant. Got to know people. Saved near about everything he made. Seed money for this place."

His face began to buckle, but he contained himself and went on. "In those days I was a pretty bad one to carry on. Rowdy. Thought I was a dandy with the ladies. A big businessman. As I said, I did some pretty bad things. I could tell you stories that would curl your hair." He paused to look at her, then resumed. "Sorry. Some of it was just being young and stupid and a blowhard, and part of it was the place . . . this was a real outlaw kind of place. When the Culebron Field came in, you wouldn't believe it. Nineteen-forty. An oil boom is a terrible thing. Money, greed, land men all over the place. Everybody running around

with pie-in-the-sky and ants-in-their-pants. Grifters, crooks, and crim-
inals. Fly-by-nights. Some of those old boys knew how to put the sales
pressure on, and I was . . . you know that a contract is a promise for a
promise? Well, I'd signed my name on the promise line for two well
deals, and I had only enough money for one. I thought I could get it
from . . . Aw, hell, I don't know what I thought. But whichever deal I
went with, the other one would break my legs. So I stewed and fretted
and I went out to the levee to contemplate how to save my own sorry
hide when along came Tom, poking around with a stick in the dirt at
the edge of that first carrot field he put in. We got to talking and I
poured out my troubles. The upshot is, he gave me the money he'd set
aside to buy this place. Not much in this day and time, but a chunk
back then. I paid him back a few years ago. Took me nine years. He
never told you?"

She felt her face flush, the back of her neck go hot. "No."

He took a swig of bourbon. "Well, he just handed it over. Said, 'Meet
me at the Reno at nine in the morning and it's yours, Hart.'

"I won't tell you what a miserable night I had. It's an awful thing to
look into your own craven face and try to find an excuse for what you're
about to do. But I told myself I'd repay him at a hundred percent interest
and the next morning I was at that cafe with my pitiful hands wide open.

"Both deals were busts. Two of 'em, dry holes. Months went by and
I was still broke. I took to avoiding Tom on the street. Snuck around
for months like a kicked dog and thought up reasons to be mad at him
for being fool enough to lend me money. I hauled out every rotten
thing I'd ever done and in my mind accused him of it. A year or so had
gone by and I hadn't paid a penny. Hardly even saw a penny, and if I
had I'd have spent it on choc beer. That's home brew."

Eddie said, "I know."

"Well, one afternoon I was coming out of the pool hall in Martha
when I saw little old Tom Hatch barreling toward me. Mad as Moses.
Lord, I said to myself, don't let me run. And something held me. Something in his face told me I had to stand there and take what I had
coming."

Out of his pocket came the flask and again he offered Eddie a drink.
This time she took it.

" 'You did a stupid thing, Hart,' he told me, 'but you get a chance
to make up for it.' I blabbered something about interest, blowing hard
about a lease I had my eye on. 'Hart,' he said, 'I don't want your interest.'

I remember he laughed, and he said, 'If we could buy our way out of it, there wouldn't be a need for trouble in the first place.' And then he said something else that I couldn't for a long time figure out. He told me that there was going to come a time when the right thing was going to stare me square in the eyes. He said I'd know it when it happened, in the same way he knew it when he saw me there on the levee, low and miserable. Said this thing would be a hard thing, the hardest, and that it might even look a lot like the wrong thing. But it would be the very thing I'd have to do. The harder it is, he said, the righter it'll be."

He stood and shook out his trousers, straightened his belt. "Eddie, I don't know if you can understand the kind of shame that would lead a man to do what Thomas did, but I do. I'm not saying what he did was right, but I understand it. The money would be to protect you. I don't want a nickel of it."

She sat still for a time, feeling cottonmouthed and leaden. Part of her wanted to feel sorry for Thomas, to feel grateful to Hartley; another part wanted to feel sorry for herself; still another felt foolish and betrayed and angry, and she had no energy to sort the feelings out. The worst of it was that even in the face of this shock, the vision of the new house rose before her. She could sell the Hundred Acres to have it, but beyond that, how would she live? She motioned for him to pass the flask. "But how will you . . . won't they . . . the authorities?"

"It's an amazing fact of the adult life that if we live long enough we turn into the authorities. I could fix it so it could look like a murder, and I know how to do up the papers so . . . well, you know."

She swigged the bourbon and felt its amber burn at the back of her throat. She coughed.

Hartley went to the window and pulled the curtain aside. "Eddie, I already did it. I can't even say why. It just seemed like the thing to do." He let the curtain fall, returned to the desk, and reached for the flask. "So maybe some good would come out of it."

He tilted the flask to his mouth and took a long swallow, then he looked at her so closely she wanted to look away. "It's as hard to live with a lie as it is to live with a truth you don't want to believe. A lie can eat at you. But so can the truth. Near as I can tell, the lucky ones are those who know what lies they can tolerate from the ones they can't. Do you understand what I'm saying?"

She nodded dully.

"On the way over here, I knew you had to be the one to make the choice. Was wrong for me to . . . Thought I was doing you a favor, him one. Anyway, you got to make the call. I'll abide by what you say. Take whatever comes of it. Whatever happens." He took his hat from the desk and solemnly fit it onto his head. "I need to start proceedings. Do you need some time to think?"

Her body seemed to grow weak, as though if she tried to move she wouldn't be able to, but her face felt suddenly rigid and tight. "No."

He looked away. "Whatever you decide, it might be a good idea for you to let your boy think his daddy had an accident. At least for a while. A murder's a terrible thing to grow up with. Or the other."

"I will."

"I'm going on the county clock now," he said. "What do you want me to do?"

Eddie rose from the chair, walked past Hartley, and went to the window. She looked out into the dark. "Will you tell my maid what happened?"

"Which?"

Eddie rested her forehead against the pane. The glass was strangely cool. She closed her eyes. "The second way."

"I will."

"And everybody else?"

"Whatever you want. Your boy—"

"What . . ." She had almost said, "What will I tell him?" But before she could finish her question, in the darkness outside the window she saw headlights, and she stood watching as a car approached on the Mile Six Road, imagining that it carried all the choices of the moment. She watched as the car slowly passed by the house, watched until it was gone. "What," she said, "will you say?"

Behind her, Hartley was silent. In the quiet room she waited, fearing she would turn around, take back this last choice, wanting to, fearing he would take it from her. Finally he spoke. "That while his daddy was out walking his land he tripped and his gun went off."

Eddie let the curtain fall and turned away from the window to face him. "And the others?"

Hartley reached into his pocket for his badge, pinned it to his shirt. "That in a cottonfield near the Boca Chica road your husband Tom was killed, shot twice in the head and once in the back. That we're looking for the outlaw Kid Mapuche."

las azucenas

On the day before they were to move to the new house on the outskirts of Rio Paradiso, Luisa, who had packed all her possessions in the little house, went to the garden to dig up some of her lilies. There would be, Madama promised, a little house even better than the chicken house. She was to be happy. She was not to cry for the Hundred Acres. One door closed but another always opened. Joe Bonillas had paid top dollar, Madama said, and was glad to get the farm. Luisa's new house would be bigger, better. It would have a bathroom. A good kitchen. Room outside for numberless flowers and shrubs, whatever she wanted. Tavo and Tonia could walk to the school. At the funeral, Madama had embraced her, saying don Tomás would want her always to have a home, and Luisa, numb with guilt and shock and worry, had nearly fallen to the floor with relief.

Now, on her knees among the roots and bulbs and corms, digging and sorting, she mourned. Even though she could move some of the plants, they would not be the same. They would lie differently in different earth, turn their heads toward a different sun, sway in different air, close in a different night. Once she had known the beautiful old names for the many seasons, the words to mark the passage of time on the great wheel of years. This time too should have a name, but she searched her memory and found no words for what it meant.

In the big stone Episcopal church in Martha her throat had swelled with a feeling that was like remembering. The beautiful music—music like none she had ever heard, low, deep with mystery, then high and shining—seemed to pull her into a powerful river, a river of something that couldn't be said, of souls who had known great longing, great joy, and she was among them, at peace, but when the music ceased and the church fell silent, she was again alone. That night she walked through don Tomás's grove, trying to hum, to bring back the feeling of the music, but the memory of it slipped away, as though the river flowed beyond her, its sound overtaken by the rustle of wind in the mesquite.

In the old days, if you left a door or window open, los aires entered with their evil. Against those winds what door, what window, might she have closed? The answers—mysterious and changing—horrified her. A few days after the funeral she had found the blue bottle of beans. Among the brittle husks of weevils, one bean remained, and she knew it was this one that had stood for don Tomás. She walked out into the night and threw the bottle so it shattered against the washhouse. In the big house, a light flicked on. Upstairs, Madama moved across a window, but the children didn't wake, and soon the light went out. Love, she should have wished for him. Someone—even if she couldn't be the one—to love him in the way she knew he loved the world. Love. He had spoken of it only once, and in another language, but everything he did had been a picture of it.

Years before, she had planted an avocado seed. Now the tree shaded the little house, and the leathery fruits grew ripe and soft. She went to lean against its trunk, to let it hold her for a moment before she finished her work. In her mind there formed a prayer that don Tomás might know what was in her heart, but even in the forming of it came the answer, and she understood that love could not be contained in bottles or hidden in a heart. God and the dead saw into secret places, but the living were bound by acts, and those acts should be always good, so God and the dead could see them and know. Standing against the trunk, she promised to devote her life to don Tomás's family, to Madama, in his name, to make up for everything she'd done. For everything she hadn't. Her work would be a picture of her love, a way of seeking God, who had not been lost to her at all, as she had sometimes feared, but as Rafael had been so long ago beside the river, only hiding.

She surveyed the work before her. She would need more containers. She remembered that behind the oleanders she had seen an old refrigerator drawer half-buried in the dirt. It would hold most of the bulbs. She pried a stick under a corner to loosen the drawer and to warn away the snakes. When the drawer shifted, a small lizard raced off. With her foot, she turned the drawer over. Beneath it, nearly buried under leaves and dirt and an open package of firecrackers, she found the box.

Even before she opened it, she knew what was inside. Her mind raced, trying to remember the children's fight that day: Who would have hidden it, Tavo or Raleigh? She couldn't think.

The box was cool and damp from earth and darkness. She lifted the lid and found a curl of yellow hair bound with a ribbon, a broken watch, some baby teeth, an agate marble, a handful of nickel slugs, one remaining candy wrapped in red foil, its sticky pink syrup hardened. Over all remained the leaf and sugar smell of cured tobacco, a faint chocolate aroma, and the corn-and-soap-and-pepper scent of don Tomás. At the bottom of the box lay two envelopes; one contained a paper with some writing in black ink, the other a stack of gray-green bills.

She untied her apron and spread it on the ground, then placed the box at the center of the fabric. She wrapped it tightly, then went for the shovel. She buried the bundle, and over the mound of earth behind the oleanders, she placed stones, so that when she knew what to do with the box, what to say about it, she would be able to find it.

• • •

They had been at the new house for several months when Ann Dell Jenkins drove up the driveway to say that in the middle of the carrot field and in the space of thirty days, Joe Bonillas had drilled into two salt domes, bringing in four wells. Madama stalked the house for days, making phone calls behind her closed bedroom door. Though Madama's voice was muffled, Luisa could tell she was angry with someone, but she did not know who. Luisa kept the children quiet and made sure she herself didn't anger Madama further, and after a time Madama busied herself again with her new house and seemed contented.

Though Madama continued to blame his death on Kid Mapuche, in the colonia Luisa heard the truth, and she now knew that don Tomás had put a pistol to his head. She didn't know if this made what she'd done about the box better or worse, and she knew she should tell Madama, but each time she tried to frame the words, they seemed to grow beyond their meaning into something else, something terrible and dark, and so she put off the moment until the days and weeks and seasons began to grow over what she knew to turn it into something that she didn't and she forgot until the sight of a green car would remind her of the foolish belief she'd had in Salsipuedes as she'd come out of the darkened canyon imagining that there would be no price for what she'd done. When she learned that Sonny López had been sent to prison for robbing a gas station in La Feria, she was glad.

BOOK V

•

n o s o t r o s

1966

•

Ocho y diez vueltas del Sol,

era el espacio florido

de su edad; mas de su ciencia

¿quién podrá contar los siglos?

—Sor Juana Inés de la Cruz
Villancico VI from *Santa Catarina*, 1691

better homes and gardens

It was always hot in the little house, even in December. Antonia, lying on the floor, arms above her head and braced against the mirrored bedroom door, thought how cool it was in Madama's house, where the big air conditioners hummed, pumping cold air through all the louvered vents in the spacious rooms. Raleigh strained above her, drops of his sweat pooling like warm coins on her breasts and belly, his movements grinding her hips into the wool carpet until they stung, but it was cooler. She drew up her knees and curled her toes; even the carpet was cool, and she wondered how far down the coolness went.

All the houses in the Valley were slab houses, built on concrete. There were no basements; hurricanes came this far inland. Few peaked roofs; there was no snow here. Ever. Under the slab, she knew, and in the space between the walls, lived thousands of lizards: stripebacks, chalotes, brown anoles. They came out to bask on the hot packed dirt around the foundation, to crawl up the screens. Madama hated them. If she saw too many she called the exterminators down from McAllen. Then Antonia's mother was set to draping the furniture in sheeting, removing dishes, food, and clothing from the house so the pesticide wouldn't contaminate Madama and Raleigh. When the exterminator's immense plastic tent was pulled from the house and all the lizard carcasses were shoveled into bushel baskets, her mother would come back in to give the house a thorough cleaning: Pine-Sol the terrazzo, scrub the stuccoed walls, shampoo the carpets. Then she would move everything back in, washing each dish and glass and fork in hot detergent water while Madama supervised, giving orders in her swooping, self-important voice.

At the little house behind Madama's, lizards entered and departed through the gap between the screen door and the flagstone sill, unremarked. Geckos made their way around the walls, eating insects, spatulate toe pads mocking gravity. But it was so hot there. There were no windows on the south to catch the breeze. Antonia thought about the house she and Raleigh could have when she finished high school and moved from the Valley, a little college house with a peaked roof and an air conditioner in the window, a Boston fern hanging above the table, her biology texts and notes spread out beneath it.

"Squeeze them together," Raleigh said.

She braced her feet against the floor and took her hands from the door. She tried to place them on the sides of her breasts, but his movements inched her too far up. "I can't. I'll hit my head."

Raleigh balanced on one arm, pushing his glasses farther up on his nose. She didn't understand how he could sweat so, when it was as cool in the room as it was in the big stores in town. His glasses were fogged. She wondered why he wore them, what he saw as he watched in the mirror, if he saw the two of them as a watery image, the edges of their bodies blurred and running together. She looked up at him, under the rims, at his eyes, and their blue startled her. It was an uncommon color, she thought, a surprise of a color, a color she marveled that the human body, with its browns and tans and pinks, could produce. She couldn't look at it long without imagining it was from another place; foreign, vaguely holy, like the blue of the Blessed Virgin's mantle at the church of San Benito; cool and infinite, like the blue of the sky when the heat lifted and the haze that sealed the Valley blew away in the wind of a norther. It was a blue like ice and snow.

It snowed sometimes in Austin, even in San Antonio. Where Tavo had gone, to Fort Dix, New Jersey, it was probably snowing now, great fat flakes floating and floating, covering the barracks until they looked like rows of sugared loaves, and Tavo, inside with other soldiers, maybe some from other warm places, would be laughing from the surprise of it. As much as she hoped Tavo wouldn't have to go to Vietnam, she envied him his chance to be away, to open a window and draw the coolness in. She closed her eyes and imagined she could smell the snow. It must be sweet and powdery, she thought, like coconut. She looked again at Raleigh, his neck cords straining, watching in the mirror. "Have you ever seen snow?"

"Don't talk," he said. "I'm almost there." He clenched his jaw. She hoped her question hadn't irritated him.

Raleigh went to school at the University of Virginia. He was home for winter break. Madama had picked him up at the Brownsville airport, taking Pompilo along to drive the big car. A few weeks before, tailgating although she denied it, Madama had slammed into a bale truck, breaking her nose, and she now refused to drive the highway alone. All the other drivers in the Valley were drunk or stupid, she'd told Antonia's mother. Antonia didn't believe this reason; she knew Madama liked pretending she had a chauffeur, even if it was only Pompilo, who was so nearsighted that when he drove he looked like a sleepy turtle straining his neck out of his shell. On the day of Raleigh's return, Antonia had seen Pompilo pull the car into the driveway, Raleigh and Madama in the backseat. When Pompilo piled Raleigh's red plaid luggage on the tiled steps beside the tall white poinsettias, Antonia thought they looked like Christmas packages from another country, from England or Scotland. All this year, when she had thought of Raleigh, it was of their games in the shell-flecked dirt around the roots of the live oaks in the backyard of the old farmhouse, Raleigh's hair bleached almost white with the sun, tanned until he was nearly as brown as Tavo. But when he stepped from the car, she saw that he was different, stranger, not a brother-boy. A man.

Antonia was ten when she'd overheard Madama's order. The children were not to play together any longer. Madama had stood by the laundry shed, her mother at the clothesline. "Lu," she'd said, "that girl of yours isn't mine to boss, but she's about to bust out of herself."

Her mother pretended she didn't understand Madama's English, and it irritated her; her mother smiling, nodding, an impassive, half-comprehending look in her eyes, wiping her hands on a dish towel or patting little balls of dough into flat round tortillas: pat-pat-pat, smile, nod, shuffle around the big kitchen in her starched blue work dress and apron, her backless sandals. They had lived in the little house for a long time, long enough to learn English. Her mother was fierce in her defense of Madama, but still she pretended she didn't understand, or understood only dimly, forcing Madama into a fractured mixture of languages: "Lu, poner all that laundry sucia in el whatchamacallit."

Antonia and Tavo had laughed about it, about their mother getting the best of bossy Madama in such a funny way, but it made Antonia angry that her mother could let Madama think she was stupid; her mother understood everything Madama said. After Madama's card parties she entertained Tavo and Antonia with stories and imitations until they collapsed on their beds in the little house, wrung out from laughing at the dressed-up stupidity of Madama and her henna-rinsed friends. Las girls, Madama called them, but she and Tavo called them las chachalacas, for they looked like wrinkled old grackles ruffling their feathers, sniping at one another. On the day of Madama's order, her mother had gotten Madama to repeat herself three times, but she complied, keeping Tavo and Antonia from Raleigh. Antonia remembered how unfair it seemed, and that Madama saw it as her fault: *that girl.*

"Hurry, Raleigh," she said. "They'll be back."

"Maybe if you did something more than lie there," he said. "Move a little."

She tried moving her hips in a small circle. She wasn't sure if it was the right way, the way he expected or was used to, or if there was a right way. Their first time, two days earlier, when they had stood behind the door in Raleigh's bedroom, she hadn't had to move at all, and it had been over sooner. That time, Madama and her mother had gone to the grocery store, and Raleigh had come around the side of the big house to the clothesline where Antonia was hanging towels. He held a radio to her ear, as though the years they spent avoiding each other had been no more than a few weeks. She heard a rasping female voice.

"Janis Joplin," he said. "She's playing up in Austin. I usually hate country-western, but she's going to be a big deal, I think."

He lowered the radio when she nodded.

Raleigh didn't look the same as he had in high school, when she would glimpse him around the yard, or see him at football games surrounded by other boys in the same kind of clothing, madras shirts, wheat jeans, loafers they wore without socks. They dressed as if they were already in college, and everyone knew it was where they would end up. The other Anglo boys, those who would stay in the Valley to work and marry, to hunt whitewing dove in the fall, javelinas and coyotes the rest of the year, wore blue jeans and white T-shirts. Most of the Latino boys went to the public high school. Raleigh's hair was still cut in Beatles bangs, but he had grown sideburns, the earpieces of his new wire-rim glasses cutting into them. Something more had changed, though she didn't know what it was.

"Are you at Harlan Bloch?" he asked.

She looked at him, trying to decide if he was joking. She reached for a clothespin to clip the corner of a towel over the line. She was the daughter of a maid, and the public high school was her only choice. When she nodded, he asked her what courses she was taking.

She wanted to tell him about the frog dissection they had done the week before in biology, how she had cut into the pale, pearlescent belly to expose the first layer of organs, the ventral abdominal vein like a tiny, delicately branching river, the torsion of the small intestine giving way to the bulk of the large intestine and how both of them, when held aside, revealed the deeper viscera, the long posterior vena cava, the testes, kidneys and adrenal bodies; how the heart and lungs lay over the perfect fork of the aortic arch; how surprisingly large the liver was, its curves, its fluted edges, and how she could hardly catch her breath, not because of the formaldehyde or out of revulsion, like some of the other students, but from awe, for joy at the synchrony and mystery of the working of the body laid out before her, its legs splayed on the cutting table, the fragile mandible upturned and yielding to her touch. She wanted to tell him how she felt as her probe and scalpel moved through the frog's body, about the sacred, almost heartbreaking invitation of it, but she couldn't. "I'm taking biology," she said.

"Mohesky still there?" When she and Raleigh were in grade school together, Mr. Moshesky had taught health.

"He still forgets to zip his fly."

She became aware of Raleigh looking at her breasts, and when she stooped to pick up another towel from the basket she checked the buttons of her blouse. She hoped he hadn't noticed the downward glance that meant she'd noticed.

"Come in the house a minute," he said. "I want to show you something."

She had been in the big house only a few times, and never in his room. When they were just inside his bedroom he closed the door, telling her how beautiful she was, how sweet. She was all he thought about during his first semester away at school.

Her breasts were beautiful, and he'd bet they'd grown—would she show him? She was surprised to feel her nipple tighten when he took it into his mouth, the whole breast seeming to swell around it. He lifted her skirt and eased his fingers past her panties until he touched her. He unzipped his pants.

In the past days she had imagined such a moment, but she had not imagined it this far, this soon.

"It hurts," she said, and he stopped moving his fingers. "A little."

"You don't act like it," he said. He slid his fingers out and together they worked to guide him into her, her knees bent, his hand pressing against her hip.

"That doesn't mean it doesn't."

"You like it, though." It wasn't a question, and Antonia didn't bother to answer. She did like it. She liked it that he wanted her. She liked the push of it, the tip of him pushing past the part of her that felt like a small, rugate tunnel into a bigger part that had less feeling. She worried that she was too big. Anglo boys said Mexican girls were built for breeding. She wondered if this was what they meant, so much room inside, if Raleigh was small. She had seen other men; several times she had surprised Tavo, and she had seen braceros relieving themselves in the groves. She hadn't looked closely, but it seemed that most of these were more substantial, their color fuller, more nearly like the rest of their skin. Raleigh's was the color of sunburn, almost purple at the tip.

When it was over he had gone into the bathroom. She'd heard the tap running, a flush. She'd cleaned herself with her panties, not wanting to use the lacquered box of tissues beside Raleigh's bed. She noticed only a slight pink tinge, no more blood than from a paper cut. She'd tucked the panties into the waistband of her skirt and pulled down her blouse to conceal them.

This time, two days later, he had come up behind her as she emptied trash from the little house onto the burn pile at the back of the property. "Nalgas," he said, patting her bottom. She laughed at the pachuco word for buttocks, at the growling, mock-salacious way he said it, the furtive waggle of his eyebrows behind his glasses, and she had gone with him again to the big house, this time to Madama's bedroom, where he locked the door and showed her the full-length mirror behind it. Facing the mirror, with Raleigh behind her, Antonia watched his hands, nervous and more intent this time, move up her body, the tips of his fingers tapered, almost delicate, nails bitten to the quick. She could see ragged cuticles and dark flecks of dried blood as his fingers worked at buttons, at the elastic of her shorts. She remembered that even when they were small he had been nervous.

He pressed himself closer, sweating already, his breathing shallow and uneven, and when they were on the floor, Antonia on her hands and knees, Raleigh upright, kneeling behind her, she looked at their image in the mirror, at Raleigh watching, his head thrown back and arms extended so his hands grasped her hips, his movements regular and insistent. She thought of the mice they had mated in biology lab, of the male, a solid black, his motions powerful and concentrated in mount, of the female, a pink-eyed white, hunched and holding her ground to help him, her neck at an angle of submission, and she knew they were more alike than different, the mating mice, herself and Raleigh; that this impulse shot through all of life, through male and female, and made them do the things they did, made men and women lie down together. We are mating, she marveled.

Around his neck was a leather string with a peace symbol. It swung as he moved. He seemed to go deeper this time, deeper than when they stood against his bedroom wall. She felt her belly swell from him, a soft cramping like her menstrual cycle, pleasant at first, then almost painful. She'd asked him to stop, and he had waited while she turned over to face him, her arms braced against the door, then he had continued. Again she tried to hold her breasts for him and to move her hips at the same time. "You have to take it out," she said. "Before." She had forgotten to tell him this the first time.

He said nothing, concentrating on their image in the mirror. Finally he moaned, withdrawing, and she felt slow, warm spurts against her thigh. She squirmed beneath his weight, and when he rolled over she got up. "We'll leave a spot."

She went into the bathroom, looking for a cloth for the carpet. She didn't want to use the pale yellow towels folded in a complicated way across the bar, so she tore a length of paper, setting the roller spinning, and hurried to dab at the wetness where they had lain. The paper pilled and shed, leaving lint on the close shear of the wool. She tried to pick it off with her fingers, but it stuck here too. Raleigh laughed and got up to go to the bathroom. "Don't worry so much," he said, closing the door. He pointed to other spots on the carpet. "Look at all those. Dog pee." From Miss Evelyn Posey's last litter, Madama had selected a puppy whom she called Little Dixie. "Lu will get it."

His mention of her mother startled her; she and Madama would be back soon from McAllen. She dressed quickly, tucking the wad of paper into her pocket. She was halfway down the galería to the stairs when she heard the bathroom door click open and Raleigh calling out, but she didn't want to risk the time to answer.

The little house felt hot and close after the expanse of the big rooms. Even before she opened the door she smelled the heat inside, the dust, warm cominos simmering into the beans in the big cast-iron olla. Miss Evelyn Posey, ancient now, napping, almost invisible on the brown chair, perked up her ears and opened one eye as Antonia entered, but she didn't rouse herself. As she crossed the room to her bed she compared what she had seen upstairs in the big house with her mother's attempts to brighten things, a scattering of secondhand bathroom rugs across the dull linoleum, knickknacks cast off from Madama, paper flowers at the single window. Antonia's bed was the lower bunk of a government-issue set, curtained with a sheet tucked under the mattress of Tavo's top bunk, where boxes of clothing and household things were stored now that Tavo had gone. The beds were white, but the paint had chipped, exposing leopard spots of army green. At the head and foot the letters *US* were carved into the wood. When she was learning to read, she had thought the letters meant herself and Tavo; us, *nosotros,* and she felt special, good, tracing the letters with her fingers, with a purple crayon, lucky: No one else had a bed that told of herself and her brother, of their place in the world. She hadn't wanted to believe Tavo when he'd laughed and told her what the letters stood for. Her mother slept on a daybed in the opposite corner, behind a partition made of crates and a blue shower curtain with a picture of an egret wading among green rushes. Antonia lifted her sheet curtain and lay down, letting the heat and dimness envelop her.

She heard the car pull into the driveway, Madama's voice telling Pompilo to wash the car. She heard the slap of her mother's sandals on the flagstone path, coming toward the little house. She wished she had washed; the girls at school said other people could tell by your smell if you had been with a boy. In the stuffiness of the room her mother would notice it. She lay still and hoped her mother would think she was asleep.

Through the sheet Antonia saw her come in, silhouetted in the light streaming through the doorway. She could see well enough to tell that her mother still wore her apron. Madama insisted on it, especially when they went to town. She watched as her mother took off the apron and folded it over a wooden chair, then began taking dishes and pots and pans from the crates that were stacked to form shelves, wisps of hair springing from the bun at the back of her neck.

She tried to remember how her mother looked when her skin wasn't glistening with sweat, when her hair wasn't escaping from the bun. Saturday before church—she had started going only a few years before, though Antonia could never predict whether her mother would return serene or angry—sometimes for whole days in winter if a norther came in and work at the house was light. Even through the sheet Antonia could see the patches of darker blue under her mother's arms, around her waist, between her shoulder blades. They were as much a part of her mother as the starched work dress, as the apron, as the low song she sang while she worked, a song that irritated Antonia for its persistence, its quality of being a song yet not a song, more a droning, melodic murmur made low in the throat that had the power to remove her mother, lift her beyond Antonia's reach and back into the time before, a song from her mother's earlier life in the foothills, a place she never talked about.

When she and Tavo asked about it, their mother said little. All they knew was that Raleigh's father had found her walking along the road, fourteen, pregnant with Tavo, on one of his trips below the border to find workers. He didn't like the migrant teams but preferred to find whole families who wanted to come across the river, to live in the blockhouses at the bend in the levee until they found something better, or even asked about something better, and then he would help them, with papers, by getting their children into school, with medicine and food. Her mother had been alone on the road, in the last months of pregnancy, but he had idled the truck alongside her, asking questions in Spanish, inviting her to join the families in the truckbed. Tavo had been born in the blockhouse by the levee. Antonia was born three years later. Her father was a soldier from Fort Hood, her mother had told her, working a few months with the Army Corps of Engineers on an irrigation project before he moved on. This was all she knew. She and Tavo had stopped asking; their mother didn't welcome questions about the other life.

A stack of Melmac plates clattered to the floor, causing Antonia to jump. Her mother must have heard.

"¿Estás aquí?"

Antonia swung her legs over the edge of the bed. "I'm here, Mama."

She made it a practice to answer her mother's Spanish with English, as though she were talking to a toddler just learning the words for things. "What are you doing?"

Her mother ignored her and continued picking up the scattered plates. Antonia sighed and repeated the question in Spanish. Her mother was stubborn enough to ignore the question all day if it was a matter of will.

Her mother smiled at her, setting the stack of plates on the wooden table. She said that she and Madama had gone to an appliance store in McAllen. She described the shining rows of silver and white, and a new color for stoves and refrigerators called avocado green. They had picked out a new stove for the big house. It was to be delivered tomorrow. And guess who, as a gift for Christmas, was to have the old one?

Antonia smiled in spite of herself. "We are!"

Her mother crossed the room and stood behind the big chair next to the window. "Ayúdame."

Antonia helped to move the chair. They placed it at an angle by her bed, then lifted the table from the corner where the new stove would go and put it by the window. While her mother dusted the tabletop, Antonia went outside to get one of the potted aloes that lined the step. She arranged it in the center of the table.

"Mira, Mama," she said, gesturing grandly toward the plant. "*Better Homes and Gardens*." They laughed, and Antonia felt good, good and happy, like Tonia-nine-years-old, Tonia of no secrets, her mother's chula niña in a ruffled skirt and braids stretched tight for church. She watched her mother poke the broom into the cleared corner and shoo a lizard along the baseboard toward the door, her throaty song rising in the heat, happy with so little, and suddenly she was angry.

"A stove," she said. "An old stove. How much did the new one cost?"

Her mother continued sweeping, the hem of her work dress swaying stiffly with the motions of the broom. "No importa."

"It *does* matter!" She felt like grabbing the broom away and forcing her mother to listen. "We don't need a stove. Let her sell the old one and give us the money. Let her buy us an air conditioner. She has enough. She has everything."

She thought of nights in the little house, of trying to sleep with only the old black fan to cool her, its woven cord stretched from chair to chair, tripping her if she got up to get a drink of water, the frayed fabric encasing it reticulated like the backs of the water snakes she sometimes saw in the canal. "It will only make it hotter in this place!" She pushed against the screen door hard enough to wedge the flimsy frame against the bump on the edge of the step and walked out.

She cut through the live oaks, through the rows of oleander set out like railroad tracks to shield the little house from view, around to the back of the property to the overgrown area that she and Tavo and Raleigh had called the jungle. Madama had intended a swimming pool but had never gotten around to it. The jungle was mostly scrub pecan choked with ololiuqui vines, oleander, crotons, and yucca, but a few banana and papaya trees survived, making the place seem exotic and lush. The spears of a saw palmetto slashed her legs as she ran past the boundaries. She looked down to see the thin lines like razor cuts across her thighs. She darted through the algarroba thicket and came out on the other side, to Grand Texas Boulevard. A fine name, she thought, for the rutted road that led to the highway toward Reynosa. When the house was built, the developer had plans for an esplanade, but only the dirt lane remained.

She slowed down, thinking about what had just happened, thinking that she now knew what made people run away. It wasn't a simple matter of not liking home, it was far more complicated than that, and at the point when things became too complicated to think about any longer, people ran away. For whatever reasons they had that were too entwined to sort out. She imagined her mother walking along the road, and she imagined a man in a truck, a man in khaki work pants and a Panama hat. He would be smiling. Kind. She would have climbed inside the truckbed, too. She saw herself riding away from the Valley to a different place, any place, maybe a place with snow. To Fort Dix, where Tavo was, Tavo a soldier in uniform, able to be what he was without people thinking they *knew* what he was just by looking at him, by knowing where he came from, a place with more to get excited about than avocado appliances, where he made his own money and didn't have to depend on a bossy old woman like Madama, where he didn't have to care what such a woman thought of anything he did. Tavo would understand how she felt. He had been glad to leave the Valley. She picked up a stone and threw it at an irrigation pump.

She knew what Tavo would think of what she and Raleigh were doing. He would spit and make the jerking-upward jab with his wrist, like stabbing. He would stab Raleigh if he knew. He wouldn't see that Raleigh wasn't like the others. Tavo would see only his side of it, the side that hated all Anglos. He wouldn't see that it was different with Raleigh, that the two of them were what they were, male and female, Raleigh and Antonia, as simple as that. Raleigh wanted her, he found her beautiful. The feeling made her stomach tighten as she walked along, slower now. She held her shoulders straighter and began to sway her hips the way she had seen other girls do, feeling the heads of her femurs articulating deep in her pelvis. She knew now why those girls walked this way: A man wanted them.

She stopped to watch the sun go down behind a grove of navels. The fruit hung ripe and brilliant, orange as the sun, as the bright new tennis balls Madama kept in canisters on the laundry shed shelf. She heard the big trucks start up, loading braceros for the trip back to the colonia. Traffic on the highway quickened and she turned to go home, the trucks rumbling by. When she heard the clicking noises the men made, their high-pitched yips of appreciation, she toned down her walk, but she thought: Let them look, let them want.

Raleigh didn't come for her the next day, or the next, though she made many trips between the house and the laundry shed, the laundry shed and the burn pile, watching the back door of the big house. She began to think that Tavo's version of the way things were with Anglo boys and Mexican girls might be right. She could hardly bear her mother's excitement about the stove, and she snapped at her to stop polishing it so often. She snapped at her to speak English, to pick up her feet when she walked and stop shuffling. Her mother stared at her when she said this, and Antonia had seen her face close down.

On Saturday Joe Bonillas brought two chickens and her mother baked them, filling the house with a rich yellow smell that made her queasy. She couldn't touch the chicken and she didn't go with her mother to church. She knew it was far too early, improbable, given the dates of her cycle, but she began to worry beyond reason that she was pregnant.

At sundown Saturday a norther blew in, rattling the rickety door and filling the house with random pockets of cold air. She pulled a sweater from the box under her bed and put it on, then slid the shutter panel across the window and shut the heavy storm door. She sat at the table in the dark, not bothering to pull the string on the light overhead. When the first knock came she thought it was the wind, but it kept up and finally she opened the door.

Raleigh wore a zippered red windbreaker and his hair blew up behind his head like a rooster's tail. He was smiling. "Did you miss me?"

She wanted to slap his glasses away so they would skitter across the flagstone into the cans and pots and basins of her mother's garden and he would never find them. She wanted to tear off her blouse and sweater and show him her breasts, press them into his chest so hard that they burned him. She remembered the days just after they were told to stay apart, and felt as mad and helpless now as she had then. "No," she said.

He tried to look around her to see inside the house. "Can I come in?"

She looked behind her into the dark room, at the silly rugs and the shower curtain and the stove in its corner like a squat white ghost. "I'll come out."

They walked around the house to the jungle, Antonia with her arms folded across her chest, her hand tucked into the sweater sleeves, Raleigh with his hands jammed into the pockets of his windbreaker, neither of them speaking. They sat on the rim of a discarded tractor tire where Tavo had once found a coral snake. She shivered, glad it was too cold for snakes.

Raleigh bent to flick an oleander leaf from the toe of his loafer.

Alarm surged through her. He had found someone else, she wasn't good enough. Madama had found out. She wanted Antonia gone—that girl, her mother, gone.

"I'm busted at UVA," he said. He looked at her. "Kicked out."

She hoped she kept a straight face, kept from smiling: This is *all*?

"Miss Eddie's been hauling me all over south Texas for the last two days, throwing her weight around." He laughed, but Antonia could tell he didn't think it was funny. "She thinks she can get me into A and I or Pan American. I guess it's better than getting drafted."

This last Raleigh said in a voice that mocked Madama, and Antonia laughed. Raleigh had told her that because his father was dead and Raleigh was the only son, he was exempt from the draft. Madama, he'd told her, had kept this knowledge from him—he'd learned when he'd gone to register—and she continued to play out the school/draft drama, most likely because she wanted him to stay in school. To get her goat, he had played along, throwing out the draft threat to watch her squirm. "I don't know why I started it," he'd told Antonia, "but it gets her going, and I figure any little thing I can do, well . . ." Antonia wasn't sure how she felt about this deception. It made her think less of Raleigh, though, and so she tried to pretend it didn't exist.

She waited to see if he had anything else to say, but he was quiet, drumming his knuckles on the thick black tread of the tire. "Maybe it's not so bad," she said. She wanted to tell him what Mr. Mohesky had said, that if she continued to work hard he would help her apply for a scholarship to Pan American, but she couldn't think of how to say this.

He shrugged, then pulled a jeweler's box from his pocket. "Anyway, I got you these." He handed her the box. "For Christmas."

"Not yet," she said.

"You don't want it?"

"I mean, it's not Christmas yet." She held the box, stroking the nap of the black velveteen.

"Soon enough," he said. "Open it."

Inside was a pair of earrings, tiny gold chains with filigree humming-birds at the ends, red stones for each eye. In the moonlight she could make out the store name on the inner lid: Didde's of San Marcos. She imagined him on the streets of the college town, going into the jewelry store while Madama waited in the car, poring over hundreds of boxes until he chose these, for her. "Thank you," she said, and when he stood and held his hand for her she went with him through the jungle to the laundry shed. He waited while she removed the silver hoops she wore, then he inserted the posts of the new earrings into her lobes. She tilted her head to each side to help him, and she was reminded of the female mouse. The thought came to her that staying still was just as powerful an act as moving, just as necessary, and she again felt linked to the everlasting, perfect cycle of things.

They made love on the floor of the laundry shed, her hips lifted, supported by a pile of towels. They felt damp against her skin and smelled of Lifebuoy soap and Clorox. Her carotid artery throbbed from the rush of blood to her head, but she didn't complain, and she didn't tell him to withdraw. It would be all right, no matter what. What they were doing, this act, was a promise of that, a pact. She felt the earrings slide back and forth against her neck.

She made it back to the little house and into bed before her mother returned from church, and when she woke up Sunday morning, the first things she felt were the hummingbird earrings. She thought of Raleigh. Was he waking up just now in his room in the big house, remembering what they had done? She moved her hands down her body to the warm pocket between her legs and wondered how she felt to him. How could they ever know, male and female, what each felt like to the other? She heard her mother stirring and she sat up to part the curtain. Her mother was tying her apron over her work dress.

"¿Café?"

"Coffee," Antonia repeated automatically. Sunday mornings they usually sat at the table drinking coffee, Antonia reading the paper to her mother. It was her mother's day off. "Why are you wearing that?"

There was no answer. Antonia sighed, repeating the question in Span-ish. Her mother explained that Madama needed her to help with a party. She had to clean, prepare food, set things up. She would come home in the middle of the afternoon to rest, then she would go back in the evening to serve.

"On Sunday?" Antonia pulled out a chair and sat at the table, pouring coffee into one of the Melmac cups, adding sugar.

Her mother shrugged, and the helpless gesture irritated her.

"Why didn't you tell her no? You always do everything she says. 'Sí, Madama, no, Madama, ¿algo más, Madama?' " Antonia rose from her chair and went to the small refrigerator for milk.

Her mother stood at the sink, calmly tucking wisps of hair into her bun with bobby pins, her back to Antonia. Antonia thought she may as well have been talking to the stove, for all the effect her words had. Even her mother's back looked obstinate, her hips wide and stolid, square and stupid, the apron bow at her back as ridiculous as the daisy garland around the ear of the cow on the milk carton she took from its shelf. She stirred the milk into her coffee and looked at the older woman. She knew her mother's life would always be the same, shuffling back and forth between houses, going to church, easing her knees and elbows with salve she made from Vaseline and aloe, waiting on others, obsequious, stubborn in her obsequiousness, taking her small revenge in pretending she didn't understand English, forcing Madama into pidgin silliness, and all of it because of stubbornness, because she wanted nothing more, because she thought no further than the day after tomorrow. Antonia banged her cup onto the table, sloshing coffee over the edge and onto her cotton shift. "Why don't you get a better job?"

Her mother turned, and Antonia saw her face, hurt, defiant. Because she was ashamed that she'd never learned to read, her mother refused to get another job. Antonia didn't believe this reason.

"You could *learn*, Mama."

She felt suddenly defeated; there was nothing she could do. "It's your only day off," she said weakly.

She watched her mother rinse her own cup and dry it; she took it with her to work because Madama didn't believe in sharing dishes. Her mother left the house, closing the screen door gently, leaving Antonia alone at the table sipping coffee she could barely swallow for her welling sense of injustice. She got up from her chair, then ran after her mother, catching up with her along the flagstone path. "Don't do it, Mama. Say no. Say it for once in your life. Show her what you think of her."

Her mother shook her head and resumed her walk.

"You work for nothing. For a house too little and too hot. For a stove! And she doesn't even appreciate you." She grabbed her mother's arm and shook it. Her mother looked away, across the yard toward the laundry shed.

"Leave me alone."

"English, Mama. Your English is good. Use it. Make her *see* you!"

Her mother looked at her hard, and Antonia felt suddenly exposed in her cotton shift, as though she were standing naked on the path. Her mother shook off her hand. "No."

Pompilo came around the corner of the house with a wheelbarrow full of sand and a box of candles. He began placing brown paper bags around the patio. Antonia stood still, watching her mother walk toward the service entrance. Her mother had almost reached the door when she whirled, throwing her cup to the ground, then started back down the path toward Antonia, her face dark and angry. She reached out and with a violent flick at Antonia's ear set one earring spinning. "¡Éstos son de Madama!"

Antonia's hand flew to her ear, to the sting. She was dumbfounded by her mother's anger. Then she realized her mother thought she had stolen the earrings from the big house. "They are mine," she said, proud that they were, glad her mother was wrong. "Raleigh gave them to me."

Her mother's eyes widened. Antonia watched as her mother took in the information, as she looked at her daughter for clues. More than seeing her mother's look, she felt it on her body, a hot pressure through the thin shift at her breasts, which seemed in that moment huge and bobbing, giving away her secret, deeper, to the place inside her where the way she wanted Raleigh was suddenly confused, a solid, pulsing thing, a cluster of red capillaries, tangled, spreading. It was as though her mother saw this tangle, pierced it with her look so that it bled.

Her mother's look felt worse than a slap. "Fool!"

Antonia ran to the little house, to her bed, where she cried until her eyes were red and swollen and her throat was raw.

At last she got up to dress. Her hands felt limp as she pulled her skirt up over her hips. She didn't want to be home when her mother came back for her nap, but she didn't know where to go. She didn't want to go for a walk, and the few girls at school she could call her friends were just that, school friends; they rarely saw each other outside, and if they did they only teased Antonia about studying so hard and taking everything so seriously. When she opened the refrigerator to look for something to eat she realized it was Raleigh she wanted to talk to.

She sat at the table most of the afternoon, pushing cold rice around her plate with the tines of a fork, watching the activity at the big house, Pompilo arranging the luminarias, raking palm trash from the drive, pulling the car around for Madama. When she saw her mother come out the service entrance, she left the little house and hurried to the laundry shed.

The pile of towels was still on the floor, flattened slightly from when she and Raleigh had lain on them. She fluffed them up with her foot to make them look more natural. She looked out the window to see her mother going into their house, then she took a tennis ball from one of the canisters. She planned to stand behind the poinsettia outside Raleigh's window and throw the ball against the screen.

Her first throw fell short of the window, and her second, thumping against the wire mesh, was louder than she imagined it would be. The ball bounced into a plot of white azaleas, where its presence looked miraculous and unreal, like one fully ripened orange in a grove of still-in-blossom trees.

As she crossed the front yard to retrieve the ball, she heard the heavy carved door swing open on its wrought-iron hinges. Raleigh stood in the doorway, the fingers of his right hand kneading his left biceps, the blue stone in his class ring glinting in the sun. He walked toward her. His face looked fuller, younger; he had shaved his sideburns. She couldn't make herself meet his eyes.

"What's the matter?"

She couldn't look at him. "My mother knows," she said. "I'm sorry."

She hoped he would tell her it was all right, that he didn't care, that he was glad: Now they could be together, without hiding.

When he crossed his arms the fabric of his windbreaker made a slick, sliding sound. "What does she know?"

She couldn't think of what to call what they had done, the way she felt, what it had meant. "Everything."

Raleigh laughed.

She looked at him, relieved beyond words.

"It's not like she hasn't done the same thing," he said. "She's been around the block."

She was puzzled. "What?"

"You know. When we were kids. Nobody ever said, but just put two and two together. With my father . . . you know how uptight Miss Eddie is."

Antonia never thought of her mother in that way; her mother was just what she was: aproned, blue-dressed, patting tortillas, sweeping; working. She started to ask Raleigh what he meant, but all of a sudden she knew. She remembered a time before they had come to live at the new house, her mother, younger, thinner, sitting on the floor with them, showing them how to cut circles of colored paper and twist them into the shapes of bougainvillea, oleander, the blue trumpets of jacaranda, her hair loose and fragrant from the jasmine shampoo she kept on the shelf above the sink. Laughing, her mother had tucked one of Antonia's flowers behind her ear, and in the hollow of her throat a small blue vein seemed to pulse. Antonia had reached up to place her fingers on it, moved to joy, to longing at the happy mystery of how beautiful her mother was. Her mother had scooped her up and hugged her with a strength that surprised her.

In the hot still nights after she and Tavo were in bed, her mother would leave the house. Just for a walk, she said, to putter in the garden. Antonia would try to stay awake until she came back in, but the hum of the fan would always put her to sleep. In the morning her mother would be at the sink, running water for coffee, draining the soak water from the beans, and Antonia would forget. Maybe it had been then. It had been Raleigh's father who brought the fan, taking off his Panama before he entered the little house, patting the top of her head, "Qué chula, niña." She now remembered: He had looked longingly at her mother. He had brought the beds.

"Come inside," Raleigh said. "You can see the preparations for the big shebang." From his tone Antonia could tell what he thought of Madama's party, but she hesitated.

"She's not here," he said.

She followed him into the house. As they passed through the big hall she caught a glimpse of the sala with its grand windows. At the far end of the room stood an enormous fir, its branches flocked with white, shimmering with gold and silver birds. She thought of the plastic Santas she and her mother would hang on the potted Norfolk pine they would bring in from its place among the other plants that rimmed the little house, the red suits nearly pink from sun and age, the white of the beards and fur trim gone yellow.

"She's got it all decked out," he said, starting up the stairs. When they were inside his bedroom he locked the door and took a mirror from the wall, propping it on the floor against the bed. He fingered one of her earrings. "Pretty," he said.

She pushed his hand away, but then stood still, her arms lifted as he pulled her blouse over her head. He kissed her, unhooking her bra. She felt her nipples draw and tighten.

"My mother isn't what you think," she said. The words surprised her.

He eased himself down and took her nipple in his mouth, but she drew away. "She speaks English. She only pretends she doesn't so your mother will look foolish." She felt the beating of her heart, shuddering and rapid, almost hot, astonishing as anger.

He laughed, nuzzling her, pulling at the elastic of her skirt. "I know," he said. "It's been a joke for years. I used to spy on Mother's bridge club just to hear her do the Lu imitation. She's really got the routine down." He did an imitation of a placid, nodding sleepwalker.

Antonia stared at him as he unbuckled his belt and stepped out of his jeans. "Lie down, chula." His hands on her shoulders, he pressed her down with him until they were kneeling beside the mirror. She looked at him, at the dark triangle of hair against his pale skin, at his penis rising, then to the mirror, where she saw the flexion at the side of his buttock where the gluteus inserted. She saw herself, smaller, a fool looking up at him, a fool somehow more beautifully made, browner, smoother, more round.

She tried to meet his eyes, fixed on his own, but couldn't, and she had the feeling each of them was seeing something different in the framed rectangle, like two people looking at the same slide under a microscope, trying to adjust the focus to accommodate both their visions, failing.

She removed his hands from her shoulders and stood up, gathering her clothes, starting to dress. "I have to go," she said.

"Wait," he called out to her as she walked along the galería. "Tonia!" When she heard her childhood name, she nearly turned. "I love you," he called as she descended the stairs, but she kept moving away.

She walked out into the early dark of December. Light shone from the little house, and as she got closer she saw her mother's form moving back and forth against it. Antonia knew she would be eating her supper, standing over the olla eating beans rolled into a flour tortilla, alternating beans with bites of pepper, waiting to go back to work. She looked up when Antonia entered but didn't meet her glance.

"Coffee," her mother said, gesturing toward the pot on the stove. Antonia saw that the light came from behind the pot, from a small bulb under the hood of the stove that cast the shadows of the olla and the coffeepot onto the floor. She sat at the table. Her mother took cups from their hooks, poured them full, and placed them on the table. Then she sat across from Antonia.

Antonia looked at her, at the crease from her nap across the smooth brown of her cheek, her hair freshly brushed and fastened back, in her eyes the sleepy distance of the saints, the prophets, as though she knew something Antonia could only guess at, and that this knowledge pleased her. Her mother lifted the lid of the sugar bowl. "Sugar?"

Antonia nodded, and her mother spooned the sugar into their cups.

They were small things, not calling attention to her mother's use of English, sitting still to let her mother serve her, but she could tell they had pleased her mother. She heard the low song begin in her mother's throat, masking for a while the faint metallic buzz of the stove light rattling under its enameled hood. Then the song trailed away.

They sat for a long time at the table. Even the presence of a small green anole skittering across the top of the stove to bask briefly in the harsh white glare, the ruby throat it expanded when threatened now a flaccid sac, was not enough to disturb their silence. Something had happened, Antonia knew, though she could not say what, but it was as though a loop, a slackened thread, had been drawn tight.

2

When Antonia looked back, it seemed as though the months had passed like the flocks of swallows that now flew over the Valley. You looked up to see them, specks on the horizon that grew larger until the low-flying clusters, violet tails iridescent against the sky, were so close overhead you could hear their shrill, clipped flight calls, *dee-chip*. Their shadows fell across you as you stared up at them, dappled you with moving shade, and then were gone.

She had been on her way across the yard to the tractor tire, but now she stopped walking. Above her, toward the outer reaches of a branch, a swallow moved in a side-to-side fashion along the tip of the limb, flicking his tuxedo tail. She held her breath, careful to make no sudden movements. The bird cocked his head, seeming to appraise her. He didn't fly away. Antonia began to breathe. She had been on her way to the jungle to think, but at this moment, she couldn't move.

As long as the bird stayed, time would stand still. She could stand this way forever, she thought, through days and nights and weeks and months, a statue-Tonia on the carpet grass of Madama's back lawn, unmoving. She let her gaze go distant, taking in the field beyond the jungle, the burn pile smoldering in its packed-earth pit, the silver glint of the trailers in their rows beyond the field, the spindly palms along the far road with their fringed topknots like the crests of prehistoric birds.

The afternoon was quiet, only a slight breeze that did no more than flutter the leaves, the lazy drone of a wasp somewhere behind her. Her mother was napping in the little house after the morning's work; soon she would wake up and begin to bathe and dress for church. From the direction of the little house, she heard one chachalaca startle the air with its buzz saw call, its warning then taken up by the rest of the flock roosting on the power line like a row of black, scruff-feathered priests, their din rising to a raucous cackle, their message: something out of order in the world.

From the machine shed came the sound of Pompilo trundling the lawn mower down the planks of the ramp, the cough and sputter of the engine as he yanked at the rope start, then the steady growl as the engine caught. When she glanced up, the swallow was gone. She went through the jungle and sat on the rim of the tire.

When you started showing you quit school and stayed home. Boys laughed when you walked downtown. They smirked and sneered and looked you all over with eyes like metal. They wrote your name on walls. Some fought over who had done it. When Rose Figueroa quit school, stupid Felix Cruz offered her five dollars if she would promise to tell people the baby was his. His cousin Fonso, who had really done it, had cut Felix, cut his face, taking a slice of his ear. Fonso kept the trophy in a Sucrets box and showed it around. She had seen the little black nub, wrinkled as a raisin. When Fonso shook the box, it rattled.

In February she had first said the word. Ripe, globular, it made her think of the trilling, full-throated calls of the spring peepers in the rushes by the canal, calling over and over through the long nights when she lay in her bed trying to sleep. *Pregnant, pregnant, pregnant,* louder, louder, until she had to get up, pad to the door, and look out to see that nothing had changed. Outside, the same leaves moved with the same wind, the same lights shone on the same silver trailers the same distance away, from far out on the levee came the yips and howls of the coyotes. Once, standing at the doorway, Antonia had run her fingers across the screen, pressing them so that the wires left dusty little waffle prints on her fingertips, and she stood in the moonlight at the door, staring at the marks as though they would tell her something. She must have made a noise. Her mother sat up in bed. "Antonia?"

"It's nothing, Mama. I just can't sleep."

Her mother muttered that she hadn't been eating enough. She started to get out of bed.

"Go back to sleep," Antonia said. "I'm just listening to the wind."

That had been the first time she hadn't gone—fooled by the funny cramping feeling in her abdomen—to the bathroom to check. It was an immediate, buried, soft feeling that began to take on a kind of bulk, a hardness inside, pressing against the other organs—her bladder, her bowels, the lowest part of the abdominal wall where the bones joined. There. She had returned to bed and lay behind her curtain, arching her back, raising her hips, moving her hand along her belly, pressing as deeply as she dared. There.

Lately all her mother talked about was graduation, about how proud she would feel as she watched her daughter get her diploma. She spoke for the first time of a brother in Mexico, a poet, she said, and educated. Her mother seemed animated these days, and happy, as though there would be a great surprise in store.

She couldn't tell Raleigh. He was away at San Marcos; she didn't know how to reach him. Funny, but he really didn't seem to matter in it, anyway. Nothing she could say to him would make her not pregnant. She had been a fool at Christmas break, she wouldn't be the same fool again.

Tavo? She almost laughed.

She missed her brother. She scuffed her foot in the dirt at the base of the tire, making a row of Z's in the soft soil. Z for "Zorro," the Mark of the Man. Tavo and Raleigh had played Zorro, Raleigh taking the part of the hero because he had seen the show on TV, Tavo, who hadn't, following his lead, playing his sidekick, Sergeant García. Even in the game, Tavo would trick Raleigh. Just when Zorro was about to jump from a tree onto the back of the stagecoach they'd rigged with ropes and boards and empty oil drums, Sergeant García yanked on the rope and Zorro landed in the dirt. She laughed, remembering the look on Raleigh's face, his black plastic Zorro mask askew, his nose sticking through one of the eyeholes.

Since January, when he had sent her money for her birthday, they had heard nothing from her brother. When her mother fretted, dusting the bottles of the bath salts he'd sent from Thailand, arranging them on the shelf, Antonia told her that his company was probably in a place where there was no mail. But she worried, too. She had heard about pungee sticks and snipers, minefields and children who carried bombs and grenades in their bicycle baskets. In his letters, Tavo had said nothing of these things. He wrote about how hot it was and the mosquitos. He said it was just like the Valley in the summer, only with more trees, more snakes, and more bugs. Not so many Anglo maricóns in pickup trucks. He wrote about his friend called Amp who rigged some speakers into a huge tree and made them boom so loud it shook the snakes from the branches and all the men started shooting at them. He wrote that he was in such a safe place that the only danger was that you got so bored, even shooting snakes seemed like action.

She would write to him again, even though her last two letters had gone unanswered. She would tell him her plans for Pan American, the scholarship Mr. Mohesky was going to help her with, that Mr. Mohesky said when Tavo came home he could go to school with government money—all he had to do was take a special test.

She should do this soon, because in June she would go away. In Corpus Christi there was a home she'd heard about from Donna Tomlinson, whose cousin had gone there to have her baby. The cousin was an "unwed mother," Donna had said in biology class as they worked on their fetal pigs, her voice a whisper.

"What do they do with the babies?" Antonia had asked.

"Oh, adopt them out, I guess." Donna wiped her fingers on a paper towel. "Yuck," she said to the smell of formaldehyde. "This is really sickening."

Antonia held out her hand for the probe. "I'll do it if you want."

Antonia began to separate the intestines from the inner wall. "Does she have to pay?"

Donna smoothed her hair, adjusted her velveteen headband. "I'm sorry?"

"Your cousin. Does it cost?"

Donna shrugged. "I doubt it. My aunt and uncle are tight as ticks."

Antonia discovered in herself a reservoir of craftiness. "I'll bet that place has one of those jail-y names. Like Alcatraz or something."

"It's just Booth Memorial. Salvation Army."

Pompilo had moved now to the back lawn, was mowing in a square of diminishing proportion, even though Madama wanted him to mow diagonally; "catty-corner," she called it. His movements seemed hurried; he yanked the mower out from under the firecracker bushes as though he was afraid of something. She hoped he would finish before Madama returned, so he could pull another one over on her. If she caught him, he would smack his forehead, shrug, tell her he forgot. He would act ashamed. As punishment, Madama would make sure he went without the bottle of Coca-Cola she gave him after the job was finished, handing over the bottle as though it were precious. At his house Pompilo had cases of Coke, stacked to the ceiling.

Madama's sharp green eyes noticed everything; they would take one look at her body, at her face, and they would know. She ran her palms along the rough, cracked rubber of the tire. She had done her best to avoid her, but a week before she had gone to the clothesline and she'd noticed Madama's speculative gaze. The very thought of Madama finding out made her feel queasy. She leaned back slightly, imagining the tire she sat on was a great round door she could fall backward into until the ground closed over her.

Next Saturday she would make the arrangements. She would tell her mother there was a class field trip. The bus ride to Corpus would take up most of her twenty dollars, but it would take her only an hour or two to sign up, and she wouldn't need to spend anything on lunch. What she needed to figure out today was a story to tell her mother about why she would have to be gone the entire summer, maybe almost to the end of September.

She became aware of a stillness in the afternoon. Pompilo, finished with the yard, had cut the lawn mower engine. He drew a red oil rag from his back pocket and wiped his brow. He looked around, surveying his work, then he pushed the lawn mower to the far corner and began crossing the yard in diagonal fashion, using the dead mower to make wheel tracks to suit Madama. When he approached the edge of the jungle and looked up, he saw her and waved, grinning.

"Better hurry," she called. She mimicked Madama's voice. "I've got ojos in the back of my cabeza, Pompilo!"

When he laughed, Antonia thought again of Tavo, wished he were home, then, remembering, changed her wish to one that he would come home safely, when it was over. A glint of sun on chrome flashed through the jungle: Madama turning her big car into the drive. Pompilo swore.

"Now you're in for it!" Antonia called, laughing.

He began to jog the mower toward the machine shed, his red rag flapping behind him. "No Coke!" he yelled. "¡Ay de mí!" He made elaborate motions of parched throat, comic supplication. He crowed, "Hee hee!" Then he disappeared around the corner of the machine shed.

Madama pulled the car beneath the arched side portico nearest the rear entrance to the house. Antonia shifted her weight on the tractor tire, trying to arrange herself so she was hidden by the shrubs and trees of the jungle. Madama got out of the car and shut the door. "Pompilo! Groceries!"

The afternoon seemed to echo with her call. No movement came from the machine shed. Antonia held still, watching Madama walk to the edge of the driveway where the lawn began. She saw her put her hands on her hips and shake her head, looking at the grass. "Pompilo," she called again. "I know you're out there, and if you think for one minute that I don't know what you're up to, you can think again!"

No answer from the machine shed.

"I've got ojos in back of my cabeza, Pompilo."

Madama was looking toward the jungle. "Antonia! I see you in there. Come out here."

Madama marched toward the laundry shed, the heels of the spectator pumps she had worn to town sinking into the thick grass. She looked like a large, pale heron. "Come here!"

Antonia wanted to call to Pompilo. If he were to appear, Madama would seize on him and she would be safe. She would escape, saying she had to help her mother with something. But she had been afraid to call out to him. Slumping as she walked, she followed Madama.

Inside the laundry shed, Madama pulled the light chain on the overhead bulb, then pulled it off again. "Too hot in here," she said.

Antonia stood beside the big galvanized sinks, the same kind—she noticed for the first time—as the sinks in the zoology lab. She almost wished the woman would just come right out and say, "You have to go."

Madama fidgeted with a rusted jalousie crank at the window. "I've told him and told him to get these oiled."

Outside, at the tire, the breeze had cooled her; now, in the still air, she felt sweat running down her sides. Madama, too, looked hot. Along her forehead where the reddish blond hair swept up to begin its wave, moisture glistened in tiny beads that looked faintly pink. Madama reached into her purse for a tissue and dabbed at her hairline, then tossed the tissue into the trashcan. Antonia tried to keep her eyes on the holes in the drain. They made a pattern, starlike, if you looked at them a certain way.

Madama crossed her arms. "You might as well tell me. I wasn't born yesterday. Who's the boy?"

Antonia kept her gaze on the drain.

Madama let go of the crank. "Your mother doesn't know, does she?"

Antonia shook her head.

"Well, it'll kill her," Madama said. "She'll just die."

Antonia felt tears running down her cheeks, salty at the corners of her mouth. Madama opened her purse and drew out another tissue. She handed it to Antonia.

"Spilt milk," she said, her voice somehow comforting. "Cry if you want, honey. But what's done is done. I suppose the boy is long gone."

Antonia looked closely at Madama. Her voice had sounded understanding, and it felt good, suddenly, that she wasn't alone with the terrible secret. And Madama didn't know about Raleigh.

"I'm going away," she told her. "To a home in Corpus. Next Saturday I'm going to go make the arrangements. I have some money." She wiped her eyes with the tissue and tried to smile.

Madama eyed her. "You're not seriously planning to *have* this baby, are you? That's just about the worst thing you could do."

"It is?"

"Why, sure." Madama appeared to think for a while, then moved forward to pat Antonia's arm. "Even though what you did was wrong, you're not the only girl who's ever found herself in trouble. You remember that Strecker girl?"

Antonia nodded. Marilyn Strecker had been homecoming queen the year Raleigh graduated.

"Well, her daddy got it fixed."

Antonia didn't understand.

"Mexico. That way, nobody has to find out, and you can wait until you're married, then have all the babies you want. It's what people do."

"But it's . . . they're not supposed to, are they?"

"You mean because of the law? Down there, it's practically a rule. Besides, it all depends on which 'not supposed to' you decide to pay attention to. You're 'not supposed to' get yourself in a family way, are you?"

Antonia shook her head.

"The worst thing you could do is go to Corpus. You'll wonder all your life where that baby is. It'd be like giving up your right arm." She stood back to appraise Antonia. "You're only a little bit along, right? And so now it isn't even . . . it's just trouble you don't need." Madama shook her head sadly. "And neither does your poor mother."

"I'd be all done with it in September," Antonia said. "I've got everything figured out."

Madama's look had turned severe. "I won't be blackmailed."

She tried to speak but Madama cut her off. "Don't you dare try to work me." Madama turned on the sink tap so the water splashed into the deep basin. "It's an oven in here!" She bent toward the sink and began to splash her face with water.

When Antonia turned to go, Madama shouted, "Don't leave this room yet!" Madama stood, her face dripping, her hair gone wiry and disheveled, pointing her index finger at Antonia. Then, as though she realized how harsh she had sounded, she said, "Let me just calm down a little." She grabbed a towel from the shelf and began to dab at her face. "It's just so hot."

"Your mother has worked for me for a long time, and she's almost a part of the family. I couldn't sleep at night if I couldn't make things better for her."

Madama crossed to the washing machine, her hands twisting at the towel. On the white terry cloth Antonia could see the pinkish dye stains from Madama's forehead, a smudge of makeup. Antonia wiped her own brow with the back of her hand. Her blouse was soaked and she could smell herself. Her hair, where it clung to the back of her neck, felt like a thick blanket.

"Do you understand what I'm offering? That I'll help you . . . that I'll pay for it? Out of . . . because of your mother?"

Antonia nodded. Although she was sick at heart that she would owe Madama money, and that Madama would probably find a way to hold it over her, her body went limp with relief.

Madama's look was firm. "You're never to tell a soul."

"I won't. I promise."

Madama gathered her things. "Good. It's settled, then. I'll make the arrangements."

"Could we do it on a Saturday so I won't miss school?"

When Madama pursed her lips, Antonia saw that her lipstick had feathered into the tiny crevices around her lips.

"Is that all you can say?"

"I don't know what I'm supposed to—"

"How about 'Thank you'?"

But before she could get the words out, Madama turned away and left the shed.

a map of the known world

In her history book there were maps Antonia loved to look at—maps that showed the world crisscrossed with many-colored trails. Black dots to show Columbus crossing the Atlantic, an X at San Salvador. Magellan's red scallops, sewing up the parts of the world like a seam. In orange, two dots and a dash for Pizarro, two dashes and a dot for Balboa. From Spain to Cuba to Vera Cruz ran Cortés's green curves, and then the straight line between the twin volcanoes that marked his entrance into Tenochtitlán. Coronado's crooked search for the Seven Cities of Cíbola. Antonia's favorite was the little Spaniard Cabeza de Vaca, shipwrecked on an island off the Texas coast, who had zigzagged across the very land she now saw from the window of Madama's Buick. She liked to imagine the man with his silly name—Cow Head—poking about in the lowlands and the arroyos like a curious little steer.

The map of Antonia Cantú would show a squat X on Rio Paradiso, a dotted line that led down the highway to Harlingen, there another X for standing with her class in front of the Iwo Jima sculpture. Now there would be another line. Straight down the highway to Brownsville, then across the International Bridge into Matamoros. Madame's Whore House, everyone at school called it; each weekend carloads of Valley boys paid drunken visits.

Why did the maps of men show something they were seeking, while the maps of girls and women, if there were such things, would show them moving away from something? She tried to remember a girl's map from her history book, but she could think of nothing unless she counted Sacajawea guiding Lewis and Clark. The closest she could come was the map of the Virgin that she could see in her mind's eye: Bethlehem to Egypt, hiding the baby from Herod, then back to Nazareth.

It was not the same for her as it had been for her mother. No man in a truck to pick her up; she rode in the backseat of the big car that belonged to that man's wife. Her mother had ridden through the sunlight in the open bed of a truck, other people packed in around her like warm melons. Madama smoked cigarette after cigarette, and the cool air inside the air-conditioned car was nearly blue with tobacco smoke.

As they neared the outskirts of Brownsville, Madama pulled the car into a Texaco. She turned to Antonia, resting her arm on the seat back. "I'm going to tell a little fib when we get to the bridge, and you have to go along with it. They might think we look suspicious."

Antonia nodded.

"You're going to have to sit up here with me to make it look good." She pointed to the front seat. "Come on, now."

The sun was bright even though it was just mid-morning, and the cement gave off heat that seemed to bathe her legs in warmth; she realized how chilly it had been in the car. Traffic on the highway was light, and Antonia felt a sense of unreality, as though she had come out of nowhere to be standing on this strand of concrete, above her the red Texaco star with its green *T,* the tall pole like a signpost from another world. She blinked in the light, then shook her head slightly to clear it. From her hair as it swung against her cheeks came the scent of stale smoke.

She opened the front passenger door and asked if they had time for her to use the toilet.

Madama looked irritably at her watch. "Our appointment's for straight-up noon."

"I'll hurry."

As she walked toward the door marked LADIES/DAMAS, she heard the faint buzz of the power windows being rolled down, the ticking of the Buick's engine.

Inside the tiny room, she sat on the toilet. Above her was a window through which she could hear the pump bells, voices, the whoosh of air from cars out on the road. The window was too small to crawl through. What if now, at the last moment, the stain was there? At eye level on the cinder-block wall someone had written *Chinga.* She looked away. When she washed her hands at the rust-stained sink, the mirror showed a girl with dark eyes but nothing in them.

She had never been in the front seat of the car. Ahead on the flat road stretched great puddles of water which she knew to be mirages, but always before she had seen them as she walked along the highway. Madama's big car traveled so fast and so quietly that she was certain the front wheels would splash into the water, splatter the car with cool drops. There were hundreds of resacas, dry lake beds, around Brownsville, and she imagined for a moment that the shimmering mirages on the road ahead were reflections of the ancient lakes, lost in the sky for a thousand years but remembered by the air.

"I'd stop and buy you a Coke, but they said you shouldn't eat or drink anything."

"That's all right," she said. "I'm not thirsty." She looked out the window at the houses and stores of the outskirts of Brownsville. It was strange to be sitting in the seat beside Madama, and she had the feeling that the air had become fuller, that if she turned just now to face Madama, some strange language would pour from her, a language made of all the unsaid words that made the air so thick between them.

Beside the road grew some tall weeds with yellow flowers, and she began to think about how plants sent messages to each other through their color and their breathing and the spiked dust of pollen, all their knowledge of how to cover what earth where, and all of it without one spoken word. "It's hot today," she said.

Madama took her hand from the wheel to smooth her French twist, her fingers deftly tucking in the pins. "Just be glad we've got the air-condition."

"I've never been to Mexico," she said.

Madama brushed ash from her skirt. "Well, it's filthy. It'll make you appreciate how good you've got it."

"I do already." She hoped Madama understood that she was grateful, not only for what the woman was doing for her now but—suddenly— for everything, in spite of everything. "I really do."

"Good," Madama said. "You don't know how bad things can get."

Madama pointed toward a structure on the road ahead of them. "There's the bridge," she said. "That little house is the border station." She glanced at Antonia. "Sit up straight," she said, "No. Slump a little. Like the air-condition's got you chilly."

Antonia crossed her arms over her chest and bent forward.

"Not like that. You look like you've got the grippe. Just a little."

Antonia tried again, but Madama wasn't satisfied. "Here," she said, picking up her purse and dropping it in Antonia's lap. "Hold on to this."

When the car pulled under the arcade that stretched above the row of booths, Madama rolled down the window and a tall blond man in a uniform and a wide-brimmed hat leaned toward them, resting his hands on his knees. "Morning, ladies." He winked at Antonia, and she hoped it was her imagination that was making her believe his look meant he knew exactly what a girl like her was doing in such a car beside a woman like Madama.

The man walked around to the back of the car.

"Don't turn around," Madama warned her. "He's just checking the tag."

At last the man returned to Madama's window.

"Hidalgo County?"

Madama straightened her sunglasses. "Just a day trip. Shopping. This is my little niece. We'll be back this afternoon." When she smiled and patted her hair, Antonia realized for the first time that Madama had once been young, and that she thought herself still beautiful. "My goodness, it's hot down here," Madama said, fanning herself with a fluttering hand. Her voice was soft and flirtatious.

The guard stepped back from the car. "Pass on through, ma'am," he said, waving them along.

Madama drove slowly across the bridge. Once when Antonia looked over, she saw Madama's mouth working in a strange way, but she looked away, more interested in her first view of the river.

On maps, the river was a crooked blue line that started in the green Rocky Mountains until it grew into a wider blue at Santa Fe, even wider as it reached El Paso to form the border between Mexico and Texas and split the continent all the way to the Gulf. All the maps showed the United States like an enormous fish swimming west through the oceans, a fish with puzzle-piece scales that were all the states, the ventral fin that was Texas cutting through the land so the fish could swim westward into the clear Pacific. She liked to think of herself in Rio Paradiso at the tip of the fin the river made, carried along toward the sea with the millions of other riders. The edge of that fin, in her imagination, had always been a silver blue, and so she was surprised to see that the water was brown as the dark coffee her mother laced with milk, no more unusual than the muddy water that ran through the canal.

On the Mexican side, Madama pulled the car onto a side street and parked in the dirt lot beside a store that advertised liquor and cigarettes. "I'm going to run in and get the limit," she said. "As long as we're down here."

A group of ragged little boys appeared from around the corner and swarmed around the car. The oldest looked to be around seven or eight, the youngest no older than three. Each carried a tray of brightly wrapped gum. "Chicle," they called, scratching and tapping at the windows of the car. One of the older ones pressed his cheek to Madama's window, his skin flat and suddenly green-looking, and looked sideways into the car, batting his eyelids. Madama sighed. "Oh, never mind. If I get out of the car they'll be all over me."

She yanked the gearshift into reverse and began to pull away from the adobe wall of the liquor store. There was a thump against the back bumper.

Madama braked, cutting the wheels sharply, then shifted into drive. "Don't you dare get out. I'm going to drive around through that alley and don't you even try to look back."

Antonia looked back. The boys were clustered around the rear of the car, looking at the ground. One boy was holding his hands over his eyes, others were jumping up and down, yelling.

"You hit one!"

Madama lifted her foot from the gas pedal. "That's the oldest trick in the book."

When the car began to move, the pack of little boys ran around to the front and began waving and gesturing frantically. "Ignore them," Madama said.

One of the biggest boys hoisted himself onto the car hood. Spread-eagled against the windshield, he pounded against the glass. Gum boxes spilled from his tray and skittered across the hood.

"Stop!" Antonia was surprised at the strength of her own voice. "Stop now!"

When Madama slammed on the brake, Antonia got out and ran to the back of the car, where a little boy lay facedown in the dirt. The others knelt around him. All were crying. The injured boy was the youngest, the three-year-old, a tiny body in dirty cotton shorts. She knelt beside him and put her hand on his head.

The others began to speak in rapid Spanish, saying that his neck was broken. They called him Nestor. She bent to listen for breathing. His skin was warm when she touched his neck. She put her ear to his side, and beneath his rib cage she heard the sound of his heart, a series of steady beats. She told them he wasn't dead. She smiled at them, but they continued to look skeptical, wiping at their eyes. She looked up toward the car, where Madama remained seated behind the wheel.

Suddenly the boys broke into an excited chatter that she could hardly understand. They all talked at once, and the only words she could catch were "doctor" and "hospital." She couldn't believe Madama could stay in the car.

"Momento," she told the boys, and she stood up to walk back to the car. The boy who had jumped onto the hood still stood in front of the car, as though guarding it.

Madama rolled down the window. "Get in this car this instant."

"We have to help him. He needs a doctor. We can take him."

"Are you defying me?"

Antonia looked at the ground. The dirt was littered with bottle caps and broken glass and cigarette butts.

Madama rapped her knuckles against the door. "Look at me when I talk to you. I didn't hit that child. This is a trick."

Madama's green eyes looked sharp and her mouth had become a grim line. Antonia thought of Madama's broken nose, the lie about tailgating.

"The minute we drive away, that little thief will jump up and run down the street. Get in this car!"

"We have to help." She looked at the little one in the dirt, and then looked Madama squarely in the eyes. "If you don't help him, I won't do it."

Although it was only a few moments, it seemed to Antonia that hours passed. Madama at last opened the car door and, clutching her purse to her chest, stalked toward the rear of the car.

The group of boys began to talk wildly, jumping, waving, crying, and again Antonia heard them talking of doctors and hospitals. At their feet lay little Nestor. Antonia worried that by now he was dead.

Madama elbowed away the crowding boys. "How much?"

The boys began to speak in a tumble of words.

"They think his neck is broken," Antonia explained to Madama. "They want the ambulance."

"Oh, foot. Ambulance, my eye." She turned to the oldest boy, who had come up behind her. "I suppose you're the ringleader. ¿Cuánto?"

The oldest boy hitched up his shorts and walked over to the injured one. He shook his head sadly, then crossed his arms over his chest.

Madama opened her purse. "Five dollars."

The boy shook his head. He explained to Antonia that the doctor was very expensive, he was a rich man who had no time for boys who sold gum on the streets, he had a very bad dog he kept on a chain in his yard and unless you could prove you had the money for treatment, he would turn the dog on you. He charged twenty American dollars just to look in your throat.

"Hump. Tell him five."

Without waiting for Antonia to interpret, the older boy squatted beside the little one's body and began to pat his head. He rubbed at his eyes and looked away.

From her purse Madama took a five-dollar bill and waved it over the older boy's head. The other boys watched the green flash of the bill. "Take it or leave it."

The boy stood. "Fifteen." It would cost at least that if the police had to be called in. The police in this town were very bad; they put people in jail for nothing, even gringas.

Antonia looked away. How could Madama bargain over the life of a little boy? Did she think the whole world turned around money, that you could buy anything and anybody? She pushed into the circle of boys and knelt beside the still body, her ear against his thin rib cage, angrier than she had ever been. When she looked to the front of the store she saw people passing on the sidewalk, but no one bothered to look. She stroked the little boy's back and listened again for the sound of his heartbeat, for the sound of breathing. He was still alive.

"Get away from him," Madama barked. "You'll catch tuberculosis. Ten," she shouted at the boy. "And that's it."

Along Nestor's skin there ran a quiver. Antonia drew back, frightened, then again lowered her head to listen. There came a choking sound, as though he were struggling for air.

Above her, Madama threw two bills into the air. The boys scrambled.

"Wait," Antonia called to them, "he's waking up." Nestor's eyes were squeezed tightly shut, his mouth struggling to stay still. She gasped: He was giggling. When she had bent to listen to his chest, her hair must have tickled him. He jumped up and ran after the other boys, who had reached the corner of the store where it met the street.

Madama went back to the car and jerked open the door. She blew three loud blasts of the horn, then started the engine.

They careened through the streets of Matamoros. Madama smoked. Three in a row, lighting one from the other, until the car was thick with smoke and Antonia thought she would be sick. She was just about to ask permission to roll down the window when Madama coughed harshly, rolled down her own window, and threw the half-smoked cigarette out into the street. "If you ever put me in a position like that again . . . I know how things work down here and you don't. All you know is the soft life you've had at home, but I'm here to tell you, Missy, down here they'll eat you up and spit you out. You'd have been working at the shirt factory by the time you were nine years old and if you were lucky you'd have a pair of shoes to call your own.

"You people just don't understand how hard it is to work for a dollar, to save, to do without so someday you can have something. You all want everything everybody else worked hard to get, and you want it all yesterday. Steal, beg, cheat. If I'd been lazy enough to think the world owed me a living, I'd be just where I deserved to be, in a filthy town with goats and dogs running wild on the streets. Flies so thick on everything you can hardly see what you're looking at. You'd better count your lucky stars your mama works for me. You don't *know* what trouble is. Just look out there."

A yellow dog scratched his skinny haunches along the wooden platform that formed a porch outside a storefront. On a bench outside the open doorway sat three men in T-shirts and tan trousers. Even from this distance Antonia could see that they were drunk and that their arms were covered with the patterns of vein-blue tattoos. A young girl in a tight pink sweater and a skirt so short her buttocks showed when she walked was crossing the street in front of the car. The men called to her and she sauntered toward them, choosing the middle one's lap to sit in, stretching her legs across the knees of the one on the end. As the Buick passed, Antonia could see that all three men had their hands on the girl and that she squealed and laughed and mock-slapped their hands away. In the space between buildings she saw a group of children jumping on three stacked mattresses, laughing and shrieking. Antonia crossed her arms; the children looked happy enough.

"That's what your mother ran from. You may be a citizen, but she's not, and if she had to . . ." Madama craned forward, looking out the window. "That turnoff ought to be around here somewhere. Look for Calle Cruz Street."

"On the right or left?" Antonia asked, glad the lecture was over, ashamed at her own gullibility, and when she heard her easy response to Madama's change of mood, she was suddenly angrier and more confused than she had been at any time since she learned she was pregnant. She wished she had never confessed to Madama, she wished she had held to her plan. In the days leading up to this one, after Madama had made the arrangements, when she had tried to sort things out, to put names to feelings, to decide right from wrong and good from bad, she either fell asleep, or ate until her stomach hurt, or cried. It wasn't that she didn't want to think about these things, it was that she couldn't.

"Get that little paper in my purse. Oh, never mind." Madama slowed the car while she dug in her purse and drew out a piece of paper that had been folded and refolded many times. "Don't lose this. The damn thing cuesta plenty."

Antonia looked at the map. It showed a straight line from the International Bridge through Matamoros to the western outskirts, where it made several turns to end at a starred spot on a dead end road. She thought of tossing it out the window, but again, she couldn't think beyond the act.

At the outskirts of town, the houses became even more tumbledown. Some had no windows or doors, others looked smaller than the Buick, than the machine shed at home. Children were everywhere, and dogs roamed the barren yards between hulks of rusted machinery. At one house near a dry arroyo, several goats stood on the hood of a car, and as the car passed by, Antonia saw one goat butt another off into the dirt.

"There," Antonia said, pointing at the wooden sign for Calle Cruz. "Turn left."

In the center of the small patio at the house's entrance grew a broad-crowned catclaw acacia, its yellow flowers like ragged cotton bolls against the roof tiles. Two red hens and a barred rock rooster scratched in the raked dirt around the tree.

Madama took an envelope from her purse and handed it to her. "There's a hundred dollars in there, and I'll find out if . . . I'll pick you up in two hours."

a routine procedure

The room seemed nice enough, the walls whitewashed; against one wall was a bed with bright woven pillows, a card table, two chairs. A curtained doorway led to another room Antonia could not see into, but a chemical smell reminded her of the biology lab at school and she was reassured. "It's Martha Ann, but you can call me Marty," the nurse said, smiling.

Marty took a white smock from a peg behind the door and put it on over her jeans and the pretty blouse with the lacy sleeves that Antonia thought looked like angel wings. She wanted to ask where Marty had bought it; she would like to have such a blouse. She supposed Marty was older than she looked—she would have to be in order to work here, she imagined. She wondered when the doctor would arrive.

Marty pulled her long, straight hair into a knot at the top of her head and secured it with a rubber band, then took a seat at the card table and motioned for Antonia to sit across from her. From her pocket she took a notebook and flipped through the pages. "You're eighteen, this says."

Antonia nodded.

"Well, that's good, at least. If I see one more thirteen-year-old in here . . ." Marty scanned the information in the notebook. "Eight weeks along."

"Maybe a little more than that," Antonia told her.

"Well, a few days won't matter. You have the money?"

Antonia gave her the envelope and followed Marty through the curtained doorway into another room, where a large enameled cabinet lined one wall and in the center stood a sheet-covered table. For the first time she noticed how tiny Marty was; her smock seemed to swallow her. The hem of her jeans was ragged, cut in a kind of scallop where her heels had rubbed at the denim. She had a peace sign necklace like Raleigh's. "In a few hours you won't even remember this," Marty was saying. She went to a basin and dipped her hands into the water, then took a bottle from beside the basin and uncapped it. A sharp, clean aroma filled the small room.

She patted a high table, indicating that Antonia should use the wooden box at its foot to step up and be seated. Then, abruptly, she said, "No, wait. Stupid me. You need to get undressed." From a chair she took a folded length of white cotton cloth. "Everything off. Wrap this around your middle. Do you need to pee?"

Antonia shook her head. "They said not to eat or drink anything yesterday or today."

"Sure? Sometimes it helps to try."

"I'm fine," Antonia said. She began to undress, turning her back to Marty. She felt weak, suddenly, and when she rose from bending to pick up her shoes, she felt her vision blur. She folded her skirt and blouse and underthings and placed them on the floor in the corner.

"All ready?" Marty stood at the foot of the table. "Hop up here and let's have a look."

Antonia climbed onto the table and followed Marty's order to lie flat. Beneath the sheet covering the table, she could feel the roughness of the wooden planks.

"You'll get used to it," Marty said. "Pretty soon you'll even be glad. But I'll get you a pillow when it's time."

When Antonia heard Marty taking what sounded like metal objects from the enameled cabinet, she began to shake as though she were cold. She propped herself on her elbows. "It's so cold," she said.

Marty's laugh was comforting. "That's normal," she said. "Lie back and try to relax, Toni. Do you go to school?"

Though she knew Marty was just making conversation, she felt better. "Harlan Bloch High. I'll graduate in a few weeks."

"Far out," Marty said. "What do you want to do after?" She gave a little laugh. "Not get married, I hope."

Antonia shook her head. "I was thinking of college. Maybe Pan American."

Again Marty said, "Far out," but her tone was disinterested. "Scoot all the way down so that your bottom feels like it's ready to hang off the edge. Knees up and apart."

"Wider," she said when Antonia opened her legs. "Like a little frog, okay?"

Something was wrong with the tendons in her thighs. She felt as though they had locked, like steel rods beneath the flesh of her legs; to open them wider would tear her in two. Marty had draped the cover sheet across her knees. Again she began to shake. "It hurts," she said. "When will the doctor be here?"

"I'm just going to look," Marty said. "Relax." She patted Antonia's knees, applying pressure to widen the distance between them. "Think about something else. Something nice. Think about college."

Antonia tried, but nothing would come to mind except the vision of Raleigh's plaid luggage beside the poinsettias. Suddenly, she wanted her mother.

"Get ready," Marty said. "I'm going to put the speculum in and it'll be a little cold."

When Antonia felt the push of the metal, her hips seemed to shrink and she felt her knees clamp shut.

"I can't do this if you're going to clam up every time I come near you."

"Sorry," Antonia said.

"I have to open you up this way so I can work." Marty's voice was businesslike, removed. Antonia felt a steady clicking of the metal between her legs, felt the motion of Marty turning something, a hard, steady widening. "There," Marty said, "that wasn't so awful, was it?"

When Antonia laughed, she felt contractions around the metal instrument. "No."

"All right, then. So far, so good." Marty's face disappeared behind the drape.

For what seemed like a long time, Antonia heard nothing, felt only slight probing. Trying not to think about what Marty was doing, about how she must look to her, she let her gaze roam the walls of the room, taking in the high window she hadn't noticed before. The window had a curtain made of what looked like a baby blanket, pale blue with a print of yellow ducks and rabbits. Again, she wondered when the doctor would arrive.

Her neck felt stiff and again she felt cold, but she tried to make her body go limp and supple; it would hurt only a little, Madama had said. If it hurt a lot, they would give her medicine. Suddenly, deep inside her, she felt three quick tugs that felt raw, metallic, like a blunt-edged knife scraping against something hard. Like the knife her mother used to shred the dense flesh of jicamas. Antonia tried to tolerate it, but the sound of the scrapes and the sick, sharp piercing against the hard thing bone-deep in her belly were more than she could bear.

"Hold still." Marty's voice was a scold. "I can't do this if you're moving."

"But it hurts."

"Grab the side of the table. I'm only looking now. Haven't you ever had a pelvic? Jeez, you're all over the place."

Antonia moved her hands to the table's edge and held on as Marty continued the movements. She felt herself straining upward from the planks of the table; only her hips and the back of her head were touching the wood.

"Stop," she shouted, "take it out. Take that thing out!"

There was a long silence, then she noticed that Marty stood at her shoulder. "Your friend . . . that woman . . . she said you were just a few weeks along. When *was* your last period? The truth."

Antonia started to sit up, but the speculum kept her on her back. "The middle of December."

"Oh, man," Marty said. She counted on her fingers. "Oh, God."

"I know." Antonia felt tears trickling past her ears. "I'm sorry."

"That woman told me . . ." Marty broke off, shaking her head. "You're four months along, at least. No way I'm going to mess with this. You'll just have to tell her—"

"What about the doctor? Doesn't he know how to—"

Marty's laugh was rueful. "You think for a hundred dollars you get a doctor?"

Marty removed the speculum and helped Antonia get cleaned and dressed. Her touch was brisk but tender, and Antonia sensed a dry sadness in the tiny woman. She was much older than Antonia had thought; the skin around her eyes seemed thin and bruised. When they got into the outside room, Marty lit a cigarette, then propped it in a bean-shaped metal basin. She handed Antonia the envelope. "I won't charge you. You might want to get a napkin or something. There might be some bleeding," she said. "And maybe some cramping. Good luck, kiddo."

The bright sunlight as she stepped outside into the patio was nearly blinding. After her eyes adjusted, she noticed that the hens and the rooster still scratched for insects around the base of the tree. Madama's car was not in the street. Antonia didn't care. She started walking.

a letter from los aires

The letter she'd dreaded for twenty years had finally come.

In all the time she had worked for Madama, Luisa had stolen nothing. Not a cup of sugar had entered the little house without Madama's permission. Other maids laughed about what they'd made off with. Her friend Altagracia Castañeda had once taken a whole baked ham from los Jenkins. The ham, Alta insisted to Señora Jenkins, had fallen to the floor at the exact moment Foster, the Doberman pup of the neighbors los Sissoms, burst through the open screen door. Señora Jenkins was forced to serve egg salad for Easter dinner. Later Altagracia had produced the shank as proof, pointing out the toothmarks along the bone; her son Henry had worked half the night with a kitchen knife and a piece of sandpaper. Others took little things—forks and knives, salt shakers. Today, for the first time, Luisa wanted to steal. She didn't know what. Just something to count for all those times she hadn't.

All morning she'd kept the letter tucked in the pocket of her apron. She had found it wedged into the screen door of the little house. It had not been left by the mailman; the other letters she had collected from the box she'd laid on the desk for Madama when she returned from her business today, but this one was for her. She brushed her hand across her pocket and felt the crackle of paper. She drew it out to look at it again: Luisa Cantú. In the corner, the official print of the United States Government. The envelope was thick, white as starch, in the center was black printing from a typewriter, and she could tell, by the way the printing at the top corner looked, that the letter meant she would have to go back.

Two days before, she had seen the men knock at her door. She had been coming around the corner of the big house with the laundry basket when she saw them, stiff in their uniforms. For one wild moment, she'd thought Antonia's father, the soldier Ben, had returned, but then she realized the men were INS, and she stepped back until she was concealed by the cocopomosa. Her mind raced. First to Sonny López. She had heard he was dead, just two months after his release from prison, but she didn't believe the rumors. There was no one else who would do such a thing. Madama, though crabby and bossy, could not get along without her. How many times had she said so? It had been years since she had threatened to send her back. At last the men had driven away.

The next day, Friday, when Madama had gone to town and she was alone in the house, from the upstairs window of Raleigh's old bedroom where she had been dusting she saw the car again, parked in the big circle driveway in front of Madama's door. When the doorbell rang, she crouched under the windowsill, her heart beating in bursts. She wondered if they could search. She had heard stories of people yanked out of bed. It struck her that both times the men had come, Madama had been gone. She crouched until she heard the crunch of gravel as the car pulled away.

Today they must have come as she vacuumed. She had not seen them. But they had left the letter.

Twenty years should count for something. She had walked the steps between houses as many times as there were stars at night. Antonia said the stars were there in the daylight too, but hiding in the light. How many more were there she couldn't see? That was how many steps she'd made. How many breaths she'd drawn, how many times her eyes had taken in the trees and flowers and birds, promising to look longer at them, to fix them in her mind so they would never leave? The years: the flowers she'd planted, row after row ringing the house—cannas and cosmos, daisies, poppies and snapdragons, lilies and azaleas, aloe and geranium, so many whose names she didn't know but whose ways she knew so well it was as though they were written in her blood. These meant more than paper, than one paper. Antonia said that every seven years a person had a whole new body—new skin, new hair, new muscles, and new bone. Here, she had become a new person two times over. How could some writing on a letter mean more than that?

Careful not to disturb Madama's papers, she began to dust the beautiful dark wood of the desk. She brushed away the web a spider had spun between a lamp and the framed picture of don Tomás and Señor Ike. At thirty-seven, she was too old to run away. You ran away once, and what came to you from that first running was what you were to stay with. You didn't run back to what you'd run from. And where else could she run? To the northern towns, where people worked in factories dark as great square monsters and there was no sun? Those who went to the hill country came back with fingers like raw meat from the spikes of cotton bolls, fingers stained black from picking pecans. Besides, once la migra caught you, you were caught; they knew who you were and where you went. Nowhere you could run would be far enough. She saw herself in the migra truck with its bars in the back like a big cage. Dropped in the dust of Mexico with nothing but her clothes. Sometimes, lately, she caught herself remembering her former life with smiles for her mother, for Rafael, for herself barefoot in the dry hills, carrying the corn but dreaming of blue heaven. But it had not been sweet there, not at the end. And her house, her precious home. Her daughter. Her beautiful, smart Antonia would walk away from everything she could have here toward the nothing that was waiting for her in Mexico. That was if she chose to come. She didn't have to. Luisa hoped she wouldn't. And, beyond all reason, she hoped she would. She wondered how Tavo would find them.

Madama had been mean-mouthed and angry for days, and Luisa searched her memory for what she might have done wrong. There had been a chipped plate. Another spot on the bedroom carpet from Little Dixie, the puppy Madama had chosen from the last litter Miss Evelyn Posey whelped before she died. Madama had trained Little Dixie to wet on newspapers. So severe had this training been that now each time the nervous little dog found paper on the floor, she squatted, automatic. It had been Madama's custom to drop her *Better Homes and Gardens* magazines on the floor beside her bed, and every morning, though she'd ceased the practice, there was a damp yellow blotch, sometimes a foul-smelling pile, and stubborn Madama would not put her foot on the floor in any other place. The bedroom was beginning to smell. But these wrongs, Luisa decided, were not enough.

There was only one thing that might make Madama angry enough to send her away, but she was certain she knew nothing of the fools Antonia and Raleigh. She finished dusting the desk's legs and stood up, suddenly light-headed. A chill began in the center of her back, just between the two wings of her shoulders, then raced along the skin and down to her hands. It was as though los aires, having searched for her, had sewn themselves into the currents of air and wind and had made their way into the big square ducts of the air conditioner in Rio Paradiso, Texas, to find her with her dust cloth idle. Something bad was going to happen; she knew it like she knew her own breath.

Alone in the house today—with Antonia on a class field trip and Madama gone to Brownsville—she felt as lonely as she had ever felt, as unsure of her place in the world. Deep in her stomach there was a kind of buzzing, at the back of her throat a taste like old pennies. She wrapped the cloth around a toothpick and began to work the point into the carved wood of the desk legs. Maybe it was just the large, cool rooms. Nothing was true yet. Inside the envelope was what was true, but until she opened it, she didn't have to know. The letter in her pocket seemed heavy as iron, and she wanted to sit down. But sitting in the house was not allowed. She would go home at lonche, rest, then in the evening Antonia would be back to read the letter to her. She tried to imagine the terrible words.

To keep los aires away, you shut the doors and windows, the way you boarded up for a hurricane, taping glass, nailing plywood, shoving furniture in front of windows. Here was the answer: Shut the door. Here was the net to fall in, to hold her up: She couldn't read. If she couldn't read, how could she be expected to obey the letter?

She would hide it under her mattress. If they caught her and pointed their fingers and asked her why, in twenty years, she hadn't tried to get papers, she would say she didn't know about the law. To pass the test, Amparo had told her a long time before, you had to know how to read. How could she know about a law if she couldn't read? It would all work together. And it would not be a lie. And if they came again and caught her and she had to go, at least she would have more time to think about what to do.

When Antonia was in the first grade, she had tried to teach her to read. "Now we'll play school," her daughter would announce, and she would make Luisa sit on an overturned lettuce box while she pointed the end of a wooden spoon at words in her book, a bossy little teacher. She could write her name, *Luisa,* and Antonia taught her to print *Cantú.* She had learned the English ABC's, and how to shout out *Stop, Go, Run, Spot, Dick,* and *Jane.* She did not tell Antonia she could say them only because the first letters were bigger and she had memorized them that way. After the first letters, nothing made sense. She thought of herself at the Bible school in Salsipuedes, and burned with shame that she'd believed Señor Miller when he called her his best pupil. With her daughter, she always mixed up *Spot* and *Stop,* and Antonia would get so angry that Luisa would have to laugh and tickle her for being so stern. And the game would be over.

On Madama's desk there was a pug-faced doll with wild green hair, naked and no bigger than her fist. A troll, Madama called it, saying, with what seemed to Luisa to be great satisfaction, how ugly it was. Luisa picked it up. It seemed that in its face there was the same amount of good as there was evil. It reminded her of something, something from the old time, but she didn't know what. She dropped it in her apron pocket, where it made a hard lump she felt throughout the day. In a way, it took her mind off the letter. But when the time came to return home, she retrieved the troll and set it on Madama's desk, fluffing the hair so it looked like green flame.

That evening as she knelt beside her bed, preparing to slide the letter into the coil of a spring, she realized that her solution was wrong. Fifteen years and still she didn't know what to do with the box she'd buried behind the oleanders. The longer it stayed there, the larger it grew, and sometimes in the night she would wake to a horrible quiet and know she'd again had the dream. The box had become her house, dark and buried and covered with piles and piles of soil, roots growing through the windows, white and furred and smelling of old onions. Someone was digging, and she felt the bright slice of shovel above, the ground shaking and crumbling.

Briefly, she wondered about the last time she had seen don Tomás, the papers he had spoken of, whether they had to do with her, but then she pushed the thought away: That time was past, buried as surely as the box.

She propped the letter on the sugar bowl in the center of the table. Honesty was the best policy. This was one of Madama's favorite sayings, and Luisa decided it was true. When Antonia came home, she would have her read the letter. Together they would go to Madama. She sat down for her cup of cold, sweet coffee and began to daydream that the reward for honesty would be that Madama would allow Antonia to stay in the little house until she finished school, and she spent the evening working on the white dress she was making for Antonia's graduation.

the fence

Antonia wanted to take off her shoes. They were the white canvas sneakers she had worn for school all year, but now they burned her feet as she walked. She had tied one of the laces too tightly back at the house on Calle Cruz. The knot seared into the bones at the top of her foot. But to bend down to loosen it might disturb some balance inside her. In the quiet stretches of walking, when no voices and no music came spilling out of the little shacks and cantinas she passed, when no cars rumbled by on the dirt roads, it was almost as though nothing had happened.

She kept to the side of the street—sometimes there was a board sidewalk she could have walked on, but to do that would have put her close to the open doors of cantinas and little stores, to the people, mostly men, who lounged outside them. Many of the little stores had big red and white Coca-Cola signs nailed along the walls, or Pepsi or 7-Up signs with their green bubbles rising to break into the air. Her throat felt dusty and she could almost smell the sweet fizz. She wished she had money to buy something to drink. She patted her skirt pocket to make sure Madama's envelope was still there.

She continued along the road she was almost sure had been the same one she and Madama had taken on their way through town. Sometimes the things she passed—rusting cars, weed-grown vacant lots where people had planted vegetables, tomatoes, squash vines trailing over the old tires that seemed to be everywhere she looked—looked exactly the same, but at other times nothing seemed familiar. Had she seen the tall, barbed-wire-topped fence around this factory with its smokestacks casting thick shadows all the way to the road? She was certain of her direction, though: north. The sun was over her left shoulder. Back in Rio Paradiso, school would be letting out and her mother would be waiting for her to come walking down Grand Texas from the bus. She didn't want to think about her mother. She had left for simple reasons, Antonia was sure, the clear difference between what was right and what was wrong.

Antonia stopped walking. From deep in her pelvis there rose a clench-
ing movement, as though something inside her was trying to swell at
the same time it was trying to turn inward, and she nearly doubled over
from the strength of it. Then, just as swiftly as it had come upon her,
the pain ceased, and she was left standing on the side of the street, her
head suddenly clear. She took a deep breath; she hadn't breathed, she
realized, while the cramp held. Now, however, nothing remained of
the feeling, and she resumed walking.

Ahead of her there appeared a wide-hipped woman carrying on her
shoulder a large basket. As Antonia drew nearer, she let herself look at
the woman's face. "Do you need something?" the woman asked.

Antonia asked her if the river was ahead.

The woman shifted the basket and pointed toward the east. "But the
bridge is on a different street." She shrugged. "You need something?"

"I'm looking for someone," she said. "My aunt is meeting me at the
river."

The woman set down her basket and took from the clothes piled
inside it a child's T-shirt. "Take this," she said, pressing the thin fabric
into Antonia's hand. She bent to pick up the basket and, shouldering it,
began to walk away, muttering, shaking her head.

The T-shirt's neckband was frayed and the fabric had gone gray with
washings. The woman was probably a loca, carrying old clothes in a
laundry basket, pressing them on people as gifts. Carrying the T-shirt,
Antonia began to walk faster; if she could believe what the woman had
told her, the river was close. At the next alley, she would cross over to
the other street where the bridge would be. Maybe Madama would be
waiting for her there.

Cooking smells—onions, peppers, cominos, the acrid odor of some
kind of meat—wafted toward her from a small cinder-block building at
the corner of a dirt alley and she felt a knot form in her stomach, a
tightening twist that rose to the back of her throat, sour-tasting and foul.
Suddenly, from the open windows came a noise that sounded like several
large pans crashing to the ground. She heard a curse, then a yelp and
squeal that sounded like a dog being struck, then several dogs yapping
and snarling. The cursing and pot banging grew louder as she neared
the open doorway of the kitchen, and just as she passed the door a pack
of yellow dogs boiled out into the alley and streaked past her. The lead
dog carried in his teeth what looked like a long, gray string of sausages—
menudo, maybe—and the others snapped and snarled and chased him.

Then the pack disappeared around the corner and into the street and she was again alone in the alley.

Gripped by a pain that seemed to clutch her from behind, she leaned against the wall of the next building. If she could only sit down. She waited, doubled over, her back to the wall, hoping the pain would diminish, but it seemed to pierce her from the inside out, a radiating wave of ache and pull, causing her breath—when she could think to breathe—to come in ragged bursts.

In the clear spaces during the pain when she could breathe and when her vision cleared, she was aware of a wetness between her legs, and she looked down at her skirt. There was nothing on the plaid fabric, but when she let her gaze travel to her feet she understood what the woman had been trying to tell her: Down the inside of her leg, like an exposed vein, ran a branching runnel. Her white shoe had caught it and was now dappled with bright new blood, the rust-red of older blood, drying.

She used the T-shirt to wipe at her calf, then, making sure there was no one to see, she tucked the T-shirt under her skirt, inside her panties. She would have to hurry now, even faster, and she couldn't take the main street but would have to find her way through the alleys to the river, alleys that were becoming increasingly shabby and frightening, barely more than dirt paths that led through a maze of lean-to shelters and piles of rubble. She tried to remember how the Mexican side had looked from the bridge—there had been those children playing in the tires. Surely she could find that place and wade across. The river would wash away the blood. She began to walk as fast as she could, guarding her abdomen with her forearm.

When she passed by the ramshackle structures that lined the narrow alleyway she looked away, hurrying from the calls of several women who looked up from a washtub to beckon to her. Above the women's heads stretched clotheslines strung with grayed laundry. Ahead of her in the dirt a naked baby crawled, followed by a small girl who crooned and hovered like a mother bird. Antonia side-stepped them, jerked away when the girl pulled at her skirt and asked for money. A thin white dog came out from under a pile of packing crates to nose at the baby, then began to follow Antonia, sniffing at her heels.

She made her way past clothesline after clothesline, ropes strung from packing boxes to tin sheds, reminding her of a great web. Everywhere she looked there were signs that people lived in this maze of wood and galvanized tin and old tires. She threaded her way through, stopping only once to decide whether to turn the corner where the dirt path seemed to branch. When the dog licked at her ankles she kicked at him.

Suddenly she was walking uphill and the wood and tin and clotheslines and tires seemed to fall away around her. The air was somehow lighter, and she knew she had reached the river.

A tall mesh fence separated the shanty town from the riverbank beyond. Around the base of a pole, shards of glass shone in the sunlight, sparkling, brown and green and blue. Windblown trash and paper littered the fence line. Low on the fence someone had made the design of a star by stuffing paper cups into the mesh. And there, there at the bottom of the slope made by the levee where she stood, was the river.

Children playing at the water's edge—they were not the same ones she had seen before, she could tell—threw handfuls of sand into the slow brown flow, laughing. When they saw her at the fence, they stopped their game, shouting at her. One of them began to run along the bank, waving his arms, pointing at something along the fence row and a short distance down. From the children's gestures, she guessed that what he was pointing toward must be important, but she couldn't hear what they were shouting; another cramp had closed off her senses, so strong it drove her down so that she crouched among the broken glass.

She heard them calling to her. The pain had eased and she looked up at the excited faces peering at her through the fence. "Here, here. Two centavos for a message!"

One of the larger boys cuffed the small one who had spoken. "Five, stupid," one of the bigger boys said. "She is rich. Look at her earrings!" He asked her if she spoke Spanish.

After her nod, the boy explained that they were in charge of the hole in the fence and that for five centavos they would show her how to get through. A gringa in a car was looking for her. She had offered them a lot of money to find her. But they would help her run. Many people, the boy explained, used this hole, especially at night. It was the best hole, he assured her, the lucky hole; no one who used it was ever caught on the other side. The river was perfect here for crossing—sand almost to the middle, many weeds to hide behind. Too far from the guardhouse to see. Not far enough so that the mean migra up the river got you. They had dogs that would crush your ribs.

"I don't have any money," she said. "Where is the lady?"

The largest boy held out his palm. "Give us your earrings. One for the hole. The other if we take you across."

She reached up to remove the earrings. "Where?"

The boy took the earring, gave it a quick bite, then began to run along the side of the fence. "Come this way," he called.

She had thought only to make her way across the river and back home, but now she realized that Madama would be angry when she found out she was still pregnant, and suddenly it was important that she hide from Madama.

She followed the fence line for a few yards before the next pain welled up from her belly and she had to stop moving. She grasped the fence, panting until it passed. A few posts ahead of her, the group of children waited.

There was only a slight depression in the dirt where the wires of the fence had been cut close to the pole to form a flap. Antonia stepped into the depression while the boys held the flap, and in one simple step, she was through.

She began to descend the bank toward the wide, low river. She had to walk with her back straight in order to make her way down the embankment without tipping forward, and this made her legs feel strangely unmoored from the earth. It hurt her head, now, to walk; each step felt like a shock of electricity. She made it to the flat sandbar at the bank before the next pain gripped her and she squatted at the river's edge.

She was dimly aware of the boys telling her that this was not the place to cross, aware of one of them pulling at her skirt, but she paid no attention. And then it seemed easiest just to lie down.

•   •   •

Above her was the white, wheeling passage of a flock of birds. Gulls, she thought, from the mouth of the river where it emptied into the Gulf of Mexico, with their white flash of wing, their far-off skirling calls like a high, thin lullaby, and when the men appeared above her, their white shirts bright as ghosts or angels, she knew that two of the gulls, curious, solicitous, had swooped down to find her in the warm place she'd found among the weeds beside the water, a scooped-out place in the sand where she felt as though she were cradled in the softest blankets, and the sounds she heard coming from their mouths were some kind of low gull-language meant to soothe.

She felt their feathers brush against her face, her arms; as the great birds moved above her, she smelled how warm they were, bird-warm and close. She felt them pulling at her, lifting her, brushing something from her clothes with their soft wings. And then all pain and tiredness was taken from her body and she was flying with them but it was nothing like the flying she had done in dreams. There was nothing to look down on, and she was not upright, but on her back and looking up—looking all ways at once—so that she could both see herself and at the same time be herself, and she understood that she was seeing things not through her eyes but through her body. They took her to a place where a dark lady in a white gown called to her, saying that she should wake up. But it was too warm and she wanted to sleep.

When she woke, she was in the backseat of Madama's car, wrapped in a blanket with a medicine smell. Between her legs was a full feeling, as though cotton had been packed inside her. The car was moving through the night. The birds were shadow flickers from the lights of passing cars; the sound their wings made was the whoosh of tires on wet pavement.

She thought she asked a question, but she wasn't sure until Madama said, "Nothing. You're still pregnant." For a time, they rode in silence, and then Madama said, "You're going to tell your mother that I found you trying to run away, and that I brought you back. We'll work the rest of it out later."

• • •

It was late when Antonia returned. Luisa sat at the table, the letter before her. When she saw the way Antonia looked as she let herself into the little house, she gasped at the sight of the hollowed, shrunken look on her daughter's face. She rose and went toward her, arms open.

Antonia shook her head. "No, Mama. Don't."

Luisa ignored her, taking her into her arms and holding her while she sobbed.

Later, when Antonia put on her white nightgown, Luisa would notice the blue veins in her daughter's breasts, the puffed look of the skin on her upper arms and she would remember the thought she'd had weeks before when Antonia had refused to try on the graduation dress so Luisa could fit it. Now, hugging her daughter, she felt the thickening of her waist, the round hardness of her belly, and even before Antonia could get the words out to tell her, she began to croon to her that she knew, she knew, and that it would be all right. Though her daughter didn't say, Luisa's heart ached with the knowledge that Antonia had tried to run away.

Toward morning, careful not to wake Antonia, who slept fitfully behind her curtain, she crept to the stove and clicked the knob. She waited until the element glowed red enough to light the little kitchen, hot enough to make her face give off heat as she turned away from it to take the letter from its place, and then she touched the corner of the letter to the coil until the paper caught.

7

the bleeding heart

On Monday, not two days after the fiasco in Matamoros, and before Eddie could decide what to do about it, Raleigh—she had thought he was taking his final exams—came home from San Marcos. Somehow he had bought a car, which she heard before she saw. She had been seated on the upstairs toilet, trying to be patient—Dr. Bonney had said she'd be a candidate for an operation if she didn't stop straining—when she heard a gurgling rattle, like an out-of-whack washing machine. She couldn't get up, so she sat, wondering what the noise could be. At last she'd finished, and when she went downstairs, she saw her barefoot son in frayed cut-offs and a ragged T-shirt. Sporting a scraggly beard. His glasses taped with thick black tape. He looked awful. In four months he'd turned into a hippie.

Though she was shocked, she tried to smile. He gave her a stiff-armed, formal hug; his clothes gave off the aroma of some piercing, foreign-smelling oil that made her sneeze.

Speechless, she followed him to the kitchen, where he opened the refrigerator and stood perusing its contents. He had quit school, he told her. There was no point in taking finals. The world was in a shambles, and he believed in none of what it stood for.

"D-R-A-F-T. What do you think that stands for?" She had meant to be rational, but suddenly, in the face of this news, she couldn't control herself. She felt a great swelling heat, as though the hot flashes she'd endured a decade before had returned, and her reason departed. She called him a pup and an upstart, relishing the juicy spurt of those names. "Who do you think you are," she said. "There's a war going on, in case you hadn't noticed. If you aren't in school, you'll . . ."

He took out the milk jug and sloshed the liquid around before taking a swig. "I don't believe in the war."

"Well, whether or not you believe in it, it's a fact. It's here. I mean there. And I did not—" she slammed her palm against the gaping refrigerator door—"suffer labor for nothing. It's a necessary war, Mother just doesn't want you in it."

"Why?"

"What do you mean, why?"

"Let me understand this, Mother. You're a hawk in dove's clothing—"

"Don't patronize me."

"It's a good war, but you don't want me in it?"

"That's right."

Again he tilted the milk jug to his mouth and drank.

"And please use a glass while you're under my roof."

He lowered the jug, wiped his mouth with the back of his hand, then yanked the door open. "Can you tell me why you don't want me in it?"

Skinnier than he'd been when he left at Christmas, with his scanty beard, he looked like a scrawny, unkempt mouse and made her think of Thomas. For a moment she stood, unnerved, but then she recovered her irritation. "Well, Mister Lawyer, it's because . . ."

His gaze was level, threatening, startlingly close. "Do you think I don't know I'm exempt?"

She was speechless.

"Do you know the last time you told me I did something right?"

"What?"

"Do you even remember the last time you told me you loved me?"

"That kind of thing goes without saying."

"Have you ever," he asked, his voice measured and meditative, and she could tell he had rehearsed the words, "had a simple feeling in your life? An honest one?"

She felt punched. All she'd tried to do for him. Feelings, it was! She who had been both mother and father, who had seen to it that he wanted for nothing. Her friends' children were at Baylor and SMU, joining fraternities and sororities. Joan's boy had already passed the Texas bar exam, and Ann Dell's oldest had a scholarship at Tulane. For her trouble, she was rewarded with a hippie. She wanted to march the young scut down the flagstone path to Lu's and haul Antonia away from her truculent mooning and say, "Look at this mess! I drove the streets of that godforsaken place alone. I bribed street urchins. Sneer at money if you want, but how do you think I got her out of that filthy clinic? But I did it, and I did it for you." But she didn't want him to know about the girl, so instead she said, "And just how do you plan to support yourself?"

Raleigh snorted. He muttered something about fodder for the military-industrial complex. Hunkered down before the open refrigerator, he opened the cold-cut drawer.

"Do you think you can just come down here and live off the fat of the land?"

Her son slammed the drawer shut. A bottle of catsup tipped over and rolled to the back of the shelf. "I don't want to live off the fat of the land. I don't even want to live here. The war . . . Daddy taught me that . . ."

At the mention of his father, the words rose up in her to dash his sanctified self-righteousness as he talked about principles and convictions, courage and honor and equality and oppression and the masses and how she was a dupe and a symbol of all that was wrong with the world. But she held back the words. Her son had turned Thomas into an icon. "Don't you speechify at me. What kind of mumbo jumbo are they teaching you at that place? You sound like a communist!"

He only smiled, which infuriated her.

"Your grandmother was related to Robert E. Lee," she yelled, "and your father, whom you are so fond of quoting, was a personal friend of Dwight David Eisenhower, himself a general. We are people of some standing in the Valley, and I won't have . . . don't you dare say those things about your country!"

He righted the catsup bottle and closed the refrigerator quietly. "I won't," he said. "I'm going to Canada."

In a way, she was glad.

•   •   •

The next morning, while Raleigh was still asleep, she went to town. Though they were scarce in the Valley, she found several plaid woolen shirts in Raleigh's size. She bought jeans and socks. As a little joke to make up for their argument the night before, she had the clerk gift wrap a compass. She would joke about the North Woods. Mark Trail. Or—who was that cartoon character he'd loved, that Canadian Mountie—Dudley-something? Dudley Doright! No, she wouldn't use that; he would take her joke the wrong way. But she would apologize. In the messy heat of their argument the night before, she had seen a fragile kind of pain in her son's face, as well as fear, and though he was young and shortsighted, she understood that it had cost him something to talk back to her, and her heart had gone out to him. Perhaps she had been too hard on him, but he should understand that she wanted only the best. She could afford to give a little. She would tell him he was doing the right thing. She would tell him she loved him; she was amazed that he would question this. Later, she would sort things out. On her way out of town, she turned the car around and went to the bank to withdraw a thousand dollars to give him.

When she got home, she found Lu sitting on the front steps by the driveway, apron over her face, weeping. When the woman looked up, Eddie had to look away from the sight. Lu looked just the way Antonia had with the street boys in Matamoros: a glare of blame that held her in its heat.

"What on earth is the matter?" Eddie asked, brushing past her to enter the house.

Lu stood, followed her, then drew in her breath to speak in English so perfect, so practiced-sounding, that it stunned Eddie almost more than what she said: "The children have run away."

All her motherly feelings toward Raleigh departed. At first she decided to let him suffer the consequences, but then, able to see around corners, she realized what those consequences would be, and that next the two runaways would plop themselves down on her doorstep. Her foresight turned another corner and saw embarrassment, shame, finger-pointing. Marriage.

In the Valley phone book there were two listings under "Private Investigators": Cisco Camacho, Esquire, and Eldon Wing, Jr. Though she preferred to patronize white-run businesses, there was really no choice; each time she passed the derelict Wing place across the road from the Hundred Acres, Eddie remembered the way she'd felt when she'd yelled about gas and then trotted off to her affair. She had seen Eldon, Jr. a few times in town—once at the post office, another time at the grocery store—and each time she'd had to convince herself that the curious look the rawboned, slack-jawed man gave her was more a function of his inferior intellect than of his memory.

Camacho kept a sweatbox of an office above the Mexican flea market on Temple Street in Martha. In the breast pocket of his guayabera shirt, a shirt so thin his purple nipples showed through the fabric like bruised eyes set in his hairless chest, he kept a plastic pencil pouch from Nutrena Feeds lined with neat rows of Q-Tips. Squinting as he cleaned his ears, he listened to her story. After she had finished, he asked for up-front cash. She hesitated, but wrote a check, which he eyed suspiciously but took. "I been burned before," he said. "When it clears, I go to work."

He delivered in less than a week, giving her an address in Corpus Christi where Raleigh had a job washing dishes in a diner that catered to roustabouts on the offshore rigs.

Eddie laughed. "The military-industrial complex."

"Beg pardon?" said Cisco, pulling a Q-Tip from his ear.

"Nothing," she told him. "A private joke."

"That'll be another fifty," he informed her. "Cash."

She made a reservation at the Holiday Inn in Corpus, had the Buick serviced, and packed a bag for an overnight stay. She told Lu she was going after the children, and to her maid's reproachful glances said, "You should just be glad I'm able to." Resolute and well prepared, she felt like a businesswoman as she pulled out of Rio Paradiso and onto the highway. Perhaps she should get into real estate. Get her license.

Except for the flight to Charlottesville when she'd taken Raleigh to UVA, this distance was the farthest she'd been from home in twenty years, and she reflected, as she drove up the Gulf Highway, that she ought to take a vacation after all the trouble settled. A cruise, maybe. Nila and Ann Dell had gone several times to Las Vegas, they shopped in Dallas and Houston, and Joan gushed about her trips to Santa Barbara to visit her daughter Mrs. Doctor Carol Kay, a Miss Texas runner-up now married to a plastic surgeon. And blah-blah-blah. She'd stayed home because . . . well, she didn't know. There was really no reason.

As she neared Corpus Christi, she began to practice her speech. She knew exactly what to tell Raleigh, exactly how to work Antonia. But she had to get the words just right so that over the truths she knew and the falsehoods she would tell, the shadow of possibility fell just right.

8

common law

"But when do you *think* it might be?" Antonia wanted to know.

Raleigh, hand on the doorknob in their rented walk-up just off Bayside Drive, a backpack made of a fringed Saltillo blanket slung over his shoulder, said, "We're supposed to close at three, but guys are always coming in. Maybe around four?"

She stood at the sink, washing the plates from the meal she'd made on the hot plate—Van de Camp's pork and beans with hot dogs—watching the water swirl in the drain. Many times she had imagined such a sweet, homey scene, the wife at her domestic tasks. But she saw now how quickly a simple sink could turn into something else—an anchor, an altar—and she didn't know how to move away from it to tell him what she needed.

And then it happened, as it often did with Raleigh, that he read her mind, and she felt him come up behind her. He put his arms around her waist. "I'll miss you," he said. "I'll be back as soon as I can."

This was why she loved him. That he seemed to know her when she sometimes didn't know herself. She turned to kiss him, tasting the Dial soap he had just used, smelling, in his hair, the sheets of the bed they shared. After he left, happy again, reassured, she began to straighten the room.

Two weeks they had lived together. Two weeks and five candles, five different layers of colored wax that dripped down the sides of a Mateus bottle. At the end of their first day together, exhausted by the drive as well as by their talk the night before, when they had first entered this room—large, bay windowed, a tiny bathroom off the kitchen corner—there had been a moment when they were unable to look at each other. But that had lasted only a few minutes. Now it was as though they'd lived together all their lives.

A few more weeks of work in Corpus should give them enough to get them up to Dallas, he'd told her, and from there they'd head toward

Denver, then up to the Al-Can Highway. "Why don't we just go to Mexico?" she'd asked. "It's warmer." She wished they could stay closer to her mother, but this she didn't tell him. He was never able to make his reasons clear to her, but it had to be Canada.

She would be happy to stay here. She loved their little walk-up on the winding street with its houses painted in Popsicle colors—banana, lime sherbet, tangerine—the palms and gulls, their tiny balcony with its rickety railing, where on their first night together they'd sat to share a bottle of warm Blue Nun.

He told her he had never been happier, in spite of everything. Each day before he left for work they took long walks along the beach, talking. Entranced by her first time at the water, she examined each shell, each jellyfish, each strand of sea grapes. Neither could she get enough of the smell of the sea, brine and sand, oil and fish, the wind over water.

Sometimes, she thought, it was as though they'd picked up a conversation they'd dropped a decade before. They agreed that in a way they had always been best friends, like brother and sister. When they talked about growing up, some of the things he told her made her hate Madama even more. One time, when Raleigh was eight and they had just moved into the big house, she'd sent him the half-mile to the Piggly-Wiggly, his Radio Flyer loaded with Coke bottles to return for the deposit money. She'd counted the bottles, figuring exactly what kind of change she wanted: ten quarters, seven dimes, and five nickels. Something like that. Even now, he couldn't get it straight. He'd come back with the wrong change four, maybe five times, and each time she'd yelled louder, meaner, why couldn't he carry out the simplest of orders? Then she'd sent him back. Finally, he'd quit, stopped in the wagon halfway between the store and home, crying. When she'd found him, she'd screamed that that, too, wasn't right, and that he should bear his responsibilities like a little man. "A little man," Raleigh said again, and Antonia could tell that the words troubled him even now.

"The only time I ever saw her cry was when she was watching Kennedy's funeral," Raleigh told her one day as they walked along the shore. "Crying about Jackie and Caroline and John-John. How noble Jackie was. A lady. That blood and breeding always told. Oh, yeah, and the veil! I remember the veil was this big deal. Mother went on and on about it. How it was so tasteful. Some kind of lost art or something. And then do you know what she said?"

A gull swooped low. Antonia said, "What?"

Raleigh kicked at a clot of tar and seaweed. "She said, 'Somebody should have told her that dress was too short.'"

Both she and Raleigh agreed that his mother was strange, but neither could figure out exactly what her problem was.

"I used to pretend your mother was mine, too," he told her. "She was so good and happy. I used to think my father and your mother would be the perfect parents."

She hadn't known what to say. She wondered if he had forgotten what he'd told her about around-the-block, about his father and her mother.

He did not press her about sex, and although she was grateful—she still felt sore and bruised—sometimes at night a powerful waiting feeling seemed to hang over the bed. One night as they lay together listening to the wind in the palms outside their balcony, the vast rush of the Gulf, she turned to him and moved down his body beneath the sheet. She kissed him until he grew hard and his scrotum drew up so tightly it made her want to put her hand between her own legs and she did, and when her hair brushed against the inside of his thigh he moaned and she took his penis in her mouth, tasting the faint earthy scent of wild mushrooms while he held her head and wouldn't let go. "Sorry, I'm sorry," she thought he whispered but she couldn't tell, and when it was over he drew her up and kissed her and without speaking they fell asleep.

They fought only about Vietnam. Sometimes Raleigh would stomp through the room, singing the Country Joe and the Fish song that she hated. "'And it's ONE, TWO, THREE, what are we fightin' for?'" he would yell. "'Don't ask me, I don't give a damn. Next stop is VEE-ET-NAM!'"

She would plead with him to stop, but sometimes he got wound up and couldn't. She tried to tell him how she felt with Tavo in Southeast Asia. He would say he understood, but then he would begin a harangue against the war that left her weak and confused. It was worse if he'd been smoking marijuana with the kitchen crew at the diner. Then he hated everything about everything. Nothing was any good. She wondered if he meant everything he said or if he said things because he thought they sounded good and everyone else was saying them.

At other times the grass made him placid and dreamy. "It's like nothing matters, man," he'd said, passing her the joint, trying to teach her. She tried, but the nips and sips, the breath-holding so the smoke would fill her lungs, the roachy way you had to hold the joint made her feel mean and masculine, slit-eyed and stupid. And she worried that it would hurt the baby. The three sharp tugs she had felt in Matamoros haunted her. And the cramps and the bleeding. Madama had told her that at the clinic in Matamoros they had said she would be fine, and she had taken all the penicillin Madama had given her, but sometimes she pictured the baby, still alive but torn, poked, damaged. She'd told Raleigh about her worries, but he brushed them away. On the night of the joint, she ached for someone to worry with her, and for the first time, in their second week together as she prepared for bed, she had been seized by a powerful longing for her mother. But at the moment she realized this longing, she remembered her mother's religion. Her mother's was a hybrid Catholicism, and Antonia could never tell which parts she would decide to believe at which moments. But about what had really happened in Matamoros—that Antonia had lain on the table and allowed Marty to scrape—her mother would never understand, and Madama's lie was easier than the truth.

Near dawn, Raleigh eased into their lumpy bed beside her. He nuzzled the cleft between her breasts. "You smell like plums," he said. She had fallen asleep with the radio on; Wayne Newton was singing "Danke Schoen." Raleigh smelled of cooking oil and beer, of the Volkswagen's oily, sun-beaten interior. His hand on her hip was warm, and she could feel the dishwater ridges in his fingers. As it often had in the past weeks, the question came to her—what am I doing? Sleepily, not caring what the answer might be, she made room for him, drawing the sheet over their bodies.

They were awakened by a rapid pounding at the door. Muzzy-headed, they scrambled into clothes. "Bet I'm the last person you expected to see," Madama said when Antonia opened the door. Antonia could not read her look; Madama seemed businesslike. A school principal making the rounds. She asked Antonia to leave while she spoke to Raleigh.

"Whatever you have to say," Raleigh said, moving to stand by Antonia, "you can say in front of her. We're married. Common law."

Madama made the chortling sound her mother often imitated. "Well, you might want to think again. I'm not the monster you all think I am, and what I have to say will—"

"I'll just leave," Antonia said.

Madama smiled curtly at her. "It won't take long. Give us a half-hour. Then I need to talk to you, young lady. Your mother is sick with worry. Just sick."

Antonia walked down the block toward the Gulf and sat on the sea-wall. She watched a gecko stalk a palmetto bug. She pictured her little mother twisting her apron, and Madama, who pretended to care about her, saying something mean.

Not ten minutes went by before she heard the Volkswagen start up, then chug along in reverse as Raleigh backed down their crooked street. She listened as he ground into first gear, as the little car sped away. Though he talked big about standing up to his mother, she should have known that against her he would be as powerless as the boy in the Radio Flyer.

When she returned to their apartment, she found Madama sitting at the table. "We need to get some things straight between us. So we can all go on." She motioned for Antonia to take a chair. "You know my son won't be back?"

There rose in her the urge to slap Madama, but she only nodded.

"Good," Madama said, "I knew you were a sensible girl. Now, I have a plan that makes a little bit better sense than this." Madama ex-plained what would have to happen next, and Antonia stared at the tabletop, picking at a burn scar in the Formica, understanding that she had known from the beginning that things could have been no different.

9

la llorona

Her daughter was back in the house, where she belonged. In the big house, Madama went about her days as before, and if she had not noticed the way Madama looked as though she were afraid or guilty of something, Luisa could almost believe she had imagined that the children had run away. She wondered what had gone on in Corpus Christi, but she was afraid to ask Madama, and if Luisa's conversation veered toward such questions, Antonia rose from her chair or from the bed and slammed outside. Luisa had stopped asking. Antonia seemed miserable.

Sometimes she moved slowly, and seemed hardly able to speak, as though she had been struck, at other times she was full of bitter answers to Luisa's questions. About her daughter's love for Raleigh, Luisa understood, and it came to her to use this pain to explain her own feelings for Madama, to tell Antonia there were those in life whom she would love beyond her power of reason—this had to do with time and living, difference and sameness, closeness, distance—and that when this love sent its roots into the heart there was no use to try to banish it with bitterness, which hurt the heart more than it hurt the roots, for this love would no more disappear than would the mesquite trees Joe Bonillas each year tried to poison, burn, or hack away, but which only cropped up thicker in the next one. But she held her silence. Nothing had come of the letter, and it was almost as though it had arrived in another life. She had asked at the market; all confirmed that Sonny López was dead.

Antonia went back to school to finish, although she didn't walk in the graduation. Luisa packed away the beautiful dress and threw herself into making ready for the baby, hemming flannelette for diapers, sewing receiving blankets, cutting out little shirts. "It's four months away," Antonia would say. "Time flies," she would answer.

To her surprise, Luisa's own mother's words began to fly out of her mouth at this time, and she remembered things she thought she'd long forgotten. Customs, sayings, rules, advice. Antonia rolled her eyes, and to any advice that began "In Mexico . . . ," her daughter said, "Stop it, Mama. It's a terrible place." Again she wondered exactly what had happened on the day of the letter. All Madama had said was that she had brought Antonia home, saying she'd found her trying to run away. An unspeakable suspicion rose in her mind, but she pushed it away. Not that.

But even in the face of these secrets, Luisa could barely contain her excitement about the baby. As she worked at the big house, she could hardly keep her mind on her tasks, and she made the trip down the path to check on Antonia many more times than she had to.

Joe Bonillas ordered from Sears a crib and a chest of drawers and they set them up beside Antonia's bed. For several days after that, Luisa had walked around with the ghost of a memory swirling around her head. Then, one evening when she opened her sewing box and saw a spool of red thread, she remembered, and she began to leave little bits of it around the house, stretching a length across the cradle to ward off los aires. When Antonia asked her about the threads, she shrugged, and when she found them tangled into balls from Antonia's attempts to pick them off, she silently replaced them.

One day a white wooden rocking chair tied with a yellow bow was delivered to the little house by Joe's nephew Randy Cruz. When Luisa asked him where it came from, Randy smiled. "My uncle says to tell you that you're such a wild woman that this might be the only way he can get you to settle down."

With Antonia, there were certain subjects she could not talk about. Madama, for one. Raleigh, for another. Even the subject of her work in the big house was off-limits. One day, making small talk, all she had said was, "If that dog makes peepee one more time . . ."

"You'll what, Mama? I think you like having to clean up that mess. You think somehow it makes you better. That it makes *you* right!" Luisa had shaken her head: How could cleaning up after a dog make her better? She made allowances for Antonia, though, remembering her own confusion about herself and Uncle and Chavela and the baby that would be Tavo.

Sometimes the baby was a safe subject and sometimes it was not. The weather was allowed. Her garden. How Antonia felt, her swollen ankles. Food. Luisa worried because all her daughter wanted to eat was stick potatoes from a can, washing them down with Coca-Cola. They'd gone to the doctor, who hadn't even heard of the wisdom of hot things and cold things. Still, Luisa tried to follow the doctor's advice about green things. One evening she had set a plate before her and Antonia said, "A jalapeño isn't a green vegetable, Mama," and they had laughed. In this moment she felt they had been restored to each other, and she wanted to tell her daughter about time and forgetting, but she held her silence. Whether she mentioned these or not, they would do their work.

They could talk about Tavo. Antonia loved to talk about their childhood, telling her of events she didn't know about—once Tavo had convinced some camp children that he'd seen an alligator in the canal and he'd sold them little clumps of dried refritos he said was alligator bait; another time, when she was in third grade and a boy had teased her on the playground, Tavo had punched him. "He was a good big brother to have," she said. "Just right."

One afternoon, as they were talking, Antonia said, "Something happened to him in junior high, though. I don't know what. But that was when he got so quiet and mad all the time and it was like I didn't know him anymore. You know those lost boys in Peter Pan?"

Luisa shook her head; her children knew things she did not.

"Well, he was like that. In this kind of land where there wasn't any . . . where he forgot . . . I don't know."

She sat down in the brown chair and picked up her sewing basket. She began to hum.

Antonia looked at her. "We had a wonderful childhood, Mama," she said. "I loved it here so much."

Luisa, remembering her daughter dreamy in the trees, the butterfly sundresses she had sewn, the way the children played, hoped it was true. "Did Tavo think so, too?" she asked.

"Oh, yes," Antonia said. "I'm sure he did."

One afternoon in the middle of July when she returned to the little house to rest, she found Antonia lying on her bed with a cloth on her forehead, the fan set on a chair beside her bed, blowing directly on her so that her hair blew in dark strings across the pillow. Luisa asked if she was sick.

"No, just tired. Bored. Hot. I wish we had some books. A television."

Her belly had grown large, and the sight of the stretched blue veins made Luisa's legs hurt as she crossed the room to the chest of drawers. She began counting the shirts and diapers, thinking that perhaps she should sew a few more, just in case.

A pair of plastic pants made her think of the black cord belt Tavo had once loved. Just as she began to wonder what had happened to it, she remembered her old dream of Tavo under the crowded, humming tree, the long grass ropes, and the worry she'd been holding back found its way into the room, and she said, "Sometimes I think he's hurt. Your brother."

Antonia stretched. "He just doesn't have time to write." She shifted, propping herself on her elbow. "Besides, they'd send somebody to tell us. We'd get a letter."

Luisa dropped the stack of diapers.

• • •

They used Madama's phone to call Joe, who made the other calls. And then they waited for the words: *service, courage, honor, painless, instantaneous.* A box would be sent. Not Tavo. His things. There was nothing else.

Joe saw to the arrangements. When the box arrived, Madama gave her two weeks off. Luisa wished she hadn't. She ached to work.

Antonia wept often. She raged at the war, at armies, at men, at the world. Once Luisa saw her daughter sitting beside the tractor tire, resting her head on her arms, alone, holding her sorrow with the curve of her body, like the picture of the two Marias at the tomb. "He was not your son," she wanted to shout. "He was mine!" She thought of her story of the hen who loved her two chicks the same and knew the truth, which was that in the moment of its loss a soul was dearest, and she worked to make herself remember that she was the mother of this strange grieving girl.

La Llorona had drowned her son because his father wanted to take him to a strange country. La Llorona knew that if her son died away from her, his soul would find no rest. These days Luisa thought often of the weeping, wandering mother and understood what she had not before, that there would be balm in holding in her arms the dying child, comfort, peace in sending him from her own hands into the other world. Then maybe she could weep. Here, without him, even her own body seemed a strange place, as though he had been torn from it but left no blood, no wound to mark the loss. He had vanished from the earth, inhabited a land no words, no touch, no tears could reach.

It seemed she witnessed the service from a great muffled distance, afterward remembering only the rows of soldiers, their abrupt, muscular hands, their stiff chests. There was no music, no comfort, and no river, only the feeling that she had sent her son to pass alone into a harsh, mysterious brotherhood.

• • •

One night as Luisa was preparing for bed, she heard noises outside. Thinking that the back door of the big house must be banging in the wind, which had been strong all day, blowing dust from the newly plowed bean fields south of the property, Luisa went outside and looked up the path toward the big house. Usually Madama spent her evenings in the sala watching television and arranging rows of cards in her games of solitaire, but on this night the kitchen lights had been on, and each time Luisa had checked, she'd seen Madama moving back and forth. Now she saw that the noise had come from Madama struggling to close the door while at the same time trying to balance something she carried. Luisa started up the path to meet her.

In the moonlight, Madama's face looked white and puffed. There were green shadows under her eyes. She held her mouth with the same stiffness with which she held her offering, a fruit salad, her specialty, oranges, coconut, pineapple, and sweet cream. Around the edges of the bowl she had arranged mint leaves and cherries. In the wind, a mint leaf blew away. "Damn it," Madama said. She handed the bowl to Luisa. "I made it for you. It's just a little ambrosia. I know you like it."

Luisa took the bowl.

"You can keep it," Madama said. "The compote, I mean."

Luisa thanked her.

Madama's hair rose from her forehead in a pale puff whipped by the wind. "I feel as though everything's gotten so out of hand. We need to get back on track."

Luisa nodded, but could think of nothing to say.

"You can keep the bowl," Madama said again. Luisa looked at the bowl; it was Madama's best footed crystal, usually kept on the high shelf in the china closet.

Dimly, Luisa noted that Madama looked miserable, on the edge of tears. "Lu," she said, "do you understand that I want to do right by you? That I'm sorry about him? Tavo? In the smallest of ways, I think I understand how you feel. We've both . . ."

There was a rustle in the oleanders next to the path, and then Antonia, her hair wild in the wind, her white nightgown blowing against her legs and belly, appeared at the edge of the lawn. She took a few steps toward Madama, then stopped. "You don't understand anything," she shouted. "You have no feelings!" She took another step toward Madama, but then turned away, sobbing. "I hate you." She ran awkwardly into the bean field.

Luisa, hearing her daughter's ragged breath, a thumping sound, as though of Antonia stumbling, bent down to set the bowl on the grass and started after her. She had taken only a few steps when she remembered Madama. She stopped, then turned, meaning to explain that Antonia was young, that she didn't mean what she was saying, but Madama was gone.

hurricane baby

In the wet, hot days of September, Hurricane Beulah struck the Gulf Coast. While the rest of the Valley was nailing down and boarding up, stocking batteries and ice and water, while squad cars and fire engines raced up and down the roads, their sirens moaning, Luisa and Joe drove Antonia to the little hospital at McAllen where—blue-eyed, squirming, red and perfect—the baby was born just as the eye of the storm passed over and the rains and wind began again.

The nurses joked that the baby should be named after the storm, but Antonia said her name was Beth. With the birth of the baby, Antonia seemed to shed the skin she had worn for the past months, for now her bruised look vanished and she smiled. Luisa had forgotten she was beautiful.

The nurses made over Luisa almost as much as they made over the new mother. "Mama Grande," they called her, even the Anglo nurses, and they asked her questions about her own babies, her own deliveries. Better still, they listened when she told them. They behaved as though she possessed some secret knowledge. Some moments, walking in the cool hospital halls, she could almost believe she did. She could imagine that the line between the living and the dead was like a long-forgotten language in the blood, its words the memory of breathing passed from one soul to another. But then, just as she thought she understood, her thoughts again were lost inside a terrible question, not of how as one life left the world another entered, but of how those who loved both lives should feel.

Joe stood outside the viewing window with Luisa for a long time, moist-eyed and marveling, once blowing his nose on a red bandanna. "A beautiful granddaughter," he said. "I wish she were mine." He did not ask who the father was. Not in the months before and not now. For this, Luisa loved him.

·   ·   ·

Madama paid a visit. Stiff, straight-backed, she entered the room, where Luisa sat beside the bed as Antonia dozed. "Don't wake her," Madama whispered. She'd brought a plant in a basket. "I don't know what kind it is," she whispered, "but if she doesn't want it, maybe you will." For the baby, she brought a soft blanket and a white lace christening dress, saying, "I don't know what you people's ceremonies are, but this will probably come in handy." The beautiful christening dress made Luisa think of the little suit she'd bought at Woolworth's when Raleigh was born, the automatic suspenders and buttons and the little red tie. She had never seen the garment again. Long ago, this had hurt her feelings, but she had lived long enough with Madama to learn that you could never tell what she would do or what she was thinking. "Don't wake her," Madama said again, and she looked so uneasy that Luisa obeyed.

Luisa took her to the window to see the baby. She ached to take Madama's hand. For all they had gone through. For their braided lives. For their lost sons, their common love of don Tomás. She wanted to say what a miracle it was that from the two children could come this precious life and did Madama not agree that a baby was a way of finding the lost? That in time Antonia would grow up. But she was glad she hadn't, for Madama only glanced at the baby, then hurried away, saying she had an appointment.

When she returned to Antonia's room, Luisa found her daughter fanning herself with an unopened card. Antonia handed it over. "From her. Why did she even bother to come?"

When Luisa opened the envelope, a hundred-dollar bill fell out. "I knew it," Antonia said. "I don't want it."

She told her daughter it was only right. After all, Madama was the child's grandmother. "Look. The little dress." She showed Antonia the beautiful lace of the dress. "It must have come from her family."

"She's not!" Antonia cried. "Don't ever say that."

Stunned, Luisa looked at her.

"She's paying so she can pretend she isn't!" Antonia burst into tears. "I hate her!"

Luisa remembered the outrage she had felt as a girl when her mother suggested she forgive Chavela, but now she understood her mother's reasons. Hatred hurt the hater more. But in the face of her daughter's anguish, she held her silence. Later, later, she would say what had to be said.

• • •

When the baby was four weeks old, Antonia went to work at the canning plant. Luisa was ashamed to admit she was almost glad, for this left
her with the baby most of the day. Each day after she gave Beth her
morning bottle, Luisa packed her in a vegetable basket and carried her
to the big house.

Madama seemed surprised at first, and uneasy, but when she explained about Antonia's job, Madama nodded. "Okay, but just for poco
tiempo."

"Lu, you're on another planet," Madama would sometimes say as
Luisa worked, the baby nearby.

Often she caught the older woman peering at the tiny Beth in her
basket, but Madama always made some excuse for any attention she paid
the baby. "I thought I saw a fly on her cheek," she would say, or, "Her
little feet are sticking out. I just tucked her up a little."

"Pick her up," Luisa offered. "She's so good."

But Madama the proud, though Luisa saw looks she knew were longing, would not.

Time, Luisa knew, would change this, and she waited.

Nothing, not even the births of her own children, had prepared her
for the love she bore her daughter's child. She sang every song she knew.
New songs, songs she made up, old ones from Salsipuedes which now
returned to her. In the songs she called the baby Tina, for the name *Beth*
was hard to fit into rhythm.

She neglected her garden, forgot to water, forgot to pinch, forgot to
prune. Crabgrass sprouted, grew leggy between the beds; chamico rose
stout and tasseled, higher than the daisies; careless weed sent scouts along
the border rocks, crept among the cannas. Sometimes, when she looked
outside, she would think she should tend the overgrowth, but then she
would settle back into the rocking chair, reminded of another song. This
was the greater miracle, of her body, once removed. And her own voice,
something was in it, something full of beauty, joy so wide it hurt her
throat.

As a girl, the first time she had gone to the canyon, she had lowered
herself into the water to sit, digging her toes into the sand. Wanting to
know what it felt like beneath the flow, she lay back and let the tea-
colored water cover her. Above her the world went on, she knew, but
beneath the water was a hushed, slow thump. Under the water she knew

something she no longer knew the moment she broke upward into air. Now, as she rocked the baby, she had the feeling that if she could only rock long enough, some old, lost knowledge would be restored to her.

•   •   •

One evening in early December when the baby was fretful from teething, Antonia came home late from her shift and plopped into the brown chair. "I found a place to live."

Luisa wiped the baby's mouth with the hem of the cotton blanket. "You live here."

Antonia bent to untie the thick white shoes she wore to work. "It's hot and it's crowded and it's insane for all of us to try to live in a closet."

The rocker creaked beneath her weight as she shifted. "When will you see Tina?"

"Beth. Her name is Beth." Antonia jerked her head toward the big house. "I won't stay here and let her run my life. Or Beth's. I'll take her with me. Angie Ayala baby-sits for lots of people. . . ."

Luisa felt suddenly hot. "Angie Ayala can take better care of her than her own grandmother?"

"There are things you don't know, Mama . . ." Antonia began, but then it seemed her daughter's thoughts jumped from one dark track onto another, and she continued. "You think if you just act good enough . . . I'm sick of it. You try to boss me about the baby and you act like you know everything. You don't."

Luisa listened but said nothing. She rocked. In her arms, the baby stirred, whimpered, stretched, again closed her eyes. "She has a tooth," Luisa said. She heard a rattle in her own voice, a creak, a little squawk. To cover it she coughed.

Antonia slipped on her dress shoes and picked up her purse. She opened the door. "I'm going out with some girls from work," she said, but then she stood still, looking at Luisa in such a hard way that Luisa had to look away. "I'll tell you something, Mama," her daughter said, "and after I tell you, if you can still sit there . . ."

Antonia held her silence for so long that Luisa again looked up. Her daughter was gazing out the door toward the big house.

Luisa tried to make her voice gentle. "Tonia, she is a mother too. She isn't as bad as you think she is. She's . . ."

Antonia shook her head and said, "Oh, never mind. It wouldn't matter."

Luisa was tired. Her legs hurt, her back, her feet. Even her elbows. Her head was heavy, and she rested it on the back of the rocker. The longer Antonia stood at the door, looking at her, the heavier her head became, the more her back hurt, and the more all of this became Antonia's fault. She was glad when at last her daughter left, closing the door quietly behind her. Tears formed. She pictured telling Altagracia that Antonia had decided to move out. "Why?" her friend would ask. "She has a good home, Luisa." She would like to be able to roll her eyes, to shrug and say, in the way she'd heard other mothers use to explain the headstrong behavior of their grown daughters, "Who knows?" But she knew. Antonia and Madama had made a bargain: If Antonia and the baby left, Luisa could stay.

She had waited for the day when Madama would realize her wrongs, would say, "Lu, I never knew how bad I was treating you." These daydreams had been rich and nourishing as bread. She had been good, and this goodness would never shine so brightly as it would in the moment of Madama's apology. It would be then that she would tell about the buried box, explain how it came to be there, explain her fear that Madama would blame her. One for one. Then all would be well with them. She should have left long ago. Should have.

Rocking the baby, before she knew what was happening, she had sunk into another daydream. In this one, ten years fell away and the children were small again. Madama came to her for advice about . . . No, time moved fifteen years forward and it was Tina's graduation from high school and she had made her a beautiful dress . . . Before the daydream could take hold, could blur and sweeten the truth, she snapped it off. It would never be that way. She shook her head, sickened. Her movement startled the baby, who drew a breath to cry, but then again was still.

She rocked. How could you know, at the beginning, what the end could be? How could you mark the point at which you knew a wrong was so great it could not possibly be righted? There had been school for Tavo and Tonia. There had been this, there had been that, one thing after another, and in all of it, she had tried to do her best. Only that. She had done nothing to deserve this. Someday Antonia would see her sacrifices and be sorry. Someday Madama would.

She was tired. Tired and sad and busy. Too tired and sad and busy to think. Let others find apartments. Let others make ugly bargains with the lives of the innocent. Let them blame. Let them fight and refuse to see the good. Let them be selfish. Hold grudges. She was rocking the innocent. In all the world there was no more important act.

Tomorrow, she would speak to neither. She would harden her heart against them. She would say nothing, but through days and through years she would never forget. Someday they would be sorry. Antonia, she would forgive; daughters had to blame their mothers, and someday Antonia would understand this. Madama, she would not. She began to hum, and soon she felt better, rocking toward that moment.

The next morning when Madama said, "Today you can start in los upstairs baños," Luisa nodded, but went to work briskly, noisily, downstairs in the sala. To Antonia, when she returned from her shift at the canning plant, she made her eyes wide with surprise and said, "Well, what do you think? She gave me a raise!"

BOOK VI

•

the bundle of years

1983

•

Incipit vita nova

⌒〰

the garden of martyrs and saints

In the fifteen years since she had left, it was not so much that her mother's house had changed, Antonia thought as she parked her Toyota under the hackberry that shaded the little house, but that it had grown. A mitosis of kitsch. A parthenogenesis of clutter. The same geraniums grew in the same pots beside the door, but around these pots were smaller ones—cans and pots of cuttings. Under the window the same cannas held up their birdlike scarlet heads, shrugged their wide leaf-shoulders, gathering around their stalks the green shoots of their young. Everything was the same, there was just more. Her mother would never leave, and it was as though the clutter served as both evidence and excuse.

The yard around the little house had become a wonderland of cast-offs—the old bird ball lay nested in a clump of aloe vera like a great blue egg. It had been separated from its pedestal, which her mother had turned upside down to fill with a pot of gerbera daisies. Beside the pedestal was a purple clay turtle that she thought she remembered Beth having made in kindergarten. A plaster deer, its paint faded and its antlers chipped but its nose still iron black, grazed over a kettle of petunias. In a grotto of cinder blocks, the Virgin regarded Saint Francis, on whose outstretched arm there hung a plastic hummingbird feeder her mother kept filled with thick red Kool-Aid. Everywhere were gifts from Joe, a wooden bench, her mother's name carved into the seat, more hummingbird feeders, dozens of birdhouses—some wooden, others hollowed gourds, still others plastic—that dangled from the tree branches. A string of chili pepper lights—a gift from Pompilo—festooned the oleander. Her mother loved these things, happily moving them around, her arrangement never the same, as though she had yet to find the one right way to order the world. She and Beth lived close—in Harlingen, where she was working to establish a general practice—and she visited every week. There had not been one occasion on which *something* hadn't been changed, adorned with a plastic flower, tied with a length of ribbon.

She cut the car's engine, then gathered her purse from the seat and got out of the car.

Her mother came to the door. "Tina?" she asked, peering suspiciously around Antonia toward the car, around the yard, as though a sixteen-year-old might have simply wandered off to play.

"She wants to be called Beth," she said. "She's at a friend's house, Mama." Though it was Sunday, her mother had on her blue uniform; Antonia decided not to ask the reason.

As though reading her mind, her mother patted her apron, explaining, "She's making a big party for Christmas. I'm only helping a little. Come in."

Antonia entered.

"Raleigh is coming tomorrow," her mother said, watching her face, Antonia knew, for a reaction.

"That's nice," she said.

Inside the house, the clutter was even worse. Her mother threw nothing away. On the shelves above her bed, among the bath salt bottles and the dimestore vases, her mother had made a gallery of school projects; beside Tavo's toothpick Indian village, where faded paper campfires still burned, sat the hardened blob of papier-mâché she had made in fifth grade, laboriously gluing red and blue yarn to the mass, which she had titled "The Medicle Heart," in front of which was propped a pie-plate handprint from Beth's preschool days. Stacks of magazines and newspapers cluttered the corners. Pompilo, who couldn't read them, had given her mother a set of hurricane-damaged *World Books*, their pages swollen and discolored. When the library in Rio had set boxes of old books on the curb to be picked up by haulers, her mother had made five trips back and forth, carrying the books in an onion bag. Calendars lined the walls. Under the table was a cardboard carton filled with envelopes on which her mother had practiced writing and would not throw away. To the accumulated smells in the house—cooking oil and cypress, cominos, dust, her mother's shampoo—there was added the aged scent of newspapers and old books, char from the burned pages.

Her mother had learned to read. In Spanish and in English. Antonia had found out only the year before, when she'd caught her mother puzzling over Ann Landers's column, her lips halting on certain words. At first Antonia thought the display was one of her mother's affectations, and she asked her mother to repeat what she was reading. Her mother struggled with a letter about a woman whose husband snored, but she missed only a few words. *Provider,* Antonia remembered, and *palate.* "Where did you learn?" she'd asked. "In a box," her mother said, giggling, "with a fox." In the years Antonia had spent at Pan American, she and Beth had visited every other Sunday, and while they were at Galveston for her M.D., they came at least every month. Beth might have taught her at some point in those times, but Antonia didn't think this was the case. Maybe Joe Bonillas had. Her mother now spoke English almost exclusively, though her faulty grammar made Antonia wince.

And Joe had taught her to drive. Once Antonia had seen her mother behind the wheel of his white Cadillac convertible, driving fifteen miles an hour down Acacia, her neck craned to see over the wheel, arm resting on the door, hand dangling, a middle-aged low-rider. When she'd asked, "Don't you worry about what will happen if you're caught with no license?" her mother shrugged. "What can they do? They can't take it away . . . I don't have none!" She supposed it was because there had been so little actual threat behind her mother's lifelong fear of the INS that she'd become cavalier about the lesser laws. Long before, she had given up trying to persuade her mother to seek citizenship. Half the Valley, her mother always told her, was illegal. "Are they going to put a million people in jail?"

Now her mother motioned for her to take a seat. "She likes it when I call her Tina. It was her baby name."

Antonia removed a stack of newspapers from a chair and sat at the table.

"This place is a fire hazard, Mama."

Her mother looked proudly around the room. "I don't have no matches."

"*Any.* You have electricity. Wires can go bad. Lightning. You need smoke alarms at the very least."

"Coffee?" her mother offered. "Smoke alarms," Antonia heard her mutter, "like I don't have no nose."

Antonia sighed. "Coffee would be nice."

Mounted on the wall above the table was a black metal box, a buzzer discarded from the razed high school, old-fashioned wires poking from the sides. Pompilo had carted it home from the salvage yard for his own purposes, but Madama discovered the buzzer and ordered him to install it. "I don't see why she doesn't put a phone in here for you, Mama. It would be so much easier than that obnoxious thing."

Her mother took milk from the refrigerator. "Are you hungry?"

"I just came to tell you about Christmas. Beth is going on the CYO ski trip and I'm going along to chaperone. . . ."

Her mother poured coffee into their cups. "Who?" Then, as though she'd just remembered, "Oh, yes. Tina."

Antonia told her about Snowmass, then they talked about her practice.

"Any good diseases?" her mother asked slyly. "I heard Camarena Vega had her wart cut off." She eyed Antonia accusingly. "You told me you didn't operate on people."

"I don't, Mama. A wart isn't major surgery."

"I told her not to come to you," her mother persisted. "She didn't believe me that you didn't do no operations."

"I don't."

Her mother folded her arms over her chest. "Well, obviously you do. I was embarrassed."

"I'm sorry."

Her mother pouted awhile, stirring her coffee, then said, sounding so much like Madama that Antonia had to laugh, "Hump."

Her mother wanted to hear about everyone's ailments, trying to outguess Antonia's diagnoses, the look on her face so shrewd and smug that sometimes Antonia wanted to trick her. Actually, she welcomed these times; as long as her mother was involved with medical questions, she wasn't poking into her love life, asking the eternal: "Have you met any nice men?" Her mother, expert on male/female relations. Joe Bonillas had loved her for years, putting up with God knew how many of her mother's ridiculous rules: He couldn't spend the night at the little house for fear of Madama's displeasure; she couldn't spend the night at the Hundred Acres for fear of Madama's displeasure; he had to park his Cadillac behind the hedge, and so on. She behaved like a sneaking teenager. Sometimes Joe could do nothing wrong, other times he could do nothing right, and her mother picked odd moments to stand up for herself, usually when she was clearly in the wrong. Antonia suspected menopause, always a more emotional time for the repressed, but those times she'd tried to make discreet inquiries, her mother had waved away her questions, as though she couldn't be bothered.

Today she told her mother about a case of rubeola.

"Chicken pox!" her mother pronounced. "I knew it."

They drank their coffee, Antonia taking care to avoid the subject of Madama. What talk they allowed themselves had to be along the lines of joking, but even then she could never predict when her mother might decide the joking had gone too far and there would be an argument.

The last time she had come to visit, her mother had baited her with a story about how one morning she'd found Madama dancing with Little Dixie in the sala, crooning in baby talk that Little Dixie was just a little chocolate chip, and singing a silly song that her mother remembered as, "Ho ho ho, you and me, little brown dog, don't I love thee!" Her mother could mimic perfectly Madama's big-boned intensity, the helplessness of the dog, its tongue lolling, eyes bulging as Madama twirled. Just as Antonia had begun to laugh, her mother had closed down. "I am lucky," she said. "I shouldn't make fun."

"Lucky? To work until your feet are swollen? Not even minimum wage."

Her mother shrugged. "I am blessed with the gift of forgetting."

She had grown weary of her mother's high-sounding rationalizations. "It isn't a blessing, Mama. It's blindness." She tried to explain the concept of denial.

"I'm not denying nothing," her mother said.

"*Anything,*" Antonia prompted. "You're not denying *anything.*"

"That's what I said. She does things and I forget them. That way we can just go on. You can look forward, then, and not behind you. If you forget things, they don't matter. You should try it."

"They matter," Antonia had said, "and I can't."

In her mind, the Madama of 1967—rigid behind the wheel of the Buick as they drove through Matamoros, red-faced in Corpus Christi as she laid out her plan for the baby's birth, what she would pay, how Antonia must promise to leave, as she threatened to fire her mother— was fixed as a tissue section between glass slides, and nothing could change her opinion of the woman. She was a bigot, a manipulator, a hypocrite, a liar, and a phony. Worst of all, she was mean to the marrow. Her mother ignored all this and God knew how much more.

In her third year at the Med Branch at Galveston, Antonia had received a letter from Raleigh, postmarked Portland, Oregon. She had speculated, but until the letter came, she hadn't known what Madama had said to him on that day in Corpus. She read the letter on the fly— she'd just ducked into the mailroom to see if there was any coffee in the pot and had been surprised to see the envelope in her box—then threw it into the mailroom trashcan and went back to her work.

By late morning she came down with symptoms so nonspecific but so debilitating it was difficult to move. She was weak and dizzy. She decided she was dehydrated. From a hall fountain she gulped water and waited for the tissues to absorb it. This didn't help. Her next thought was potassium depletion, and she grabbed a banana from the call room fruit bowl and wolfed it. She chased aspirin with Coca-Cola for the caffeine buzz. Nothing worked. By noon she was nauseated, hammered with headache, buzzed by scintillating scotomata. She had vertigo, nystagmus. Her ears rang and her head felt thick. At the back of her throat was a hot, sick taste. Her hands could not hold so much as a pencil without dropping it.

The week before she'd been on the infectious disease rotation and they'd seen a case of hepatitis. She found her friend Rudy Triana—the only other female student in the class—and pulled her into an empty examining room. "Do my liver," she demanded. "I've got hepatomegaly, I know it." Rudy palpated but found no enlargement. Antonia went to the required afternoon rounds, then she went to Dr. Stokes, the chief of medicine. For three years she'd endured his patronizing manner; on this day it seemed worse than ever. "You're probably just tired," he said. "You know it's a cliché to imagine symptoms from whatever rotation you're on. Do derm, you've got ringworm. Oncology, it's CA. Obgyn, you've got ectopic pregnancy and all the men swear off. Don't be a cliché, Cantú. Are you menstruating?"

She went to Serology and had a tech draw blood. All findings were unremarkable except for a hemoglobin count of 11, for which she should take iron. She felt even worse than before: sweat, myalgia, neuralgia, malaise. She was SOB: Her lungs could hardly draw a deep breath. Palpitations: She knew she was throwing PVC's. That night, desperate, she knocked herself out with Seconal and in the hazed moment before the drug took over her consciousness, she understood that the disease she had was a violent, fulminant anger.

Raleigh's letter—coming after seven years—said that he had wanted to write earlier but couldn't. He hoped she would understand after he told her the reason. He had just received a letter from his mother, who wrote from time to time to persuade him to return to the Valley. In this letter, at the very end, she'd written in an offhanded way—and this part he reproduced verbatim—"By the way, I meant to tell you that Lu has finally come clean about certain things, and I've just learned that what I told you in Corpus was not true. Antonia is not your half-sister after all."

He wrote that she hadn't even apologized, but that he would. He was sorry. He didn't know if she knew these things or not, but maybe they would explain his behavior. He asked about Beth. Then he told her he was married.

Antonia had spent hours composing terse, sniping telegrams but in the end she had not answered his letter. The only good that had come of it was that, if she chose to, she could tell Beth a more honest version than the one she had prepared, which was that her father was a college boy with whom she'd run away to Corpus Christi. At six, the child still hadn't asked. Antonia didn't know whether to feel angered or vindicated by Madama's admission, however askance.

A few weeks after she had received the letter, unable to bear the horror of Madama's lie alone, she had told her mother what Madama had told Raleigh. Her mother had looked stricken. "No," she said. "No." Although Antonia was ashamed to acknowledge it, she felt a small spark of satisfaction at her mother's reaction. But then her mother rose from her chair, brushing at her apron. "Well, that's all in the past. It doesn't matter. See how it all worked out?" Then she resumed talking about Beth's confirmation dress. When her mother went to the sink to pour the soak water off a bowl of beans, Antonia heard the low murmur of her mother's hill song, cracked and halting. Antonia had left the little house without another word, and it had taken several months before she could make herself return to visit her mother.

Even now, so many years beyond that time, her anger continued to stun her, but today she had resolved not to let her opinions about her mother's boss spoil the visit. She noticed that her mother walked gingerly and that every time she sat, she released a sigh.

"Do your feet still hurt?" Knowing her mother would deny it even if they did, she didn't wait for an answer. "You need a checkup. Why don't you come to the office and let Rudy have a look at you? You like her okay?"

"Doctors don't know everything," her mother said. "Things go away all by themselves."

Her mother looked out into the yard, focusing, Antonia thought, on the bird ball, then shifted her gaze past the garden and into the sky, and then even farther, as though she saw beyond everything. Antonia almost laughed. When she was young, her mother's faraway look had impressed her, but at some point she had begun to suspect her mother's smug mysticism. Once that look had fooled her into thinking her mother possessed some deep Indian wisdom. Now she knew better. The looks were to divert her attention, and behind them was nothing more than stubbornness, grown more obdurate with years and practice. "Well," she said to her mother, "maybe you can forget things, but your body remembers."

As Antonia prepared to leave, congratulating herself that she hadn't once mentioned Madama, her mother said, as though Antonia had inquired, "She has a job. At the New to You."

The reverence with which her mother pronounced the name of the Episcopal charity shop on Acacia Drive made her sigh. "Little old gringo ladies selling junk to other little old gringo ladies."

"Not only to them!" Her mother gripped her arm. "Did I tell you what happened to Altagracia? She bought a bedspread there for five dollars. A beautiful bedspread. Pink. With pretty flowers inside little fences. She had it on her bed already, with pillows all around, when guess what happens? Madama drives into her yard in her big black car." Her mother made the stiff-armed motions of driving, pantomimed a stern Madama braking the car, getting out, straightening her dress. "Yes, and she gets out and comes to Alta's door. She has a piece of Kleenex stuck in her glasses like a little horn. To tell Alta the bedspread cost not five dollars but seven."

Her mother's eyes were like slits from laughing, her cheekbones almost green. "And do you know the best part? Little Dixie is with her and all the time Madama is talking, Little Dixie is barking and barking and she barked so hard she made a puddle all the way down Madama's dress."

Antonia laughed in spite of herself. Over the years the Chihuahua had grown fat. Her skin was afflicted with scale, sarcoptic mange. Her front teeth—all but a lower canine—had rotted and had been removed, and the dog's tongue protruded, causing her to look slow-witted. She limped from where once Madama had stepped on her paw. But Madama doted on her and took her everywhere. She swore the dog slept on the plaid blanket she'd ordered from a catalog, but every morning when her mother went to make the bed, she'd told Antonia, there were long brown hairs. Fleas sometimes. Left in the house, Dixie made piles and peed on the carpet. By all lights, her mother should have hated the dog; it was her job to clean up, to let the beast in and out, to bathe her, but she didn't. Sometimes Antonia suspected that when her mother was alone in the house she performed her own secret dog-dances, twirling around the house with the creature, dipping and swaying and crooning her Salsipuedes song.

Her mother, who had been tying on her apron to return to work, stood stock-still, as though she'd heard a distant call.

"What's wrong, Mama?"

"I think I heard her car."

As her mother leaned over the table to look out the window, Antonia saw the spidery clots of burst capillaries at the backs of her mother's knees, her vein-shot calves like a map of rivers, thrombosed and blue. Her mother had put on more weight; she now looked squat and solid as a fireplug. Antonia remembered she'd meant to bring support hose.

"We didn't talk about Christmas," she said. "Will you be okay? I assumed you'd go to Joe's."

Her mother smiled an odd smile. "Did I forget to tell you? I'm taking a vacation. On Tuesday, tomorrow. All by myself." She nodded proudly. "I'm going to be a world traveler. To South Padre Island."

"But where will you . . . how can you . . ."

Before Antonia could finish her questions, the bell sounded from the big house, Madama's lunatic code—three shorts and a long— urgent, buzzing like a firehouse alarm, and her mother was out the door and halfway up the path. As she got into her car, Antonia saw that Madama stood at the back door. "Lu, voy al post office," she shouted. Madama began to shout something else, but Antonia started the engine to cut off the sound.

a storybook christmas

Trashy was the word Eddie put to the way downtown Rio Paradiso looked this Monday morning, a week before Christmas. Ropes of foil spangles had been tacked to storefronts, stretched between the palm trunks that lined the business district, spangles the poisonous color, the bellyache blue of a Hailey's MO bottle. A tattered star swayed from a traffic light over the main intersection, bobbing in the cool wind. Paper cups blew along the sidewalk and a crumpled beer can rattled in the gutter; the place looked more carnival than Christmas. Even the weather had turned sour. A blue norther was expected.

Eddie parked the Buick, and with Little Dixie—a jingle bell tied with a red ribbon around her neck—nestled in the crook of her arm, began walking up Acacia toward the post office. It had been a bad morning. Lu, in a dither about her ridiculous trip, had neglected to dust the louvers in the closet doors. There had been words. Then she'd refused to help Eddie move the Christmas tree so the drapery pulls wouldn't mangle the ornaments. Finally, Eddie'd had to say, "Oh, just take today off, too!"

Years before, this never would have happened, but now the Valley had changed. Now everybody spoke Spanish all over the place. Stores carried signs in Spanish, hand lettered and tacky. Even she could tell many of the words were misspelled. And Mexicans ran things. The chief of police was Mexican, and so was the sheriff. Hartley Rowell—the last of his kind, the paper reported—had retired. Word had it he spent his afternoons at the Coyote Club on old 83, reminiscing with other codgers, leaving when it was time to watch *Dallas*. *Dynasty*. Something. The mayor was Mexican, and Valley politics were even more crooked than before. Even the postmaster was Mexican.

It was because of Mexicans that she had to make this trip into town to get her mail. For years she'd had a mailbox on its post at the end of her drive, clematis vining over it, their blossoms like stars. How she had loved to see it there, her name in Roman script, the mailbox like a guard, a sentinel on the road beyond which the groves stretched regular and lush. But teenagers spray-painted its sides with "Chinga" and even worse. This, when they hadn't outright stolen it. She couldn't order from a catalog and expect to receive a package. One by one, all the big estates on Grand Texas Boulevard had taken down their mailboxes, and at last she, too, had given up.

She entered the crowded post office and stood in the line, which today was composed mostly of snowbirds, a few locals. She'd moved up two places when she remembered that Fredo Ramos had told her twice not to bring Little Dixie into the building. "It's against federal regulations," he'd told her in his officious way. "No dogs in the post office. Except for Seeing Eye." She turned away from the counter to conceal the dog.

The couple in front of her gabbed gaily about a package from Minnesota. The woman was dowdy, giggling. Eddie tapped her foot impatiently while the woman fished in her handbag, saying now where did she put that letter? *Pocketbook,* such a woman would call it.

"What a cute little puppy," the woman cooed. "All dressed up for Christmas. Like a little brown elf." She put her hand out to pet Dixie, who growled.

"Watch out," Eddie warned. "She isn't fond of strangers."

"Well, I'm not a stranger, now, am I? I'm your friend. What's your name, doggie?"

Eddie, feeling the vibrations of Dixie gearing up to yap and desperate that the woman not draw Fredo's attention, turned away. In her bag she found a square of Kleenex and draped it over the dog's head.

"Leave the puppy alone, Mother," said the woman's husband. "You'll get the lady in trouble."

Mother, as though she was now happy to be in on the deception, moved to shield Eddie from Fredo's sight. She winked conspiratorially.

"I can't help but notice," Eddie offered, anxious to keep the woman on her side, "how much you resemble Mamie Eisenhower. Are you related, by any chance?" When the woman said she wasn't, Eddie said, "Well, she was a dear friend of mine."

Mother's eyes widened. "Really?"

"Oh, yes."

"Isn't that something, Daddy? Did you hear that?"

Eddie learned that the couple had a son who practiced at the Mayo Clinic. She told them about Raleigh in Portland. "He and his family are coming for Christmas. I'm expecting a letter from him. Their flight itinerary. I always have him send me one. That way you know exactly when to send the driver for them."

Raleigh had made it as far as Seattle, where he'd taken a job at a fishery, on something called the slime line, which sounded awful. In 1972 she received his graduation announcement. He had a degree in psychology, but he said he thought he'd continue at the fishery; he liked business. How hard it had been to keep from saying she'd told him so. Military-industrial complex, indeed. From time to time she'd sent checks, but he'd never cashed them. One letter said he was proud of having gone through school on his own steam and that he'd like to hear that she was, too. Though she thought him a fool for refusing what would have been freely given, she wrote that she certainly understood that he had to do it his way. She wrote that she was proud.

In 1976 he had written to say he'd been married for a few years and there were two daughters: Caroline was two and Jeanmarie had just been born. His wife had encouraged him to write; she hoped they could reconcile their differences. Eddie invited them for a visit.

Elaine was a public defender, but she was like no lawyer Eddie'd ever seen. Her hair was lank and she wore hippie glasses. She dressed in floursack grannies. The girl's fingers were short and stubby, and Eddie's first thought as she'd shaken Elaine's hand had been *peasant stock*. "Poor posture," Eddie had remarked to Lu, but behind her hand so Elaine wouldn't hear, "and her shoes aren't nice at all. Look at the heels. Sloppy."

Raleigh had been nervous—this had been before she'd written to tell him she'd been mistaken about Antonia's parentage—and in the whole time they were there, she hadn't seen him so much as look in the direction of the little house. Lu was her usual impassive self as she went about her cleaning and cooking, but Eddie caught the look of wounded industry her maid had perfected in three decades.

The visit had been a disaster. Elaine tried to help Lu with the dishes. Offered to do the ironing. Insisted on making the beds. Lu was flustered and Eddie was aghast. During her lovely Sunday dinner, Elaine had delivered a diatribe about colonization and oppression, how Eddie was running a twentieth-century fiefdom, and finally Eddie had had enough.

"I'll tell you who's oppressed around here," Eddie'd said. She explained the complexities of the Valley, about the swollen welfare rolls, the chaos. Wetbacks. She told about how difficult it was to find good help. Elaine stared at her plate, nursing Jeanmarie at the table. Caroline picked at one of Lu's perfect tortillas and rolled the bread into pills. Raleigh left the table.

The worst was when Lu asked to hold the baby. Elaine was a cat around the four-month-old Jeanmarie, had a fit when Eddie wanted to buy her some Buster Brown hard soles. "Those little feet," Eddie told her, "should be in shoes. To form the bones correctly." Elaine barked at Eddie not to put her finger in the baby's mouth simply to see if a tooth was coming in. She wouldn't listen to reason about breast-feeding being low class. "If you can afford bottles," Eddie'd instructed her, "they're really best for baby. More sanitary." And so when she had seen Lu hold out her arms to take the baby, hoping to reassure the persnickety Elaine, Eddie had said, "It's all right. She's just as clean as any white person."

Elaine's jaw dropped in an unflattering way. "That is probably the most," she'd said, "insufferable thing I've ever heard anyone say."

Raleigh had come back once, and their visit had gone much better, but Elaine and the girls hadn't returned.

This year she'd had her brilliant idea for the storybook Christmas. Because the scofflaw Lu was leaving on her ridiculous vacation, there would be no conflict. She could certainly do for her own family for a few days. If she got into trouble, she had the promise of Nila's day girl. Maybe she would have Concha slip in at midnight and do up the laundry, like the shoemaker's elf, so Elaine wouldn't get her nose out of joint.

Raleigh accepted her invitation. Excited, she promised to cook a goose; she'd never cooked one, but she had watched Noon Nulan do dozens. She had Pompilo deliver a great tree. She draped the doorways with magnolia and mistletoe. For Elaine she ordered a Coach bag from Neiman Marcus—the last time she'd come, the girl had carried everything in a threadbare satchel. For Raleigh she found an ebony desk set. She bought "My Pretty Pony" coloring books for the girls, and a toy called Puppy Puddles that wet on a paper when you filled its body with water. She bought the last Barbie's Dream House at the Harlingen K mart, but she and Pompilo and Lu together couldn't figure out how to assemble the pink and blue plastic contraption. She herself did not need glasses to read the instructions; Pompilo and Lu were too stubborn to admit their eyes were going bad. There had been excuses, anguish, an argument, and they'd ended up wrapping the box; Raleigh would have to put it together. Candy! She stocked up on lemon drops and orange slices, french burnt peanuts and licorice whips, ribbon candy. She'd bought cute red-and-green reindeer appliquéd stockings, a music box on whose lid a train ran through a snow-covered village while the mechanism played "It's a Small World."

The people in front of her had finished their business and the man was now chatting with Fredo about the weather. "If we'd a known it would be this cold down here, we'd a stayed in Des Moines."

The woman smiled and said, "Move, Coy, and let the lady have her turn."

Eddie hung Little Dixie over her handbag. Using her elbow to hold the dog securely, she stepped to the window. "Box Twelve," she said to Fredo. She drummed her fingers on the counter. "I'm expecting a letter from my son."

"Nothing today, Missus," he said, shuffling papers, not looking up. "And no dogs allowed except Seeing Eye. Federal regulations. Read the sign."

"You didn't even look in my box."

"I checked already. You always come at the same time. There's nothing. I told you about that dog."

She stared at the ink-stained finger stall on his brown thumb. "I insist that you go to that box and check again."

Fredo shrugged, then shuffled over to the mailboxes.

"Nothing," he said. "Might be something if the dog went out."

"Open that door." At her side, at the level of her handbag, came the sound of a jingle bell. Little Dixie sneezed, shaking off the Kleenex.

"It's empty."

"What's in the back room? How many bags are back there that you haven't sorted?"

"I gotta work the window. I can't be going back there all the time."

People behind her seemed to press closer, and Eddie was conscious of murmuring. To Fredo she said in her most authoritative tone, "I know for a fact that there's at least one mail bag back there, and I'm not leaving this window until . . . It's a federal crime to tamper with . . ." She was flushed and hot. Her hands shook, and suddenly she was shouting, "I want what's coming to me!"

He rolled his eyes, then went into the back room. He returned with a thick envelope.

"Ha!" she crowed, waving the letter to the watching crowd. "I knew it."

As she walked past the line toward the door, she saw that people were looking at their shoes.

Behind her, Fredo shouted, "No dog next time!"

"I'll report you," she called over her shoulder. "For rudeness."

Pushing against the door, only to remember that she needed to pull, she heard a child's voice saying, "That lady is acting naughty. Does she need a nap?"

Eddie yanked at the door. Outside, she examined the envelope. Addressed to Occupant, Lot Six, Sunset Palms, Rio Paradiso, Texas, the envelope contained a gift calendar from a termite company.

When she arrived home, Lu told her that Raleigh had called. Elaine had a sinus infection, the girls had colds. They weren't coming.

3

laguna madre

On the road. Luisa savored the words as she drove Joe's enormous car down Highway 281 to catch the jog to San Benito. As she passed a fruit stand where an old man sat beside some crates of broccoli, she realized that she had been so busy looking at the scenery she had not thought once about Joe, the reason for her trip. Dutifully, she directed her thoughts.

For many years he had begged her to marry him. She had never told him yes or no, always wait, or maybe. Now he wanted an answer. "A real answer," he'd said. "Final." At Thanksgiving dinner, at his crowded table at the Hundred Acres, in the presence of his brothers and sisters and cousins, Antonia, Beth, and Pompilo, as he asked for the blessing over the feast, Joe had ended his prayer with the words: *And if You see fit, let the love of my life at last say Yes, to make me the happiest man on earth.* She had raised her head to meet Joe's gaze, hopeful and shy in the watchful silence of their families. But she couldn't speak. Then it seemed that everyone laughed and talked at once. "When?" his family pressed her.

"I have to think about it," she'd replied.

Joe raised his glass. "When?"

"When I have time," she'd answered. "I'm very busy."

Over dessert it was decided that she would borrow his car to take her trip. It was decided by Joe, and this was what troubled her. She loved him, it was true. He was good and capable and kind, and some nights at his house at the Hundred Acres he held her so close she could not imagine wanting to be anywhere else on earth. With Joe she at last understood the feelings in her body that had begun with Uncle but which had gone away until she felt the baby Antonia nursing at her breast. And the older she became the better this was. But this was not enough. She now laughed to think of how once she'd wondered at the mysteries of men and women, laughed not because she understood them, but because the greater mystery lay in how any person—man or woman—got along with any other. Why, she sometimes wondered, did they even try?

Under Antonia's every word ran the accusation that the course of her life had been wrong, and it seemed this was no different with Joe. If she complained, only a little, about Madama, he would tell her what she *should* do. He would tell her what to tell Madama, and the things he wanted her to say would make it so that she couldn't work for Madama any longer and she would have to give up her house. And Joe thought he was always right. Sometimes the jut of his jaw reminded her of her brother Memo. It was easier, she had decided, to go ahead with her thinking-about-it trip. If she refused to make a show of thinking, this too would be added to her long list of mistakes. But she knew already what she would tell him when she returned.

Although she had not wanted the trip in the first place, over the weeks as she prepared for it she had grown more and more excited. She'd studied the map, and sometimes, as she looked at the blue and red and green lines that traced paths to anywhere, she thought of the pictures in Antonia's medical books. Like the blue and red lines that took the blood, the roads took people. If one wouldn't work, you could always take another one and get to the place you wanted or get back to the place you started. Now she saw that she could drive fifty miles from home and still be herself, for her house was like the heart through which all roads could run.

"That's the way," she said into the wind, "I like it."

Like the road behind her in the rearview mirror, the morning slipped into the past, and it seemed the car with her inside it stood still while the road beneath her vanished, spinning the wheels with its loss as the present slipped away. Something was coming, not on the road—the flat ribbon stretched into the distance, little traffic to distract her from her thoughts—but in time. A great change. For the past weeks she had felt it in a shift of wind or in a sudden stillness as she worked among her flowers. If a bee hummed too closely behind her ear, she was reminded. In Salsipuedes there had been a name, which she couldn't now remember, for the coming changes. The name had to do with years. Fifty-two, maybe, but she couldn't be sure; it might be fifty. And there was something to do with fire—old fire and new fire—and throwing things in and taking things out.

As she neared the Gulf, the air grew heavier. Along the road were marshes, wetlands with tall reeds and thick, spiked grasses. Trying to see if the wide-leafed, low-growing vines she noticed along the shoulder were the gourd vines she remembered from the hills, she didn't notice that she'd been puttering along the gravel shoulder until the front bumper was about to hit the jut of the concrete culvert just ahead. She braked, jerked the wheel to the left, causing the car to heave sideways, its rear end coming to rest in the reeds, the back wheels sinking slowly into the marsh.

A heron rose from a cypress stump and then flapped off. She cut the engine and got out of the car. Insects whirred loudly, then ceased. In the car, the comforting hum of the engine had made her feel safe, but now, outside in the odd silence, she felt strangely frightened. She got back into the car.

First to pass her was a truck, in its bed a stack of mattresses, two boys, shirtless even in the cool air, lying on their stomachs on top of them. "Wrong way, grandma!" they yelled. One of the boys threw a Pepsi can, which clattered along the shoulder. Next along the road, moving slowly, came a big Winnebago with aluminum lawn chairs strapped to its roof. The driver, an old Anglo man, touched the brim of his cap as he passed. He craned his neck and yelled out the window something about a radio, the highway patrol, help. Inside the vehicle, Luisa saw that a blue-haired woman sat before a tiny television set, watching as she rode, and she thought of Madama and her afternoon shows. Sitting in a straight-backed chair before the screen, Madama would yell, "Don't open that door, Angela!" shaking her finger, trying to boss even the characters on TV. "I told you and told you he'd be back!"

She was thirsty and she wished she'd thought to pack a lunch. She thought of Madama's refrigerator, the Tupperware containers of

deveined grapefruit and oranges, cut and ready for the famous ambrosia.
She was sorry for Madama, too proud to admit she was hurt because
Raleigh wasn't coming. When she'd heard this news, she'd almost can-
celed her trip, but then Madama had picked a fight about the way she'd
dusted the closet doors, and Luisa had held to her plan. Maybe, when
she returned, Madama would have missed her. This notion satisfied her,
and she began to explore its possibilities. Madama would be waiting for
her at the front door of the big house when she returned, she would
rush toward Luisa. She would say, "Oh, I had no idea how much I
depended on you . . ." Even this—one word, one moment out of
thousands—would set things right and . . .

Out in the marsh, a flash caught her eye. On the same cypress knot
where the heron had been a turtle now sunned itself. In the army box
had been a photograph of Tavo in uniform, his helmet the shape and
color of the turtle's shell. The camera had caught Tavo squinting in the
sun; his eyes looked tough and frightened at the same time. Before she
could fix the picture in her mind to think more clearly about it, though,
the turtle, its shell now shining, slipped back into the marsh. She imagined she could feel the cool seal of the water as the creature eased into
the hidden world beneath the surface.

She had been watching the ripples left by the turtle and wondering
what she might have left at home to cause this strange feeling of loss,
and so she didn't notice the approach of the green truck until the vehicle
came to a stop behind the Cadillac.

Joe jumped down from the cab. "Am I interrupting your sight-
seeing?"

"You followed!" The sight of him angered her, the way he talked to
her, as though she were a fool. "This was supposed to be my trip on
my own."

"Aren't you glad to see me?"

She pointed toward the cypress. "I was looking at a turtle."

Joe smiled. "You parked this way so you could have a better view?"

She sat, thinking of something haughty to say, but he had stepped
into the ditch to inspect the Cadillac's rear end. She didn't like the way
his back looked, as though even his bones knew how straight and important he was, how ready to fix everything in just the right way.

"I can do this myself," she called to him. "A man is calling the highway patrol."

He started the truck's engine, then moved the vehicle around the car, backing toward the front end. "This will take a minute, then you'll be on your way." She tried to gauge his feelings; his voice had taken on the hurt tone that often in the past had made her feel sorry for him, then angry because she felt sorry, and then, because she was angry, not sorry at all.

When the truck was positioned, he threw out a hook and began to pay out the tow chain. He secured it, then walked over to kiss her. She turned away to avoid his kiss.

"Sorry," she said. And she was. Joe tried hard to be good. She of all people should recognize this; it was the way he went about it that maddened her. Over the years, sifting through her notions of sin, she had come to believe that the greatest was pride, for the way it fed itself on the judging of others. Joe made her feel less than she was.

He looked at her for a moment, then shrugged. "Keep the front wheels straight," he said.

When the Cadillac was back on the shoulder, he stood at her window and said, "This is a good example." He crossed his arms over his chest. "Say," he said, as though he'd just had one of his fix-it ideas, "why don't I come with you?"

"I can do this myself. You said."

He bent to kiss her again. This time she allowed it. "Don't forget," he said, "I have a new microwave oven. And a Mixmaster."

His grin made her laugh in spite of herself. She swatted his arm.

"It will make you legal," he added, risking, she knew, her anger. Several times he had tried to persuade her in this way, and each time she had shouted that he was a fool. Now she made herself answer him softly.

"Who cares about that? It doesn't matter. All my life I'm here and nobody cares." She buckled her seat belt. "There," she said, "and don't follow!"

He smiled and shrugged, then walked away. As he turned the truck onto the empty highway to head back up the road, she heard him call back to her, "Okay, okay."

Keeping her mind on her driving, she drove a few miles before she heard a siren, growing louder until the patrol car was just behind her. She lowered her speed and kept driving, but the patrol car, its red lights flashing, did not pass. Finally, she stopped the car.

A highway patrol officer walked up to her window. "You okay, ma'am? We heard there was a Cadillac stuck in a ditch."

She waved airily. "Do I look stuck?"

"You know you're supposed to pull over when you hear a siren?"

"I did. I'm stopped." She pointed to the steering wheel. "See?"

He looked at her in what she thought was an odd way, but then said, "Okeydoke. Just checking. Next time, pull over sooner."

"I will."

"And you might try to go the speed limit."

She looked at his badge, at his freshly shaved, unlined face, his smooth skin: a boy. "I have," she instructed him, thinking even as she said the words that this was the way Madama would handle him, "my own way of doing things. People are going to have to get used to that."

He stared, as though considering what he should do about her. She saw him brush his hand across his trouser pocket, where a tattered pad of blue and yellow papers fluttered in the breeze, but all he said was "Well, good luck."

She drove on. So much for legal. So much for Madama and Antonia, who thought they knew the law. So much for Joe.

She entered Port Isabel as the sun was setting. The Laguna Madre Causeway bridge frightened her for the dangerous way it swooped above the water on its long legs, but she was by then in a line of cars and there was no way to avoid it. Driving along the beachfront strip, she passed the fine hotel three times before she realized it was the place Joe had made arrangements. There were flowers in the room, a note from Joe. "Don't think too much," it read. For a moment, she couldn't think of what it was she was supposed to think about, and she was surprised to hear her own voice, low and determined in the quiet room, saying, "Well, I won't."

Though it was early, she was exhausted, and she lay on the too-big bed beneath a painting of a gull flying low above the sea and went to sleep.

to whom it may concern

Dear Son, wrote Eddie, seated at the beautiful carved writing desk she had ordered from Mexico City so long, it seemed, before, *Can you not find it in your heart to forgive an old woman for doing the right thing for the wrong reasons?* She scratched at the paper, inking out the words, and tried again . . . *the wrong thing for the right reasons?* "Oh, hell," she said into the quiet of the sala. She heard the furnace click on and felt the blast of warm air from the vent, air that carried the smell of stale oil and dust, of something deeper and lower. "Lizards," she said into the stillness. Carrying on their filthy, scurrying subterranean lives beneath the clean expanses of her floor. She would call the exterminators. She turned back to her writing, but forgot what she had meant to say to her son. When it occurred to her that perhaps her thoughts this evening made little sense, she blamed her confusion first on Fredo Ramos, then on the impertinent child who'd said she needed a nap.

The summer before, she and Buzz and Nila had gone to watch the Blue Angels when they performed at the Confederate Air Force Show in Harlingen. The jets swooped over their heads, so loud and low she'd ducked. Then they rose in formation, clustered, banking, then veering off one by one, pulling away until only one jet flew straight up. On this night in late December, as she sat in her darkened house, Little Dixie sleeping in a tight brown curl in her lap, she considered the wreck of her beautiful holiday, thinking of the lone flyer.

She took out a clean sheet of paper. *Dear Elaine,* she wrote briskly, *Blow your nose and grow up. And while you're at it, go to hell.* She felt better for a time, but then the sight of the twelve-foot Norwegian balsam framed by the windows, its lights sparkling for no one to see, sent her again into the depths. She was alone, the very picture of an old woman with a dog on her lap. As she crumpled the note to Elaine, Little Dixie flicked her ear. She drew out a clean sheet of paper.

Dear Thomas, You would hardly believe all that's happened . . . She wanted to say something about years and scars and going on in spite of them, but even after three decades, she couldn't stretch her mind wide enough to find an answer for what he'd done, for who she'd been to him. For a long time she sat, pen poised above the paper, sat through two cycles of the furnace. Early in their marriage, when once she'd asked to know how he felt about her, he'd said, "My grandpa Jack said there were three things that made a person's character. The first was where on earth you were set down, and the second was the people you were set down with." He'd smiled. "Eddie Jane, I'm glad I was set down with you. Even if I had to come and get you." Pleased by this compliment, she'd wanted more, and she asked about the third thing. "I don't re-member," he'd said at first, but then, when she pressed him, "not the things you get, but what you don't." He'd looked away. She should have known then. Should have. The furnace clicked on a third time. Eddie wrote, *How could you?* She wrote the phrase again and again.

In her lap, Little Dixie stretched in her sleep, a long deep shudder that seemed to go on and on. Absently, Eddie patted her until she was again still. It was late, hours past the dog's usual bedtime.

How could she say it? To whom could she tell the story of what she'd wanted, what she hadn't got, how one person after another had left her, how no one appreciated anything she did? A trajectory of defection and taking for granted. When she asked herself if there had been something in her that sent them running, the answer came quickly, and it was no. The reason was as simple as it was terrible: luck; she had drawn the black bead. Born to be left.

And now the feckless Lu. In the past years, her maid had picked up a vocabulary of demands. Somewhere she'd gotten the notion that Eddie owed her Social Security. Minimum wage. Health insurance. Benefits. Eddie had laughed. "I'll show you benefits," she said once, and she led the woman outside and pointed to the little house, blooming, that sea-son, with lilies. She led her back inside and showed her the stocked pantry, from which each week Eddie allowed her enough food to feed herself and enough, for many years, to feed her family. She'd never heard another word. It galled her, though, her maid's unspoken expectations, the resentments no doubt harbored in her heart. After all she'd done. It was funny, she decided, how the truth of things lay more in what you didn't say than what you did.

Eddie smiled at a thought: It was just a matter of time before Lu was picked up for driving without a license. They would haul her in. Eddie'd tried to tell her, but lately every time she tried to instruct her on the finer points, Lu made a face. Or she scoffed outright at Eddie's warnings. She'd gotten uppity. This when she wasn't wandering around acting holier-than-thou and put-upon. Eddie blamed Joe Bonillas for putting ideas into her head. After all the years of Eddie's kindness, all the things she'd given her, paid for, Lu would take his word against hers. *Dear Lu, You don't know how good you've got it.* That said it all. This letter she signed and folded, placed in an envelope, and propped on her antique inkwell.

But at issue tonight was her own life, the wreck of it. The agent, she decided, was lust. Take lust out of the world, and half its trouble would vanish. Maybe all of it. Look at Lu, at her age, racing off to shack up with Joe Bonillas, at grandfather-age himself! Long before, she had grown out of romance, but at seventy-three, she still thought about sex. She imagined a hard, urgent coupling, spitting and growling, more animal than human. On a PBS special, she'd seen two beasts mating. Komodo dragons. Graphic, it was, the camera catching the push of the leathery penis, the give of the female tissues. She'd jumped up, thinking to call the station to complain that children might be watching, but she'd stood watching as though mesmerized, her heartbeat rapid. Now on a sheet of her stationery, she wrote the terrible truth of her life. *I didn't get enough.* And it held for almost everything.

Dear . . . For a moment that seemed to stretch back through the years as she tried to bring into focus his face, she couldn't remember his name. Something buoyant and insubstantial, flippant . . . *Bobby.* She crumpled the paper. Old. She was finally, unremittingly, old.

Of the original las girls, only she and Nila were left. In the latter years, it seemed something had gone out of them and they had turned into old ladies, and when they met for cards it seemed that four husks sat around the table, each in her own world. Most often the talk was of grandchildren, and dutifully Eddie trotted out photos of Caroline and Jeanmarie, cataloging their accomplishments—the ballet recital where Jeanmarie had played a Queen Mouse, French horn lessons, Caroline's high score on the Iowa Test of Basic Skills—but their lives seemed far removed from her own, and she might as well have been talking about strangers.

She had watched as her friends' houses filled up with the desperate evidence of old-ladyhood, of too little to do: tatted toilet paper covers, door pulls of pompons and felt, feathered lampshades, shell picture

frames, things sequined, embroidered and macraméd, shellacked maca-
roni mosaics, trivets, potholders, ceramic cats and angels, plastic fruit
compotes, Modge-Podged trinket boxes, gold-spray-painted doorstops
made of folded *Reader's Digests*, stained-glass suncatchers in the shapes
of hummingbirds and cherries, driftwood seascapes studded with plastic
gulls on pipe-cleaner legs.

A month after Ann Dell's funeral, her children had given what they
called a parting party. The plan was that each of the children, the nieces
and nephews, the grandchildren and their children would draw lots for
the choice of some article he had loved. Each, having selected, would
tell what the article had meant to him. Eddie and Nila and Joan were
invited, seated in places of honor. Joan had said, behind her hand, "Isn't
this a bit maudlin?" But Eddie, dabbing at her moist eyes, had been
touched, as well as envious, as one after another of the family told a
story of Ann Dell, as often as not tearfully. In her own cool, tasteful
rooms, there was no homely artifact, no handmade vessel into which
she had poured her life and her longings, even if it had been only a doily
tatted into the shape of a cluster of grapes that somebody—someone
who loved her—would weep over. All she'd wanted was what other
people seemed to have so easily.

My dear Beth, she began on a clean sheet, *You don't really know me, but
I'm your grandmother. In a world where grown-ups do certain things children
don't understand, it sometimes happens that . . .* Eddie crumpled the paper
and took out another. *My dear Beth,* she tried again, *I am a woman of
independent means and I would like to . . .*

The terrible question that had lurked over her that evening now descended. What, in her life, had she loved truly? Worse, whom? Worse
still: Who had loved her back?

She crossed out the line of words. *I do not need,* she scrawled across
the page, *a nap!*

Little Dixie had grown stiff and heavy in her lap, and she reached
down to stroke her, thinking she would carry her quietly to bed, thinking that here, in the dog's small body, was faithfulness, the one soul she
knew fully, on whom she could depend. But when her fingers touched
fur, she found it strangely cool. Cold. At some time amid the pen
scratchings and the click and wheeze of the furnace, in the midst of her
darkest night, Little Dixie had died, and Eddie hadn't even marked the
moment.

"Oh, honey," she wailed brokenheartedly into the silent house. "Oh, honey." For a time she stood still, stunned to think that there was no one who would say those words to her.

She wrapped the little dog in a tea towel and carried her outside, where she found the shovel propped by Pompilo's toolshed. She began to dig in the dirt of Lu's bed of cannas.

5

south padre island

On her first morning on South Padre Island, Luisa watched as the hotel maids rolled their carts up and down the galleries. They chatted, laughed, going in and out of open doorways through which she could see unmade beds, trays of dishes, bags of trash. In every room, a television blared. She would get nothing done if there were a television in every room. Her neck would be sore from working one way, watching another.

On this morning, she longed for work. She made her bed and tidied her room, then went to stand on the balcony to look out over the water, determined to think long thoughts about what she wanted and what she did not. But with nothing to do, no thoughts would come. For a time she watched a flock of chachalacas squabble over a pizza crust in the courtyard below. Still no long thoughts would come, only quick ones no more lasting than the peck of a beak or the flurry of feathers and wings as the birds, startled but still greedy, rose and descended.

On the balcony was a ponytail palm, root-bound in a plastic pot too small, its peeling debris like a ragged skirt, untended. She busied herself with the plant, roughing up the soil to give it air, picking off the dried fronds. She unwrapped a water glass in the bathroom, filled it, watered the palm, then looked around for something else to do. There was nothing. Finally she left her room.

In the lobby, business was slow. People were talking about the coming freeze. There was free coffee, and she drank so many cups her mouth felt dull. She walked up and down the row of shops off the hotel's lobby. She sat in one chair, then another. She flipped through magazines. She watched *Sesame Street* with a group of children in the playroom, happy to find that she could say the answers in her mind before the children shouted them. But the minute the program was over she jumped up. Again she walked up and down the shop row, looking in the windows. She wanted to go home.

"The world's not as simple as you think it is," Madama had said. "You'll be back with your tail between your legs."

"Pah," she said now to a diamond ring in a window. "Pah."

A sign said there was a beauty shop in the lower level. She walked down the stairs and into the shop, and before she knew it, she was in the shampoo chair and the girl was unwrapping her knot of hair. Exhilarated, she heard herself telling the girl—her name was Sofia—that she wanted her hair cut. "All of it off. Short."

"You must have a lot of Spanish blood," Sofia said, fingering her hair. "It will be curly if you cut it."

Her mother's hair had been straight and black. Hers must have come from Old Father. She could not say why, but this knowledge, even so late, pleased her. "That's just what I want."

Sofia shook her head but began to cut. "Do you want me to save it for you as a keepsake? Or maybe you could sell it."

This answer seemed somehow important, although she could not say why. Luisa looked at the long lock Sofia held, streaked with gray, no longer part of her, and said, "Throw it away."

She walked out with her new head, feeling younger and lighter than she could remember. Like one of Chula's kids, springy and light, with little goat feet. Frisky. She felt a silly urge to prance down the thick carpet in the long hall of the hotel. An urge to bleat and laugh. She caught her reflection in a shop window: Who was that kid, that little goat kid, so springy and funny and light? If anyone—Antonia, Joe, Madama—fussed at her, she would . . . she would think of something to say, something frisky, and it would be good. "I wonder," she said, looking into a shop window at a display of turquoise jewelry, "whatever happened to Amparo." The last time she had seen Amparo, her friend had boasted of her new boyfriend, a line supervisor at the juice plant, but Luisa had seen finger bruises on Amparo's thickening arms.

In the souvenir shop, she bought Beth a T-shirt with a picture of a lioness dressed in a business suit. "Hear me roar," read the words. For Antonia, she purchased a clock made of varnished driftwood, and for Madama she bought a birdhouse made of beads and seashells. It would look perfect hanging from a low branch of the live oak in the center of the circle drive.

Where had the time gone? It was late afternoon, time to go to the water; she had been putting it off.

Antonia said—Antonia who thought she knew everything—said that there was something about the sea that made people remember who they were and what they'd known already and didn't know they knew. Luisa, standing at the water's edge, decided that her daughter might know much about the things that could be seen and how they worked, but about the things that couldn't she knew little, and about the sea she was wrong. Here, there was too much sky and too much water and there was no answer to who she was in all of it, not the way there was at home, where all around were things she knew and touched and loved. Here, surfaces looked flat, as though beyond their colors was no meaning. Still, she took off her shoes, determined to test Antonia's words.

The sand was wet and clinging, the water cold. She waded in up to her ankles, stricken to realize that she didn't know how to swim. Frightening creatures, she knew from Pompilo's encyclopedias, lived beneath the water. For a moment she couldn't move for fear of them. But she made herself wade out a little farther, noticing how at close range the water was a different color from the sky, gray green, and how the sky held itself above the water, but when her gaze moved toward the distance the colors ran together and it was hard to tell where the water left off and the sky began and in the place where they met there was something she ought to be able to see but could not. Alarmed by nothing she could name, except the same terrible feeling of loss she had felt after the turtle slipped into the marsh, she turned, churning and thrashing, breathless, stumbling through the little waves and back onto the beach. Her heart would not slow down. Between her legs she felt a wetness, warmth. At some point as she'd looked out to the sea, she decided, she must have lost control and wet herself. As she walked along the beach toward her hotel, she felt as though she had avoided some great danger.

the leopard and her spots

In the blank television screen Eddie saw a bloated hag, death-green shadows beneath her eyes. Beside her on a table lay the sticky ruins of the fruit tray Raleigh and Elaine had sent from Oregon. Dried apricots and figs, dates and candied pineapple, walnut halves and macadamia nuts, banana chips and kiwi. "Coals to Newcastle," she'd snorted when it arrived that morning, the morning after she had buried Little Dixie, like a horrid consolation prize. Into this lush valley, at a time when the oranges hung full and ripe and ready to be picked, her son sent wizened apricots that smelled like dirty feet and left a sharp acidic taste along the sides of her tongue.

But she had eaten nearly all the fruit and had started on the Christmas candy. She planned to finish off the jellied orange slices, then cut the sugar with the salt of the French burnt peanuts. All afternoon she had sat in the chair before the television, eating, and now her stomach felt stretched tight. It hurt to move. A pain under her arm told her that her gallbladder would be next to go.

It was time for the five o'clock news. She clicked the remote control and the announcer voice of Alfonso Cárdenas blasted through the room. The big freeze was on its way, he said, and citrus growers were taking precautions. "I don't need you to tell me that," she sassed him. "I know smudge when I smell it!" She felt a little better, and settled back in her chair.

The county government continued to uncover evidence of another election scandal, the news went on. The Fonseca political machine had voted the cemetery rolls, the names of the dead. "Vote me," Eddie said. "I might as well be."

She clicked and saw Billy Graham's wavy hair and potato-jawed face. She started to click again, but something stopped her, and she turned up the volume to the swell of organ music, voices singing "Just as I Am."

She hadn't heard the hymn since she had been a girl, when she'd gone

Sunday evening to the Baptist church with her friend Ruth Williams. Brought up Episcopalian, she'd been horrified by the emotional service. Pastor Bunch had ranted and raged, blistering the congregation with its sinfulness, then he'd had the gall to cry at the end of his own sermon. Awful. At the invitational she had been afraid she might stand up and go forward with the rest of them. Anything to feel better than she felt in that hard pew, mad and miserable. But now something about the song touched her; it made things sound so simple. "What a crock," she said aloud, to steel herself against the feeling, but she didn't click the channel.

Now Billy Graham was calling the congregation to dedicate their lives. His Carolina voice led her back to Lynchburg, and she remembered one of Noon's practices. "The cure for trouble's in the Book. I don't waste my precious time and tears. I head smack-dab to the Lord," she'd once said. "I close my eyes and think my trouble and then I open up that Bible and I put my finger on the answer and it's always, always right."

Feeling silly, Eddie jumped up and rummaged in the bookshelf, where she found Thomas's old Bible. She closed her eyes, opened the book, then stabbed her finger onto a page. She had hoped for comfort, but what she got was a garbled, half-cocked passage from Ezekiel 37:1: "The hand of the Lord was upon me, and carried me out into the spirit of the Lord, and set me down in the valley which *was* full of dry bones." Over and over she read the words, but they made no sense. She read on. There were cloven-hoofed creatures and fires, wheels in the middle of wheels. She remembered Noon singing a song about Ezekiel's wheel. *De big wheel turn by love and de little wheel turn by de grace of de Lord.* Or was it the other way around? Who could tell? Ezekiel was—all the prophets were—fire-breathing, bug-eating madmen.

She went back to the television and clicked the channel. This time it was an old western in black-and-white, and she began to think how much simpler life must have been in those days, when bad was bad and good was good. Lulled by the images on the screen, she must have dozed, for when she woke up, she was in the middle of a buffalo stampede. The television air was black with dust and the herd snuffled and bawled, galloping, snorting and chuffing, their hoofbeats a thunderous tattoo. On the screen, under a fallen log, a pioneer girl crouched, her shawl pulled over her face so that only her frightened eyes showed. "Uh-oh," Eddie said, not knowing where the disturbing feeling of dread came from, only that it was coming, and not only for the pioneer girl but thundering toward her. "Uh-oh."

On the screen she saw the massive, horned heads of the buffaloes, their wild eyes rolling, bodies thick and shaggy at the withers, the devil-black hide at their haunches glistening as they ran stumbling, bellowing and spooked.

She turned off the television but the menacing image remained. In her darkened house, she was afraid. She hurried through the rooms, turning on lights, but her ears still rang with the sound of the stampede. Her stomach was upset. As she walked along the upstairs gallery, she remembered again, for no reason she could detect, Ruth Williams. Vain, pretty Ruthie and her blue eyes. China. Cerulean. That had been her friend's favorite game, to think of new names for the color of her eyes. The list went on and on: robin's egg, Wedgewood, ocean, sky, aqua-marine, blue grotto, Chinese vase, turquoise, sapphire, cochineal—all of the names beautiful; there was no ugly word for Ruthie's blue. Eddie's eyes were green. Jade, emerald, celadon—these were the only words they could think of, and soon Ruthie's suggestions became silly: arsenic, slime, bread mold, fungus, swamp water, garden hose. Green could never be as good as blue. One afternoon as they lay in the heat of Ruthie's bedroom, Eddie, wanting to sting, had said, "Isn't it just awful? How can you stand it? Williams is such a *colored* people's name."

Now, after sixty years, she was wracked by shame. She thought of returning to the television to see if the pioneer girl had survived, but she was afraid. Her stomach hurt. She hurried to her bathroom for Bromo Seltzer, but found in the medicine cabinet next to the cotton box marked with a blocky red cross her cousin Nellora, sweet, tender-hearted, the friend of her youth, who one day had been too sad to play with Eddie because her cat Brindle had died. Hurt, Eddie'd waited, planned her ambush, and one day not long after Nellora had recovered, as they played in their grandmother's carriage house, Eddie, knowing what her cousin would say, started one of their well-worn games: What Will You Be?

Nellora's eyes shone. "A nurse. So I can make people well."

Eddie struck. "You'll have to pull fingernails off babies if they have infections. You'll have to give them a shot. You'll make them cry and they'll hate you. And if they get scratched by a cat, you'll have to cut off its head to see if it has rabies. And you'll have to do it in front of them!"

Now she braced her arms on the bathroom sink, sickened as, one after another, her past meannesses rose in her memory, a rueful parade, and she saw her younger self in the saying of every hateful utterance, lies petty and hurtful, every comment she'd uttered, intending to wound or one-up.

Aunt Bean, the day after Eddie had brought Thomas to meet her, had said fretfully, "I fear you're marrying beneath you, dear."

"That shows what you know," Eddie'd said. "His family has ranches and oil. His grandfather founded . . ." she'd rummaged in her brain for the name of a college in Texas ". . . Baylor!"

Wide-eyed, Bean said, "Oh, dear! He's a Baptist?"

"At least," Eddie remembered saying to Bean, Bean of the African violets, the cats, the linen antimacassars, the narrow, the girlhood bed, her thyroid syrups arrayed on crocheted dresser scarves; Bean with her bulging eyes and her thin hair slicked back on her fragile skull, who looked, Eddie now saw, like a human Little Dixie; dear Bean, to whom she had once said and could never take back, "at least I'll *have* a husband."

And Thomas. She had married him for several reasons, only one of which was spite and all of which were wrong, and she had never forgiven him for what she'd done.

"Oh, oh," she said in the mirror. "Oh."

How must she have looked, all her life? Had her bitterness shown as much as she'd felt it, with the same clarity as she now saw it? Had anyone at all been fooled?

In a moment she hoped was sanity, she tossed her head and then held her chin and mouth in a haughty position. "Phooey," she said to the mirror, "on everyone," but instead of the righteous disdain she had hoped for, the mirror showed her a wrinkled old face, the lines around her lips as puckered and creased as the drawn flesh of a desiccated apricot, a face trying hard to look defiant and sassy, but behind its eyes some great, some hidden hurt.

She composed herself and appealed to her reflection. "Am I that bad?"

Though she had the feeling that the jury had been rigged, that any test she made would have given her the same answer, her own eyes in the mirror, hollowed, bereft, newly wise, said yes.

los hijos del sol

Shaken and cold from her time in the water, Luisa started back toward the hotel. Her legs felt wobbly and numb, and as she walked, she marveled that her feet kept taking steps along the sand. She went to her room and lay on the bed, but she couldn't hold still, and she jumped back up. She went into the bathroom, intending to clean herself from her accident.

It had been many years since she had last bled. Exactly when her cycle had ceased, she couldn't have said, but now there was blood, a single bright stain, round as a coin. "Oh," she said, addressing the spot as if it were an object she had lost or mislaid, only to find it much later, in just the place she had left it, "there you are." And she laughed that this moment had come to her, alone in a faraway room, on a toilet. And then, after she rose and went to the mirror without knowing she would, for this strange new feeling of the past and future in the present as she looked into her face and saw that she could understand no more now than she had in the beginning, for all she had lost, for time and forgetting not making things right but only the past, but then suddenly—now—not beyond her at all, she began to cry.

To push away the terrible feeling, and to cover the noises she was making, she ran water into the tub, then sat on the rim. Each time she thought she would grow calm, another cry came from her throat. When at last no more sounds would come, she stood. She felt a thickness behind her eyes, a heavy feeling in her chest. Her ears rang, but her head seemed strangely clear. She took a bath. She dried herself, and in case there would be more blood, she tucked a tissue between her legs, then dressed in the new orange pants suit Joe had bought for her in Harlingen. "Very stylish," he'd said as she drew the garment from the box. "Polyester. No ironing." Wearing the gift now for the first time, she felt silly and buttoned up, the thick, puffy fabric so different from her cotton dresses, and she imagined she looked like a plump little man in a gas-station suit. She left her room and as she walked down the hall she could hear the lumpy, *swish-swish* sound of her thighs rubbing to-gether.

In the lobby was a poster of a mariachi band. Los Hijos del Sol wore frilled shirts and sequined ties, black trousers with thick shiny belts. She imagined what Joe would say about them; to him, any man who didn't work outside was not a man. "Hump," she said, and she went into the lounge, where it was dark and cool and people were drinking bright-colored drinks from large glasses, some with paper umbrellas perched on their rims. She found a table and settled herself in a chair. In the corner, a couple sipped some kind of drink that came in a coconut shell with a flower on top. "That, please," she told the waitress.

"The Zombie?"

"Yes. And a little umbrella with it." She would take the paper um-brella to Beth as a present. She settled back in her chair, determined to have a good time and to forget what had happened in the bathroom.

The drink was delicious, tasting of bananas and coconut, so cold it made her head hurt when she drew long pulls of it with a straw that was far too little. The taste reminded her of something, of the piñon and agave drink Uncle had given her, then of the wine she'd had on the night of falling stars. She laughed and took another sip; at least this time she would not become pregnant.

Suddenly the lights went down even dimmer than before and the stage lit up. With a flashing commotion of spangles and colored lights, maracas and tambourines and trumpets, accordions and guitars, Los Hijos ran out from behind a curtain and began playing and singing so loudly she wanted to cover her ears.

There was a sticky, sweet taste at the back of her throat, and she felt as though she'd swallowed something heavy, a wet sponge, maybe. Again her legs felt funny and everything looked strange and wavering. Her head felt even lighter than before, as though it turned too easily. She felt again the familiar worry that she had forgotten something im-portant. When the waitress came around, she told her to take the drink back. "But it's gone," the girl said. "You drank it."

"So I did," Luisa said, her mouth strangely loose, a bubble of a feeling just beneath her tongue. "I'll have a Coke now. My stomach is very fuzzy." The waitress looked at her oddly, but removed the coconut shell and returned with her order.

She began to look around the bar. People weren't paying attention to the music, but were talking and laughing and clinking their glasses. On stage, the tallest hijo, the one with the guitar, was singing "Las Mañanitas," singing quietly, and his voice was beautiful.

Everything, suddenly, was beautiful. She wanted the noisy room to be still, to honor this. She focused more closely on the singer. He reminded her of someone. Of Tavo if he had grown older. Of her brother Memo. Of Rafael. Of someone. Someone she had known. Someone she had loved. She could hardly wait for the song to end, and she was out of her chair, dizzy but waving, before the final note trailed away. She called out to him, "Hey!"

The room went quiet as the tall hijo squinted at her. Her mind spun past Señor Miller and Memo and Rafael and Uncle and don Tomás and the soldier Ben and Joe and all those she had known, and in this moment she was certain she was seeing before her the face of her son.

"It's . . ." Just as the words "Your mother" rose to her lips, the room shifted shape and instead of her son, the man became Memo, and she started to say, "Your sister," but again the room spun and the man became someone else but she didn't know who, and she said, for there being no way to say who she was to him, "Me."

Around her, she could see faces turning her way. Then she remembered: She hadn't eaten. All day she'd had only coffee, and at this moment she marveled more about this than she did about the tall man making his way past the tables to her.

This close, he no longer looked familiar. His hair glinted blue black and shiny, his eyes seemed hooded; he was no boy, but a man. A stranger. What had happened in the bathroom had made her imagination wild and reckless. She was a fool who looked among the living for the dead. "I made a mistake," she said, when he stood before her. "I forgot to eat."

She sat down and made herself busy by wiping the table with her napkin.

The man did not go away. He rested his hand on the back of her chair and leaned toward her. "María Luisa?" he asked. "Villamil y Cantú?"

Later she would understand that when she heard her name it was as though a long spell had been broken, and that the message of the blood was that she had been dead in life but had not left her body, which had carried her through time until the moment she would know this, that

this death in life had dealt a wound to others—to Tavo, to Antonia—
one she hadn't seen. Though it seemed to press against her heart until
she felt a shudder, she took this knowledge for a miracle even greater
than the miracle of finding him when she asked, "Which one are you?"
and heard his answer, "Rafael."

She cried and hugged him for a long time, then for a longer time she
couldn't speak except to repeat his name. What Sonny López had told
her was true: Rafael cried a lot himself. It was true, too, she learned,
after he told the group to go on without him and they moved to the
restaurant so she could eat, that he had been to the university, that he
was a poet. He had written a book and it had won a prize. "A little
one," he told her. He would send a copy to her. After all, she was in it.
"Only sort of" he said, when he saw her alarmed look. "Not by your
real name."

"It's a red book," he said, smiling in a way that made her think this
must be important. She didn't understand, but she smiled.

"I knew you lived somewhere in the Valley. Everywhere we've
played I looked for you in the phone book but I couldn't find you."

"I don't have a phone," she told him, astonished. "I live in Rio
Paradiso. On Grand Texas Boulevard. But in the back. How did you
know I lived in the Valley?"

"Years ago somebody said so. I was a kid, but I remembered. When
I got out of school and started trying to find you and couldn't, I thought
maybe you didn't want to be found."

She looked at her hands. "I wasn't hiding. I wasn't lost."

His look was sorrowful. "Sister, did you not know what you meant
to me?"

She looked away. Nothing she could say could make up for the years
she had forgotten him.

"What are you doing here now?" he asked.

She told him about her job, Madama, her first-ever vacation. "What
about you?"

"I teach in Monterrey, but sometimes on holidays I travel with the
group."

"Your other job doesn't pay enough?"

"I do this for fun, mostly. It makes a little extra, but not much. I love
the music."

"Me, too," she said.

She had ordered, pointing at the menu, a dish with a confusing name which turned out to be some kind of chicken with ham and cheese, and she felt much better.

Rafael and his wife, Gloria, had a little boy named Jacobo, named after the teacher, and as Rafael talked of their lives in Monterrey, his classes, she was reminded of what Sonny López had told her.

"I heard Memo went to Monterrey."

"He did at first. But after that no one heard from him again."

"So he is still lost."

"I think so."

She asked about Uncle.

"Still there. He hobbles around. He's probably a hundred years old by now. Too old to arrest. But he's not putting on any more ceremonies." From his tone, she could tell what he thought of Uncle.

"It wasn't what you think," she said. "There was a reason."

He looked at her oddly, but then nodded.

He had seen to Chavela's burial. There was something she had wondered all her life. "Why," she asked him, "did they make a hole in the back of the house to take our mother out?"

He told her that according to the old beliefs, a woman who died in childbirth was a messenger between two worlds, and therefore the most dangerous and sacred.

She had so many questions. Did he remember this song, that saying? What was the name of the barren season? That yellow plant with the narrow leaves, the one they had called butterfly bush, did he know another name? What was the name for the time that came when the old passed away and the new began, the fire time?

"The Bundle of Years." He explained about the old calendar, the names of the eighteen seasons. "It's a dangerous time. A place between places, where it is determined what to burn and what to save."

"I knew that!" she said. "Just when you said it, they all came back, the names. Sometimes," she told him, "I think I forgot more than I ever knew."

"If you remember that you've forgotten, you can't have forgotten entirely." Her brother pointed to her head, then to her heart. "You need to come for a visit," he said, "so you can remember."

"I will," she said. "I will."

"The house is just the same," he said. "Well, we've fixed certain things. New tiles for the roof, a bathroom, that kind of thing. But mostly we've kept it the same. I found out that it was built in the year of the treaty. Sometimes we stay there in the summer if I'm not traveling. Did you know that it was yours?"

"Mine?"

"They passed it down through the women."

She thought of the way the house sat on the curve of the hill, the catclaw tree, the good, thick adobe walls, and the dusty, fragrant vigas. She thought of her bean bottle, tucked into its hiding place beneath the loose board, wondering if it could still be there.

"Anytime you want to come," he was saying.

"Oh, but I don't need it." She told him about the little house on Grand Texas Boulevard. "It's so beautiful," she said, "just the way I like, with everything in it. At night I turn off the light and I walk around and touch things. Sometimes in the morning I sit at my table and look out my window." As she spoke of her garden, her house, a great pride swelled in her to think of the life she had made for herself. She talked of Antonia and Beth, telling him about Antonia's practice, Beth's school.

Rafael looked at her closely. "A long time ago we heard you had a boy."

"I did," she said, but she found she couldn't say more. She folded her napkin into a small square. "I do."

Rafael put his hand on her arm. "Can you talk about him?"

The tears that had come to her in the bathroom returned, and she lowered her head to hide them. "I don't even know what happened."

"Did he die?"

She nodded. "Rafael, a strange thing happened only today. He has been gone for so many years. It was the war. Other things happened and then . . . I don't know. It was as though I put him in a drawer and closed it and never looked in it again. The way I did with you in Salsipuedes. I don't know why."

"To save yourself from pain."

"Rafael, I will tell you something terrible. Only today did I cry for him. Cry truly. In so many years. And I didn't even know it was for him I was crying until now." She told him about the turtle, her fear of the water, the bathroom. "When I first saw you, I thought you were Tavo. Even now, when I look at you, I see him, too." She looked at her placemat, its pictures of water and islands and fish. "I was going to say that maybe this means that I'm supposed to see him, that I never did, but I think that's not the truth. What happened was that I did see him and I looked away. Because I didn't want . . . and then he was gone."

For a long time she looked at the placemat, then Rafael reached for her hand. "What happens will happen."

She smiled at him. "You sound like our mother."

"We were very young to lose her."

"Do you remember that day in the canyon? The day she died?"

He nodded.

"I thought it was my fault. Chavela—"

"Luisa, she was sick."

"I know."

"But still—?"

"Yes."

"Have you tried to see that time in other ways?"

"To blame yourself for nothing is worse than to blame yourself for everything."

He shook his head. "I don't know. I think they both come from the same place, from the dark." He looked at her as though thinking, and she thought he would say more about the dark, but when he spoke again it was to ask, "Do you know what Jacob Miller said about you?"

"The teacher?"

"He told me that when he first came to Salsipuedes he was troubled by many things. How poor the town was, how little we had. Our backwardness. But he told me, 'When I started to question whether any good at all was in this place, all I had to do was look at the light behind your sister's eyes.' "

"He said that?"

Rafael nodded. "He blamed himself that you left."

She laughed. "Just as well to blame the stars. I was such a little fool."

"Luisa, do you think maybe you need to forgive yourself?"

"For what?"

He laughed. "For everything you think you've done, maybe. Maybe for not forgiving yourself."

"Once he told me I would do a great thing. That I would be called to do it. But I haven't done nothing." She picked up the salt shaker, tilting it one way and then another so the grains shifted slightly. She set it down. "I thought I would be better than I am."

"You mean perfect?"

"No. But better."

"Maybe it's just living, what we're called to do. Our work. What love we put in that." He shrugged, grinning. "Maybe it's sex."

She nudged him, ducking her head to show she knew that he was teasing, but in a deep part of herself she knew that this was true.

They were quiet for a time, and then she asked, "This book I'm in but not by my real name, in it what do I do?"

Rafael looked surprised, as though seeing something for the first time, and he laughed. "You leave. I look for you."

Delighted, she spanked the table with the palm of her hand. "And now look! You find me!"

"In the book, I don't."

"This is a sad book, then. Not true."

"Maybe not." He smiled. "But there are other ways of finding people."

The restaurant was closing and the waitress gave them cups of coffee to take to the lobby. "They treat you so nice here," Luisa said as they settled into chairs, then, without knowing why she was telling him, she said, "I'm supposed to decide to get married or not." She told him about Joe and his proposal.

"Do you want to?"

"The problem with Joe is that he always thinks he's right. About everything."

"Have you told him this?"

"All the time," she said, but suddenly she was not sure this was true.

"Tell him," Rafael said, "that you are the famous and wonderful María Luisa Villamil y Cantú, sister of el Netzhualcoyotl, the poet-king. Tell him I said to stop treating you . . ."

She laughed. "Like a pet!"

Suddenly she thought of Madama, of the way the woman had treated her, but how ready she had always been to forgive her if only she would ask. Joe and Antonia thought she was a fool for this, but they didn't understand. She decided to ask Rafael what he thought. She scratched creases along the side of her Styrofoam cup. "If a person does something bad to you, it's best just to forget it, wouldn't you say?"

Rafael looked at her as though considering. "Do you mean Chavela?"

"No. Just anyone."

Rafael put his palms together and brought his hands to his face, resting his chin on his thumbs, and she smiled for the way he looked in that moment like Señor Miller. Then he took his hands down, saying, "It depends on why you're forgetting, I think. Whether you're really forgetting or whether you're saving it to hold against them without even knowing that's what you're doing. Storing it. The same can be true of forgiving. The one who forgives most can hold himself above the one he forgives, and that is the worst of all. Then it's not true forgiveness, which is somehow mixed up with forgetting as well as with remembering."

"I try to think of all these things, but then I get too confused and so I stop thinking and just go on."

"Do you know what our mother used to say about the night and the day? That the night is the forgetting time. She said, 'The night hides things from us.' " Again he rested his chin on his thumbs and was quiet for a time. Luisa waited, trying to decide whether or not this was true.

Rafael cleared his throat. "I'm not explaining it very well, but anyway, there was a reason the day was made. So nothing was hidden or made to look like it was something else. To show us what things truly are and what we have to do—"

"Our mother said this?"

With a bewildered look that pained her because she understood that this was the way she often must look to others, Rafael said, "I don't know. I get mixed up about what I write and what I read and what really happened."

Luisa laughed. "My daughter says I forget things so I don't have to look at them."

Rafael had moved back to the subject of marriage. "If Joe would admit that he was wrong—"

"Even one time," she added, setting down her cup so hard the coffee sloshed over the rim.

He smiled. "If he would, could you?"

For a moment she was confused; his question was not the one she'd expected. "But I'm the one in the right. *He* was the one . . ."

Rafael laughed, a full-bodied sound that was comforting and unsettling at the same time. "Let's say that's true. Could you?"

Luisa snapped her fingers in the gesture she'd seen Antonia use. "Easy. Like that."

He looked at her for what seemed a long time, and in his smile Luisa saw her mother's, loving and warm, yet faraway, as though he knew something she didn't.

"Like that," she repeated, again snapping her fingers, this time to bring him to earth, remembering a phrase she didn't understand but which she'd heard Beth use for how fast, "in a New York minute."

Rafael laughed. "Good," he said. "Then you're ready for marriage."

They talked on, far into the night and the early morning, their conversation looping from present to past and back again. Behind the registration desk, the clerk shuffled papers, rattled keys. It was late and they were tired, and at last they parted with promises to write, to meet again. Rafael would bring Gloria and Jacobo at Easter. Joe, she promised, would love to meet them; he was not as bad as she'd made him sound, but a good man, and she loved him in spite of everything. When Rafael asked if that meant she'd marry him, she gave his arm a playful push.

As she lay waiting for sleep on her last night in the wide, cool hotel bed, she resolved to let the night hide nothing from her, and she began to think of her life, to remember. This taste and that moment, this sight and that act, this sorrow, that joy, the scent of ripe corn, the death of a child, and when these were difficult to look upon she made herself look harder until she pushed beyond them into the place where who she had been became who she was.

At some point in the night she was shocked awake by a dream of fire, but then she remembered the Bundle, the throwing in of years and from their burning, new ones, and she went back to sleep. Toward dawn, she rose again, this time to check for blood. Finding none, she smiled to think she knew it had been there, then cried, but only a little, to remember what it had meant. She pictured Antonia receiving the shock of her life to hear her stubborn mother say that she was sorry.

Tomorrow, she would go home. She didn't yet know how, but things would be different with Madama. Luisa put herself back to sleep by going over in her memory all the items in her house. Even in these objects was the proof that she—her life—had mattered.

the miserable comforter

Between Rio Paradiso and Martha on old 83 was a roadhouse called the Coyote Club where Thomas had occasionally gone with other growers and where on weekends an array of dusty pickups nosed haphazardly toward the Alamo-shaped facade. Once Eddie'd asked him what they did there. "Jaw," he'd told her. "Tell whoppers and play poormouth." Eddie turned off the television, knocked the fruit tray and the candy jar onto the terrazzo floor, took a coat from the closet, and left the house.

By the time she was settled in a dark back booth, she had almost forgotten why she had come. "Some kind of beer," she told the waitress, "any kind. And a package of . . ." she hadn't smoked in fifteen years ". . . Lucky Strikes." She gave the waitress her most winning smile. She thought she caught a strange look on the waitress's face, but she ignored it and began to look around the room.

On the far wall was a long bar behind which a television flickered. Another room held pool tables. Wagon wheels and mounted horns lined the walls. From the rafters hung bridles, collars, horseshoes, lariats. In the blue neon light from a beer sign hung in the flyblown window, a sick-looking cactus sent off one magenta bloom.

Hartley Rowell, his stained old Stetson beside him on the bench, sat at a corner booth. He saw her, saluted, picked up his hat, then walked over to her table, hitching his pants as he came.

She fanned herself with her napkin. "I'm just catching my breath before Christmas. I had to get out of the house."

"Mind if I join you?"

"Didn't know I was coming apart." Her own laugh sounded feeble. "Ha, ha." Again she smiled her most winningly, hoping to bring off a devil-may-care effect. "That was a joke."

Hartley ducked his head, seeming suddenly to be more concerned with fiddling with the pocket of his pearl-snap shirt than with her presence. "Eddie, there's some kind of orange goop between your teeth."

While she used her napkin to pick out the clumps of jellied candy,

Hartley took a seat and began to chat about the weather. "Pretty dead in here tonight. Everybody's out watching for the freeze. Maybe it'll come tonight, maybe tomorrow. I think it's a day away, at least. Nothing they can do about it."

When he saw that her glass was empty, he got up and started for the bar. "Let me get us some more beer." His seat-sprung khaki trousers, the legs bunched at his knees and ankles, rode low on his backside, so low she could see the frayed tops of his boxer shorts, below that, a sight even worse. She noticed that the heel of his left boot was loose and wobbling.

"Hart," she called after him, wanting to save him from embarrassment, to tell him to hitch up his pants, but then a Bible verse about sins and first stones rose up with the primary-colored clarity of the robed and sandaled Sunday-school flannel-board pantheon, and when he turned, she said, "Never mind."

The evening wore on. Hartley, with so many digressions she was nearly stupefied, told her the latest developments on *Dynasty*. She listened, pretending to care about the video perfidies and turpitude, pretending shock, when the truth was that none of it seemed very bad at all. Dressed-up, made-up Hollywood sin.

She grew maudlin with the second beer, and she told him about Little Dixie. To cheer her up, Hartley went to the bar and came back with pickled eggs and Slim Jims and a bag of barbecue-flavored pork rinds. He spread the feast on the financial pages of the Houston paper.

Though she'd vowed never to eat again, the food made her feel better. She was careful to check her teeth with her tongue. "Hart, how did we get so old?"

"You think it's a conspiracy?"

"Seriously." She bit off a hunk of her Slim Jim, which tasted awful, like dried-out bacon. "You know who I miss? Thomas. He was a good man."

Hartley nodded. "Old Thomas." Into his mouth he slid a whole pickled egg, which he chewed meditatively, then swallowed. "Tried to be the best man in the world. It's what killed him. Just couldn't live up to his own expectations. Personally, I aim low. That way . . ." He broke off suddenly, as though realizing his choice of words had been unfortunate.

Eddie waved away his embarrassment. She worked her cud of jerked beef. "Do you think he loved me?"

Hartley brightened. "Now, that's a female question if I ever heard one. Man marries a woman, that's proof of the fact thereafter, and a man sees it that way. No need to keep saying so." He looked at her quizzically. "But yes, ma'am. I know he did. Matter of fact, he said so. Plenty times. Didn't I ever tell you what he said about you?"

She shook her head. "No."

He scratched his forehead. "You sure?"

"Hartley, don't tease. I need to hear something nice."

He squared his shoulders. "Well, it happened in this very bar. That table right over there." He pointed to a round table in the center of the room. "One day old Tom is out here and a bunch of us're playing Liar's Poker and he's losing bad. But that don't matter. What's important is that the talk turns to the subject of wives and women. Buddy Baines says his wife's kicked him out of the bed for no reason on earth and so we talk about that for awhile, everybody trying to top the other fellow's story. I remember Dub Sissoms says his wife once set a board down the middle of the bed until he admitted he couldn't tell the difference between her mix biscuits and his mother's baking-powder jobs."

Hartley picked up a pork rind and twirled it between his fingers, examining it as though the pattern in its bubbled convolutions could provide the answer to the tortured questions of ladies and gentlemen. "Fits and tricks. You all got ways men couldn't dream up. Put twenty smart men lawyers in a room together, and they couldn't invent half the devices known to woman. Makes you think men ought to just lay down and give up. Save a lot of trouble. Anyways, we're talking like this and I'll admit there was some complaining going on, when old Tom ups and says, 'I bet you all can't think of three nice things to say about your wives.'

"Well, it'd burn your ears to hear the ring-tailed fibs those old hounds told each other. Near about broke their necks trying to make their wives out to be sex goddesses and Betty Crockers. Finally it comes Tom's turn. Now, he's been quiet all along, just listening with this Tom-look on his face, like he's got a mouthful of something good and can't nobody taste it but him, and now he speaks up and you know what he says? Says, 'Fellas, I won't waste your time in the kitchen and the bedroom. Why, any woman at all can . . . ' " Hartley looked at her, then at his hands, then at the pork rind, as though considering. "Well, you get my drift. Tom says, 'Boys, my wife's done the guaranteed one thing a man can't resist in a woman.' "

He leaned across the table toward her, so close she could smell his scent of beer and dried beef and beneath that his old-man smell of unwashed, hat-worn head. "He says, 'That woman has made herself so danged hard to love, you just *got* to.' "

To cover the tears she felt welling, Eddie folded her arms on the table and rested her head in their shelter. When she again looked up, Hartley said, "I'm trying to cheer you up, Ed."

The waitress came by. "Happy hour. Two for one."

Hartley said, "Fix us up."

Eddie dabbed at her eyes. "Hart, you made that up, didn't you?"

He busied himself by dusting crumbs from the table, arranging the pork rinds into a square. "Sorry."

She picked at a pork rind and allowed herself to feel sorry for herself. "Why?"

"Sounded good. Because you needed some stiffening up." He examined his nails, then began to chew on a hangnail. "I guess mostly because I could."

Again she dabbed at her eyes, hoping her lids hadn't swollen. If she were to cry, with her fair complexion, she would take on the bleared, white-lashed look of a sleepy Hampshire white shoat.

"Hart, I don't even know what the truth is anymore. I'm old. I'm lonely."

Hartley guffawed. "You ever think we wouldn't be?"

"But it hurts," she said. "I didn't think it would. I wanted . . ."

The words were nearly out before she caught them. *People to love me,* she'd almost said. She sipped on her beer; the taste seemed flat and metallic. "Did you ever . . . did anybody think Thomas was . . . that I was . . . ?"

Hartley wiped the condensation from his beer bottle. "Spit it out, Eddie. Did anybody think what?"

"That Thomas was . . . I don't know what men would call it . . . a sucker?"

"You asking for a reason or just idling your engine?"

"I just wondered if, you know, people ever said anything. Anything at all. I just wondered."

He looked at her closely. "You sure that's the only reason, honey?"

All it had taken was one tender word, one listener, and she had confessed it all, leaving out nothing. Her many meannesses, the awful feeling of not enough, the something missing, the hollow self, the ruin and the want. The lies she'd told that had sent Raleigh running, though she'd tried—too late, maybe—to right them. The lies she continued to let him believe. Sniffling and hot-faced, she told it all. "It was all my fault. I'm paying for it now."

Hartley, who had listened all the way through, shaking his head, patted her hand. "Be right back." He left the table and returned with two cups of coffee.

"Here. Congratulations."

She blew her nose into a napkin. "What for?"

He smiled. "That's the most terrible story I ever heard."

The coffee was hot and she blew on it. "You really didn't know?"

He shook his head, then pointed to the package of Lucky Strikes. "You haven't smoked a lick."

"Want one?" she asked, pushing the pack toward him.

Hartley pulled the cellophane string and removed the foil, tamped the pack, then cocked one toward her. She took it. He drew a box of matches from his shirt, struck one on his boot heel, and held the flame for her. He lit one for himself, and for a time they sat, smoking.

"Tastes good, don't it?" he said.

She nodded. Her eyes were tearing, not from the smoke but from the way the taste reminded her of her old self, the self that thought she was better than everyone else.

Hartley blew a series of rings. "Want some advice? Some lies you can't undo. And you probably shouldn't if it don't serve anybody but yourself." He leaned back in the booth, pointing to the rafters where a coiled lariat hung from a baling hook. "You know how a rope can get all knotted up? The more you try to yank it right, the tighter the knots'll get?" He waited until she nodded. "Now put that rope in a barn under some weight and let it set. Take it out and even if you do get it all undone, it'll never lay flat. It'll kink up when you least expect it. I wouldn't tell him. What good would it do? Let him be who he thinks he is."

"I don't know," she said. "I just don't know."

Hartley shook his head. "To tell the truth, I don't either. And I'm no one to talk. Back when Thomas died . . . I been sorry about that for a long time, warring with it. . . ."

She brushed away his confession. "If it's anyone's fault what happened, it's mine. I hounded him and hounded him. You don't know what I did."

Hartley leaned forward. "Don't think that anything's ever only one person's fault." He propped his cigarette in the ashtray and spread his hands on the table, picked again at his hangnail. "See, there's degrees of things, and only a idiot tries to make it come out even. I figure that most of the trouble with the world is that too many people think that way. Hell's accountants. Trying to fix blame all the way back to the beginning. Add it up and weigh it out. Say this one thing is worse than two of those or five of the other. Never happen. I'm not talking about the big evil. There's big evil and that's a fact and I don't have an answer for it. I'm talking about everyday bad. Though there's a touch of big bad in the little business, too. But never mind. It takes two to tango and what matters is . . ."

Hartley paused to survey the room. The bar had filled up with the late-night crowd. It was noisier, someone called across the room, "More wine!" and someone else yelled back, "Hell, more ever'thing!" She heard the chink and whir of the jukebox selector, static, then the slow, sweet twang of Hank Snow easing into "Now and Then There's a Fool Such as I." Hartley put out his cigarette. "They're playing our song." He stood and offered his hand. "Would you dance with a foolish old man?"

"You were going to tell me what mattered."

He looked puzzled.

"About degrees and accountants? Two to tango?"

"Well, I don't remember a word *of* it." He reached for her hand and pulled her from the booth. "Must not have been important."

"Do my teeth look okay?" She smiled for his inspection.

"Beautiful." He squinted, cocking his head to get a better look. "They real?"

"Hartley," she said, "I'm not sure I agree with you. About two to tango."

He shrugged, then slipped his arm around her waist in preparation for their dance. "That's fine," he said. "Most of the time I'm not sure I agree with myself."

Though he smelled of cured beef and pickled eggs and, when she moved closer and into his arms, the human scent of his unwashed shirt, she was comforted. She rested her cheek against his whiskery one as he began to shuffle and turn. His grip was strong. She held on tight.

ezekiel's vision

In the middle of the night Eddie woke from a dream that was a memory that became a vision. In Lynchburg on the next street over in a stone mansion had lived two doddering sisters whom the town called the Panatier girls. Widows of the War Between the States, their boy-husbands sixty years among the honored dead, they dressed alike, held hands when they walked along the sidewalks of Diamond Hill. They died a day apart.

Eddie woke with an ache for a hand to clasp, the comfort of a face as battered and wrinkled and sorry as her own, someone to love and to love her back. For a long time she lay in the darkness, her hand on the pillow beside her where Little Dixie had slept for so many years, round as a cushion, her nose tucked into her hindquarters. She felt tears well but she blinked them away, trying to understand why she would dream of the Panatiers.

And then it hit her: Lu. She would get her to move in with her. They would become friends. It was a brilliant plan, and one, she marveled, that might never have occurred to her if she hadn't been through the fires of hell and now had one foot poised to step out onto the cooler side.

The Hacienda plan had come with a maid's room off the kitchen. Of course Lu had never used it; she had the little house. The room—with its own bathroom—had become a storeroom over the years. Though it was the middle of the night, Eddie sprang from the bed and went to work. She moved the ironing board and she carted boxes, piling them willy-nilly in the back hall. She swept. She dusted. Work felt good. Sweating—how long had it been since she had sweat?—she stripped off her nightgown and raced to Raleigh's old room, where in the closet she found a pair of his sweatpants and a T-shirt that read "Property of Alcatraz." Though her feet were hot, she decided not to take off her terry-cloth mules; she hated the feel of a bare floor. Feeling strangely young, she hurried back to survey the fruits of her industry. The room still looked empty, and so she went upstairs to bring down lamps, little tables, anything she could carry. She tried to move a mattress from Raleigh's old room, but it became wedged on the stairwell and so she left it. Crawled underneath, slipped through, and just left it. Before Lu returned tomorrow, she would get Pompilo to move the bed, other furniture.

In the linen closet she found sheets, and these she tossed into the room. She considered her work, her big, funny, bony self doing it, and she laughed. The house was a mess, but when Lu returned, together they would put it right. What mattered was that she get the room to look homey and inviting.

Though her joints hurt and her back was knotting up from her exertions so that when she raised her arms an electric jangle traveled down them, she hurried outside and down the path to the little house. She would move a few of Lu's things inside, so she would get the idea.

She had never been inside. The small room was dark and close. She groped her way toward the table and pulled the light chain, and then she choked at what she saw—cast-off curtains, mended figurines, dime-store gewgaws, everything she'd ever thrown away, in every object evidence of poverty and love and someone who didn't know the difference between trash and beauty—but mostly at what she felt. She felt as though she had been squeezed into the narrow chambers of her own constricted heart, a walled-in place, a place that made her want to run from it while at the same time revealing itself as the place she should have come many years before. "I didn't know," she wailed. "I didn't!" But the quiet horror of it was: She had known, and how she had treated Lu, had treated Tavo and Antonia made her pride, her girlhood mean-nesses, her sassy lies look no more terrible than pranks. "She loved me!" Eddie wailed.

She straightened up and looked around the room. After the events of the past days, she wondered if she was getting carried away. Like Scarlett O'Hara at the end. Susan Hayward in *I Want to Live*. Maybe this wasn't so bad. Maybe she hadn't treated them badly at all. "It wasn't my fault," she said to a familiar-looking crystal compote filled with bobby pins and pennies. "She didn't have to stay," she told a doorknob around which were stretched a year's worth of rubber bands from the morning paper. "It wasn't that bad!" she shouted. She tried to remember what Hartley had told her, but all she could summon was the memory of the dusty lariat, and Hartley was—the phrase came to her from a long way off, from Noon and the Book of Job—a miserable comforter. She took a deep breath and sat down hard in a seat-sprung brown chair she thought she remembered from Thomas's bachelor days. It was that bad.

Raleigh's old accusation came back to her: Had she ever in her life had an honest feeling? Of any she'd had, this one felt the most real, the most painful and true. And, in a strange way, she wanted it to be. But how could she know it wasn't something else, something messy and selfish and confused?

Eddie sat forward in the chair. *Dear God,* she began, but then she stopped. A shameful question struck her with the force of a voice. Who did she think she was to sit in a chair? She rose, turned around, then eased herself down on her knees, stiff from her activities, folded her hands, and bowed her head. *Oh, boy,* she began, not knowing what to say, *I mean, O God.* She covered her face with her hands. *Oh, boy,* she said again when she realized that the last time she'd prayed she had asked for more, and that this time was really no different. *I'm so sorry,* she said, but nothing else would come, and into the silence she sent her remorse and her will—whatever they were and whatever they meant—upward, propelled by a desire she knew was earnest, and which she hoped was good. Then she said, *Amen.*

She opened her eyes. She still felt the same: a need she couldn't put words to. But the feeling was honest and real and she knew it, so true that if it were a coin she could bite on it and not leave a dent. And the best part was that on the other side of the feeling was the knowledge that in her was the power to make things right. She hoped this knowledge wasn't just her own pride, and she prayed one last time—hearing her own voice cracking but determined not to feel sorry for herself— *Please let me start again.*

She could not have said where the voice came from or whose it was— it sounded a little like Hank Snow's when his hit a mellow-throated patch of song, a little like Thomas's when he'd caressed the names of oranges, a little like Lu's in the old days before she'd stopped humming her maddening song—but when she heard the voice and what it said— *Okay,* that simple—she felt her face give out, her heart, though pummeled and raw, begin to beat a different way, as though she'd come unstuck, and she cried, "Oh, thank you all!"

She rose from the floor and looked again at the room, feeling battered and foolish, but new. "Okay," she said, and she would have laughed at the picture she must have made if it hadn't felt so true. "Tell me what to do."

But the voice would not return. At first she felt angry, to be brought to this place and then deserted, but then she understood. "Hmmm," she said, thinking she sounded like that ratty TV detective—Peter-something, Columbo—figuring things out on his own. "I get it."

As though by an answer, she was visited by the facts: Lu was stubborn, would never move as long as her house remained. Another inspiration struck her, and she left the little house and went toward Pompilo's toolshed. As she passed the mound of earth where she had buried Dixie, she felt a pang. She and Lu together had loved the dog, but now that common love was gone. But then she understood a sudden, perfect truth: that the creature had laid down her life toward the greater good. *And a little child shall lead them,* came the Sunday school words, and Eddie smiled. It was true, except that in their case it was a little dog. "Oh, honey," she said again, but this time the words held in them an impulse that went past grief and stretched all the way to gratitude. On a shelf in the shed she found a box of kitchen matches, the gasoline can behind the door.

It might even seem like the wrong thing. Who was speaking? Who had said the words she heard now as she hurried back across the yard, her flesh a riot of goosebumps in the cold? *But it will be right. And you'll have to do it. The harder it is, the righter it'll be.* Hartley had said it. Said Thomas had said it. She hoped it wasn't another of his fabrications. But how could it be? As she entered the little house for the second time, she was certain of the rightness of what she planned to do.

She hoped for a conflagration, a pyre of atonement, billows of smoke, burning ashes like wickedness departing in air, but a house was harder to burn in reality than it was in her vision. When she struck a match to ignite the curtains, the fire raced up the cheap fabric but at the metal curtain rod, quit, refusing to jump to the window frame. The batting in the brown chair was nearly ossified. It caught, but only in fits and starts. The smoke from the chair was black and awful smelling, and she flapped at it with a tablecloth until it went out, then she ran for a glass of water to make sure. A stack of newspapers smoked and smoldered but wouldn't flame. Though it had seemed a good idea when she'd thought of it, she was afraid to use the gasoline; she'd already singed her hair when the fire licked up the curtains. Her eyes watered and she began to cough. Little by little, though, she was able to do enough damage to the inside to make the place uninhabitable.

Outside it had grown even colder. She shivered on her way back to the big house. Her teeth rattled. In the distance she heard sirens, but from the little house there rose no smoke, no flames. Somebody's smudge pots must have set fire to something. Exhausted, she let herself in. In the bathroom she washed the black from her face and brushed her hair. She could do nothing about the singe, gray and malodorous and frizzed like a scouring pad, and she was glad for its presence, the proof of her remorse. She thought of sleep but decided to wait for Lu, to explain what she had done and why, to ask if they could start again. When a sigh escaped her lips, she nearly cried to think of what she'd been through on the way, at last, to doing right. Though a nameless fear nagged at her, she opened the front draperies and then eased herself onto the sofa to watch the sun rise on the first day of her new life.

• • •

When she woke up, the sun, though feeble, was high in the sky, and she guessed it was afternoon. The norther had arrived, and frost, which she hadn't seen since 1951, rimed the carpet grass. From outside she heard a hacking sound, as though of someone choking. When she went to the back door and looked down the path to the little house, she saw Lu wandering as though dazed, making the dry, choked noise, in one hand a trowel, in the other a contraption that looked to be made of seashells. Eddie, arms outstretched, started down the path.

Even from a distance, she could see that something was different about her maid, and though she'd meant to clasp her in a hug, when she got close all she could say was "What in the samhill have you done to your hair?"

Lu's face was a terrible mask, her breathing ragged. She still made the hacking sound, and though Eddie hadn't heard her speak Spanish for years, she finally understood that her maid was asking what had happened.

"I made you a room in the house. We can live together. Like the Panatier girls." She tried to pull her toward the big house, explaining about the matching dresses, the hand-holding, that they'd died a day apart, the rightness of it all. "Come see."

Lu balked. She threw off Eddie's hand. Her noises grew louder.

Eddie backed toward the big house, still trying to explain. Finally, exasperated, she shouted, "Stop it!"

"Who did this?" Lu cried.

Eddie saw her mistake. Suddenly, in the face of that hideous stare, it occurred to her to blame Pompilo, teenagers, even Lu herself for the hazard the little house was, but her new self, her better self, made her raise her gaze to Lu's and say, "I did."

The choking sound became a shriek which lowered into a frightening bellow, a noise like no human sound she'd ever heard, a terrible, dark language. A disjointed thought crossed her mind: how good such a sound would feel to make. But the sound went on and on and it seemed there was no way to make it stop and this made her furious. She started to yell, "I'm sorry," but, suddenly, she wasn't. She had reached the door and she opened it and stepped inside. "Just stop it!"

When Lu lunged toward her, the trowel raised, Eddie shouted, "I did it for you!" She slammed the door and locked it. "And it was mine to burn!"

Outside there was a growl, then against the door there came a sharp thump, a clatter.

Eddie waited awhile, then opened the door. "It isn't that bad!" she yelled over the sound of the Cadillac's engine. On the tile floor of the porch lay a pile of plastic beads and cowrie shells and tangled twine. The Cadillac, Lu behind the wheel, careened out of the drive. Eddie hunted through the house for her own car keys, grabbed a coat, then set out after her.

the river

As she sped along Mile Six Road, the Cadillac's speedometer hitting eighty, Luisa yelled. Her throat was raw but still she felt the need to have a stream of noise emerging from her throat. As she drove toward Joe's, she yelled until her vision blurred and her blood rang in great waves deep inside her head. In the moments of stillness, she was amazed to think that just the night before she'd found her brother, that she was in a book. She wondered what a book person would do about what happened.

It was not so much the way her house had looked when she opened the door but what Madama's act had told her, which was that all along her life had meant no more than this: burned paper and charred curtains. All Madama's wrongs piled up before her like a dark, thick cloud and she saw herself beneath it, shadowed, small, a fool to try to have the first kind of heart, the grateful heart, thinking that this made her rise above, when all along it hadn't mattered.

Her first impulse had been to drive toward Antonia's. Then she remembered that her daughter was gone and that even if she weren't, Antonia would find a way to blame it on her. "It's your fault, Mama," Antonia would say calmly. "You let her walk on you for years. What did you expect?"

"Not this!" Luisa had yelled out the window into the swirling dust left by a passing car. "Not this!"

She braked, then fishtailed onto the La Feria exit, made the loop, and headed back toward Rio, thinking she would go to Joe. He would be glad to see her. She would fall into his arms and tell of what she'd come back home to.

On Farm-to-Market 10, she again slammed on the brake. Joe would be even worse than Antonia. First he would tell her what she *should* have done, then he would turn things around to prove the whole thing meant she should come to live with him.

Others could do things, leaving the rest of the world to pick up after them. This time she would be the one to do. She saw that it didn't matter what she did, or even why, just that she *do,* to show them she could. She pulled into an oil lease road to think, gunning the engine so hard it shook the car, as though in the next roar would come the answer to what she could do that would be so strong and so powerful, so right and so final . . . She pressed the gas pedal and knew she would do something bad. So bad it would not be forgotten, so bad it would stop the world, so bad it would prove once and for all how good she had been and how wronged.

And then she knew what the bad thing was. Luisa backed onto the road, shifted into "Drive," and continued through the night, yelling at slow drivers, on her way toward Madama's house on Grand Texas Boulevard.

When she pulled into the drive, Pompilo ran toward her car, shouting, but she swerved around him, steering the Cadillac across Madama's lawn as fast as she dared. She plowed through the firecracker bushes, the azaleas and crotons. She flattened the tall poinsettias. She wished she knew how to drive like a teenager, to make the great circular scars in the grass, but she settled for weaving across the wide lawn, sorry to remember that long ago the mailbox had been removed. Pompilo ran behind her, but she didn't stop. She made two passes around the house, careening through Madama's flowers—blooms the woman didn't even know the names of! The threshing noise of the plants against the undercarriage made her think of the satisfying spill of corn against her mother's metate. But this act was not the bad thing, and she drove on toward Joe's.

As she neared the head of his lane, she slowed the car. She saw Joe's truck in the Rio Red grapefruit grove, some of his workmen around it, tending the smudge pots. Instead of taking the main lane to the big house, she cut over onto the back road that led to the little house, now used to pen Joe's goats. She parked behind the oleanders, in just the place Sonny López had long ago parked his alligator car, then she got out and went into the jungle.

The oleander hedge had grown dense, and to the pile of discarded tires in the children's jungle many more had been added, but the stones were where she'd left them in the spongy, leaf-thick ground. One by one, she set them aside gently, taking care not to let them chink together and alert Joe. She began to dig with her fingers, thinking of where in Joe's car she could hide the box so the border guards wouldn't discover it when she crossed the bridge, then, as the hole grew bigger, that she would take only the money and leave the rest for Joe and Madama to find, and that this would be better.

She had buried the box deeper than she remembered. The earth was damp and cold, and mud clotted her fingers, but finally she felt the tatters of the apron she'd used to conceal the box, and she worked to scrape away the wet earth, the insect-eaten cloth shredding as she dug. The tin had rusted, and she could no longer make out the cross-stitch design, but the box was there, bound in a thready tangle of roots that gave way as she pulled.

From the road she heard the sound of a car's horn, honking frantically. Madama's Buick screeched into the driveway and Joe ran toward it from the grove.

She wanted to run but she couldn't move. She watched them as they talked, but they were too far away for her to hear what they were saying. Then she heard Joe shout, "There she is!"

They hurried across the yard toward her. "You don't understand!" Madama shouted. "I did it for you."

"She burned my house," Luisa yelled at Joe.

Joe had reached her side. He put his arm around her shoulders. "This can't be that bad. You've . . ." He looked more closely at her. "Your hair?"

She shrugged off his arm. "She burned my house!"

Joe looked at her sternly. "Luisa, let's be reasonable."

For the many times she had told Joe stories of Madama and he'd only laughed, or tried to instruct her about how to handle things, for there never having been a reason for anything at all, she shouted at him, "Shut up!"

"You need to get off your high horse," Madama said. "You need to understand. I wanted you to come and live with me. I wanted . . . I'm so sorry."

"I don't care!" she shouted, because now Joe would think she was the one who was wrong. Thick with rage, a yell rose to her throat, but when it came out of her mouth it was soundless.

Then Madama saw the box. Head cocked, she asked, "What's that?" then, "Thomas?"

Luisa moved back, shielding the bundle with her arms. "I didn't do it!" she shouted. "Tavo and Raleigh . . . I found it."

"I should have known," Madama said quietly. "You've been hiding it all this time."

She would hit. For the many times Madama had wronged her, for the one time—only one—she had said so, and now she was the one who was caught, she would hit. The box raised over her head, Luisa lunged.

But Joe gripped her from behind and held her, prying the box from her hands.

"Open that this minute," Madama ordered, reaching for the box.

"I'll take care of this," Joe said. Luisa wrenched away, flailing at him. In the struggle, the hinges gave way and the box fell open, spilling the contents. The nickels plopped onto the wet leaves. A brown agate marble struck metal. A ribbon-tied lock of hair fluttered to the ground beside Madama's foot. She stared at it. "Thomas . . ."

Joe bent to retrieve the parts of the broken box. From the bottom of the larger one he pried loose a hardened gray-green mass spun over with whitish webs.

Madama stared. "The money?"

Joe dropped the lump, then kicked at it. Bits of paper fell away, paper the texture of ash. "Ants. A nest. They chewed it all up." He bent to poke at the lump, peeling away from it the remains of a ruined envelope. "Some kind of legal paper, probably. Nothing left of it. Ink's all gone."

They were quiet in the chill air until Joe stood up and rubbed his hands together briskly, looking toward the grapefruit grove, then at Madama. "Señora Hatch. With all respect, I'm asking you to leave. We'll settle this in the morning."

He turned to Luisa. "It's too cold for you out here. I'm ordering you to come into the house."

But when Joe took Madama's arm to lead her to her car, Luisa ran for the Cadillac. As she pulled out of the lane she yelled back, "Nobody orders me nothing!"

•   •   •

In the Buick, which was running low on gas, Eddie followed Joe as he drove his truck up and down the roads, looking for a sign of Lu. She'd told him to start in Harlingen, at Antonia's, but he wouldn't listen. He had waved her away.

She knew now that burning the house had been a mistake, but she was certain that once Lu understood, all would be well. It was funny that in the middle of admitting what she'd done, it had turned out that Lu had done something even worse. A secret she'd kept for years, a terrible secret. When it occurred to Eddie that she could work this to her advantage, however, she pushed the thought away. It didn't matter; gone was gone and done was done and why was not important. All the reasons in the world could never change this.

Her head buzzed with exhaustion and she was ready to give up. If she knew anything about anything, Eddie reflected, Lu would eventually return, her old righteous, stubborn self. She allowed herself the small pleasure of imagining Lu's sheepish look. But something—again a nameless fear, but one she decided she would heed—made her continue driving, following Joe.

It was full dark when they found the Cadillac parked on the levee road, the headlight beams illuminating the withered brown grass of the slope, the driver's door standing open. Though her legs hurt and her muscles were sore, Eddie climbed the levee behind Joe, then gingerly picked her way down to the sand. Joe trained his flashlight along the bank: red dirt, hollows and washes, ratty reeds, a pile of batteries and tires. Downriver, a set of footprints led into the water.

Up and down the bank Joe played the flashlight's beam, searching for a trail, but the footprints did not come back out.

"The channel's pretty deep here," he said. "Can she swim?"

"I don't know."

For a long time they called, but there was no answer. Joe waded out as far as he could, holding the flashlight over his head, training it along the banks on the opposite side. When he was chest high, he turned around and waded back out. "There's a bad drop."

"Do you see anything on the other side?"

He shook his head.

Eddie let herself down onto the sand, let herself think the thought that had come to her when she'd first seen the footprints: *twice.*

Joe walked up and down the bank. Finally he sat on a rock and buried his face in his hands.

For a long time they were silent, then Eddie, her teeth chattering, rose from the damp ground and said, "We have to call the police."

Joe rose from the rock. "What can they do?" His wet shirt and trousers clung to his skin. "She was an illegal." In the moonlight his face looked beaten and old, familiar and yet somehow strange. Though she had known him for almost forty years, Eddie realized, this was the first time she'd looked into his eyes.

"You go on home," he said. "I'll let you know when I know something."

Eddie turned away and started for her car, then stopped, suddenly, remembering. She turned back to Joe. "That paper in the box? I think I know what it was. A long time ago Thomas said something about papers for Lu. That he'd fixed something. I only just now remembered." She shivered in the cold. "I guess it doesn't matter."

Numb, Eddie got into her car and slowly headed toward home. In her rearview mirror, she saw the Cadillac's headlights switch off, the dome light go out as Joe closed the door. Before she had gone even a mile, his truck sped past her on the road, peppering her windshield with dust and caliche.

"That's okay," she said, waving absently toward his receding taillights. "I deserved it."

She drove on through the night, heading home, too numb to think, until she began to feel a presence in the car, a warmth, as though of someone breathing just beside her, and she saw, as she looked to her side to the passenger seat, that the presence was Thomas, who said, "No, you didn't."

Eddie wept.

• • •

From a hollow in the levee a short distance upriver, Luisa, wrapped in layers of clothing from her vacation suitcase, had watched the scene below. She hadn't meant to hide, but when she heard them coming, she couldn't move. Wrecking the yard was not enough, the box was not even enough. This, she saw, this hiding, was worse; they had pushed her to it. They could suffer.

She had intended to walk across the river, to find her way to Salsipuedes, money or no money. She had done it before and she would do it again. But the water had been too cold and too deep. She'd walked out into it until it reached the tops of her legs, but she'd been afraid to go farther into the channel. Her arms hurt from holding her suitcase over her head. She'd trudged through the water, hoping to find a shallower passage, but there was none. She'd come out of the water farther from the point she'd started from, moved up a bit on the levee, and sat in the hollow, watching while Madama and Joe searched for her along the riverbank.

To make herself strong, so she wouldn't rise and call out to them, she focused her gaze on the opposite bank, concentrating on the way the land rose and fell and the light of the moon made shadows among the hollows. The rocks told her she could not, she would not, and she didn't have to, and with this knowledge came the vision of the sky above her scoured, barren of all memory, all meaning, only darkness stretching up to further nothing. She tried to throw off years and acts to make herself again the girl in Salsipuedes, holy, dreaming, clean, and good, and she looked along the bank, wishing the word which long ago she'd written on the sand, her name, *Luisa at the river at the bottom of the canyon,* would magically appear, to know again what sweet, lost thing had been inside her as she'd traced the letters, for she understood that here she had been closest. But on the sand there was no message, and she couldn't draw that girl into this time. She looked again at the rocks. Just when she was concentrating hardest, when the picture was sharpest, she saw a movement below her, and when she looked toward the bank she blamed Madama—it was at the moment when the woman sat down on the sand—when in the absence of her gaze the rocks shifted shape, and when she looked back at them the shadows fell differently and would not look the same. She bit her thumb to remember her ruined house, to let the pain tell her what mattered and what didn't, what she could help and what she couldn't, but in the stillness, in the dark, no answer came.

11

the morning after

Because she was too exhausted to crawl under the wedged mattress in order to go upstairs, Eddie had again slept on the sofa, wrapped in a bathrobe she'd found among the old clothes when she'd moved them from the storeroom. An ache in her legs woke her. She had a cold, a rattling cough. As she shuffled toward the kitchen to make coffee, through a window she saw Joe's truck nose into the drive, and she turned around and went to wait for him at the door.

He seemed to be taking his time, and so she stepped to the door and opened it, meaning to let him know she was ready to hear the news. But the door opened on Lu, as though risen from death, who stood with her fist raised, ready to knock.

"How could you!" Eddie shouted. She slammed the door.

Luisa looked at the big carved door, where stiff wooden vines and leaves intertwined. For most of the night she had wandered the Hundred Acres, the Valley roads, practicing the speech she would give Madama. In the cold air, in each puff of breath, she imagined the gathering of los aires, of dark birds. At dawn she had gone to Joe's and, looking through the back door window, found him sitting at his kitchen table, asleep in his clothes. When he looked up to see her at the door he began to sob so brokenly that she wanted to run away, but she waited for him to let her in and stood still to let him hold her. At last he pulled away, holding her at arm's length, gripping her shoulders. "I am so mad at you," he said. "So mad." Luisa stood while he looked deeply into her eyes, fearing he would say more, but he dropped his hands to his sides, then turned to go back to his place at the table, where he rested his forehead on the wooden surface. "So mad," he said over and over, his voice a sorrowful rasp. She crossed the room to stand behind his chair, placing her cheek against the back of his head, and she waited, her arms around him, until he was still.

He refused to lend her his truck when she told him she needed to go to Madama's, even when she explained what she planned to do. "Look what happened the last time I let you borrow the car," he said, and she could tell he was still upset, but then he said, "I'll drive you. I'm not letting you out of my sight."

Silently they'd ridden toward Madama's, Joe shaking his head, Luisa determined not to leave until she told Madama what had been bottled in her heart from the first day she'd arrived at the Hundred Acres. She would tell Madama the truth, that no one could love her because she chased everyone away with her meanness. That she, Luisa, had done nothing wrong, and if it looked as if she had, well, this too was Madama's fault. She would back up all the way to the beginning to prove this, a chain of becauses linked so tightly there was no room for but-what-about-this or and-then-you-did-that, a tunnel of doors that slammed in her face. She would have the last word, and then she would leave.

Behind the door, Eddie took deep breaths, trying to collect her thoughts. She pulled the bathrobe around her, smoothing its folds, tying the belt. She ran her fingers through her hair; she had forgotten the singed tuft and her ring caught in the snarl. She yanked her hand loose, then patted her face for color.

Luisa prepared to knock again when suddenly the door swung open and in the frame it seemed there stood a new Madama—a different Madama from the one who had looked at her angrily before she slammed the door—a smiling Madama, trying to gather her into a hug. "I'm sorry. I'm just so surprised . . . so glad. I thought . . ."

Luisa pushed her aside and then stepped past her and into the entry.

"Come in, come in." Eddie bustled into the sala, righting a vase, snatching up a ball of crumpled stationery to bring some order to the wreck of the room. "Sit down. I have so much to tell you. I thought . . ."

Luisa walked toward the desk, stepping over a pile of candy wrappers, then stopping, turning back to kick at them. "Pah," she said.

"Don't say it," Madama said. "I know it. I've made a terrible mess." She indicated that Luisa should sit down in the desk chair but then she sat in it herself, then quickly jumped back up. "I'm not an emotional woman, but certain things have come to my attention. I've come to understand . . . I've come to believe . . ."

Eddie couldn't say what she felt. And trying to say it, she suddenly didn't know what it was that she wanted to say. Something too full of feeling, something embarrassing, something naked and hopeful and wanting, words that would lay her wide open and gut her like a fish. She sat back down.

Luisa stood beside the desk, her arms crossed over her chest. "I want to . . ." But before she could finish her statement, Madama jumped up and said, "I want to give you the little house. Fix it up and deed it to you. An acre, too." She rubbed her hands together. "I'll just give it to you."

Luisa shook her head. "I have some things to say." She drew in her breath. She meant to start at the beginning, but she heard herself saying, "That money . . ."

Madama began to pace around the room, shaking her head and covering her ears and saying "No, no, no."

Luisa looked at her, hard, waiting until Madama took her hands from her ears. Then she began again. "This is about the box. I didn't do nothing. I want to tell what happened about the box."

Again Madama covered her ears. "I don't care if you stole it or hid it or gave birth to it behind a bush." Madama waved her arms wildly, as though trying to be generous, to give Luisa something she didn't want to receive, then she lowered her voice and said sadly, "It doesn't matter. Do you see? Or else . . . or else . . . I just don't know. If I held that over you, what would I be?"

Again Eddie sat in the chair. She drew a hoarse breath, trying to quell the rising want that would make her ask for an immediate answer. "Lu, I wouldn't blame you if you never spoke to me again. I know what I've done. All of it . . . everything . . . all of it. But do you think you could think about forgiving me?"

Her voice trailed away and in the silence Luisa noticed for the first time that no Little Dixie had trotted across the tile floors to dance at her feet, no brown fur cushion lay sleeping in a chair. At some point in the night, she had realized that Madama had at last said she was sorry. Walking through the dark, she had tried to shake off this knowledge, to make the words unsaid, for she had seen how all the years and what she'd made of them and who they told her she had been would have to vanish. She had seen how the wanting of the words had grown far greater than their power to heal. In her daydreams, when Madama apologized, she, Luisa, would accept it easily, she would forgive, but as she walked along the real roads, Chavela's scornful laugh found her once again, and once again, she had thought bitterly, she had been a fool to think a sacrifice cost nothing.

Luisa looked at the floor. It came to her that at last she stood before the great good thing, not in the way she had imagined—a moment beautiful and full as she stepped across a clear line to be numbered among the good of earth, the serene, far-seeing saints of heaven—but in emptiness and anger, loss. No voice had called to her, there was no map, no book, no sign to tell her what to do, and here she was, a foolish beanself in a foolish bottle, her very skin more brittle than a paper shell, beneath this skin a feeling deep and large and terrible, and danger in her next breath.

Long ago her mother had told her the second great sin of the world was not to forgive. God himself had committed it when He hadn't given the first people another chance. He had done this to show how easily it could happen, how even the greatest could do it. Thousands of years it had taken to right that wrong; who was she—Luisa thought now— who was she, a person, a maid, the right and the wronged, to try to be better than God? God, too, was stubborn. Unfair. All through her life

He could have looked into her heart to see what was there, how she had always meant to do what was good. This, she saw, made no difference at all, for now when He looked He would see only her fault, and nothing of how unfair it was that Madama—who believed that *she* was the one who had forgiven—could expect Luisa to forgive.

Later, she decided. Later she would think. About fairness and forgiving, if they lived in lands which shared no border, if hiding in the heart of goodness was a shadow that was pride, the secret of martyrs who held themselves so high above or else so far below that there could be no living on the earth, if God was tangled up with people, so tightly and mysteriously bound that she could not tell where one left off and the other began. Later she would determine which things to throw away and which to keep, but only when she knew why they had mattered. Later, she decided, she would think about the way that although a moment might go past mattering, a feeling never would, how in a moment you could not know what you were doing or even why, and only on the other side could you know what you had done.

"Will you?" Madama, her face blotched and drawn, waited for an answer.

Looking at Madama but picturing herself walking out into the sunlight to Joe's truck, picturing herself as she rode away, and speaking only to push herself closer to the door, past the awful question of what more she wanted, Luisa waved away Madama's hopeful look and muttered impatiently, "Okay, okay."

She turned to go, but then, realizing she hadn't said what she'd come to say about years, about chances, realizing that in her answer there had been no sting, no satisfying spill of blame, and thinking that selfish Madama might take her muttered words in a way she hadn't meant them, she turned back to shout at her: "But not now!"

But before she could speak, she saw that a look she had never seen before had come over Madama's face, a look she recognized as like the one her mother had worn as she'd worked among the statues, moving her hands along the folds of stone, humble, wonderstruck, as though she had received a gift she knew to be more costly than its giver could afford. Then this look vanished, its radiance shattered as another took its place. Now Madama began to cry so bitterly that Luisa wondered what she'd said. Whether she'd said something else.

"Oh, Lu, I don't—" Madama began, but whatever she had meant to say had turned into strange, cracked, bleating sounds that seemed to catch in her throat. And her face, before she hid it in her hands, had looked so worn and battered, so sorrowful and broken that Luisa ached to comfort her, and she moved toward Madama's chair through what seemed a great blurred space where one need met another, nameless and no difference between them, only distance.

But when she stood beside the chair, her hand held just above Madama's shoulder, she couldn't think of anything to say.

"What," she finally asked, "has happened to your hair?"

Madama's eyes were swollen, red and small, and Luisa worried that the woman's face would again smear into the weeping mask. But instead Madama smiled weakly, brought her hands to her hair in a funny, primping gesture. "Oh, do you like it?"

They were quiet for a time. Twice the furnace ticked before it caught.

Eddie asked hopefully, "Do you think you could call me Eddie?"

Luisa looked away, at the window, the desk, at her hands. "I don't think so." Then, to soften her refusal, she offered, "I'm in a book."

Madama looked at her sideways, her lips pursed in an odd way, as though considering, but then she said, "Well, aren't we all?"

Luisa started to be hurt that she wasn't impressed, but then she smiled for the way Madama looked suddenly like an eager fox, green-eyed and curious, youthful and alert.

Eddie stood up. "Randy Cruz can fix the house. It'll only take a few days, and I'll throw in an air conditioner. You'd like that, wouldn't you?"

Luisa crossed her arms over her chest and looked around the sala, appraising. "This house is messed up pretty bad. Two days I go away. Looks like goats got in here."

Eddie thought she saw where Lu was heading and decided to play along, delighted that joking would figure in their new relationship. "Why, yes. It's just terrible. My maid . . . well, she left. Of course, no one could replace her. She was a treasure. Now of course I'll have to hire a new one and I was thinking . . ."

Lu's face had closed down. Eddie scrambled for words. "I only meant—"

"A maid," said Luisa, "is not enough. You need a housekeeper."

When Madama stared at her blankly, Luisa, thumping herself on the chest with her fist, prompted, "*I* am a housekeeper."

Awash with relief that threatened to turn into more tears, Eddie leaned forward to clasp her hand. "Oh, Lu, the job is yours. You don't have to apply for it. Do as much or as little as you want."

Luisa drew back her hand. "I do a lot. You didn't know how much."

"You're right," Eddie said. Though Lu had promised to think about forgiving her and Eddie believed her, this would take time, she saw, and she promised to tread carefully in honor of its passage. "I never did. I'm sorry."

There passed across Lu's face a look that Eddie, though she'd known her for over thirty years, could not interpret—pride, surprise, a look that might have been astonishment or love. The only certain thing was that she'd never seen the look before.

"I charge minimum wage. And benefits. I won't start until tomorrow. And I want papers."

Eddie nodded. "Would you like some coffee? I was just about to make some." She patted her middle. "And I'm so hungry I could eat a horse."

"No, thank you," Luisa said. She turned away and started for the door, then stopped to face Madama. "But that's very nice of you."

"Say," Eddie said, moving toward Lu. "I have a wonderful idea. We could get in the car and go out to get a bite to—"

Luisa shook her head. "I have to go."

Eddie stopped herself from asking where and Luisa stopped herself from saying. At the door they parted, each nodding to the other, and then Eddie closed the door.

Eddie decided to bring some order to the place, and she went to the kitchen for the trashcan, the dustpan, and the broom, but then she stopped to look outside the kitchen window, midway in her mission: The grass, the trees, the road, the sky stretched out before her and she stood transfixed. There would be time. Not infinite, and maybe not enough, but time. She went back to her desk and eased herself into her chair, where she sat marveling, for no reason she could determine but that it was the simplest of miracles, one meant for her to see, so plain that even she could see it, at the way her bones fit together, each onto the other, at how the flesh lay over them, fitting desire to deed. She sat for a long time in her disordered house, drained and quiet, old and singed and sorry, glad before the complex living heart of grace.

BOOK VII

·

the land of the living

1994

·

Even memory is not necessary for love.

—Thornton Wilder, *The Bridge of San Luis Rey*

Each new life bears some burden from the old, and Eddie, ever vigilant to ensure that an occasion go the way she planned, had prepared detailed instructions for her funeral. Around the house Luisa found scraps of paper in odd places, and when Eddie grew too weak and raddled to remember where she'd left them, much less file them, Luisa took over, binding them in a notebook that she gave to Raleigh when he came in the last weeks of his mother's life, which she spent in bed in her upstairs room. The scraps bore messages and orders in Eddie's crabbed hand-writing. One requested: *Rich color for my dress, depending on the season. See closet: Chestnut for fall, Ivory for winter, Jade for spring, Violet for summer. No reds and no pastels. They wash me out.*

Make me look, she wrote on another scrap, *serene. Comfortable would be good, but if I get too stringy, try for sweet. I never was in life. Ha, ha.*

If there's a choice, Rite II from the Book of Common Prayer.

Sing "Just as I Am," even if it causes a stink, and kick anyone who tries to make me out a saint.

In her later years, Eddie had grown kind and generous and friendly to all, and so the service at the beautiful Church of Christ and Saint Luke was well attended. Eddie would have been happy to see that many of the mourners wept, to know that their tears were heartfelt, and that no one required kicking.

Luisa sat in the front row, on her right the newlywed Antonia with her husband, Daniel, beside him Beth, home from graduate school at Stanford. On Luisa's left sat Joe, holding her hand with his three-fingered one in a husbandly grip. It had taken many years, but after he had admitted he didn't always know best and Luisa had done the same, after each had pledged to help the other to remember this, she had married him, as there no longer seemed a reason not to, though for many more years they would maintain their separate houses, in the interest of the times they would forget.

Toward the end of her life, his mother had seemed haunted by something, and this, Raleigh told Luisa, troubled him. "Was I a good mother?" his mother would ask him, her withered hands pulling his jacket straight. "Was there anything you wanted that you didn't have?"

Among the paper scraps with her funeral instructions, they had found other notes, scribbled questions: *Is it better to learn a truth that hurts or to believe a lie that makes you comfortable? When does it not take two to tango?* The questions were abstract and mysterious, and he couldn't imagine what could have troubled her so.

"Do you know what she's talking about?" he asked Luisa.

Although she knew Madama's secrets, although she ached for Raleigh, Luisa shook her head; she had promised.

One night as they sat their watch beside her bed, Raleigh told Luisa that although he once would have been glad to see his mother humbled, he was in a way sorry for her doubts, for in the years of his fatherhood he had lived through those times when his own children—sometimes joking, others not—weighed and found him wanting. He had lived, too, through those times when he would take his own measure, charting the distance between how he wished to be and how he was. Luisa smiled to comfort him, thinking how like don Tomás he had become, then, remembering the truth that seemed not to matter at all, she patted his hand. "Your parents were so proud of you," she told him. "Anyone would be proud to have a son like you."

Raleigh covered his eyes with his hand, then he said, "Luisa, I was so sad when he died. When Tavo . . . I was gone . . . I am so sorry." But then he couldn't speak for crying and when she saw that maybe this was better, Luisa cried with him for the many times she hadn't. "I know," she said. "I know." Just as God heard prayers, the dead heard tears, and she knew Tavo knew they loved him.

At the funeral, Luisa followed Raleigh through the viewing line and heard him whisper to his mother that he knew she'd done her best. When Luisa passed, she lingered, touching Eddie's hand. She murmured, "Mi hermana," and then words in a language no one understood, and then some more in Spanish, among which Altagracia swore she clearly heard the word for *pardon* but which Antonia heard as *loss*. Pompilo maintained that she had spoken of a long-lost parrot, but no one believed him. Luisa wouldn't say.

After the burial, all gathered in the sala of the house on Grand Texas Boulevard. The mourners started out somber and ill at ease, but little by little, between sips of the California wine Joe had discovered in the machine barn at the Hundred Acres, between bites of tea sandwiches and chocolate cake, they began to tell stories of who Edwina Jane Harmon Hatch had been—this to one, that to another—and soon there was laughter and good humor. Pompilo, whose capacity for remorse exceeded his tolerance for wine, repented lavishly of all the times he'd tried to trick her. Nila Nimrod, two years widowed, holding court in her wheelchair, told in her papery voice about Eddie's famous luncheons, on which she worked so hard but at which something always went awry. "I remember some kind of bird salad. Turkeys, they were supposed to be. It must have been Thanksgiving. Anyway, she used so much food color our mouths were green for days. Or blue. I don't remember. I hope she knew," Nila mused, her left eye tearing, "we loved her for it."

An uneasy moment occurred when Antonia, at forty-four happier in marriage than she'd dreamed was possible, eight months pregnant and beautiful, her husband told her, beyond his comprehension, Antonia, awash in a sea only partly hormonal, a sea of sorrow, resentment, and bliss, daily astonished by the miracle of—and to discover that during her first one she had been prevented from having—a joyful pregnancy, Antonia, unaware that all these feelings would come to a head when she stood up to act out the tale of Altagracia and the seven-dollar bedspread, which she thought would be funny, felt her lower lip begin to quiver, then protrude, her face pucker, then stretch into a brokenhearted grimace she couldn't control. When she could finally speak, she blurted, "She was so mean to me."

No one spoke. In the kitchen, after the clank of a pot and the rattle of flatware in a pan, even the volunteer servers were silent, and it seemed the afternoon stood still to honor the knowledge that for certain hurts—those gone beyond apology and time and reason, those which cleave to bone—the only help for them is to say they happened.

At last Raleigh stepped forward and took her hand and said the words that made things right between them. "Yes," he said, "she was."

The noise rose again, people talked, someone laughed, and the company returned to the business at hand.

A new family bought the big house on Grand Texas Boulevard. Timeless, the real estate agent called the interior design. Immaculately kept. For a time, Luisa stayed on, but eventually she moved in with Joe.

Though she would live many more years, Luisa began to wonder about death. When would it come, and where, how it would feel; would she know the moment? She wondered if her heart would take her, for sometimes at night she felt a rise, a flutter, in her chest. There were times she hoped it would come while she worked among her flowers. She knew that, having loved the earth, the trees and rocks and water and her place among them, she would try to stand up to the moment, tell it: Later. No, not now. At other times, she imagined death might come to her in sleep, as she lay beside her husband. Though sometimes Joe nudged her if she snored, especially when she had a cold, or she would have to poke him when he laughed aloud in one of his strange dreams—dreams, he told her, smiling and astonished, of shuffling a deck of cards, ten-fingered—and his laughter shook the bed, here too she felt at home. She hoped there would be time to move close enough to feel against her skin the broad warmth of his back, as though the place their bodies met could hold all mysteries, their earthly answers.

Of these mysteries, she understood only that in each loss was finding, in each found thing, something lost, and that the line that separated what she couldn't know from what she could had been no wider than her next breath, and always just beyond her. But if she caught herself dwelling too long on these matters, she worked harder—dusting, digging, stirring—not to push the thoughts away, but as a promise to be glad in living, hard as it was easy, a sign she was content in knowing death might be the same, that only through it would she see it.